DEADLY ANCESTORS

A BERNADETTE CALLAHAN DETECTIVE
MYSTERY

LYLE NICHOLSON

Book Editing and Design;

EbookEditingPro http://ebookeditingpro.com

Book cover design by www.Damonza.com

❀ Created with Vellum

CONTENTS

1

FATHER DOMINIC ENTERED THE CHAPEL. Two candles flickered on the altar, throwing shadows onto the statue of Jesus Christ above it. A beam of moonlight shone through the stained glass windows, making a narrow path of light from the doorway.

He lit a votive candle and walked towards the altar to say his prayers, the old wooden floors creaking as he shuffled forward. This was his speed at seventy-five years old. His body, wracked by arthritis, moved at its own rate; the good Lord would take him in time, but now he would kneel in prayer.

A sound made him stop. Was that a click he heard? It sounded familiar—but why? He searched his memory for that sound and in a flash of recognition; he knew. A round had been chambered in a gun.

How long had he been expecting this? He knew they would come; they'd find him. He was thankful for one more moment in prayer before being sent to his everlasting life.

He moved faster, pushing his old bones forward. Determined to get to the altar to prostrate before the bullet entered his body. If he was to die—it would be before God. Father Dominic couldn't ask for more.

He reached the altar and sank to his knees when the shot rang out. The sound reverberated, bouncing off the simple wooden pews and making a wave of sound from the front to the back.

Father Dominic fell forward. His head hit the front of the altar; his arms splayed in one last worship to God. A trickle of blood flowed onto the floor. The moon cast a glow onto the blood as it made its way down the aisle as if it was searching for an exit.

Dominic waited for his spirit to leave his body, for the light, the angels, the sound of trumpets and the heavens to open. A door slammed, he heard footsteps. Was it Saint Peter? Was someone coming to take him to the pearly gates?

A hand touched his head. He expelled his breath, "Yes, I'm here Lord, I'm ready."

"Father Dominic, it's Father Frederic. You're hurt! I've called the ambulance."

"I'm not dead?"

"No, but you're losing blood. I'll put a compress on your head. Please stay still, the ambulance will be here soon."

Father Dominic looked up at the altar. The figure of Jesus stared down at him. Was that a frown on his brow? He'd never seen that before. Had he disappointed him? He wasn't sure... his mind fogged over. He slipped into unconsciousness to the sound of sirens coming up the hill to the seminary.

～

CONSTABLE STEWART PICKED up the call of gunshots at the seminary. A strange call on a cold February night, the seminary was ten kilometers on the outskirts of Red Deer, a small city of one hundred thousand in western Canada, two hours east of the Rocky Mountains and five hours north of Montana. It was an estimate that locals used when driving a car in the summer; in the winter they doubled the time. Gun violence, though rare, happened downtown where the drug dealers fought over their turf.

Stewart was a tall, muscular man with a dedication to the gym that made his biceps and triceps a thing of wonder to those who'd never spent time there. His other passion was the law and the Royal Canadian Mounted Police. His father had been a sergeant and his grandfather an inspector. His red hair and freckles made him look much younger than his late twenties, but no one dared call him 'kid.'

The other units and paramedics had arrived at the scene. Stewart was sweeping North Road looking for suspects. Another cruiser was doing South Road. The countryside was flat, with large expanses of farmers' fields covered in deep snow.

If he had to leave his car to follow tracks, this was the perfect night for it. A meter of snow lay on the ground, little wind and a full moon. He could find just about anything or anybody in these conditions. He turned his headlights to high beam and slowed his speed to scan the surrounding fields.

Everything lay covered in a blanket of snow. The harvested fields of stubble lay frozen on the ground, waiting for the spring and summer heat to bring them back to life. There were few trees; someone had cut them down years ago for crops. The few trees left standing became property markers or windbreaks. They stopped the howling winds blowing in from the Rocky Mountains that could tear off a layer of topsoil in a day.

Stewart looked at the outside temperature gauge; it read minus twenty centigrade. Damn cold, but nothing like last month when a cold front had moved in from the Arctic and pushed the temperature to minus fifty at night.

Stewart looked out onto the field. Nothing was stirring. Then he saw something moving along the tree line.

"Is that an animal?" he muttered to himself.

He watched it move from tree to tree; it ducked behind a large stand of bushes when it saw the police cruiser.

"That's no damn animal, no frigging animal moves like that." He picked up his radio, "This is unit two niner, I got eyes on a person wandering in a field over here on Township Road four two one, just four klicks past Range Road, do you copy?"

Dispatch copied the message and replied that backup was on the way.

Stewart stopped the cruiser, letting the engine idle. The figure went still for a moment, then ran across the field.

He switched on his microphone, "This is the police. Stay where you are," he commanded.

The figure ran faster.

"Of course, that never works," Stewart said, climbing out of the car. He spoke into his shoulder mike, "Unit two niner in pursuit of a suspect on foot."

He was going to unlock the shotgun from the dashboard, decided against it, as it would be cumbersome to jump over the barbwire fence in the field with it. He put on his thick gloves and pulled his woolen cap over his ears. He hated chasing people in the winter.

He launched himself over the fence and trudged through the deep snow. He'd wished he'd time to pull on the snowshoes from the trunk, but suspects never gave you that luxury. They ran at the most inconvenient times.

The figure in the snow ran slowly, as if the effort in the snow was more than he or she could handle. As Stewart caught up to it, he could see it was a man. He'd fallen into the snow and lay on his back with his hands in the air.

"For the love of god, please don't shoot me, I'm just an old man lost in the fields."

Stewart stood over him, shining his flashlight on him. The man looked a mess; maybe from the effort of walking in the fields. His long gray hair lay matted in strands. His face hadn't seen a razor in days. His eyes rimmed in red. His breath came in long puffs as he exhaled clouds of steam into the icy air.

"Do you have any weapons on you?" Stewart asked.

"No, just a penknife," the man answered in a thick Irish accent.

"I'm going to check you, anyway. Stand up. Can you do that, can you stand?"

"I'm not dead," the man answered with indignation in his voice. He stood up and raised his hands in the air.

Stewart frisked him. He pulled out an object with a bone handle. He felt a small button on the front. He pressed it; a switchblade knife shot out. Its sharp edges gleamed in the moonlight.

"You're carrying a switchblade knife, sir. These are illegal in Canada."

"I told you it's only a penknife. I use it for my protection and to clean my teeth once in a while."

"What's your name?"

"Cahal Callahan is the name. And what's yours?"

"Constable Stewart. You want to tell me what you're doing out here in this field tonight?"

Cahal looked around. "That's easy to see, isn't it? I'm lost.

Why else would a man be wandering about on a miserable night like this?"

"Then why did you run when I hailed you?"

"You hailed me? On what now did you do that?"

"On the car's speaker; it has over two hundred decibels. You can hear it kilometer away. You didn't hear it?"

"I'm an old man, I'm near deaf, I am. Not a young buck like yourself."

"Why did you run when you saw my police cruiser lights on?"

"How am I supposed to know you're the real police? Here I am in a foreign country, maybe you're one of those masquerading police types like they have in South America." He huffed out a breath. "I was running for me life."

"This is Canada, Mr. Callahan..."

"Better safe than sorry, I always say," Cahal said with a nod.

They walked back as the other police cruiser came to stop on the road.

Stewart put Cahal into the back of the cruiser and walked over to the officer. It was Constable Marie Jelenick. She was new to the force and good at her job. In her mid-twenties, she had dark brown eyes and platinum blonde hair with an attitude that said all business. Stewart liked that about her.

"What have you got there?" Jelenick asked, nodding towards the suspect in the cruiser.

"The guy's name is Cahal Callahan, says he got lost. Told me as we walked back here that he hitched a ride to the seminary to see one of his old Irish friends, then he got lost on the road. Oh, and he says he's related to Detective Bernadette Callahan."

Jelenick smiled. "I'm sure Callahan will love that when she gets back from vacation."

"Well, that's all I got from him."

Jelenick squinted as she looked into the back of Stewart's cruiser. "Well, that's a delightful story, but the footprints in the snow led from the seminary to this field. I think we've got our prime suspect in your car."

DETECTIVE BERNADETTE CALLAHAN arrived at the RCMP detachment early. She was in her mid-thirties, taller than average, with red hair, green eyes, and freckles with a bronze skin tone that revealed her mix of Irish and Cree heritage. She had a lot to catch up on. Was it two weeks since she'd been away? One day seemed to collide with another, then there was the stopover in Paris; so nice being there with Chris, but here she was back at work. It was good to be back. She almost hummed a tune.

She found Jerry Durham, the chief of detectives in his usual place, at his desk with his all-day cup of coffee by his side and a stack of files. Jerry was mid-forties with a receding hairline he valiantly tried to comb into something that looked like hair on top but failed. His body was revealing the pressure of his desk by growing a paunch on his tall frame. It made him look like he could tip over when standing up.

He motioned for Bernadette to take a seat, pushing several files to one side and sitting back in his chair.

"Hey, Chief, how're doing?" Bernadette said as she sat down and sipped her coffee.

"I'm fine, but how are you? I'm amazed you're back at work. I thought you needed more time in Paris. Hell, I would have cashed in my chips and stayed there."

Bernadette looked at Durham's tired eyes. He looked older than his forty-four years, but two kids and police work can age any man, and there was no way he'd ever 'cash in his chips,' to leave this.

"Yeah, Paris was nice, but I was getting chubby on the food, and I got a job to do."

Durham looked at the files on his desk. "You sure do. A bunch of drug dealers are having a war over who controls the fentanyl supply in the city."

Bernadette shook her head, "Damn. Don't tell me the dealers are muscling in on the pharmaceutical companies again."

"Still with the terrible sense of humor." He pulled two files from the top of the stack. "Take these two; it's a good place to start. There's an armed robbery and a drug dealer to chase down."

Bernadette took the files and leveled her gaze at Durham, "And... what about the suspect in custody who claims to be my uncle?"

Durham shook his head. "You know the rules. We can't have you tainting any testimony with personal conflict. The prosecutor would be all over us, so would the judge."

"But his statement is hearsay. I've no recollection of an Uncle named Cahal Callahan. He could use this to get around us and pull me off the case."

Durham got up from his desk to pour himself a cup of coffee from his personal coffee machine. He'd brought it in because he drank so much of it. He filled his cup and looked at Bernadette. "I can't risk having you in the same room with him. He's in the Remand Center; the judge took his passport and denied him bail."

"Who has he got for a lawyer?"

"Joe Christie. He's beating the drum to have Cahal released from jail. I don't think I've seen more motions in my life," the chief said, pushing the files to one side.

He pulled some paper clippings from under the files. "These are a bunch of newspaper headlines from our local paper and some in Ireland. They're all saying we have an innocent man locked up, and an old one at that."

Bernadette scanned the pages. "Looks like the old public opinion poll works well for Cahal. How about I see him in an unofficial capacity?"

"What'd'you mean?"

"I leave my badge at my desk and wander over to see if this guy is my uncle."

"You promise not to mention the case? If you do, his lawyer will have him out of jail in seconds, and this department will experience the pain and so will you."

"Chief, I'll just drop by to see someone as a potential family member, the blood thicker than water thing," Bernadette said. She knew the defense attorney, Joe Christie, when she was a constable in another province. Back then he was a crusader for his clients. He'd do everything he could for Cahal Callahan. She'd have to watch herself to not cross him.

Durham threw up his hands. "Okay, go, but if you sign in over there as Detective Callahan by mistake, I'll hand your ass to you on a platter."

"I got it," Bernadette said, getting up and taking the files with her.

. . .

SHE WALKED out of the office and over to the serious crimes division room where she worked. Two other detectives, Marsha Evanston and Brad Sawchuck, were busy at their desks.

Evanston was ten years older than Bernadette. She'd been with the RCMP detachment for five years, pulling herself up the hard way from constable to detective. She was also a girl from the far north, just like Bernadette. Sawchuck was a recent addition from Winnipeg; they had brought in him to form a task group on drug dealers. The way the users were dying on the streets, the dealers were winning.

Bernadette sidled up to Evanston and stood beside her, dropping a pair of ice hockey tickets on her desk.

Evanston pulled her head up from her computer screen and looked at the tickets and back to her screen. "Are those for tonight's game against the Edmonton Oil Kings?"

"Yes, they are. I got other plans, thought you might use them."

Evanston swept the tickets into her desk drawer. "I love the Red Deer Rebels. I don't have to kill anyone for these, do I? I have to draw the line somewhere."

Bernadette smiled, she loved her sense of humor. Always dry, always good. "Evans, I'd never cause you grief. I just need a peek at the Cahal Callahan file, just to get up to speed."

"Aw shit, I wish you'd asked me to kill someone. I'd be better off. If the chief finds out my ass is grass and he's a lawnmower."

"Look, I said a peek, I just want to see what they have on him. I'm not on the case, I'm only... an interested party."

Evanston reached into her desk and pulled out the file.

"Take it to your desk, read it, and bring it back here. You have ten minutes."

Bernadette found a desk in the corner, far from the prying eyes of Sawchuck. He claimed he'd transferred to the smaller City of Red Deer to be closer to the Rocky Mountains and fishing, but in the time he'd been there, no one heard him talking of fishing. The squad room rumor mill pegged Sawchuck as a demotion for some screw up or a divorce. The guy didn't talk much outside of work or go to the pub on Friday. You can't trust what you don't know is a detective's best defense.

The file had the arresting report of Cahal Callahan, a photocopy of his passport from the Republic of Ireland. Birthplace registered as Kildare on February 12, 1945. He claimed he had two siblings, Aideen Callahan his sister and Dominic Callahan his younger brother, which was Bernadette's deceased father. He had the birthdate of her father and his birthplace correct.

The interview with Evanston and Sawchuk showed little. Cahal kept saying he could not remember much of the night. He'd stated that with his age and the long flight from Dublin to Calgary, he'd become disoriented.

When Evanston asked him why he visited the seminary so late at night, he claimed the jet lag from the long flight and the fact that he hadn't changed his watch from Ireland made him forget the time.

The file had a copy of the ticket from his flight. He'd left Dublin at 0835 on a flight to Frankfurt, Germany, and then a direct flight to Calgary that arrived at 1455. The flight was nine and a half hours. On arriving at Customs, Cahal gave Detective Bernadette Callahan as his contact in Canada. He'd written in her home address but not her cell phone number. Instead, he'd given the phone number of the RCMP headquarters in Red Deer.

How he made the two-hour drive to Red Deer from the airport in Calgary was another mystery. He said he found a ride with some good people he met at the airport who dropped him at a gas station on a major road into town. From there, he claims he found another lift to the seminary.

His reason for going to the seminary was that he'd tried to reach his niece, Bernadette Callahan, but was told she was away until further notice. He decided he'd go to the seminary to wait for his niece, Bernadette, to return.

Evanston had asked why Cahal didn't leave a phone message for Bernadette. He said he didn't want to spoil the surprise.

He claimed he was going to make a surprise visit to his old friend Father Dominic instead. They'd been to a boy's home together at one time. Father Dominic couldn't corroborate the report, as he was not lucid as yet.

There was also the charge of an illegal weapon. Cahal claimed he had no knowledge that his knife was illegal. The knife had been a gift. However, he couldn't recall who'd given it to him.

Bernadette sighed as she read the report. This was the most confused old man or the perfect alibi.

She pulled out the incident report and found little to work with. No witness to the shooting and no weapon. They a bullet from the chapel, but no shell casing.

From running the bullet through the IBIS, the Integrated Ballistics Identification System, from an uploaded scan of the bullet and an exhaustive check, Evanston had determined the gun as a Sturm Ruger pistol and the bullet a twenty-two caliber.

Bernadette let her finger rest on the information. Who the hell brings a twenty-two to kill someone, unless you get close in? The chapel was small and the range close, but if you wanted to knock someone off, why not bring along a nine-millimeter?

The report went onto say that the bullet grazed Father Dominic; had it been a millimeter more to the right, he would have been dead. The injury had resulted in a concussion. Something he would recover from, but at his age it would take time. There was also a note on the report about a screw up at the hospital but it only mentioned, "a misdiagnosis resulting in a lack of being able to speak with the victim."

The last remark on the report was no GSR found on the suspect. That meant no gunshot residue on Cahal's hands. But they found him without gloves. Had he dropped them somewhere?

She rubbed her forehead; she had more questions than answers. She closed the file and dropped the file back on Evanston's' desk.

Evanston looked up at her as she slid the file back under her pile. "You satisfied now?"

"Not really. How long before you have to spring him on what you brought him in on?"

Evanston raised an eyebrow. "Wow, that obvious, huh? The Crown Prosecutor asked for another thirty-six hours for us to recover any evidence."

"Is the judge going for it?"

"I think so. Cahal's all we got. Unless a ghost fired the gun, he's the only man around. We have a team of officers with a dog searching for the weapon today. Maybe something will turn up."

Bernadette walked out of the office. The mention of the word ghost sent a chill down her spine. This man who claimed to be her uncle had the weirdest story and had appeared in her life at the strangest time. She needed to see him face to face.

3

THE REMAND CENTER was a short walk from the police detachment, so was the courthouse. The justice system worked like this: the Royal Canadian Mounted Police Force made the arrests; the accused appeared in court, then off to the remand Center while the crown prosecutor and the defense lawyers haggled over the case.

The last word was the judge. From there, the accused made their way through the Canadian legal system. An excellent defense, or in most cases a decent alibi and no witnesses, saw an accused go free. A poor defense and no alibi meant you were in remand; you stayed there until your day in court. If found guilty, off you went to a provincial or federal jail depending on your sentence.

The legal system had placed all the buildings close by to work in tune with each other, but the process churned slowly. Not enough clerks, not enough lawyers, and too many clients clogged the system. People could languish in remand for months waiting for their trials while lawyers, judges, and clerks fought over mountains of paper to deal with them.

The only get out of jail card was lack of evidence to process an accused. The system had forty-eight hours, with an allowance of another seventy-two if the police needed more time.

As Bernadette walked the two blocks from the police headquarters to the remand center, she knew the clock was ticking. The police had only circumstantial evidence on Cahal Callahan, so thin that no prosecutor in his right mind would present it to a judge without getting a reprimand and told to not waste his time.

The sun was finally showing itself at 8 a.m.; it glowed in the sky but did nothing for the February chill. Snow covered the sidewalks and streets. A snowplow roared by, plowing the snow onto the sidewalk, A man with a shovel on the sidewalk cursed as the plow destroyed his morning's work. The snowplow moved on as more snow fell and piled up behind it.

Bernadette made her way inside the center, stamping her boots to clear off the snow and taking off her gloves. Behind the reception desk, Ernest Rheingold smiled as he saw her. She'd caught a break; he was a good guy to deal with. She'd known him for the past several years.

Ernest was pushing past sixty and close to his pension. He was almost as wide as he was high, with an enormous head of gray hair and a big mustache that gave him the nickname of the Walrus. He treated everyone with a smile and wave, wanted everyone, including the inmates, to relax; hard to do in a place like this. The center had 147 beds. Ernest was so cheerful when you came in, you might think you'd entered a low-cost hotel. But that wasn't the case.

The place smelled of strong disinfectant to mask the state of many of the inmates who entered the facility. They were often drunk, high on drugs or just pulled from the street. This was not a cheerful place.

This was a place where people ended up who wondered how or when they might free or when they would start serving a longer sentence in a more hardened facility.

Ernest smiled when he saw Bernadett., "Well, Detective Callahan, a delight to see you this frosty morning. I suspect you're here on official business. Which of our wonderful guests would you care to visit this morning?"

Bernadette came right to the window and pressed her face to the glass and the speaker so the other guard couldn't hear. "I'm here unofficially, Ernest. I need to see Cahal Callahan... kind of family business."

"Ah, I see. Let me get you signed in on a regular visitor pass. I'll need a piece of ID, Ms. Callahan," Ernest said.

Bernadette nodded and pulled out her driver's license. The best thing about Ernest is he got it right away. He knew the law, that she couldn't be seeing Cahal officially. He also knew that he was violating the protocol of regular visiting hours, but that didn't bother Ernest. He signed her in and told her to wait in the sparse waiting room.

The waiting room had rows of plastic chairs facing each other that allowed you to see the misery on the faces of visitors to this place. There, you could sit across from someone and wonder if their loved ones were in as much shit as the person you were about to see.

It took all of twenty minutes before Ernest motioned for Bernadette to go through the large metal door. The door buzzed. She entered a small room with a window. She showed her visitor's badge and got buzzed through the second door.

A guard named Jenkins met her on the other side. The little smirk on his face said it all. Here was a detective to see a relative. Her hand twitched; she'd love to slap that grin right off his face. She nodded at him and followed him to the visitor's room.

Jenkins opened the door, said she had fifteen minutes, and swung the door shut behind her.

There, leaning back in a chair wearing an orange jumpsuit, sat Cahal Callahan. He had shaggy gray hair and bushy eyebrows, a long and narrow face with thin lips and pale green eyes that watched her as she entered.

"I was wondering when you might appear, my dear Bernadette. My god, you look so much like your father. What a delight it is to see you, and here I am all tied up in this infernal mess. You must wonder about the state of your old uncle," he said in rapid-fire sentences as he got up from his chair.

"Don't get up. Stay where you are." Bernadette said. "There is no touching of prisoners."

Bernadette took a chair at a table across from Cahal. "And it remains to be seen if I'm your relative."

Cahal brushed his hand through this hair. "What? You mean to say your father never spoke of me or your aunt Aideen?"

Bernadette held his gaze, "Nope, never mentioned you. I thought all his relations in Ireland were dead—or not speaking to him if they were alive."

Cahal sat up and threw his hands in the air. "Ah, me and your father, Dominic, had a bit of a falling out, as it were."

"Really?" Bernadette asked as she crossed her arms. "Why don't you enlighten me about the Callahan clan that I've never heard from until now."

"Well, it was the time of the Troubles in Ireland. Your father was all of fifteen or sixteen when he got involved."

"Got in involved how?"

Cahal wiped his hand across his face as if he was allowing his memory to reboot. "He got in with the petrol bombers. A bunch of sixteen- and seventeen-year-old boys, too young to join the IRA, would throw five pounds of gelignite strapped onto a butcher's hook with a ten second fuse, then they'd run like hell." He looked up at her. "The British army had enough of it, and they said they'd shoot all petrol bombers dead. I told your dad to get out of Ireland before he became a martyr."

"He hated you for that? For saving his life?"

"Your da was thick skinned, not taken to instructions. I had to remove him by force from his mates and throw him on a boat to get him away."

"Explain force to me," Bernadette said, unfolding her arms and leaning across the table.

Cahal dropped his head. "I put a drug in your da's pint, then dropped him off at the harbor. I put him on a container ship as a cook's helper. Cost me a fair bit to get him some fake papers and all, but he never thanked me for that. He got a nice tour of the world on that ship, sailed around Africa and all the way to Singapore. Not one postcard from the ungrateful whelp."

"I think they call the term being 'Shanghaied,' as in put on a ship against one's own will," Bernadette said.

"What's the harm in that? He got taught a cook's trade and saw a bit of the world, and might I add, he didn't end up dead from a British army bullet. I say that's a fair deal for any man."

Bernadette leaned back. "So, I'm supposed to believe this story, that you saved my father and sent him off to see the world, and he landed in Canada never once mentioning what you'd done for him?"

Cahal managed a weak smile. "Does sound like he was ungrateful, doesn't it now?"

"No, it sounds like a fantastic tale. My father never once said he knew how to cook or showed us he could. He was a musician when my mother met him, he worked in bars when he wasn't singing. He was also an alcoholic, did you know that?"

Cahal nodded. "Aye, the Callahan's have been known to suffer the sins of drink. I have been accused of such a thing. It doesn't surprise me your father was a musician, your great Uncle William, well now, that man played a hell of a fiddle."

The door opened, Jenkins yelled time's up, and stood there waiting for Bernadette to leave.

Bernadette got up from the table and leaned forward so Jenkins couldn't hear her. "I think you have a hell of a story, Mr. Callahan, if that's your actual name. Whether you're related to me remains to be seen. So far, I've heard nothing that makes me believe it."

Cahal lowered his voice to a whisper. "But, you've got to get me out of here. I'm your blood, can't you see it in my eyes? We're kin. How can you not see that?"

"Sorry, can't help you there. I can't be involved in your case. If you're innocent, the courts will set you free." Bernadette turned and walked past Jenkins without looking at him.

When she hit the street, her face was burning so hot she hardly felt the cold. It took her a block before she put her gloves on. When she reached the detachment, she went to her desk and took out a piece of paper she'd made notes on when she looked at Cahal's file.

There was a phone number of Aideen Callahan in Ireland. She poised her hand over the telephone. She couldn't believe she was sweating. She looked around; she felt like a kid in a candy store about to steal something. This was police time, not her personal business. But she was dying to know.

She dialed the number of Aideen Callahan. The phone rang a long time before an old voice replied, "Hello. Callahan residence."

"Is this Aideen Callahan?"

"Why yes, it is. How may I help you?"

"I got your number from Cahal Callahan. My name is Bernadette Callahan."

"Oh my, so happy to hear your voice. I haven't seen you since you were a baby," Aideen replied.

"I don't believe I've ever been to Ireland—you must be mistaken."

"Oh no, your da brought you over to see me before he took you to Canada. I have your picture right here," Aideen said.

"Where do you live?" Bernadette asked.

"I'm in a little village called Kilmeague in County Kildare. I've lived here all my life, no other relatives around. I'm all alone here."

"Do you know that Cahal is in jail here in Canada?"

"Oh, I heard about it just yesterday in our local paper, and the parish priest came by to see me about it. A dreadful thing it is. Can you do something for him?"

"I'm afraid I can't. I'm an officer of the law and I cannot be involved if the person charged claims to be my relative."

"I see, but maybe you can help him somehow, my dear. You are his niece. And he's so far from home."

Bernadette looked up to see Evanston waving to get her attention. "I have to go now, my duties call. Perhaps we'll talk again."

"That would be nice, my dear. It's been far too long."

Evanston walked up to her. "We got another ten thirty-eight at the seminary, and Durham told me you were up on this one. Sawchucks got some kind of dental thingy going on."

Callahan grabbed her gun from her desk. She followed Evanston to the hall where they put on their winter parkas and boots. A ten thirty-eight was code for a fatality.

"Any idea on the victim?"

"I didn't say victim, I said body. Why do you think we got a murder?" Evanston asked.

Bernadette closed her eyes and shook her head. "Damn it, I said victim, didn't I." She paused for a moment. "No idea why I said that. Let's get out there."

4

THE DRIVE to the seminary was cold. They'd had to take a vehicle that had been outside overnight. The upholstered seats felt like blocks of ice. Bernadette wished she'd taken her own car with leather seats and seat warmers, a true luxury in Canada that no one should be without.

Morning traffic was light as they headed out of town. They were both quiet until Evanston broke the silence.

"So, what did your relative, Cahal, have to say for himself?"

Bernadette looked over at Evanston. Sunglasses hid her eyes. But the look of judgement was there.

"What makes you think I went to see, Cahal?"

"Really?" Evanston asked, taking her eyes off the road for a second. She looked back at the road with a slight smile.

Bernadette stared straight at the road. "Okay, I dropped in on him, but as a civilian. To check if the guy had any family resemblance."

"And...?"

Bernadette blew out a breath. "I do not understand. I phoned someone who claimed to be my aunt in Ireland, but

I'm still not sure. This is so much better, going to view a body, than talking to someone who claims to be part of your family."

Evanston chuckled. "Yeah, I hear you. I got several relatives on Frank's side and mine I would like to trade in or trade up for something that approximates a reasonable human being. But in the great DNA shuffle you get what you get."

"Yeah, I hear you. Which reminds me, I got to plan my wedding in the next few months. You got any insights into that, as in inviting relatives?" Bernadette asked.

"Sure do. The relatives you invite will be pissed they have to attend because they have to spend money for presents and travel. The ones you don't invite will be pissed they didn't get to come," Evanston said.

"Thanks, you're a great help," Bernadette said with a smile. She looked out over the frozen landscape. "You get much information on what we're attending?"

"Yeah, Stewart's on the scene. They found one of the seminary's residents swinging from a rafter in his room."

THEY PULLED into the driveway of the seminary. A coroner's van and a police cruiser were at the entrance. They went in the front door. An elderly priest stood ready to greet them.

"I'm Father Francis, please follow me," the priest said with a solemn voice. He wore a black floor-length cassock. A set of scuffed boots peeked out from beneath the heavy woolen folds. His clerical collar wasn't on straight, as if he'd struggled to put it on before coming to meet them. He looked like he was in his eighties, but it was hard to tell in the half-light of dark wood and tapestry. Bernadette put him down as beyond his prime and living on something borrowed. She followed his shuffling figure.

They made their way down a long hallway, then up several flights of stairs before they arrived at the room. Constable Stewart was standing outside with his notebook.

"What've we got, Constable?" Bernadette asked as she approached him.

Stewart looked at his notes. "One of the other priests, Father Josaphat, found him this morning. He was hanging from the rafter in his room."

"Has anyone disturbed the body?" Evanston asked.

"We couldn't in all conscience leave Father Fredericks in that manner," Father Francis said from behind them.

Bernadette turned to him. "Yes, I understand that, Father, but still it—" She stopped in mid-sentence as the coroner, Dr. Keith Andrew, came out of the room. He was removing his gloves.

"Aye, I'd like a word with you if I may, Detectives," Dr. Andrew said as he motioned for them to come into the room with him.

Dr. Andrew was a Scot. You noticed it not only by his distinct accent—he drew every word out like he was revving a car engine over his tongue—but the giveaway was he wore a kilt all year round. At this moment, he wore his kilt under his lab coat. He had on his tall leather boots and often wore a tweed jacket.

"What's up?" Bernadette asked the doctor.

"This was no suicide. If it was, this old man would have been a former Olympian to have suspended himself from that rafter."

"He couldn't have got up there with a chair?" Evanston asked, looking up at the high ceiling with the beam and the still dangling rope.

"No, not on your bloody life. Check it for yourself."

Bernadette put on her gloves and grabbed the chair. The body of Fredericks lay beside it. She righted it and stood on it. The noose was still a foot above it.

"You figure I'm about the same height as the deceased?" she asked, looking down at the body.

"Ah, a dead ringer, if you don't mind the pun."

"Thanks, Doctor," Bernadette said as she got off the chair. "I assume you checked this chair for footprints."

Dr. Andrew smiled, "Now you ask me. Of course it has. We found nothing on it. Why do you think I let you get up there?"

"Any abrasions or marks on the victim?"

"None," Dr. Andrew said. His busy eyebrows rose as if in a question mark. "I have a feeling we'll find something in a toxicology screen."

"You think someone drugged him before they placed him on the rafters?" Bernadette asked.

"Aye, the victim doesn't appear like someone with the strength to jump up into that noose on his own."

"Wouldn't the killer figure that when he strung him up?" Evanston asked. "Wait, what am I saying? Most of our killers have the IQ of a turnip. Why wouldn't he? He was probably in a hurry, chose the rafter, then found the rope was too short."

"There you go, question asked and answered," Andrew said.

"Any idea of time of death, Doctor?" Bernadette asked.

"Aye, from the liver temperature and the look on his face, I'd say around three this morning."

Bernadette walked out of the room to Constable Stewart. "You get any idea of people traffic in and out of here yet?"

Stewart shook his head. "The head of maintenance—"

he looked at his notes, "—a guy named Dmitri Vlasik. He says they never lock their doors at night. They figure they're far enough out in the country... if someone needs their help, they can find shelter."

"Great, so the killer can just walk in. They should put a sign on the door, they might get some axe murderers," Bernadette said.

Stewart just shrugged and looked back at his notes.

Bernadette looked around the seminary. "I guess we start by taking statements from everyone."

"That's about it," Stewart said. "There's only two farmhouses between here and Range Road and we had a near blizzard last night. I suspect we'll get nothing, but I sent Constable Jellenick to talk to the few neighbors. Maybe one of them couldn't sleep and saw some lights on the road."

Bernadette walked over to Father Francis. "How many residents living here, Father?"

"We have only seven residents. There is a cook, and a man who does some maintenance and shovels the snow; that's nine in all. The cook lives here and the maintenance man lives in town."

Bernadette turned towards Evanston. "I guess we got three each. Stewart, you take the maintenance man and the cook and the priest who found our victim and we'll get statements from the rest."

"You called Father Fredericks a victim?" Father Francis said, adjusting his glasses on his nose.

"Yes, I did," Bernadette said. "Our coroner believes someone helped the good Father Fredericks onto the beam in his room."

"But this is a sacrilege in this house of God. My word! What will I tell the bishop? First the shooting of Father Dominic, now this," Father Francis said. He walked to a bench in the hallway and sat down, placing his hands on his knees.

Evanston stood beside Bernadette. "What's it going to be, you going to interview him or me?"

Bernadette blew out a breath. "This is what I get for being a bad Catholic. I'll take him. I'll get a list of the residents from him and we'll get to it." She turned to Evanston. "We best tell the chief we got a murder investigation here. I doubt if this is going to make his day."

"It isn't a good day for Father Fredericks," Evanston said, and then paused. "I think that's a terrible analogy."

Bernadette shook her head. "There are no good analogies for murder, but that one will do for now."

THEY INTERVIEWED and took statements from all the residents in the seminary in the next few hours. What Bernadette learned is that the seminary was over one hundred years old. The place once bustled with students who were training to be priests, but with cost cuts in the Catholic Church, this place of fifty rooms and large acreage had become a burden.

"It's been up for sale as a private listing for five years," Father Francis told Bernadette.

"Why do you live here then? To keep the lights on?" Bernadette asked and then wished she hadn't.

Father Francis sighed. "I was an educator here once. The old halls rang with the excited sounds of young men filling their heads with knowledge before heading out to spread the words of our Lord to the world." His eyes closed as he let the memories flood over him.

"How long has it been mothballed... I mean how long since it hasn't been a school?"

"Quite some time, I'm afraid. We had our best years in the nineteen sixties to the nineteen nineties. Then, in this century, things faltered...."

Bernadette dropped her head to her notebook. The unspoken item was the storm of sexual abuse of children by priests that broke over the Catholic Church in 2002. The first to uncover it was a newspaper in Boston. It rolled over the country like a tsunami as allegations came to light all over North America.

"When did it close as a seminary?" Bernadette finally asked.

"In two thousand and five, I'm afraid. They sent our last students to Vancouver and Calgary, and we became a sanctuary for those too old to carry out their duties." Father Francis raised his eyebrows. "I guess we're a last home for the aged priest. We have a graveyard of our former residents out back." He motioned with his arm towards the outside. "It seems the ultimate destination for us all."

"Can you tell me about your residents? The long time ones and any new arrivals?" Bernadette asked.

"That's easy. All the residents have been with us for years except for Fathers Dominic, Fredericks, and Josaphat. They arrived from Ireland only a few weeks ago."

"Who sent them?"

"I received word from the bishop in Edmonton that the two priests were to be our new residents, and Father Josaphat arrived one week before them."

"Did you get a reason for their arrival?"

"Oh no, my dear detective, I would never question the directive of the bishop. We do God's work here, we would never question what they ask of us."

Bernadette held back a frown. Those very words grated on her like a fingernail going over a chalkboard. She composed herself. "I'll need the contact information for the bishop in Edmonton."

"But why?"

"Because we ask questions in the police force, it's our job, Father."

"Ah, yes, I suppose it is. I'll get it for you right away.

Bernadette finished her interviews and joined up with Evanston at their car. The wind was doing a good job of throwing snow sideways and obliterating the roads as they drove back to the detachment.

"Any ideas?" Bernadette asked Evanston as she peered over the steering wheel, trying to find the road.

"I got nothing from my interviews. I had three old priests that could barely shuffle without a walker. Stewart had the same with the cook. That lady is less than five feet and just about as round. And did you check out the maintenance guy? How does that guy gets around? He's got a limp. His wife drops him off and picks him up."

"So, you sum this up how?"

"Here's my take. You got someone who follows these two from Ireland and is trying to settle a score," Evanston said without taking her eyes off the road. She'd slowed down to a crawl as they approached the intersection. Going into the ditch on a snowy road got any officer or detective a good ribbing. Evanston had hit the ditch twice that year; she wasn't going for a three-peat.

"But why? Do you think someone in Ireland made these guys for perv's, found their case files and saw they did some nasty stuff back in Ireland, then followed them here to take them out?" Bernadette asked.

"You got me. I think we have to get their files."

Bernadette looked out at the driving snow. "We're going

up against the Catholic Church. That's going to be a lot of bullshit we don't need."

"But they have to give it to us, don't they? They can't hold out on us, right?"

"You're right, they can't, but this is going to be far above our pay grade. I'll get the chief to call our crown prosecutor who will put in the request and we go from there."

"Oh, this sounds like fun. Look, I'm heading to the Rebels hockey game, what're you doing tonight."

Bernadette smiled. "I think I'll be doing some catching up with my big hunk of a fiancé."

"Is he cooking tonight? What's on the menu? And if you say it's going to be you, I'm throwing your silly ass in the snowbank."

Bernadette smiled. She looked at her phone message. Her face dropped into a frown.

"What's up?" Evanston asked.

"The shit just literally hit the fan."

5

BERNADETTE GOT BACK to the detachment to find Chief Durham. He was in his office, pushing piles of paper from one side of his desk to the other.

"You get my message," Durham said, looking up.

"Yeah, I got it, but I'm not sure if I comprehend it. Cahal Callahan is getting out tomorrow?"

Durham tilted his head to one side. "Yep, his lawyer got the news about the death at the seminary. He filed for an immediate release. I got to admit if you want an alibi, being in prison is good."

"But isn't he still under suspicion for aggravated assault?" Bernadette asked in disbelief.

Durham shrugged. "No weapon, no witness, you can't ask for a better case for acquittal. The Crown has nothing. They'd keep him if they did. With the heavy snow out there, I can't send out the tracking dogs."

"Damn, this sucks," Bernadette said.

Durham pushed his file to one side. "We don't prosecute without evidence. That's in basic detective training."

"I sense Cahal is up to something. I can't put my finger on it. No one flies all this way to see someone and doesn't remember much of the details of the flight."

"You ever flown to Hong Kong from Vancouver? I'm sure my soul left my body halfway there on the eleven and half hour flight." Durham said.

Bernadette shook her head and looked at her watch. "It's past seven, and I told Chris I'd be home by six."

"Yeah, you better get going. Oh, and the crown prosecutor says he needs to speak to you."

Bernadette was heading for the door and turned. "What for?"

"No idea. To see if he's on the guest list for your wedding, perhaps?"

Bernadette rolled her eyes. "Sure, no really, what does he want?"

"Again, I got no idea. Go home to your man. And my wife says we're only coming to your wedding if it's in Cancun, but not if it's in hurricane season."

"Thanks, I'll take that into consideration." Bernadette headed out the door. She'd almost forgot. She had a wedding to plan.

She was happy her Jeep was in underground parking, which meant nice and warm. She fired it up and drove home in the driving snow. The snow was going sideways again with the wind, never a good driving experience.

She made it home, pulled into the garage, and parked the Jeep. She heard the sounds of their dog, Sprocket, their large German Shepherd, barking at the door. He was a two-year-old dropout from RCMP training school. Bernadette picked him up when someone told her the dog could not make the grade. It immediately attracted her to him. The dog's problem was attention deficit disorder, the same as hers. They ran together on both warm and cold days, and he got into almost as much trouble as she did.

Sprocket took to Chris, her fiancé, easily. Chris was a big, soft-spoken man who loved the outdoors. When Bernadette was working, Chris often took Sprocket on long runs or out to the streams to fish. They were like two kids hanging out.

Bernadette opened the door. The dog greeted her. He put a paw on her shoulder as she knelt down.

"You miss me, big fella?" Bernadette asked as she scratched his ears.

"How did you guess?" Chris answered with a laugh from the kitchen. He was wearing an apron, working a mixing bowl with a whisk.

Bernadette looked up with a smile. "Oh, yeah, you too, big guy." She patted the dog and walked over to Chris and let herself fold into his enormous arms.

Chris was, in the terms of Evanston, a hunk. He was six feet tall, curly black hair and brown eyes from his Greek heritage with a package of biceps, triceps and pectorals from his love of working out in the gym and being outside.

They'd had some rough patches together, got through them, and now they needed to plan a wedding.

Bernadette looked into his bowl. "What's for dinner? And so sorry I'm late."

Chris winked. "I'm throwing together an Italian sausage and potato pie with provolone. I'm about to mix it together and throw it in the oven. It takes forty-five minutes to cook." He handed her a glass of red wine. "You have time for a shower, but if you want me to assist, I can be available."

Bernadette kissed him hard on the lips and smiled. "Okay, sweetie, but let me wash off the daily grime before you come in, okay?"

"Sure, hard day at work?"

Bernadette closed her eyes and put her hand to her neck. "The usual cloak and dagger stuff. I could use a little neck massage."

"I'll be right in as soon as I put my latest creation in the oven," Chris said.

Bernadette stepped into the bathroom and undressed. She let the shower run hot before getting in. The water felt good on her back and shoulders. The biggest part of her day was unwinding. Putting dead bodies out of her mind, the sight of victims, the faces of the bystanders. So far, with the help of Chris and the faithful attention of Sprocket, she got by. But the dreams at night were the problem.

She grabbed the soap and cleaned the residue of the day from her body and her mind. The door open. She leaned into the shower and let the water run down her back. Moments later, two firm hands massaged her neck and releasing her tension. The hands moved to her breasts. She moaned softly.

"We have to be quiet," Chris, cautioned. "Sprocket's at the door, he'll bark if he hears you."

Bernadette turned around and grabbed Chris. "Cover your ears, because he's going to howl like there's a full moon."

FIFTY MINUTES later they were sitting down to dinner. Sprocket lay in the corner, his eyes regarding Chris with suspicion. The noises from the bathroom made him howl and scratch at the door. Bernadette had to call out twice to get him to calm down.

"This is an excellent dish," Bernadette said as she swallowed a mouthful of Chris's creation and reached for her wineglass.

Chris patted his lips with his napkin. "It's a little dish I picked up off the internet."

Bernadette drank a sip of wine. "I thought this might be something you got from your Greek mother."

Chris grinned. "My mother does nothing outside of Greek cuisine."

"No offense against your mother, but that's probably why I like this so much."

Chris reached behind him and grabbed his iPad. "There's something I've been meaning to show you ever since you got home."

"Didn't you show me everything in the shower? You mean there's more?"

"Hilarious. You remember I sent my DNA sample away months ago and never heard from them."

"Yeah, well, you were kind of busy doing security work in Afghanistan, that could have been the problem."

"I sent them an email yesterday and enquired. They apologized profusely and said they'd misplaced the file. They found it today and sent the results."

Bernadette pushed the light on the iPad to make it brighter. "So I'm about to find out you're the real thing, like you're related to the Greek God Apollo and a direct descendant of Zeus?"

Chris shook his head. "Look at the chart."

"Holy shit.... this means..."

"Yeah, it seems crazy. Read it out loud."

"You're four percent Greek—what the hell?"

"Keep reading it gets better."

"Fifteen percent Italian and the rest is...?"

"Ashkenazi Jewish."

"Wow." Bernadette said. "Damned if I ever saw that coming. Have you told your mother?"

Chris sipped his wine and gazed into Bernadette's eyes. She'd never seen him so serious. "I've got a feeling that I have kept a bunch of my family history from me."

"Did your mother ever talk about Jewish relatives?"

"No, according to her father, my grandfather was from Corfu, his name was Markellos," Chris said, shifting in his chair. He took the iPad from her and hit his email site. "Look at the email conversation I've been having with a person who is a ninety-eight percent match for my second cousin."

"His name is Malik," Bernadette said, scrolling over the email.

Chris winked. "It sure is. If you look at his text, he claims the Malik's hid out from the Nazis occupation of Greece by changing their names. He knows my mother and knows of me. My mother tried to keep her identity hidden so she could marry a Greek man."

"But why are you not more Greek in your DNA? I mean if you father was full Greek, wouldn't that kind of do... what's the word, like a blend?" Bernadette said. "Sorry if I'm using the wrong words, sounds like you're a cocktail."

"Don't be sorry, we're all part of a genetic cocktail. Mine seems mislabeled. As for my father, I got another hit from a second cousin in Rhodes, his last name is Eliakim and he claims my father is his great uncle."

"So, both sides of your family were hiding their Jewish identity?"

"Yeah. I wonder if my mother knew my father was Jewish. Wouldn't that be a twist of fate?"

"Did you have any suspicions growing up?"

"Yeah, here's the funny thing, they circumcised me at birth. Most Greek kids in Toronto aren't. I know it's weird, but it was something the other Greek kids pointed out to me in the showers after gym glass."

"Okay, that is funny, I didn't know you guys spent all that time checking out each other's packages."

Chris took a sip of his wine. "And you girls never looked at each other's boobs in the shower?"

Bernadette raised her glass. "Point well made. So what made you think you were different other than that they snipped you?"

"My mother was too adamant about being Greek, almost too much. We had to speak Greek in the house, the first to church, and I was only to have Greek friends and marry a Greek girl."

"Maybe that's why you were such a rebellious sort?"

"I would say that had a big part in it. And here's another thing. I remember meeting a kid, his name was Marty Cohen, a hell of a nice guy, my mother freaked out afterwards, said I couldn't hang around with him."

Bernadette put her hand on Chris's arm. "You think she was afraid for you? I heard stories of how the Nazis purged most of Greece of the Jews. Maybe, she thought by hiding your identity, she was keeping you safe from it ever happening again."

"I'm not sure..."

Bernadette's cell phone rang. She looked at it. "Damn, I best answer this—it's the crown prosecutor."

She picked up the phone, spoke for a minute, and said, "Do I have a choice?"

"What's that all about?" Chris asked.

"They're letting Cahal Callahan out of the remand center tomorrow morning. There's an arraignment in front of the judge at eight, and I have to be there as a relative of record."

"What the hell? How did you get that designation?"

"I'm a relative until proven innocent," Bernadette said.

She drained her glass of wine. "I'll clean up the dishes. I need to move around to let my head clear from all the recent information I've downloaded."

6

BERNADETTE WAS AWAKE AT FIVE. Chris lay there snoring softly with his big hand over her body, but she couldn't make herself go back to sleep. She moved his hand, got out of bed, making for the kitchen to make coffee.

Sprocket was at her heels in a second, his cold nose on the back of her legs. He wanted to run this morning, and so did she. As the coffee maker dripped the precious black liquid into the carafe, she checked the weather app on her phone. The temperature was minus twenty Celsius. Damn cold for a run, but she would dress for it.

As the coffee did its last gurgle, she pulled out her running clothes from the spare room. She kept them there so she wouldn't bother Chris getting dressed for running, which was her early morning obsession. She pulled on a pair of long merino wool underwear, put on a sports bra, then a long sleeve merino wool top. She then put on a light vest with a windbreaker, a pair of wind pants, wool socks and a woolen hat. There was also a wool neck warmer she'd pull over her face if the wind got ugly, which it sometimes did.

She came out of the second bedroom and Sprocket got excited seeing her in running gear. She shushed him and took several sips of her coffee and put the rest in an insulated coffee thermos for Chris when he woke up.

She opened the front door. A rush of icy cold air hit her in the face. She took a deep breath. The first ten minutes were the hardest. Once the body warmed up, she only had to keep her extremities warm. Her gloves and running shoes had insulation made for crazy runners like her who braved conditions like this. Her running shoes had special cleats for the snow, and she wore a headlamp with over two hundred lumens that lit the snow up and made it look like diamonds.

No new snow had fallen. The road lay before her, freshly plowed and sanded. She made excellent progress along the road to the pathway that led to the river. Sprocket ran beside her; this was his element. In this time, they shared a bond of breathing, existing, and just being in the moment.

Bernadette let her mind roll over the events of yesterday. She thought about the victim, the priest. All the residents of the seminary didn't fit any profile of a potential killer. They were so feeble they would have had to ask Father Fredericks to jump onto the rafter to hang himself. The residents of the farmhouses in the area had seen no unusual cars, but then again, none of them had been up at three in the morning.

They had cleared the pathway down to the pavement with some sand thrown onto it. The cleats of her running shoes made a clicking sound as they made contact. She got into a simple rhythm; her breath was streaming from her, covering her woolen cap in frost. Her eyes were tearing up from the cold. The tears turned to droplets of ice on her lashes. She pulled her hand out of a glove, warmed the lashes, and kept going. She was hitting the runners high where the endorphins kick in and flood the nervous system.

The thoughts of the victim came back to her again as her mind hit a point of clarity. The events of the past few days seemed like a hit squad was after Fathers Dominic and Frederick. This had something to do with them both being from Ireland, she was sure of it, and that damned Cahal who claimed to be her uncle was part of it.

Glancing at her watch, she noted she'd been out for a half hour; it was time to head back. She stopped, turned, and began her journey home.

A car came towards her on the road as she came off the pathway. She made room for the car, but it kept angling towards her. Its headlights were blinding her.

She cursed, "Hey dumb ass, can't you see my headlamp?"

She jumped into the snowbank and watched the car pass her. It was a red Honda Civic. She wondered what kind of shape the driver was in. She did a mental note of the vehicle tags to see where this guy lived in the neighborhood.

Bernadette ran the last few blocks in a sprint. By the time she reached the front door, she felt mildly exhausted. She walked in as Chris was pouring himself coffee; she gave him a kiss on the cheek and headed to the shower. The rule of outdoor winter runners—no sweaty hugs.

She toweled her hair off after her shower and joined Chris at the breakfast table. He'd made some oatmeal with brown sugar and some whole-wheat toast with cut up oranges and kiwi fruit.

"How you are doing this morning?" Bernadette asked.

"With what?"

"Ah, your whole DNA thing you talked about last night," Bernadette said.

"It's just that they have fed me a lie for most of my life," Chris said as he spread some strawberry jam on his toast. He looked up at Bernadette. "If my mother had never pushed the Greek thing so hard, I wouldn't have cared. I'd have said, hey cool, my heritage is Jewish. But this seems to be a coverup. I'll find the truth, trust me."

Bernadette sipped her coffee. "Don't burn any bridges with your family, like I have."

Chris smiled. "No sweetheart, I don't think anyone could burn or blow up the bridges you have."

Bernadette lowered her head and grinned. They had a running joke about how she'd alienated her brothers when she'd left her grandmother's home and eventually became a RCMP officer, then a detective. She had been, by her own admission, a bit of a 'self-righteous pain in the ass,' in administering the law that annoyed her brothers.

Bernadette looked at her watch. "My god, it's seven, I got to go."

"You don't start until eight, what's the rush?"

"I want to see if I can get a report of all Irish Nationals that have entered Canada in the past week. I'm sure whoever attempted the hit on Father Dominic and took out Father Fredericks wasn't from here."

"That old intuition of yours kicking in again, is it?" Chris asked as he took the dishes to the dishwasher.

Bernadette had a piece of toast in her mouth as she headed for the door. She stopped, turned around, and took the toast out of her mouth and gave him a kiss.

Chris wiped his mouth with his hand. "Thanks for the seconds on toast."

Bernadette waved her toast over her shoulder as she entered the garage. She pulled the Jeep out of the garage and headed for the detachment.

She was only fifteen minutes away; she sipped on a go

cup of coffee as she headed to work. Out of the corner of her eye, she caught the taillights of a red car heading down a side street.

7

BERNADETTE ARRIVED at the detachment by seven thirty. The morning shift would start soon with the uniforms getting a briefing of the night's activities and the things to be aware of.

The concern today would be the Queen Elizabeth II Highway. The four-lane ribbon of asphalt roared day and night with traffic from Calgary to Edmonton on the west side of the City of Red Deer. The snow from the previous night made the highway into a skating rink for the big rigs and cars that shot up and down it as if it was their personal racetrack.

The pileups on the highway were legendary. If the police placed enough cruisers in strategic spots the traffic slowed, but when an officer got called to an accident, the traffic revved to raceway frenzy. Drivers forgot the hazard of ice and snow beneath their tires.

Bernadette found some more coffee and went to the serious crimes division room and found Evanston. She was busy at her desk with her computer and scribbling things on a piece of paper.

"Hey Evans, how'd the game go last night?"

Evanston lifted her head from the screen. "Total crap. The Rebels had them until the third period, up three goals to one, then the little buggers get a bunch of penalties—we lost five to three."

"So sad," Bernadette said with a consoling pat on Evanston's shoulder.

"I never thought you were a hockey type," Evanston said. "How did you come by those tickets?"

"Oh, just by chance. Somebody gave them to me..." Bernadette said and then moved away to another desk. She didn't want Evanston to know she'd bought the tickets online and printed them off, hoping to use them for a bribe to get a look at Cahal's file.

Evanston watched her as she walked away, the light dawning on her, and she muttered, "Crafty little biscuit," and went back to her computer with a smile.

Chief Durham walked into the room. He had the same harried look as the day before, but with a fresh shirt on. "Okay, listen up. Evanston and Callahan, you're working the Catholic seminary case non-stop. Drop everything else, you got that?"

"What's up, Chief, why the push?" Bernadette asked.

Durham shook his head. "I got a call from Ottawa, from our supreme command. They got a call from a member of parliament who'd got a call from someone high in the Catholic Church. Do I have to draw pictures?"

"No, sir, you don't," Evanston said flashing warning looks at Bernadette.

"Okay then, get on this. Go find some leads and get me something so I can get our other serious crimes solved. Sawchuck, you're on the drug dealers and so is everyone else in the room."

Durham walked out of the room, trying to smooth those few remaining hairs of his onto his scalp.

"Damn it, Bernadette, you always got to ask questions and get us in shit. You know when the chief gets his ass in a wringer he doesn't like to explain himself."

"Look, sorry, it's just in my nature to ask questions. I promise I'll keep a lid on it from now on," Bernadette said.

Evanston frowned and pulled out her notes. "So what have we got?"

"We got nothing. I didn't see any perps in anyone we interviewed last night at the seminary, and the uniforms found nothing from the two farmhouses. Someone came in during last night's snowstorm and drugged our victim and strung him up. That's my take," Bernadette said.

"When can we get an autopsy report?"

"Dr. Andrew said he'd have it this morning. Maybe if we find the drug he used or how he delivered it, we could run it down. But there's something else. I think we reach out to Canada Border Inspection, have them check every Irish National who landed in either Edmonton or Calgary in the past week."

"What's the angle?"

"That Father Jo- something or the other said both the priests had recently arrived from Ireland. I had this crazy notion that someone followed them over to take them out."

"The best crazy notion we got, 'cause I got nothing outside of someone hates priests, and since I'm a non-practicing Anglican, I have no opinion," Evanston said.

Bernadette looked at her watch. "Crap, I've got to be in court in ten minutes. Can you start the border inspection search and I'll get with you when I come back. Oh, and will you run these vehicle tags? Someone almost ran me over this morning."

"Sure, glad to start the heavy lifting," Evanston said in a sarcastic tone.

Bernadette grabbed her jacket, gloves, and scarf and headed for the door. The courthouse was only a few blocks away; not that cold out; the sun was shining, but there was a major obstacle. Reporters.

They were in a huddle just outside the doors of the detachment. If she went down to the parking garage and out the other side, she'd be late. She had to charge through them.

The local television station was there, two radio stations, and a newspaper reporter. There were three of the new social media types. With camera phones ready to post anything at a moment's notice.

Bernadette could feel her skin crawl as she opened the doors and walked outside.

"Any comment on the recent murder at the seminary, detective?" a newspaper reporter asked.

Bernadette stopped for a moment. There hadn't been a mention of a murder; this was a trap. If she said no comment, then the reporter would say the detective of the RCMP Detachment in Red Deer, Alberta, has no comment on the murder of a local priest. This guy was good.

"I'm sorry, but I cannot comment on an ongoing investigation. There has been no determination of murder. I suggest you direct all your questions to our local RCMP detachment, spokesperson."

"He said the same thing you did," a girl with purple streaked hair said from behind her cellphone.

"I have nothing to add, as I mentioned, as this is an ongoing investigation," Bernadette said as she walked away.

A young man thrust a cell phone in her face. "What's

your relationship to Cahal Callahan, the accused. Isn't it true he's your uncle?"

Bernadette stopped and looked at him. He was maybe mid-twenties with a mod haircut and designer glasses. He wore an expensive arctic expedition parka and leather boots. He was instantly unlikeable to Bernadette.

She stopped for a moment to look at him, saying nothing.

"I'm Jacob Burkov of the *Daily Bleed Blog*. Perhaps you want to tell my readers how this affects you, Detective."

"As I have verified nothing, I have nothing to say. I am very busy with my duties," Bernadette said. She whirled and walked away. Who the hell was this guy, and what was the *Daily Bleed Blog*?

THE HEARING for the release of Cahal Callahan was being held in the courtroom of Judge Vicars. She didn't have a good feeling about him. He was very Irish, almost to a fault. He sometimes wore a hideous green suit with a shamrock pattern underneath his robes on St. Patrick's Day, and his little dog would accompany him to his chambers wearing a green tam-o'-shanter hat.

She walked into the courtroom. The place was full, as usual—defense lawyers giving last-minute briefings to clients, relatives, and friends sitting in the courtroom hoping for a good outcome. It looked like a three-ring circus.

She once thought of the courtroom as a parody on the ancient coliseums of Rome. Here, instead of being thrown to the lions, the truth was always on trial.

The truth did not always do well, but somehow motions were filed, summons made, and clients either went their way to freedom or followed a sheriff to incarceration.

They'd moved Cahal's case to the front of the docket so Bernadette could come from the police department and not be waiting all day. The one thing about Judge Vicars, he hated having the police spending hours in his courtroom tied up in testimony when they could be outside fighting crime and bringing him fresh cases.

Bernadette walked to the front of the courtroom and greeted Joe Christie, Cahals' lawyer, and Frank Stallenback, the crown prosecutor.

The judge greeted everyone and asked that the prisoner, Cahal Callahan, be brought in.

Cahal walked dressed in orange coveralls, his hands and legs in shackles. He looked over at Bernadette as he walked in and smiled. She looked down at the floor and found an interesting hangnail to look at.

"I see we're all here," Judge Vicar said. "Now, I believe you have a petition to grant Mr. Cahal his freedom, Mr. Christie?"

Joe was mid-forties, with a beige complexion with soft brown hair and blue eyes. His eyes always narrowed when he considered any question from a judge, as if he were about to set correct the greatest injustice in the world.

Joe Christie rose from his chair. "Yes, your honor. The defense finds no reason my client, Mr. Cahal Callahan, should be incarcerated any further. There is not one shred of evidence found against him. He was only in the wrong place at the wrong time. A mere matter of poor circumstances, and, as an alleged murder has taken place at the seminary yesterday, while my client was locked up in the remand center, I can see no other avenue than to set him free."

"Very well, council, and what does the Crown have to say in response?" Judge Vicar asked of Stallenback.

Stallenback was thin, fifty-plus with a trim pencil mustache that no one had told him was out of style. He shuffled his papers before he spoke. "Well, yes, the defendant may have been in remand during the recent incident which I might add has not been ruled a murder and is still under investigation. But we still need more time to collect evidence in this case."

"How long has he been in remand?" the judge asked.

"Seventy-eight hours, your honor," Christie said in an accusatory tone towards the prosecutor.

"Based on the evidence I see before me, I see no reason to hold this man any further. However, we have the charge of possession of an illegal weapon," the judge said.

"Well, your honor, as my client has stated. This was a misunderstanding on his part. I'm sure considering his age and no past record of any kind, we could let this—"

"Not in my court, you don't," Judge Vicars said. "You can make your arguments on his next trial date. I think we can fit you into March. If something else comes up, we'll let you know. I'll set bail at ten thousand dollars, cash or surety. Please see the clerk of the court."

Cahal stood up. "But your honor, I don't have that kind of money. What am I to do?"

"Unless, your niece, Bernadette Callahan, will pay your bail and take you into her home, I see you as being a guest of our remand center. Or you get on the phone to your people at home and get them to come to your aid. Now, next case," Judge Vicars said, rapping his gavel firmly.

Joe Christie turned to Bernadette. "Well, Detective, I guess it's up to you. Either claim him or see him back in jail."

"But I'm not even sure if he's my relative." Bernadette protested.

"He asked me to give you this," Christie said as he passed a small picture to her.

It was an old photo, yellowed with age, that showed a picture of two men. One was her dad, the other was a much younger Cahal. In his arms he held a young girl. It was her, Bernadette, her two-year-old eyes staring back at her.

"You want me to post his bail and take him in?" Bernadette asked.

The sheriff came beside Cahal. She was a young woman named Cheryl Duncan. She could see the indecision in Bernadette's facial expression. She stood there with the handcuffs, waiting. But her look said it all. The next contestant was waiting. Time to decide.

Bernadette put her hand to her forehead. "I feel like the ghost of my father has come back to haunt me over this. Okay, I'll post bail and take him into my care."

Cahal beamed. "What a wonderful niece you are, my girl. I knew you had the true Callahan spark in you. A fine thing you've done for this old man today."

Bernadette walked over to him. "Uncle Cahal, if that's who you are. I am now effectively your new jailer. You will wait at my house with my fiancé and me until your trail. I'm sure you'll be acquitted. But if you do anything silly to compromise the ten thousand bail I'm putting up for you, I will find you, and I will probably shorten your life. Do you understand me?"

Cahal's smile became wider, and he looked at Joe Christie. "See, what brass this lass has, a champion amongst detectives. Well, let's get going then."

Bernadette put up her hand. "Not so fast. I have to see the clerk of the court and make the arrangements. You can rest easy here. The sheriff will take you to a waiting area and I'll have to phone Chris, my fiancé, to pick you up. I've got a whole shift to fill back at work."

"Well, now, that's grand it is. Perhaps your man and I will drop by a pub to celebrate my release when he comes by," Cahal said.

Bernadette glared at him. "Not bloody likely. Look, you are on bail, that's just like prison but not in prison. You will not be venturing to any pubs, and you will see a court clerk once a week to report."

"Oh, I see... well then, that's fine my dear, no need to cause an uproar. I'll be a meek as a lamb, not a problem. You'll see," Cahal said.

Bernadette turned and headed for the court clerk's office. She sent a text to Chris to tell him what she'd done. He sent a text he was fine with her decision, as Cahal was her relative. He'd pick him up when he was processed.

It took almost an hour to process the bail order. She had to put up the money in a surety which meant an attachment on her mortgage on her home. As the home was still in her name as Chris and she weren't married yet, it was easy. The hardest part was signing the papers.

As she did, she realized that she'd given Cahal Callahan relevance. She'd given him bail, his freedom, and made him real. He just didn't seem real.

She left the courtroom, still livid over having been backed into a corner. Why hadn't Cahal shown her the photo when she'd met him at the jail? It was like a trump card. He played her like she played poker; never reveal your cards until the last moment, bluff as long as possible. She smiled at the thought; maybe Cahal was the real thing.

Now, she had a case to work on; she needed to see the

coroner and get the report on the dead priest. There was so much about the attempted murder and the murder at the seminary that wasn't right. Nothing fit. She was hoping some pieces would fall into place soon.

8

THE CORONER'S office was only a few blocks from the law courts, the police headquarters and the remand center. Someone knew in the city's planning that they would inter- twine the law and death. They'd made it easy to move the examination of death to the examination of the law in a few easy blocks.

Chris sent a text to her, telling her he'd already contacted Joe Christie to let him know when to pick up Cahal.

She walked into the coroner's office feeling only slightly relieved. Chris always had her back. If anyone could take care of a strange family situation like this one, it was him.

Her boots squeaked on the tile floor as she pushed through the doors that sighed as the air rushed out. The smell—she never got used to it—was formaldehyde. No matter how she breathed, the stuff went down her throat and sat somewhere in the pit of her stomach.

She'd be retching sometime later. It was just a matter of time. Bodies never bothered her; she'd seen so many in her years in the police force that she was numb to them. It's what they did to the bodies in here that got to her.

The bodies were first dissected, then their fluids drained, and every conceivable part weighed and measured.

The receptionist told her where to find Dr. Andrew. He was in his usual form, wearing his kilt covered in a lab coat. The kilt always swished as he walked. There was a running joke at the detachment. Every recruit was told to ask Dr. Andrew why he wore his kilt.

"So the boys can breathe," he'd always reply in his thick Scot's brogue that would make the new recruits blush when they understood he meant his balls.

"Good morning, Dr. Andrew," Bernadette said.

"Aye, good morning, Detective," the doctor replied. He was standing over a cadaver with his tools busily dissecting its cavity.

Bernadette didn't look away, but kept her eyes focused on the doctor. "You find anything interesting on our victim from the seminary?"

Dr. Andrew looked up. "Oh, aye. Here, let me get the file." He dropped his instruments in a metal dish and stripped off his gloves. He walked with his kilt swishing about his legs to a table. After rummaging amongst the files, he found the one he was looking for.

"Yes, Father Fredericks, aged sixty-seven years, Caucasian, cause of death was strangulation, but there was a massive amount of GHB in his blood," Dr. Andrew said.

"The date rape drug?" Bernadette asked as she pulled her notebook from her jacket.

"Aye, that's it. The stuff will knock you out silly if taken in a large dose. The victim might have been conscious enough for the murderer to make him stand on the chair, then use the rope to hoist him up. There was enough GHB in his system to knock out a horse. The victim didn't stand much of a chance."

"So, we're not looking for a tall person, just someone strong enough to pick up a one-hundred-and-fifty-pound man?" Bernadette asked.

"Well, no," Dr. Andrew replied. "If the murderer jacked him up with the drug, the victim would have stood on the chair and giggled. Sorry to give such a graphic, but that could have been the case. All he had to do was steer him there."

Bernadette rubbed her chin. "Then I've got someone who gets close enough to Father Fredericks to give him the drug. Were there any needle marks on his skin?"

"No, not a one. But the crime scene techs found a bottle of whiskey laced with the stuff by the victim's bed. Seems they knew the man to have a wee dram at night."

"So, the killer let Father Fredericks administer the drug himself. What a hell of a way to go..." Bernadette said.

"Aye, and it was a fine single malt whiskey, he would never have detected the salty taste of GHB."

"Any abrasion on the victim's hand showing a struggle?"

"No, none. And no skin under his fingernails. He was a willing victim for his own gallows."

Bernadette finished her notes. The killer must have entered the seminary and laced Father Frederick's bottle. Had to be before he went to bed. "Thanks Dr. Andrew. I'll look forward to your complete official report."

She walked out of the medical examiner's office and made it back to the detachment, seeing no reporters. She found Evanston in the office and brought her up to speed with her morning's findings.

"Ah, before we get into this too deeply," Evanston said

sipping on coffee, "tell me again how you got saddled with Cahal. That part sounds incredible."

Bernadette put up her hand. "Evans, I will hurt you if you continue that line of bullshit. Now let's get to work."

Evanston grinned. "Sorry, couldn't help it. I ran a check with border services. They had few Irish Nationals hitting our country, as most of them know we're so cold this time of year you can freeze the balls off a brass monkey. But a group of twenty landed in Calgary, then headed to Banff to do a ski holiday."

"They have a tour group name we can contact?"

"Already on it. I found the tour operator and told them they had to give us all the hotels they were staying at. I've contacted constables in Banff to check on them."

Bernadette poured a coffee and put in her sugar and cream. "Great, that will give the officers in Banff something new to do other than herd the elk out-of-town so they don't bother the tourists."

"Or to keep the drunk skiers from annoying the elk," Evanston said.

"My money's on the elk," Bernadette said. "Have we run checks on the supposed Irish ski holiday group on our international database?"

"I got them all inputted. So far no hits," Evanston said.

"That's the problem, you've got to have a record to be in the system. If our killer has never been arrested, we've got no trace on him."

Evanston leaned forward at her desk. "What's makes you think we got a male killer? If the report claims GHB, then a twelve-year-old girl could have placed the priest on the chair and told him to throw the noose over the rafter."

"You're right. I think we keep all our options open."

"So, no stone unturned?" Evanston said.

"Yeah, we look at every person on the ski holiday from Ireland."

"Oh, the car you wanted me to check was a rental out of Edmonton Airport. The rental company had Jacob Burkov on the rental agreement."

"That's the little jerk I met earlier. He was throwing some zinger questions. Said he worked for the *Daily Bleed*," Bernadette said.

"Oh gees, don't mess with that guy," Evanston said. "He runs everyone through the wringer, digs up dirt on them, and throws out all kinds of accusations."

"How do you know that?"

Evanston dropped her eyes to her desk. "Okay, I've read his column a few times. He's got great sponsors on his blog, and I get fifteen percent off of cat food for my cats Newman and Kramer. They love the stuff."

"I do not understand what is worse, you are buying cat food from a creepy blogging site or that you've named your cats after the Seinfeld show," Bernadette said.

Bernadette heard a ping on her phone. It was a text from Chris, it said, *Got the Irishman, taking him home.*

FIVE MEN SAT around a long wooden table. The room looked medieval. Candles provided the light, throwing shadows onto the shields and spears attached to the rough stone walls. A man sat at the head of the table in a robe with a hood over his head. He was wearing a golden mask.

The other men sat there waiting for him to speak. They addressed him as Master or Magda when spoken to. He struck fear into them. Men who'd questioned him had lost fingers; men who disappointed him had disappeared.

Master produced a phone and scrolled down the screen. "I don't like what I'm seeing. How hard is it to kill two old priests in the backwaters of Canada?"

"There were complications," a man named Liam said, his voice almost cracking as he said the words. He didn't want to say anything, but the fear of not responding was greater. He'd wished someone else had said his words.

Master fixed his gaze on Liam. "Yes, thank you, Liam, for voicing the incompetence of this group. I thought I'd assembled the wealth of the ancestors of Ireland. It seems I've been mistaken."

"You're not mistaken," a man named Andrew said. "There seemed to be a guardian protecting the priests. We'll deal with him. We had Father Frederick taken care of last night. Father Dominic is without protection in the hospital. It's only a matter of hours before we have this dealt with."

"I'll hold you accountable then, shall I, Andrew?" Master said.

"Yes, I will be accountable," Andrew said. There was nothing else he could say. He felt his intestines turn to water. He clenched his fists under the table. He'd signed his own death warrant if the assassins failed.

"What of the others. When will you deal with them?" Master asked.

"Paddy O'Dea is being picked up as we speak," Andrew said.

"Good, we need to rid all links to our sacred order. Soon we will operate in complete freedom," Master said as he rose. They bowed their heads as he walked out of the room.

PADDY O'DEA BOUGHT a pack of Benson and Hedges cigarettes from the newsagents on Station Road in Kildare. He took a cigarette out, placing his usual curse on the smoking kills label on the packet. He coughed slightly, put a match to the end of the cigarette, inhaled deeply, and broke into a spasm of coughing.

"Bloody hell," Paddy exclaimed as his breath returned. "That was a wicked spell." He looked across the road. Cara and Brennan, his two grandchildren, were playing on the swings in the small park.

He'd buy the wee ones off with the ice cream and cram them full of sweets so they wouldn't tell their gran that

Granddad had been puffing again. But what was he going to do at his age?

A car pulled up beside him, and two young boys with crew cuts and leather jackets got out. They looked like they were about to go into the shop, but they turned and walked toward him.

"Paddy O'Dea?" the ginger haired one asked. He had a ring in his ear and a tattoo of a Celtic cross on his neck.

"Aye that's me. Who's asking?" Paddy demanded. He didn't like young gobshites like these two. He was old but fast with his hands. He could give as good as he got. He wasn't in a mood to be screwed with.

"You're coming with us." Ginger hair said.

"Who says?"

Ginger hair moved his hand over his jacket and revealed a large handgun. "This is Mr. Smith and focking Wesson. He rules the street today, mate. You get in the car or we gun you down right here in front of your little ones. You want they should see you laying in the gutter? I can make your wish come true, old man."

Paddy shook his head. "You're right. Please let me go say goodbye to me grandkids."

"Do it from here. Yell to them, you got to go. Do it quick now or I'll blow your focking head off. You hear me?"

"No need to swear," Paddy said. He turned to his grandchildren, "Hey, kids, your granddad is going for a pint with these nice young men. Now go straight home to your gran, I'll be along with sweets. Mind me now, you run along home."

The two young kids stared at the men with their granddad. They didn't move.

"Now, mind your granddad," Ginger hair yelled. "We'll bring him home in a bit."

The kids ambled, taking each other's hand, looking over their shoulder.

"Nice kids, that," Ginger said with a smile. "Now, get in the car."

Paddy folded his body into the back of the little car. He was a tall man, with a wiry frame. His age had wracked his body with pain; he hurt in all his joints. He had to raise his knees up to fit in the back.

The car pulled away, making its way out of town, then took the road east towards the sea.

Paddy stared out the window for a bit, then looked at the two men. "If you don't mind boys, I'd like it if you left my body somewhere to be found. My wife would like to give me a proper burial. I'd hate for her to find I'd been disappeared."

"We'll be deciding your fate, old man. Don't worry about that," Ginger hair replied.

Paddy blew out a breath. "Yeah, I know you're feeling all God-like and omni-bloody-potent now with your gun, but if you're good Catholics like myself, a proper burial is the least you can allow a man, even for one you hate."

The other man, dark-haired with sunglasses, said, "He's right, Jamie, we owe it to his kin."

"Ah Jesus, what the hell you are calling my name, you gobshite," Jamie replied. "And we have orders to drop him over the cliff and let the sea take him away."

"Okay, Paddy, my name's Sean, and this here's my mate Jamie," the driver said. "We'll make sure they find your body."

"Aye, that's kind of you. Now, if you don't mind, who's ordered me dead?" Paddy asked.

"None of your bloody business," Jamie yelled as he

turned around. He pulled the gun from his waist belt. "I could put a bullet in you right now if you like."

"Settle down," Paddy said. "You don't want to mess your car with my blood and brains, now do you?"

Sean turned to Jamie. "He's right, Jamie, there's no need, he'll be dead soon enough. I just cleaned this car; you think I got time to clean it up before my date tonight?"

"You're taking your girl to hear the band at the James Nolan Pub tonight?" Paddy asked.

"Yeah, they're brilliant," Sean replied.

"The fiddlers a bit off, the one they had before him... not sure I remember his name..." Paddy said.

"Seamus?"

"Aye, that's the one. He could play a mean tune, that one."

Sean smiled at him in the rearview mirror. "He's my cousin, went off to Dublin to join a big band, he did."

Paddy shook his head. "All the good ones go away." He sat in silence for a while. "Now, if you could tell me what this is all about, then."

"Someone asked us to settle an old score," Sean said.

"Ah... that then. The troubles come back to haunt us all in Ireland. I figure I caused enough grief in my time. I know the government pardoned all of us in the IRA, but those I killed and those I left as widows and orphans need a reckoning. Thanks for letting me know."

THEY DROVE ALONG THE COAST; Sean pulled the car into a park overlooking the sea. Paddy got out of the back and walked away from the men toward the cliff and looked out towards the ocean.

"Nice calm day on the waters," Paddy said. "Might be a good day to fish for bass."

He turned and faced the men. Jamie pulled out his gun and came towards Paddy. He stood with the pistol aimed at his head.

Paddy advanced on him. "You damned idjit. You'll not shoot me in the head. The wife needs an open coffin." He grabbed onto the gun and pointed it to his heart. "Now pull the damn trigger."

Jamie stood there. With Paddy's hands on the pistol he could feel his fingers on his. He froze.

"What's got into you, man?" Paddy demanded. "You've no the balls to do this?"

Jamie's hand shook on the gun. He stared into Paddy's eyes, seeing the blue green flecks; the aged wrinkles, the bushy eyebrows. He became lost in his gaze.

Paddy moved his hands forward on the gun. His two powerful thumbs pressed over Jamie's trigger finger. Paddy pushed hard—with one jerk the gun fired. Paddy fell backwards onto the ground.

The sound of the gunshot echoed over the cliff. It died away slowly to the sound of seagulls and the waves crashing on the cliffs below.

Jamie lowered the gun and walked towards the car.

"You've got a bit of blood on you," Sean said.

Jamie didn't respond. He got in the car and put the gun in the glove box.

Sean started the car, reversed it out of the car park, and headed back to Kildare.

They drove in silence for a while, then Sean turned to Jamie. "Did you know he was done for with cancer?"

"What do you mean?" Jamie asked.

"He was on a list for the hospice but couldn't get in. He had maybe a week or two before he was dead."

"Then what the hell did we kill him for? We did the old focker a favor, didn't we?"

"Aye, I guess we did. There's no telling what our higher ups want in the order, but it's done."

"But, I was to shoot him in the head and drop him over the cliff, wasn't I? How do we explain that?"

"We tell them we got interrupted by some passersby. Some tourists. We had to get it done and do a runner. Don't worry, we'll be fine."

Jamie looked down at his shirt. "Ah, bloody hell, I got blood on my shirt."

"We'll drop by your ma's for a fresh shirt, then off to the pub for a pint," Sean said. He shifted the car into fourth gear and sped up. His nerves needed at least three pints of Guinness to get over today.

10

BERNADETTE AND EVANSTON went over the reports from the seminary and realized how little they had. No one had seen anything, no one had witnessed anything. The seminary doors were open all night.

"I think I want to talk to that Father Jo..."

"His name is Father Joesophat," Evanston said, reaching for the witness statement.

"Okay, yeah, that guy," Bernadette said. She picked up her phone and dialed the seminary. A woman answered, sounding like she was in her eighties, told her that Father Joesophat was visiting with Father Dominic in the hospital.

"I'm going to head over the hospital and meet this Father Jo guy," Bernadette said. "You want to come with me?"

"No, I'll stick here and keep my eyes on this incredible computer screen as it churns up useless information on a bunch of Irishmen and women on a ski holiday. And I hate hospitals. You can pick me up a Subway sandwich on the way back. Roast turkey on whole wheat—loaded with no pickles."

Bernadette grabbed her coat. "Did you want the cookie?"

"No, trying to lose weight," Evanston said.

BERNADETTE DROVE the fifteen minutes to the Red Deer Regional Hospital and went into find Father Dominic. Now that Cahal was cleared from the case, she could talk to anyone from the seminary. But she wasn't sure what shape Dominic was in. Last she'd heard, he was recovering slowly from the concussion.

Front reception gave her his room number on the third floor. He wasn't in intensive care anymore, but in a regular room on the third floor.

Bernadette disliked hospitals as much as Evanston. Her dislike was from the many times she'd had to interview victims of knifing and gunshot wounds. The problem was, with most of the victims, it was often gang related. They somehow had cloudy memories, and it wasn't from the drugs they were on for the pain.

She walked into Father Dominic's room and found him lying in bed with an IV in his arm and an oxygen tube in his nose. He looked peaceful as he slept.

Father Joesohpat was sitting beside him reading. He was in his early sixties, balding, with silver rim glasses that made his face look more oval. He was slim, wearing jeans and a large wool cardigan and boots.

He rose from his chair as she walked in.

"Detective, good to see you," Father Joesophat said.

"How is Father Dominic doing, Father Joso..."

"Please, just call me Father Jo." He looked down at the patient. "Father Dominic has woken up a few times, but he's quite confused about events. The doctors say he'll be okay in a few days."

"That's great, Father Jo," Bernadette said, taking a chair

near the bed. "But heard there was something about a misdiagnosis. Do you know anything about it?"

"It seems the local resident doctor on call for the neuro unit was a little green but eager to start the induced coma he'd just learned. Later, the EEG readings showed Father Dominic wasn't as injured as the doctor thought. So, they brought him out of the induce coma. But at the Father's age, it's hard for him to get his bearings."

Bernadette shook her head. "Yes, that's why they call medicine a practice, not a science. I'm glad he made it through. Now, if I may, could I ask you some questions about Father Frederick?"

Father Jo took off his glasses and rubbed his eyes. "Yes, how may I help? I told you all I could of how I found the poor soul. Such a horrible way to die. I was in the chapel saying prayers for him this morning."

Bernadette nodded. "Yes, I'm sure you did, but I need to ask you what Father Frederick and Father Dominic where doing at the seminary."

"What do you mean?"

"Were you at the seminary when they arrived from Ireland?"

"Yes, they flew into Calgary from Dublin. I picked them up at the airport," Father Jo said. "Two delightful men, I must say."

"Did they tell you of anything they were working on?"

"Working on? We're all involved in the Lord's work. That's our mission until our last breath leaves our body."

"Yes, I understand. But was there something from their past in Ireland? Were they involved in anything political or something or of a criminal nature?"

Father Jo paused for a moment and adjusted his glasses and leaned forward. "Father Frederick told me that Father

Dominic was working on some serious memoirs. I believe now I can't be certain, but it had something to do with their time in Ireland."

"Do you know if there is any record of this in the seminary?"

"I'm afraid not. The police searched Father Frederick's room and there was nothing there."

"Do you think they stole it last night?"

Father Jo shook his head. "I have no way of knowing. I saw no manuscript on his desk or that of Father Dominic. In the two weeks prior, they worked on a computer in the old main student study hall."

Bernadette wrote a note: Look for a USB stick, search the seminary computer. "Thanks, Father Jo," Bernadette said, putting her notebook away. "Will you let me know when Father Dominic can answer some questions? I'd like to come back and talk to him."

"Yes, but I'm afraid he's had a bit of a setback."

"What do you mean?"

"When I spoke to him briefly this morning, he didn't seem to know who he was. I tried to tell him, but he seemed confused. The doctor thinks it's temporary amnesia. He may come out of it, but they think it may take a week or more, if at all. It could be permanent."

Bernadette felt her case slipping away from her. Another old man with a case of lost memory, the same as Cahal. This seemed to be an epidemic.

"Let me know if there's any change, Father Jo," Bernadette said as she got up.

A woman appeared at the door in green scrubs with a tray and a syringe. "I hope I'm not disturbing you. I need to administer some medicine."

Bernadette was about to step aside to let her get to the

IV. Then she stopped. The woman had no name badge. And the scrubs were surgical green. The nurses on the ward wore the usual patterns with floral tops and pants with many pockets. Another thing, she wore boots. Something was odd about this woman.

"What medicine are you giving him, nurse...?" Bernadette asked, leaving it open for the nurse to give her name.

"Ah... it's a sedative to help him sleep," the nurse replied with a smile.

"He's already sleeping." Bernadette said. "Perhaps you'd like to give your name—mine's Detective Callahan."

The nurse backed out of the room. "Oh so sorry, seems I've the wrong room. Sorry to have bothered you."

"Wait, tell me your name," Bernadette demanded.

"I'm late on my rounds; I must go," the woman said as she rushed out the door.

Bernadette ran out behind her. The woman was charging down the corridor.

"No way she's getting away from me," Bernadette said as she ran after her.

"Stop, I want to talk to you," Bernadette yelled as she ran after her.

The woman rounded a corner. As Bernadette turned the corner, she found a big food trolley in her way. She was moving too fast. She crashed into it and sent the food trays flying onto the floor. Nurses came out of patient rooms, the hospital food staff looked on in amazement. There was food everywhere.

Bernadette lay on the floor with food wrapped in cellophane on trays, buns, and little portions of Jell-O and mini fruit cups rolling around.

"Are you okay?" a nurse named Constance asked, walking into the corridor.

Bernadette brushed off a plate of meat loaf that had landed on her. "Yes, I'm fine. I was chasing a nurse that I suspected shouldn't be on this ward. She was trying to administer something to Father Dominic."

Nurse Constance bent down and helped Bernadette up. "What did she look like?"

"About twenty-five, blonde hair, blue eyes and wearing only surgical scrubs, and she was wearing boots."

"There's no one matching that description on this ward. And we don't administer any medicine of any kind until well after we serve the lunch. Did she have any ID on her?"

"That's the thing, no name tag and no ID," Bernadette said, straightening her jacket.

"I'd better call security. This sounds serious," Constance said.

"Here's my detective ID, tell security to come and see me," Bernadette said.

She scraped some spaghetti off her sleeve and pulled out her cellphone to call the detachment and tell them to send some uniforms over to the hospital. They'd need to have an officer outside Father Dominic's room and to search the hospital to see if the fake nurse was still in the hospital.

A hospital security guard named Corporal Fawcett came towards Bernadette. He had his radio blaring as other security officers were calling in their positions and their search for the nurse.

"I heard you need assistance, Detective. I have my entire team of officers ready to assist," Fawcett said.

Bernadette looked at him; he was young and eager. He wore his black utility belt with flashlight and handcuffs attached as if he was a policeman in uniform, another wannabe police officer, but he was keen.

"Corporal, you need to get your eyes on a female, five foot three, blonde, in surgical scrubs who's masquerading as a nurse. She has no ID badge. I want her treated as extremely dangerous. Your personnel will report only—no engagement. You copy that?"

"Copy that," Corporal Fawcett said. His hand almost went to a salute, but he stopped himself.

"I need a guard on Father Dominic's room on this ward, one of your men will direct the police to this floor so they can start a search, and I must see your CCTV tapes for this area," Bernadette said.

"Yes, Detective," Corporal Fawcett replied. This time he couldn't help himself. His right hand made a crisp salute. "Follow me."

Bernadette waited a moment until they had a security guard at Father Dominic's door and then met with three uniformed officers to give them an account of what had just taken place.

Constable Stewart was in the lead of the uniforms that arrived. "I think we search every laundry bag and disposal unit from here down to the main floor. She must have dropped that needle and the scrubs somewhere," he said.

Bernadette put her hand on Stewart's arm. "Damn it, Stewart, I'm glad you're thinking. I'll check the CCTV cameras to see where she went—I'll call you."

Bernadette followed Corporal Fawcett down to their security guard center on the hospital's main floor. One female security officer was watching the monitors with a radio at her side.

Corporal Fawcett came to her side. "You see anything yet?"

The female officer named Sydney pointed to a screen. "I pulled this up. This blonde lady is wearing a hoody and jeans. She goes into this linen room and comes out with the scrubs on."

Bernadette grabbed her cellphone and dialed Stewart. "We've got a description of the perp. She's wearing a gray hooded sweatshirt, jeans, blonde hair, five three, slight female. Treat as dangerous, you copy?"

"Copy that," Stewart said.

Bernadette turned away from the security officers and walked out the back of the room, still on the phone with Stewart. "I think we got a killer on our hands, Stewart."

"Copy that," Stewart responded.

Bernadette disconnected her phone. "Damn it," Bernadette said as she went back up the ward. If she'd acted sooner, she would have had the suspect. She hesitated. What the hell was she thinking?

Her cell phone rang; it was Durham. "What's going on?" Durham asked.

"A suspect tried to get to Dominic with a syringe. She fled and we're searching for her in the hospital," Bernadette said.

"I'll send all units and all the detectives in the area."

"Good, tell them to be careful. I saw a look in that woman's eyes. She looked deadly."

11

CORPORAL JELLENICK ARRIVED at the hospital. Detective Sawchuck asked her to go come with him to check the hospital's basement. With her gun drawn, she walked through the doors with Sawchuck that led to the morgue.

They stopped in front of the morgue.

Sawchuck tried the door. "It's locked."

Jellenick called on her radio, "Dispatch, we're in front of the door to the morgue. It's locked. Can you ask hospital security if it's supposed to be locked?"

Sawchuck stood beside Jellenick. "You think someone locked it from inside?"

Jellenick shrugged. "No idea, but a hell of a place to hide out in."

Sawhuck nodded. "I hope it's supposed to be locked. I hate going in there."

"They're all dead, Sawchuck, what's your problem?"

"Corpses give me the creeps," Sawchuck said.

Dispatch came over the radio, "Hospital security says it's locked at all times, the entry code is one niner seven zero."

Sawchuck holstered his gun. "There you go. We can leave."

"Yeah, but what if the suspect forced someone to let her in?"

"Aw Christ, Constable, you watch too many episodes of that Nine One One show—it's all crap."

"Humor me, Detective. Or does that mean you're too scared to enter... the house of the dead?" Jellenick said, raising her eyebrows and making her eyes wide.

"Aw, bullshit," Sawchuck said as he punched the keypad and walked inside.

Jellenick got on the radio and told dispatch they were entering the morgue.

The place was dark, but for one light shining from an office in the back. Rows upon rows of stretchers lined the hallway. Their rubber-soled shoes squeaked on the floor as they walked.

With guns and flashlights drawn, they walked through the long room with Sawchuck leading.

"You see any light switches?" Sawchuck asked.

"Why'd'you need a light? I thought you didn't want to see the dead. You're not afraid they'll come creeping up on you, Sawchuck?"

"Ha, you're a comedian. I'd like to clear this room and get the hell out of here. The smell is enough to knock a skunk off a gut wagon."

"That's just formaldehyde, Sawchuck, the dead are very sanitary." Jellenick said, sweeping her gun with her flashlight attached left and right.

"This is going to put me off my lunch—wait, what the hell's that?" Sawchuck said. He shone his flashlight to a corner. A pair of legs stuck out from underneath a stretcher.

They approached slowly, sweeping their weapons left and right as they did.

As they came closer, they saw the body of a man in coveralls. He lay face down with his hands spread out. Blood flowed from his neck.

"Damn it. The suspect is here," Jellenick said. She reached for her radio, dropping her gun to her side.

She didn't see the object come hurtling at her. She felt it hit her head—she blacked out.

Sawchuck whirled his gun and flashlight to the right. A figure was already in the air, coming at him. He fired one shot, screaming as something sharp entered his neck. Falling forward, he pushed the emergency button on his radio.

BERNADETTE HEARD the emergency beacon from Stewart's radio beside her. "Where's that coming from?"

"The morgue," Stewart yelled as he started down the hallway. "All units, all officers, the morgue, now. Officers in trouble."

Bernadette ran behind Stewart as he hit the fire door to the stairs with all his force. The door swung open, banging into the concrete sidewall.

They pounded down the stairs. Two other officers joined them. No one talked; they ran, taking the stairs two by two, grabbing the side rails to keep from falling.

The only sound was their feet pounding the stairs and their breathing. Stewart hit the bottom floor, pounding the exit door open. The others were right behind. They drew their weapons as they reached the morgue.

A female constable named Kendal Jenner was on the ground on top of Sawchuck, she'd placed a towel over his neck to stop the bleeding. His eyes were rolling back into his head.

"Sawchuck, can you hear me?" Bernadette yelled. "Hang in, we got medics everywhere. You'll be fine. Hang on!"

"Where the fuck is the medic?" Bernadette screamed.

Two men with a stretcher came running in. They pushed the officers aside and took over. One started chest compression, the other inserted an IV and started wrapping Sawchuck's neck.

Stewart stood beside Bernadette and pulled her up. "You okay, Detective?"

"No, I'm not okay." Bernadette whispered. "If I'd stopped that bitch, none of this would have happened. This is all on me, Constable. This is all on me."

12

BERNADETTE DIDN'T GET HOME until midnight. She'd filed reports at the station, gone back to the hospital to sit in the waiting room with other detectives and officers, and somehow had eaten a sandwich and drank a coke. She wasn't sure what time that was. It seemed to happen in a vacuum of grief as the police waited to see if Sawchuck would be okay.

By eleven thirty that night, the doctors said Sawchuck was stable. He'd lost a lot of blood, but the scalpel the assailant used had missed his major artery.

Corporal Jellinick had a concussion and was being kept overnight for observation. Some officers hit the pub for a quick nightcap and relieve their stress with alcohol. Bernadette wanted to join them, but needed to get home to Chris and her new houseguest. Uncle Cahal.

She drove into the garage and parked the Jeep. There was no sound from the dog; he must have given up waiting for her. She entered the house as quietly as possible and headed for the bedroom. The light was on.

Chris was sitting up in bed with his t-shirt on, reading a book.

"Hey, honey, you didn't have to stay up for me."

"I heard you had a shit show today. Is everyone okay?"

Bernadette took off her shirt and wiggled out of her pants. "Yeah, Sawchuck is out of the woods. Jellinick's going to have a hell of a headache and our perp escaped with help from yours truly."

"You want to take a shower? I'll get you a scotch and we can talk about it." Chris said.

"Sounds good," Bernadette said going into their ensuite bathroom, throwing her bra and panties onto the floor and stepping into the shower. She made the water as hot as she could stand it and got in. She found a pleasant-smelling soap, lathering herself until she looked like she'd been through the soap cycle of the carwash, before rinsing off.

When she walked out of the shower in her bathrobe with clouds of steam following her, Chris had a small tray on the bed with a glass of Scotch and some salted almonds.

Bernadette sat on the bed and sipped her scotch. "Thanks, I needed that." She looked at Chris and stroked his cheek. "Sorry, I should have called you today to give you an update and see how you're doing with the ersatz uncle I've had dumped on us."

Chris moved beside her on the bed, pulled her bathrobe off her shoulders and massaged her neck and shoulders.

"No worries, I got a call from Evanston. She gave me an update on what happened. I knew you'd be wrapped up tight for the day. I took your uncle shopping to get some clothes; bought him lunch at our local diner and got him a six-pack of Guinness. We had a friendly chat by the fire while he regaled me with stories of Ireland, and I made him my famous chicken with dumpling stew and he retired to his room."

"So, is he the real thing?" Bernadette asked, putting her hand on Chris's and lifting her head to the side.

"I may not be as good a judge of character as you, but he seems genuine enough."

"Why do you think I'm a better judge of character than you?"

"Because you agreed to marry me," Chris said with a chuckle.

Bernadette pulled his hand across her chest and hugged him. He placed his head on her shoulder.

"You've had a hell of a tough day, my girl. You need to get some sleep," Chris said.

"What, you're not going to seduce me?" Bernadette asked, kissing his arm.

"Only if you want me to. If you're not too tired."

Bernadette chuckled. She put her scotch down. "You know me, always ready. But maybe I'll grab a few moments of shuteye. I'll ravage you later."

"Whatever you say, sweetie," Chris said, massaging her shoulders.

She snuggled down and in seconds she was fast asleep. She slept soundly for three hours. Something woke her with a start. She sat up in bed.

She'd seen the nurse in her dreams. Seen the blood on Sawchuck, the blood on the dead hospital worker in the morgue.

The thought nagged at her—what if she'd stopped that nurse? What happened to her intuition? She'd made the connection—the nurse wasn't real. She'd stood her ground, protected Father Dominic, but she hadn't acted fast enough. The nurse had escaped.

She'd written it all down in her report and given it to Chief Durham. A reprimand or a demotion would be in order in Bernadette's mind.

Durham had said, "We can't second guess everything we do, Callahan. You did a hell of a job stopping her from killing the priest. We found the syringe in a bin; it was full of enough barbiturates to kill him in a second. You alerted everyone to her presence. Shit happens in our line of work. You've got a tough skin. Use it."

Bernadette mulled over Durham's words in her mind. A beam of moonlight came through the window. Her arm was outside the covers. She ran her hand over her arm, wondering how tough her skin would have to be to survive her line of work. A few minutes before her alarm sounded, she fell asleep.

13

BELFAST, 10 AM.

A MAN WALKED into the bank. The place had just opened at half-past nine, an old man joked with a teller at the counter as she stamped a piece of paper for him. Three other tellers were at the counters, only one looked up to see the man who entered.

He wore a gray raincoat with a large brim fedora on his head. His glasses were black rimmed with a tint. Though he looked like a man in his seventies, he moved quickly as he made his way to the automatic cash machines and pulled out a sheaf of papers.

The tellers lost interest in the man and went about their business. It was Friday, the rush of customers would be in soon, and they needed to be ready.

The man shuffled his papers, dropped some refuse in the bin by the auto tellers, and walked away. He raised his umbrella as he left the building, although it was only sprinkling a few drops of rain.

He walked two blocks down the street, found a deserted lane way and took out a cellphone. He dialed 999, the emergency number.

"What's your emergency?" the operator asked.

"This is the Real IRA, there's a bomb in the Bank of Ireland on College Green. You've got twelve minutes. Don't be tardy now," the man said into the phone.

The operator patched through to the police who notified the bomb disposal.

Bank security staff had the bank emptied in six minutes and the police arrived in three.

As the bomb disposal unit arrived, they knew they had no chance. A twelve-minute warning was enough time to vacate the building. Two of the bomb techs stood side by side. They'd jumped from the truck and thrown their gear on, but waited behind the safety of their armored vehicle.

"What do you reckon, Seamus," the bomb tech named Steven asked.

Seamus peered around the corner of the vehicle and looked at this watch. "If it's a timer, it's about to go off in five seconds from now, but if this is a remote, he could wait for us to go inside before he lights it up."

"But the caller said the real IRA," Steven said. "I thought all those bastards were dead or in jail."

"Aye, I thought the same thing. My father told me stories of diffusing bombs they'd left, sometimes they were on the money as to timing and other times, they left false information to cause more destruction," Seamus said. He looked at his watch again, "Counting five, four, three, two..."

An explosion tore through the silence. Steven and Seamus ducked behind their truck. Dust and glass rained down on them. A frenzied flock of pigeons took to the air.

As the dust settled, a Belfast Police Constable walked over to the bomb techs. "Well, there you go, you found your bomb. Now if you'd have gone in there, you could have diffused it."

Seamus looked at the constable. He was a young man in his twenties, his name badge said O'Rourke. "We got here only three minutes ago. That may be enough time for you to give your wife a proper shagging, but not enough time to locate a bomb you've no idea where it is in a building this size and diffuse it."

Constable O'Rourke's face went red, and he backed away. "Right then, I'll leave you lads to it."

The man in the raincoat and fedora heard the blast from two blocks away. There was no need to see it; they'd already have an all-points bulletin out for him. He threw his disposable phone down a gutter and changed his clothes. He no longer looked the same. Gone was the old man. A now hip-looking university student walked down the street in search of a coffee shop. He had fired off the first salvo. There would be many more to come by the end of the day.

14

BERNADETTE THOUGHT of a quick run that morning, even though she'd slept little, but her running gear was in the spare bedroom, the one they'd given to Cahal. She poured herself a coffee and briefly glanced over the news on her cellphone. Something was happening in Ireland. Some kind of bombing; she couldn't get into the full context of the story. There was too much to think about here.

Her dog Sprocket spent the night outside Cahal's door, as if he was guarding it. He looked at her with those big searching eyes, wondering why they weren't off on their usual run together.

"Sorry, buddy," Bernadette said, scratching his ears and running her hand over his head. "Chris will run with you later, and Harvey will take you out for a walk. You'll like that."

At the mention of Harvey, their next-door neighbor, Sprocket let out an agreeable woof. Harvey Mawer was in his mid-seventies, retired several times from working in the oil industry and Bernadette's best neighbor.

When she'd moved in several years ago, Harvey shoveled her snow in the winter and mowed her lawn in the summer. He told her he needed something to do and didn't mind the exercise. Before Chris came on the scene, Harvey would invite both Bernadette and Sprocket over for dinner, claiming he'd made too much food and wouldn't mind the company.

Harvey took to Chris easily. When Chris couldn't find work when he first moved in with Bernadette, he took him out to his local fishing spot where they spent hours shooting the breeze, as they called it, and catching fish.

Now, they invited Harvey over for dinner, as Chris was one hell of a cook. Harvey was like the uncle she never had. She'd send him a text later and Harvey would pick up Sprocket, take him to the park and go for a walk. What they all knew about Harvey's walks with Sprocket is he used the good-looking German Shepherd to meet women. Harvey accumulated a collection of gray-haired ladies with poodles and dachshunds who called him regularly.

One day Chris put the relationship of Harvey and Sprocket into word:, "I think Sprocket has become Harvey's pimp."

They both agreed but decided not to say anything to Harvey, lest he know they were on to him.

The guest bedroom door opened, and Cahal Callahan stepped out. Sprocket turned; he made a low growl as his ears went back.

"Easy boy," Bernadette said. She rubbed the side of his head and placed her hand on his collar in case he made an unexpected lunge at Cahal. The dog was a dropout from police dog school. Too much attitude, they'd said. He was showing it now.

"Ah, good to see you, Bernadette," Cahal said as he walked towards the kitchen table. He made sure not to make eye contact with the dog. He knew that would only aggravate him further.

"Would you like some coffee?" Bernadette asked. She motioned to the kitchen counter while holding Sprocket.

"Splendid, I'll get it," Cahal said as he walked past the dog.

Cahal poured himself a coffee and seated himself on the far side of the table, away from the growling dog.

Bernadette bent down and looked Sprocket in the eyes. "That's enough now. You've registered your opinion of our guest. He gets it. Now, keep your comments to yourself. You hear me?"

The dog's ears lay flat. He realized he'd crossed Bernadette's line of tolerance with his behavior. He lay down on the floor at her feet.

"That's quite the animal there. He hasn't quite taken to me yet," Cahal said.

Bernadette took a sip of her coffee. "The feeling is mutual. He monitors my mood."

"Aw, I see," Cahal said. "We'll have to change that, won't we?"

Bernadette looked at her watch. "It's seven a.m. There's a double homicide and a killer on the loose. I'd love to catch up with all the family news of the relatives who dropped my family like a stone once my Irish dad married my native Cree mom. I'm sure you have some rousing anecdotes to share, but I need to make tracks."

"Ah, well then... perhaps tonight," Cahal said, standing up as Bernadette got up from the table.

"Sure, we'll meet tonight," Bernadette said. She grabbed her badge and gun from the bedroom, and gave Chris a kiss as he came out of the shower. "Hey, sweetie, Cahal's up, he's got a coffee, and I gotta go. Make sure the dog doesn't eat him, I don't want to make out the incident report."

Chris gave her a big hug. "You two conversed?"

"We fired the opening shots," Bernadette said. She headed for the garage.

Bernadette hit the garage door opener that pulled up with a groan as it dislodged itself from a patch of ice and started the Jeep. As she pulled out of the driveway, her phone rang on her dash. She hit the hands free.

"Detective Callahan," Bernadette said. She didn't recognize the number; she thought it might be someone calling in a tip on the murder suspect.

"Is this Ms. Callahan?" a female voice asked.

"Yes, it is, how may I help you?"

"This is Melinda from the Emerald Lake Lodge in Field, British Columbia. You'd sent an enquiry about having your wedding here in May. There's been a cancellation, and the good news is we have your exact date, and I have twenty rooms available," Melinda gushed over the phone.

Bernadette pulled her vehicle into the parking lot of a convenience store and threw it into park. She picked up the phone and stared at it for a second.

"Are you still there?" Melinda asked.

"Ah, yes Melinda, I'm here. I had to pull off the road. You kind of took me by surprise. We didn't expect to hear from you."

"Well, today is your lucky day. We have both the Vice President's Room and Cilantro on the Lake available for the wedding. I can put a hold on them, but I'll need a credit card for a deposit. Do you have one handy?"

"Just a minute," Bernadette said. She sat there for a moment. This had been her bright idea. Chris and she had spent a weekend there when they were first getting to know one another. They'd had sex there until they almost couldn't stand, then had sat on the veranda in the bent wood wicker chairs and stared out at pristine lake sipping wine, watching the clouds move over the mountains.

Bernadette pulled her credit card out of her wallet and gave Melinda her number. "How long do I have to decide?"

"I can give you until Tuesday next week, but then I'll need an answer. We get a lot of May weddings here, and very few cancellations. So, if you don't want it, I just go down the list."

"Yes, I understand," Bernadette said. "I'll be in touch soon." She closed her phone, put the Jeep in gear and joined traffic. *"Damn me and my bright ideas,"* she said under her breath. Chris had wanted the wedding to be in their little city. No fuss, then off to Emerald Lake Lodge after. But, oh no, Bernadette had asked and got what she wanted. *Be careful what you wish for,* she thought.

She drove passed the RCMP detachment and saw the line of news trucks. This was no longer a local event. The big national news networks had shown up. She could see some lead anchors from CBC and CTV and Global TV, a who's who of celebrity anchors. They must have taken the redeye from Toronto to get here. She kept driving, using the back entrance to park. The shit show, as they called it, had begun.

15

BERNADETTE WALKED into a beehive of activity in the detachment. They involved every officer in the meeting as the chief inspector went over last night's events and today's duties. The sole focus was on the murderer, the blonde women, the unidentified suspect who'd got away.

Inspector Davis was a lifer in the RCMP; he'd come up the ranks like the rest of them and had done his time from the desolate far north to the suburban streets of Vancouver. He was pushing sixty and sported a bushy mustache and eyebrows to match. Standing ramrod straight in his blue uniform, he addressed the troops.

"I can't emphasize the effort you need to put into this search. Check every store and gas station with a CCTV camera. Interview all persons in that hospital who might have had eyes on our suspect. We've set up a roadblock around the perimeter of the city. Officers have been there all night. You'll be replacing them."

"Were there any cars stolen from the hospital parking lot last night?" a constable named Parks asked.

"Good point," Constable, Davis said. "We have no stolen car reports. The suspect is on foot or had her own car."

Evanston came into the room. "Inspector Davis, we got a hit on our suspect from the officers in Banff."

"What have you got?" Davis asked.

Evanston read from her notes. "Two of the Irish Nationals, Alana Cassidy and Joseph Nolan, left the group on landing in Calgary. They told the group they had a sick relative in Ireland and had to take the return flight home. There is no record of them boarding a return flight from the Calgary airport."

Evanston put the pictures up on the screen. Bernadette stared at it, doubting the woman used her actual name. There were the same eyes she'd seen yesterday. But the eyes had no light, killer eyes. Why hadn't she acted?

"We sent the pictures to the police at the Calgary airport. They'll be checking every car-rental desk for their CCTV cameras and the airport hotels," Evanston said.

"Excellent work," Davis said. "Now, we have ID's of our suspects. We need to check every hotel, every motel, and every VRBO and Airbnb house in this city. We'll have the pictures sent to the news media as persons of interest, do not approach."

Bernadette stood at the back of the room, wondering where these two could hide? They'd come as a team, that was certain.

Evanston came to the back of the room to join Bernadette. "How you are holding up?"

Bernadette closed her eyes, then opened them. "Like a rag doll with a broomstick up her ass to keep her upright. Thanks for asking."

"Same as usual," Evanston said.

"Yeah, pretty much."

"What's our plan?"

"We run the two suspects into our facial recognition software to see what it comes up with," Bernadette said.

"That takes days before it comes up with a match, and hopefully the two have a sheet on them somewhere, otherwise we'll get nothing," Evanston said.

"You're right. In the meantime, we start with our victims. We need to find out why someone is after Father Dominic and who wants him dead, and why they killed Father Frederick. I said I thought we might have someone coming from Ireland to attempt the murders. I was right."

"Here's the problem with that. I tried to find the ID's of Dominic and Frederick. They are kept by the Holy See of Rome. You must know about that, you being a Catholic," Evanston said.

"No, that is news to me. And remember, I'm a barely practicing Catholic; I go to confession once a quarter to keep my mother from turning in her grave," Bernadette said. "We must get on the phones and go through channels. This might require time and coffee."

IT TOOK THEM HOURS. Both Bernadette and Evanston worked the phones to go through numerous levels of Catholic administration until they finally received an email of the former identities of the two priests.

"I'll be damned," Evanston said with a whistle when the files arrived. "Look at these two. They were really good-looking back in their day. I don't mind saying I would have flirted hard with either of these guys."

Bernadette looked at the file. "Brendan McLaughlin was Father Dominic, and Padraig O'Reilly was Father Frederick." She looked up at the clock on the wall. "You think we still have time to call the Garda in Ireland?"

"Why the Garda?" Evanston asked.

"I got a feeling all of this stems from something to do with the IRA, and I have a feeling the police in the Republic of Ireland might know more about them than the one's in the north."

"That's as good a hunch as any," Evanston said.

Bernadette looked on the website and found a contact number for the serious crime's division of the Garda in Dublin. It rang several times before an Irish accent that she could barely understand over the long-distance line told her it was The Garda.

After a long pause and some background noise that sounded like someone clanging teacups, another voice came on.

"Detective Patrick Sullivan here, how may I assist you?"

"This is Detective Callahan of the Serious Crimes Division of the RCMP in Red Deer, Alberta, Canada. I'm calling to identify the records of two individuals involved in a serious incident here."

"You calling from Red Deer, are you now? I've read about the sorry business you have going on there. Must be one hell of fix you're in trying to sort that out," Sullivan said.

"Yes, Detective, you're right, it's one hell of a fix. We've identified Father Dominic, who was injured, as Brendan McLaughlin and Father Fredericks, who was murdered as Padraig O'Reilly." Bernadette said.

"You're calling it a murder? The papers said you were still investigating."

"This is for your ears only, Detective. The assailant was a woman who arrived in Canada as Alana Cassidy. We believe her accomplice is Joseph Nolan. Both names were fake when we ran them through our files."

"Your two priests were high in the IRA ranks. I'd always wondered where they'd got to. They both disappeared back in the nineties. I thought maybe they retired and moved to Spain. Looks like they sought redemption as men of the cloth," Sullivan said.

"I was told by another priest that they might have been writing a memoir of some sort. You have any knowledge of that?" Bernadette said.

Sullivan blew out a breath. "My God, there's so many memoirs written about the Troubles in Ireland. I thought at one point we'd have a lack of paper to print them on."

"Is there anything the two could have been writing about that could have made them targets?" Bernadette asked.

"That's a good question. The IRA had so many factions between the official IRA and the provisional IRA that it was hard to keep track. I'm sure that somewhere in there, McLaughlin and O'Reilly must have witnessed something that others wouldn't want to come to light."

"Is it possible I could see their files?"

"I'd have to have that cleared at the highest level. Most of the IRA was pardoned and their files sealed. But as this is a murder investigation, I'm sure I can do something."

"Thanks, I appreciate that." Bernadette said. She paused for a moment and glanced at Evanston. "There's one more thing. Do you have any records of a Cahal Callahan?"

Evanston was beside her and shot her a look. She was going too far. If the chief of detectives found out, she'd be in deep trouble.

"Do you have a DOB?" Sullivan asked.

"Yes, December fifteenth, nineteen-forty-four." Bernadette said, trying to avoid Evanston's look.

"Let me take a quick look," Sullivan said.

During the long pause, Bernadette wondered if she'd find the actual truth about her so-called uncle.

"No, there's nothing here. This man has no arrest record, not even a traffic ticket. Where did he grow up?"

"Kildare," Bernadette replied.

"Kildare. That's a small town of about eight thousand close to Dublin. I'd only hear of this man if he'd been in some kind of trouble. Seems he hasn't."

"Thank you, Detective, you've been a great help. When we get a positive ID on our suspects, we'd like to send them to you to get further information," Bernadette said.

"All of Ireland is buzzing with the news of the two priests in Canada. We've got no end of speculation as to the cause. We're ready to help in any way we can."

"Thank you, Detective Sullivan, I'll be in touch," Bernadette said. She put the phone down. "This case gets more complicated all the time."

Evanston looked at Bernadette. "You know, we checked Cahal Callahan's record when we arrested him."

"Yes, but I wanted to double check," Bernadette said.

DETECTIVE PATRICK SULLIVAN went down the hall to see his partner Dennis Bishop. Sullivan had been a detective for ten years. He was forty-five, medium height and stocky. He played soccer with a local pub team on weekends and spent the rest of his time with his wife, who put up with his long hours of work. The branch they worked for was the Special Detective Unit (SDU) based in Dublin City on Harcourt

Street. They worked with the Defense Force Directorate of Military Intelligence, referred to as G2.

Dennis was holding a sheaf of papers, looking over the latest bombing reports in Northern Ireland. Dennis was just past fifty with the stocky body of a prizefighter who looked like he could still go several rounds and keep standing. Twice divorced, his hair had turned a silver shade of gray and his deep blue eyes kept him in trouble with the ladies.

"You find anything that connects the bombers to known suspects?" Sullivan asked as he sat down in front of Bishop's desk.

Dennis looked up with a look of exasperation. "Not a bloody thing. I was just about to come find you to go for a pint."

"Then who do we think these unsubs are? Hasn't MI5 or G2 come up with anything?"

"No one has a clue. To top it off, there have been some killings of old IRA men. O'Dea was murdered at point blank range, and Brady was shot in his car as he drove to the bank."

"But these guys are past ancient, for Christ's sake. What good would it do to kill them now? Didn't both of them have a terminal illness?"

Dennis nodded. "Doesn't make a damn bit of sense. And the bombings... someone claims they're the Real IRA, but no communication to the media."

"Sounds daft, as usual. But I've come to see you about something else—the two Irish priests in Canada."

Bishop sat back in his chair. "Yes, I've heard of that, what's it all about?"

"The one who is wounded is Brendan McLaughlin, the dead one is Padraig O'Reilly."

"I'll be damned. I thought they'd gone to Spain and fell into a vat of sangria."

"Seems they became men of the cloth," Sullivan said. "As good a place to hide as any, I suppose."

"The priests do get served wine, so I'm sure they did okay. Do the Canadian's have any idea who killed the one and attempted to kill the other?"

"They had an Alana Cassidy and Joseph Nolan as suspects. They made a positive ID of the female as the one who attempted to kill Father Dominic."

"Do the names check with any known priors?"

"None, both clean. Fake ID's, fake passports, the usual."

"You suspect a hit team?"

"Yes, I do. The Canadian detective is sending us pictures of them. I'll run it through all our known databases and check our sources. I can't see how these two haven't shown up somewhere."

Bishop leaned forward in his chair. "Aye, most killers have practiced somewhere. Now, how about that pint?"

"I'm as ready and thirsty as you are," Sullivan said. "But one more thing..."

"What's that?"

"The detective, she told her name, was Callahan. She wanted to know if we had any records of Cahal Callahan."

Bishop was about to grab his coat; he turned to Bishop. "Not *the* Cahal Callahan?"

"She gave me his exact birthdate and place of birth in Kildare."

"You know, I'd seen his name come up in the papers last week, but they had him pegged as a younger man. I didn't make the connection. Did you tell the detective we know him?"

"No, there's no record of him in our system or anywhere else that I know of." Sullivan said.

"The man has been a true ghost. Never let his picture be taken. No driver's license or identity card. It must have given him a fright to have sat for a passport photo."

"But that's just it. Why would he venture there?"

"I have no idea. Right now he's a problem of the great cold north of Canada," Bishop said. "Now, let's get that pint before the pub gets crowded with all those young winkers."

16

"HAVE WE HIT A WALL?" Evanston asked as she sat back in her chair, thumbing a ballpoint pen and making a clicking sound that Bernadette found was getting into her head.

"Not until we find out what the hit team was after," Bernadette said. She looked up at the clock on the wall. "Damn it, how did it get to be ten o'clock?"

"Time flies when you're following leads that go nowhere?" Evanston ventured.

Bernadette got up to get a coffee. As she poured her coffee with her mix of two sugars and cream, she wondered what they'd missed. Instead of going back to her desk, she headed for the squad room.

Constable Stewart was there, going over his computer. She leaned over his shoulder. "You find anything as to hotels and rental cars on our suspects?"

"Not much," Stewart said. "We got a positive hit on the car they picked up from Hertz at the airport. It was a white GMC SUV. We ran the tags through all of our highway cameras, and we didn't come up with much."

"They might've taken the back route into the city. There are no cameras on Highway twenty-one and twenty-two."

"That's the long way around," Stewart said.

"When you're coming to kill someone who doesn't expect you, you got time on your hands," Bernadette said.

"You're right. Constables on those roads can check with the gas stations to see if they stopped there. We might get another visual on them."

"Great," Bernadette said. "Any luck on hotels and motels?"

"There we got a big goose egg. The city is quiet this time of year. Everywhere we've checked have few registered guests and none matching the description of a man and a woman of the age I've given them."

"She's hiding out somewhere. There's no way she got past our roadblocks after her attack yesterday," Bernadette said.

"Like I said, this place is like a ghost town for guests this time of year, so if they were here, we'd find them. We did out-of-town searches and got nothing."

"Out of town..." Bernadette said.

She walked back to Evanston. "I think we need to take a ride."

"Where are we going? Can we pick up lunch on the way back? I missed it yesterday, with all the situations and all..." Evanston's words trailed off as she realized what she was saying.

"Sure, we're heading for the seminary," Bernadette said.

"Why? We interviewed everyone there. You got someone you want another shot at?"

"No, I want to go through the rooms out there."

"What for? Are looking for the ghosts of old priests?"

"Our suspects haven't shown up anywhere in town.

There was no evidence of traffic at the murder scene of Father Fredericks. What if they're staying at the seminary?"

"But how could that be? The place is mostly vacant—whoa, hell yeah, the perfect place to hide out. If this is for real. We need some backup."

"We'll get two units to back us up," Bernadette said. "I'll let the chief know."

17

EVANSTON AND BERNADETTE drove in silence to the seminary with two police cruisers behind them.

"Just how crazy does the chief think you are for searching for suspects at the seminary?" Evanston asked.

Bernadette pulled down her sunglasses and looked at Evanston. "No crazier than usual, but he figured we'd be out of his hair, what he has left of it, for a few hours."

"I hope you're right, I'd like to see the look on the detachment's face when we make a collar on one of your crazy ideas," Evanston said.

Bernadette shook her head. "I guess that's a compliment?"

They drove up to the seminary with no lights or sirens, thinking it best not to alert the suspects in case they were there. Father Francis met them as they made their way into the entrance.

"I received your message," Father Francis said. "I doubt fugitives might hide in our seminary. I'm sure someone would have seen them if they were roaming our halls." He stood there in his cassock, with his arms crossed. He looked and sounded indignant that the police would have suggested such a thing.

"We like to eliminate all possibilities," Bernadette replied with a smile. She thought it better to humor him than to explain her reasoning. "Please show us to the rooms that are unoccupied."

Father Francis pointed behind him. "It's the entire west wing. We closed it off years ago. We keep it heated with the water running so as not to damage the infrastructure, but no one goes in there."

"Does your maintenance man ever go in?"

"He goes in every three days, makes a complete check of the area, and signs off on a sheet near the front of the wing. We need the documentation to keep our insurance up to date," Father Francis said.

"I see. Thanks, Father, we'll do our checks and then see ourselves out," Bernadette said.

They walked down the great hall and into the West Wing. A clipboard was on a side table with a scrawl of dates and times.

Bernadette picked up the clipboard. "Hmm, looks like the maintenance guy has been pretty regular. But this is interesting. It's all the same pen."

"What's strange about that?" Evanston said.

"How often do you have the same pen with you for several weeks? And it's written in almost the same style," Bernadette answered.

"So, that means we're still going in then?"

"Yeah," Bernadette said. She turned to the officers. "We go in as teams, and no one separates. Cover each other, weapons drawn. If these two are here, they're armed. Copy that?"

They had Constable Stewart and Simmons with them.

Simmons was a mid-thirties, single mom with dark hair and brown eyes and devotion to the force and her ten-year-old daughter. Somehow, she managed her job and her growing daughter in a way that made most in the force envious.

"We copy," Stewart replied. "I'm not about to get stuck by that bitch."

Simmons looked at Stewart. "Be nice now, you don't even know the lady."

They entered the wing slowly. Enough light came from the outside to see well at first, but then it got dim as they progressed down the hall. The old wooden floors creaked under their feet.

Pictures of past priests looked down on them from the walls. The place smelled of old carpet and wallpaper.

"Did you see something crawl across the floor?" Evanston asked.

"Probably a mouse," Bernadette answered.

"I hate mice," Evanston said.

"Try not to get too excited. There might be a lot of them around."

"You know, if the maintenance guy came in here, they'd be traps set," Evanston said.

"There you go, never believe what you read—did you hear that?"

"What?" Evanston asked.

"I heard a door slam up ahead."

Bernadette turned to Stewart and Simmons. "Yeah, I copy that. We each take one side of the hall and clear each room. Copy that?"

Stewart waved he'd understood. He moved with Simmons to check each room. The rooms were small, holding two single beds with a four-drawer dresser in between and an armoire.

To ensure the room was clear, they opened each armoire to ensure no one was hiding inside. After swinging many open, Stewart turned to Simmons. "This feels kind of silly."

"If the suspect jumps out of one of those with a scalpel, it won't be."

"You're right," Stewart said as he pulled the next one open as Simmons stood behind him with her weapon drawn.

Bernadette and Evanston made it down the hall, going room by room, clearing each armoire and looking under beds to see if there'd been any sign of activity.

"It's colder in here," Evanston said.

"They must have closed a bunch of heating vents. They only need to keep the pipes from freezing." Bernadette said as she swung an armoire open.

"They didn't have much did they," Evanston said.

"No, they were giving themselves to God. That's the whole point. Abandon worldly possessions to attain the kingdom of heaven," Bernadette said.

"You believe in all that stuff?"

"Doesn't matter what I believe, it's what they believed. Thousands of men and women have become priests and nuns over the years trying to pursue heaven."

"You didn't answer my question."

"You're right, I didn't. Now, let's get these rooms cleared," Bernadette said.

They came out of their room at the same time as Stewart and Simmons, who gave them the all clear sign.

"This is the last one," Evanston said. She opened the door to the room and jumped back. "We got company."

Bernadette motioned for Stewart and Simmons to cover them. She opened the door slowly and swept the room with her gun. There were two sleeping bags and food containers on the floor. A mouse was busy with one.

Bernadette entered the room and checked the armoire. A shirt and pair of pants hung there. She pulled on a top drawer. A find a gray hooded sweatshirt lay inside. With a pen, she moved the sweatshirt to reveal a blonde wig.

"I guess we know how our blonde disappeared," Bernadette said, holding the wig up with her pen.

"Damn it, they were here all along," Stewart said from the door.

A door slammed down the hall. They jumped and turned in unison.

"Do we call for backup?" Evanston asked.

"By the time they got here, our suspects will have fled. Let's move forward," Bernadette said. She took the lead with Evanston and the officers behind her.

Pushing open a large door that separated the dormitory from the bathrooms, Bernadette swept the room with her weapon and the others followed inside.

The only light came in from frosted windows. Toilet stalls lined the room. Beyond them were rows of sinks and shower stalls. They moved in, opening toilet stalls as they went.

A toilet flushed at the end of the room.

They surrounded the stall, crouching low with guns pointed. No one breathed.

The door opened. "Police—freeze—down on the ground now. Get down now."

A frightened man in coveralls hit the ground so fast it looked like his legs had failed him.

"Don't shoot, don't shoot," the man whimpered from the ground.

"Hold up, everyone. It's the maintenance man,"

Bernadette said. She bent down and helped him off the floor.

"Yes, yes, it's me, Dmitri Vlasik, the maintenance man." He got up from the floor and brushed the dirt off his coveralls.

"You didn't sign into the book you were doing a check," Bernadette said.

"I came in the back way, from the parking lot."

"Did you know, Mr. Vlasik, that there's been someone living in the rooms on this floor?" Bernadette asked.

Vlasik's eyes grew wide. "That's not possible. I was here last week, I saw no one."

"So, you don't come in every three days like the sheet claims in the front hall."

Vlasik shifted from side to side, his eyes dropped to the floor "How can I? I do everything here, the boiler is one hundred years old, the electrical system hardly functions, and half the time the toilets back up. I do what I can." He raised his head and looked at Bernadette. "Are you going to tell Father Francis? I need this job, I'm a pensioner and my pension pays me shit."

Bernadette shrugged her shoulders. "Sure, you can tell the Father you couldn't possibly check every room and maybe he'll cut you some slack. I'll put in a good word for you. Now, show us how someone could have got in here without being seen."

"Okay, no problem, follow me. The priests lock up nothing here. I've told them they should lock the doors at night, but they won't hear of it," Vlasik said as he led them out of the washrooms to a set of stairs.

They followed him down two flights of stairs to a doorway that led to a small parking lot in the back. Five cars occupied spots outside the doorway. Four cars sat covered in snow; one larger vehicle had a tarp thrown over it with no snow on it.

"Who owns these cars?" Evanston asked.

"Some priests who have lived here left their cars behind. Some of them are junk, but the seminary hasn't had time to dispose of them," Vlasik said.

"What about the one under the tarp? Someone moved it recently," Bernadette said.

"That's strange. That's a Toyota van that we used to take priests into town. The priest who drove it became ill, so they parked it back here. I should be covered in snow."

Bernadette walked into the parking lot and lifted the tarp on the back of the vehicle. She looked at Evanston. "Looks like the Toyota van has miraculously become a GMC SUV."

The other officers came over to the vehicle. Stewart pulled out his cellphone and pulled up the license number. "We got a match. This is the suspects' vehicle they rented from Hertz back in Calgary."

Bernadette got on the phone and called the detachment, ordering a complete team to come out and sweep the vehicle and the room in the seminary for prints.

"We now know why we haven't seen them in a hotel in town. They've been living here most of the time," Bernadette said. She turned to Vlasik. "Can you get us the vehicle license number of the van?"

"Yes. I'll do that right away," Vlasik said. He hurried as fast as he could with his limp to the office.

Bernadette watched him leave. "I feel sorry for that guy with all the work he has to do, but he's lucky he didn't give the rooms a thorough check."

"Why is that?" Evanston asked.

"Because they would have killed him if he had."

18

BY LATE AFTERNOON, the crime scene techs swept the room in the seminary and the vehicle for prints and any DNA. They'd found the shower the couple had used and the garbage bin. A news team had gotten wind of the tech's activities, parking themselves outside the front door and raising their antennae on their truck to broadcast to reports to their stations.

Bernadette walked outside. A young woman reporter approached her with a microphone. She wore a red parka with her news logo emblazoned on it. A stream of vapor ascended into the air from her breath.

"Detective, have there been any recent developments in the recent murders?" she asked, thrusting the microphone under Bernadette's chin.

Bernadette stood there, careful not to look frustrated or annoyed. A cameraman was rolling footage in back of the reporter.

"This is all part of our ongoing investigation. If you go to our detachment, our spokesman will fill you in with the latest events."

"But they've given us nothing. They only say everything is part of an ongoing investigation," the young woman complained.

"Well, there you go, we're consistent now, aren't we?" Bernadette said with a smile and started walked away.

Jacob Burkov blocked her way. He had his cell phone in one hand, using it to record. "Well, Detective Callahan, I hear you've sprung your uncle, and he's now living with you. Do you have anything to say to these recent developments in your life?"

Bernadette looked at the smiling, well-dressed man and saw red. She put up her hand and knocked his cell phone to the ground. "Listen to me you little shit, you almost ran me over the other morning. I could have you charged for that."

Burkov put up his hands. "Your headlamp was in my eyes. It blinded me. It wasn't my fault."

"Following me is obstruction of a police officer. I can have you hauled into jail for that."

"You'd never make that charge stick," Burkov said. "I'd be out in no time."

Bernadette smiled. "You haven't seen the backlog in our jails. Perhaps you can write a story about that—oh, but you won't have your cellphone. We confiscate those."

"I'll gain more followers and more sponsors," Burkov said. "Go ahead, take me in, I dare you."

Bernadette bent down and picked up his cell phone and handed it to him. "Here, you dropped this."

She walked away, knowing she'd screwed up. Her grandmother always said to never fight with a pig, you get dirty and the pig enjoys it. She walked back into the seminary where Evanston was waiting.

Evanston took her aside. "What the hell are you doing? You fed right into his hands. That's what he's hoping you'd do. That whole thing of him trying to run you off the road—that was him getting under your skin, so he'll have something to write about."

Bernadette shook her head. "Yeah, damn it, you're right. I screwed up. But on the bright side, you'll probably get a bargain on catnip on his blog next week."

Evanston put her hand to her forehead. "Oh, my God, girl. You're something else."

Bernadette shrugged and turned back into the seminary to work with the crime scene investigators.

As the morning turned to late afternoon, CSI left the scene and so did Bernadette and Evanston. They grabbed a sandwich on the way back, wolfing it down with a Diet Coke at the Subway Stop so they wouldn't be getting mustard and relish on their desks back at the office.

They had a meeting with Durham and the other detectives, with Durham taking the lead.

"What have we got?" Durham asked.

Bernadette looked at her notes. "The murder and incident took place at the hospital at eleven hundred hours yesterday. If the suspects returned to the seminary and changed vehicles, that gives them almost twenty-four hours driving either east or west."

"That gives them Vancouver, Calgary or Winnipeg. They could be anywhere by now," Evanston said.

"We'll put out a BOLO to all units both east and west and have them check all gas station CCTV's. I'll get some units to set up roadblocks at mountain passes in British Columbia," Dawson said.

"That's all good, Chief," Bernadette said. "I sense they're still in the area."

"Why is that?" Durham asked.

"Because they're not done. Father Dominic is still alive.

That's who they came for. These two will go back into another hole and wait. If they hid from us in the seminary, they'll do something off the grid. I suspect an abandoned house or they'll do a push in of some single person and take over their house," Bernadette said.

"You seem overly certain of that," Durham said.

"I just got a of sense of the dedication of the mission of these two. We're not dealing with average criminals. These two are serious about getting their job done."

"Okay," Durham said. "We'll send out a notice."

"We also need to get onto every senior citizen's Facebook site and tell them to watch out for these two, then broadcast they need to check on their single relatives to make sure they're okay," Bernadette said.

"Your certain of this?" Evanston asked.

"I'm deadly certain."

Anna Lindkvist lay on the sofa with her hands and feet tied with duct tape. They had stuffed a dishtowel in her mouth. This had happened so fast. The two young people had seemed so nice.

They'd knocked on her door just after she got in from her taxi ride back from the store. They said they had a grandmother in the neighborhood, but they'd gotten lost, and their cell phone had no battery power left. Did she have a phone?

They looked so lost and so cold. She couldn't refuse them. She opened her door to them.

The moment they got in the door, everything went horribly wrong. A dark-haired man with a bristly beard and pock marked skin started swearing at her. He pushed her onto the sofa and started yelling, asking her if she lived with anyone else. They frightened her. Then he slapped her.

She'd broken into tears. "I'm an old woman. I'm eighty-nine years old."

"You won't reach ninety if you don't speak up," the man said.

So, she told them everything. She lived alone. Her husband had died several years ago, they'd had no children, and she'd outlived her two siblings. None of her nieces or nephews ever called her.

The man had turned to the woman. "We've found the perfect hidey-hole."

"She's got no Internet and no television," the woman said.

"It was too expensive," Anna had replied. "I needed the money to feed my two cats."

"Well Grandma, if you want to keep yourself and your two cats alive you'll do as we say then," the woman had said.

Anna lost track of time. The two left her bound and gagged on the sofa while they moved their van into her garage. She'd sold the car long ago; she took taxis to the store or walked.

Her neighbors, Mary and Karl Stucky, lived in Mexico in the winter. Sometimes a local boy came by to shovel her walk, but he'd done it yesterday. He wouldn't be back until it snowed again.

She closed her eyes, prayed for snow, prayed for deliverance from these two and asked herself why she'd never moved into a senior home like her friend Erna had once advised her to do.

Bernadette and Evanston came back into their office and looked over their notes. "What's our plan?" Evanston asked.

"I figure these two need to find shelter somewhere. They

have to stay off the grid and away from cameras. They were successful in hiding out at the seminary, but they must have got spooked and lit out in a hurry," Bernadette said.

"Not just messy young people?"

"They left too much information about themselves. We know from the black hairs in the wig we found that our female suspect isn't blonde. We got enough DNA and prints to ID them in the system without going through facial recognition."

"What made them run?"

"Maybe the maintenance man scared them off. The boiler room is directly below the dormitory. They probably heard him and made a run for it.."

"How do we track them down? We've had units out all over town doing gas station camera checks; that's a big zero. The highway cameras came up with nothing and the hotels, motels, and sleazy flop houses have no reports," Evanston said.

"Which tells me they never left town," Bernadette said while pouring a coffee.

She came back to the desk and clicked on her laptop. "I think we check the parking lots of every major shopping mall, grocery store, and big box store in the city."

"You think we'll see them trolling the lots looking for their next victim, or in this case their next abode after they take the person hostage and force them into their own home?"

"That's how I see it," Bernadette said.

Evanston was clicking her ballpoint pen, which was getting into Bernadette's head, again. "Okay, I say we run with your idea because I got nothing at this point. How many can we get to work on this?"

"We got you and me and Stewart and Simmons. That's

all Durham would give us. The rest of the force is out doing neighborhood patrols. The city is scared witless with the murders. Durham knows the city needs to see our people in the streets to feel safe. Otherwise, we'll be fielding calls day and night about people seeing things in the shadows."

Evanston nodded. "He's got that right. Where are we heading first?"

"I figure the big supermarkets. There's lots of parking and places for our suspects to grab someone and take them and their car without being seen."

"Okay," Evanston said. They grabbed their coats, met Stewart and Simmons in the parking garage, and headed out.

The first three big supermarkets took an hour each. They introduced themselves to the store manager who took them to their security room to view tapes. Even with fast forwarding, it still took time at each place.

They hit a stroke of luck when the head of the private security firm in charge of the store said he'd have all the other stores under his command review their tapes for suspects and forward them to the RCMP. "I've got eyes to help. I'll put all my security team on it." He said.

They thanked the security officer and took a break. They drove to the local Tim Hortons where Bernadette got herself a double sugar and cream coffee and steeped tea for Evanston with a side of chocolate glazed donuts.

"OMG, Bernadette, you're ringing my bell. I love chocolate," Evanston said as she bit into the donut and closed her eyes.

"The extra sugar will help us watch the fast-moving videos better," Bernadette said.

"This will perk me up. I still got to get home and make

dinner for my kids and see if my husband ever wants to have sex with me again."

"Oh yeah, it's Friday night," Bernadette said.

"Yeah, we send the kids over to their friends to play video games and my husband Frank gets frisky. Well, not always. If the Red Deer Rebels are on a losing streak, I have to put some extra spice in his taco. Then we're back on track," Evanston said with a laugh.

"Way too much information," Bernadette said.

"Hey, you're still young. You and Chris are what? Mid-thirties? You glance at each other and you're doing the nasty. When you hit late forties like me, you got to take a run at it."

Bernadette bit into her donut and sipped her coffee. Across the street, a large pharmacy super store had ads for toilet paper and coffee. She wondered if she should pick some up; it looked cheap.

She watched as a taxi pulled up to the front of the store. An elderly lady with two shopping bags got in the back. As the taxi pulled away, another car drove behind it.

"I got an idea of another avenue we got to check," Bernadette said.

"Can we do it from here?" Evanston asked. "I could use another donut; I should get one for Frank. The sugar in this would definitely get him in the mood."

"I just realized how many older people take taxis in the winter when they come out to shop," Bernadette said.

"Doesn't everyone have things delivered now, I do? I don't have the time to shop. I order online and they drop it by the door when Frank gets home from his shift. Thank god he works for the post office and he's off at three."

"Yeah, but a lot of older people either aren't comfortable ordering online and many of them want to get out of their house for a while."

"I hear you, it's what we call cabin fever in the winter. You need to see some civilization. So, how we going to run it down. There's maybe five taxi companies in this city. We call them up and ask for all of their fares of elderly people from large stores like the pharmacy super store across the street."

"But why not some smaller ones? There's that cool little Latino place where I get Frank his spicy taco mix. What about them?"

"It wouldn't fit the M.O., the van would stick out. If you look at this parking lot, they could have parked on the outer edge and watched the store with binoculars. Their van would be out of closed-circuit TV range, and then they follow it at a safe distance. The taxi driver wouldn't know and neither would the intended victim," Bernadette said.

"Okay, I like your plan. When do we start?"

"I'll leave a note for our night shift to call the taxi companies, and I'll follow up tomorrow."

"But it's Saturday tomorrow."

"They run twenty-four seven. I'm sure there must be someone in operations or they can get someone. I'll tell them it's regarding a murder. I'm sure they'll help us."

"Okay, then I'm off the clock. I need to go home and get into my other world; you know, the one that is supposed to be the reality of the idyllic Canadian family with no murder and mayhem."

"Yeah, you go ahead, I'm going off duty. I'll text our new ideas to Durham, then I'm going to drop in on Sawchuck on my way home," Bernadette said.

"Hey, I talked to him on the phone this morning. I'm seeing him tomorrow. I gotta bring him some pirogues. My mother makes them, he loves them."

"Sure, I'll tell him that. I'll see you Monday."

"But you're working tomorrow."

"Well, yeah."

"Then I'm working. You text me on what cab companies you're looking into and I'll take the rest," Evanston said.

"Hey, thanks," Bernadette said as she got up. She realized how good it was to work with Evanston. She was a mom, a wife, and detective. She juggled it all and found time for Frank and her to do the nasty on a Friday night. She was truly a class act.

The traffic was light as she headed to the hospital. She realized she was delaying her arrival home so as not to have to cross horns with Uncle Cahal. Everything about the Callahan clan annoyed her. It was more than annoyance, and they'd pissed her off.

They had dropped her father, her mother, and her entire family like a stone. They'd never said why in so many words, but they knew why. It was because Bernadette's mother was a full-blooded Cree Indian.

As her father had explained, his family believed that he had tainted the bloodline of the true Irish family by marrying his native wife.

And now this man, this full-blooded Irishman dared cross her doorstep. She let the thought drop from her mind as she entered the hospital and found Sawchuck in his room.

He was in bed, propped up with a bunch of pillows, watching a hockey game.

"Hey, Sawchuck, someone told me you were feeling better. You're looking good," she said as she approached his bed. She wanted to reach out and touch him. She clasped her hands together in front of her to stop herself from doing that.

Sawchuck turned to Bernadette. An IV stuck into his

arm, a bandage over his throat displayed a black and blue bruise up to his chin.

"Hey, I'm okay," he said with a raspy voice. He reached beside his bed and took a cup of water with a straw and sipped it.

"I wanted to stop by. Se how you were doing and you know... to say I'm sorry." Bernadette fumbled with her hands and looked down at the bedcovers, then back up to Sawchuck. "I shouldn't have let that suspect get away. I saw everything about her that was wrong—the clothes, and the boots. I should have grabbed her, but I hesitated."

Sawchuck put the cup down and took Bernadette's hand. His grip was warm and strong. "Callahan, if you'd have jumped her, you might have been here instead of me. She glanced at my jugular as she shot past me. If you'd grappled with her in the hall, she might have slit your throat. And, another thing, it was Jellinick who talked me into going into the morgue without finding the light switch. I went along with it."

Bernadette squeezed his hand. "Thanks, Sawchuck, I'm glad you're both okay. They discharged Jellinick this morning. How about you? When can you come back to work?"

Sawchuck shifted in his bed and moved his hand back under the covers. "I won't be coming back to work. I told Durham I'm putting in for retirement. I transferred out here to be closer to the mountains, to forget the death of my wife, and build a new life in the force." He let out a sigh. "Turns out my new life here was the same as back home, getting shot at, spit on, and having knives and scalpels thrown at me daily. It's wearing me out."

"Where are you going to go?"

"My younger brother found a little lodge on Vancouver Island, a place up near Campbell River. We'll be doing eco and fishing tours. The most trouble I can get into is sticking myself with a fishhook. I'll get used to that."

"I look forward to some pictures of some enormous salmon," Bernadette said. She wished him well and left.

As she headed home, she knew she wouldn't tell Chris about Sawchuck's plans. Chris was an avid outdoorsman; he'd jump at the chance to take them out to the woods and open a lodge. But Bernadette wasn't ready for that yet. Being a detective was still her life. The hunt for suspects, the take-down, that was in her blood. She couldn't let it go yet.

Her mind had to deal with meeting Uncle Cahal, and in her usual fashion, she talked to herself about it, *Okay, Bernadette, don't let him get under your skin. He knows you don't like him, he's going to reason with you and change that... aw Christ.... you can always shoot him...*

She laughed at her own thoughts as the Jeep turned into the street of her home. She almost hit the brakes when she saw the pickup truck in the driveway.

19

THE PICKUP TRUCK was a 1970s Ford that held together with Bondo body filler and some duct tape on the hoses in the engine. But it ran. It drove Grandma Moses all over the big province of Alberta, Canada and sometimes to Montana to meet relatives or go for Pow Wows, feasts and ceremonies or sometimes, like now, to drop in unannounced to check in on Bernadette's life.

Grandma Moses had raised Bernadette from the time she was three, and then on and off as her mother had picked her up and taken her on the road with her father to tour as traveling musicians.

Bernadette's mother had a look and sound like Shania Twain. Audiences loved her, but they never made it past the bars, and Dominic became a drunk. He became a really good drunk, the one thing he excelled at.

It tore apart the family and Bernadette stayed with her grandma until she got into trouble on the reservation. The native boys had called her a half-breed and her mother a whore; Bernadette had answered them with her fists and her boots. Grandma Moses sent her to live with her Aunt Mary in Edmonton.

Bernadette parked her Jeep in the garage and took a deep breath. She knew that her grandma would not react well to Uncle Cahal. *"Let the fun begin,"* she muttered to herself as she entered the house.

Grandma Moses was sitting in the big chair by the television, watching *Dancing with the Stars*. Chris was in the kitchen. The smell of onions and garlic being sautéed made her realize how hungry she was.

"Hey, Grandma," Bernadette said as she entered. She wrapped her in a hug and kissed her on the cheek.

Grandma Moses always looked the same with her long hair braided on both sides. She wore a print dress, a wool sweater with white socks and running shoes.

Bernadette wasn't sure how old Grandma Moses was. Her face had some wrinkles, but her eyes twinkled with a vibrancy that missed nothing. If she said something, she meant it. Small talk to her was just something that was small. She could ask you about your dreams and have you wrapped in her gaze for hours.

"I wish you wouldn't drive all the way from Lone Pine in this weather," Bernadette said. "The roads are terrible this time of year."

Grandma Moses looked back at the television. "I have snow tires, I drive slow. Other people drive fast, and they go in the ditch, not me."

Bernadette squeezed her hand. "I'm glad you made it safe, and I'm so happy you're here."

As she walked into the kitchen, she realized just how much she meant those words. Her two worlds of Irish and Cree were colliding right now. Having Grandma Moses here tipped the balance.

Chris gave her a big hug and a kiss; he smelled like food. She almost wanted to lick him.

"How's it going? Have the battle lines been drawn between Uncle Cahal and Grandma Moses?" Bernadette asked.

Chris chuckled as he resumed stirring a large pot of vegetables. "Oh, yeah. Cahal was expressive and jovial until your grandma came to the door. He fled to his room after a half hour." He poured her a large glass of red wine.

Bernadette took a sip of her wine. "Well, this is going to make things cozy here. I must tell Cahal he's got the sofa."

"I've already got it covered," Chris said as he checked the oven to see how the roast salmon was doing.

"Harvey dropped in from next store to introduce himself. Cahal and him got along like old pals. I think Cahal likes Harvey because he's German descent."

"And why is that?" Bernadette asked, taking another sip of wine and starting to feel human.

"Check your history. The Republic of Ireland got help from Germany in their feud with England in early nineteen hundred," Chris said.

"Ah, the old saying, the enemy of my enemy is my friend."

"You got it. So anyway, after your grandma showed up, Harvey came back over, saw the situation and offered his guest room to Cahal," Chris said.

"That's great," Bernadette said, "but can we impose on Harvey like that."

"Harvey said he won't take no for an answer. He's already told Cahal he has some good Irish Whiskey and several DVD's of the American Civil War. Cahal is packing his bag. It's best for all. Your grandmother might take him apart if they're together too much."

Bernadette nodded her head and looked in the living room. "You got me there. It would be Custer's last stand all over again."

Chris topped up her wineglass and made her way to the bedroom, where she changed out of her jeans and t-shirt and into a pair of casual cotton pants with a comfy sweater.

After she'd washed her face and put on a tad of make-up to look less like she had just been through the world's worst day of crime detection, she at at the small desk they had in the bedroom.

She scrolled her texts. Chief Durham liked the idea of checking with cab companies. He authorized extra shifts and overtime to work on anything that would solve the murders. He also said he'd received the identities of the suspects. He'd sent them in an attached email.

Bernadette opened her laptop and downloaded the suspect's files.

The woman was Emily Murray, the man Dylan Quinn. Both of them had priors of some fraud and break and enters, but all of that was as juveniles. These two were in their late twenties.

Bernadette looked up and down in the file and found nothing that seemed to be in the realm of the average hired killer. But was that what they were? They didn't seem like professional assassins, not that she'd run into any, but when gang members in the drug trade hired a hit man to come to town, they did the job quickly, hardly missed, and never stuck around to finish the job. These two were committed, almost fanatical.

She sent the files to Detective Sullivan of the Garda SDU in Dublin and asked him if he'd found anything of interest on Brendan and Padraig.

Closing her computer, she went into the living room and

sat beside her grandma, who was still watching television. Chris had brought her a cup of tea and she was watching the dancers in the tight outfits that had been glued to stay on. It was time for the elimination round. A big football player towered over his slight professional dance partner.

Grandma Moses had a smile on her face and chuckled as she watched.

"You find it funny, Grandma?" Bernadette asked as she watched the show.

"The tall man has legs like tree trunks and the ass of a deer. But he moves on the dance floor like someone who is learning to walk."

Bernadette had to laugh. She'd seen *Dancing with the Stars* a few times, and most times, it was professional dancers trying to make a bunch of B list celebrities look good.

The football player got eliminated as the oohs and ahs sounded as the credits rolled. Grandma Moses shut off the television and turned to Bernadette.

Bernadette put her wineglass down and met her grandma's gaze. Her deep brown eyes seemed to hold infinity somewhere behind them.

"I came to talk to you because of my dreams," Grandma Moses said.

"I've had some troubling dreams myself, Grandma, but I hope I can help you.," Bernadette said, placing a hand on her arm.

"My dreams are about you."

"Oh."

"I've had them for three days now, they are always the same. That's why I got into my truck and came south. I needed to warn you about them."

Bernadette almost picked up her wineglass again. The

dreams of Grandma Moses were serious. She'd once fore-told in a dream she'd get in serious trouble on a case in Mexico, and she had. Grandma Moses claimed she was in touch with the spirit world, and they told her things.

"Ah... what exactly did you want to warn me about?"

"The ocean and the castle. You need to stay away from the castle with the cliffs by the ocean. That's what I saw," Grandma Moses said, her eyes clouding over.

Bernadette felt a shadow pass over her, as if an ancient spirit had flown across the room. She picked up her wine-glass and took a drink.

"Thanks, Grandma, but I don't have any plans for castles and oceans. Matter of fact, Chris and I have our wedding planned at Emerald Lake Lodge in May, and we want you to come as our guest—don't we, Chris?"

Chris looked in from the kitchen. "You booked Emerald Lodge? Since when?"

"I got the call this morning on my way to work. We have until Tuesday to confirm."

Chris smiled. "Are you kidding? I have splendid memo-ries of that place."

Bernadette smiled back and raised an eyebrow. "Yeah, me too."

"The fishing was amazing there, don't you remember?" Chris said with a wink.

"Yes, I do, and I'll take you down later, in your sleep." She winked back.

UNCLE CAHAL CAME out of the guest bedroom. He stood at the door and surveyed the room, his gaze resting on Bernadette with a smile.

"Ah, there's my darling niece. How are you, girl?"

"I'm fine, and you?" Bernadette asked in a flat tone that exuded as much warmth as a skating rink.

"Wonderful," Cahal replied. He couldn't help noticing Bernadette's voice. He avoided the icy stare of the grandmother and made his way to the kitchen.

"What are you cooking there, lad?" Cahal asked of Chris.

"A simple baked salmon with sautéed vegetables and potatoes au gratin."

"Smells lovely," Cahal said, rubbing his hands. "Are there any bottles of Guinness left? Or did I drink them all?"

"You left one lonely bottle from last night," Chris replied.

"Well then, I best rescue it," Cahal said with a smile. He opened the fridge and took the top off the bottle. He took a big swig and looked at it, "Ah, we Irish have a saying that beauty is in the eye of the beer holder." He looked around, saw no one laughing, and took another swig.

Chris took the salmon and potatoes out of the oven and placed all the food on platters. Bernadette set the table and placed wine glasses on the table.

"I invited Harvey to join us, but he might not be over for a bit. He said he had to do some errands," Chris said.

"That's great," Bernadette said. She knew that Chris had invited Harvey to be a referee in between Cahal and her grandmother.

Her grandmother liked Harvey, although she thought he talked too much, but he was a transparent sort. He meant no harm to anyone and tried to do good things for people. To her, that was an honest man.

They sat at the table, leaving a place for Harvey. Chris poured wine for Bernadette and himself. Cahal decided he'd stay with his beer.

"Should we say the lord's prayer before we eat, to bless this meal and this company?" Cahal asked.

"I don't pray," Grandma Moses said.

There was a moment of silence at the table. They looked in Grandma Moses's direction.

She was staring at Cahal. He stared back. Like two bulls locked in battle.

"Now why is that?"

"When the white man came to Canada, he had the bible, and we had the land. He said, here's the bible, let us pray. We did. When we opened our eyes, the white man had the land, and we had the bible," Grandma Moses said.

"Ha, that's a grand story," Cahal said with a laugh. He drained his bottle of beer, took a water glass, and filled it with wine. He'd apparently decided he needed the wine after all.

"But it's true," Grandma Moses said without a smile.

"Well then, so it is, but bless us one and all in the lord's name," Cahal said. He took his glass and raised it in a toast to everyone.

Bernadette served her grandmother some salmon, vegetables, and potatoes and did the same for herself. This conversation was going downhill fast.

"I never got to ask you about the picture you showed me of my trip to Ireland when I was very young. I don't seem to remember it, Cahal."

Cahal served himself some food on the platter and looked up at Bernadette. "Ah, you were very young, I think about two years old. Your dad wanted to see if he could connect with some of his old music lads from the past, but it didn't go well. He left with an awful experience. His old pals didn't like his new sound from Canada, so off he went back to Canada."

"Did you remember my dad traveling to Ireland, it must have been thirty-five years ago, grandma?" Bernadette asked.

"Your mom and dad disappeared for a while. They were angry with everyone, with your grandfather and me, with their family, I think even the spirits made them mad."

"I have to ask you, Cahal, was my mother accepted by your family in Ireland?" Bernadette asked.

"She was. She was a wonderful mother to you. We all thought she'd taken to you right away," Cahal said.

"What do you mean, taken to me?" Bernadette asked.

"Well, as you weren't her child, we didn't know if she'd feel right taking you as her own."

Bernadette's fork dropped to her plate. She looked at her grandmother, "Is this true?"

Her grandmother's eyes narrowed for a moment. "Your mom and dad brought you to me when you were two. Your mom said you'd been born on Vancouver Island. But I believe you're my granddaughter, and that's what matters."

"Are you trying to tell me I was born in Ireland, Uncle Cahal?"

"Well, yes, as delicate a subject as that is. Your father had a dalliance with a lass from another village, a bit of a roaming girl, as it were."

"What's a roaming girl?"

"You call them gypsies. Some call them Tinkers in Ireland, but that's a bit derogatory. They are an ancient clan, made their way, the legend says, all the way from India and into Romania and then spread out throughout Europe. Some still call them the Roma."

"I can't believe this," Bernadette said.

"Why not?" Cahal asked. "Chris told me today about your tremendous instinct and your courage. The gypsies have that, it's a trait of theirs, and they are wily and intuitive."

Bernadette took a drink of her wine and set her glass down. "And so are the Cree natives of the northern forests of Canada. That's where I was raised."

"Well, that's wonderful," Cahal said. "Your grandmother did a grand job of raising you, and look at you now, a prominent detective with the famed Royal Canadian Mounted Police. Your aunt is thrilled back home. I's all she talks about."

"There's one problem with your story, Cahal," Bernadette said.

"Now what might that be?"

"I have a birth certificate from the Royal Jubilee Hospital in Victoria on Vancouver Island. It's how I got into the RCMP. You must be a Canadian or a naturalized citizen. I'm listed as a Canadian by birth." She took a swig of her wine and smiled. This conversation was getting interesting. Especially when she was winning.

"Ah yes, about that. Your father had a man commit a bit of forgery on your behalf when he arrived back in Canada. I told him it was a bad idea. That he should never hide your true identity. That is when we had a bit of falling out, your father and me. He wouldn't speak to me again after that."

"Again, that's a great story, Cahal, but I've seen my birth record online with the Canadian registry. Hard to forge that," Bernadette countered.

"Really now, you couldn't pay a person to enter a birth date onto a computer in your government. Your father told me he knew just the man who worked in the city of Victoria. Cost all of one hundred dollars back then and the man registered the hospital, your birth weight, and date of birth.

You changed from one hundred percent Irish to a half and half, just like that," Cahal said with a smile.

Bernadette leaned forward. "That is the greatest load of bullshit I've ever heard."

The front door opened, and Harvey Mawer walked in. "Am I too late for dinner?"

Chris jumped up from the table. "Perfect timing." He grabbed a wine glass off the counter and poured Harvey some wine.

"That's just great. What are we all talking about? The conversation looks lively."

"Just doing some catching up," Bernadette said as she poured herself more wine. She looked across the table at Chris. Tonight's conversation in their bedroom would be interesting.

20

EMILY MURRAY and Dylan Quinn sat in the kitchen waiting for the kettle to boil on the stove for tea. They'd found some biscuits in the cupboard and placed them on the table.

"I'd best see how the granny is doing," Emily said.

"Why not leave her?" Dylan asked. He pulled a biscuit out of the box and held it held between his thumb and forefinger to examine it.

"Because she might pee or shat herself and we get to deal with the stink, don't we? Must I think of everything?" Emily asked, getting up from the table.

"We'll stick her in the basement with the cats and be done with her," Dylan countered.

"And if we're stuck here for days on end, who cleans up the mess? I do, that's who." Emily grabbed a chef's knife from the kitchen drawer and headed into the living room.

The house was small, with tiny rooms, and long hallways, built in the mid-1960s. Emily realized that was a good thing, as these places were soundproof.

She entered the living room. "Hey, granny, do you need to go toilet? Nod your head if you do."

Anna Lindkvist nodded her head up and down several times. She'd been lying there with her ever-growing bladder and the shame she'd feel if she had to pee on herself and her lovely sofa.

"Well then, let's get you to the toilet," Emily said. She lifted her up and cut the duct tape from her feet. "No clever stuff now, granny, I'm quick with this knife. I'll stick you if you get silly on me. You understand me?"

Anna nodded her head again. Emily took her to the toilet in the hallway.

"Nice addition this, a toilet in the hallway. Did you put that in, granny?"

Anna nodded her head; her husband had put in the toilet and sink after they'd moved in ten years ago.

"Okay, in you get," Emily said. She pointed Anna to go into the toilet.

Anna put up her hands and motioned to them and pointed to her dress. It was obvious. Unless Emily was going to lift her dress and pull down her underwear, she needed her own hands.

"Aw, Christ. I'll let you use your own hands because I'm not about to be wiping your privates for you, granny. Here you go." She cut the duct tape off her hands.

Anna proceeded into the toilet and relieved herself. She pulled the towel out of her mouth as she did so. "Thank you, dear, I was getting desperate."

"Oye, I didn't say you could take that out," Emily said.

"Sorry, I'll put it back as soon as I'm done. But if you wouldn't mind, a spot of tea and maybe a biscuit before you muzzle me again would be welcome. I haven't eaten in hours and I'm dehydrated," Anna pleaded. "I promise I won't do anything silly."

"Aw jeez, Dylan is going to kill me for this. All right, granny, walk ahead of me into the kitchen."

Anna washed her hands, straightened herself up a bit and walked in front of Emily to her own kitchen, that her hostage takers occupied.

"What the hell are you daft, Emily? Why did you take her bonds off?" Dylan asked, standing up at the kitchen table.

"She had to pee, and she's hungry and thirsty," Emily said in her defense.

"I'm not having this. This is insanity, you bringing her in here," Dylan said.

"I don't care what you think. Sit down, granny. Do you take milk and sugar with your tea?" Emily asked.

"Just milk, my dear," Anna replied.

Dylan stormed out of the kitchen muttering to himself.

Emily poured Anna some tea and put a plate of biscuits beside her. "There you go, granny. Now eat and drink up, before I tie you up again."

"You can call me Anna if you wish."

Emily shook her head. "I prefer not to."

Anna sipped her tea and held Emily's gaze. "You plan to kill me before you leave, here don't you?"

Emily stirred her own tea and stared at a biscuit. "There's no telling what can happen. It's all a bit fluid now, as they say." She looked up and held Anna's gaze.

"I can see you're desperate. I've heard about the killings at the seminary and the hospital."

"I thought your television didn't work."

"I'm old-fashioned. I listen to the news on radio. It's free," Anna said with a smile.

"Well, you know who we are, so be on your best behavior, granny."

Anna nodded her head and sipped her tea. She took a biscuit and held it up. "I'm not afraid to die."

"If you do something stupid, I'll make you afraid," Emily cautioned.

"You don't understand. My husband has been visiting me at night. He's been standing in that hallway right behind you. He told me it's okay. So, I'm ready."

"Are you talking crazy now?" Emily asked.

"No, we old people know when it's time. But I do have a favor to ask."

"And what the hell would that be, then? You're not in a position to ask favors, granny."

Anna shrugged. "I wanted to ask if you'd take a bunch of the sleeping pills in my medicine cabinet, grind them up and put them in my tea. I'd rather leave this world in sleep than at the end of your knife."

Emily smiled. "I'll see what I can do, granny."

"Oh, and there's one more request," Anna said as she picked up another biscuit.

"You are pushing the edge there now, granny."

"Sorry, but if you'd keep the cats in the basement after you've killed me, I would appreciate it. I love them dearly, but if I'm not found in time, they will feast on my corpse. I don't want to give the police a fright when they discover my body."

Emily shook her head. "That's enough of your nonsense now, granny. Finish your biscuit and I'm tying you up again."

Anna used a napkin off the table to dab her lips. "Thank you, you've been most kind."

Emily took her back to the living room and bound her feet and hands with the duct tape and put duct tape over her mouth instead of using the tea towel. She returned to the kitchen, Dylan sat there with a look of disgust on his face.

"She's a daft one," Emily said, sitting back at the kitchen table and pouring a cup of tea.

"Don't get attached to her. We need to off her before we leave tomorrow."

"What's the plan? Are we to make a run for it?" Emily asked.

"Not until we finish what we came for."

"How's that to happen,? He's surrounded by armed guards now. We'll never get close."

"You're right, *we* won't, but I can," Dylan said as he looked out the window into the chilly night sky.

Emily shook her head, putting her hand on Dylan's arm, "Don't be a daft bugger. They'll shoot you on sight. I tried to get to him dressed as a nurse, and it didn't happen. What are you going to do—dress up as a doctor?"

"No, I'll go as a janitor. When we were there, I saw the maintenance rooms are unlocked. I nicked shirt and trousers from the maintenance man at the seminary. They're the same color as the hospitals. I get me a bucket and mop and make my way to the Father's room and I pull out this," Dylan said holding up a handgun.

"And what, you're going to kill everyone in the room with that and shoot your way out of there?" Emily asked, staring at the gun.

"Yeah, that's the plan," Dylan said.

"And what of the police? Are you daft? They'll not sit by and let you kill everyone."

"It's the element of surprise, isn't it? They won't expect a bold attack. I kill the security guard, they don't carry guns here—I shoot the priest and leg it out of there into the crowd after I've changed clothes."

"And where am I supposed to be? How do I cover you? We've only one gun."

"You stay here, wait for my call. We'll call our minder and get our pickup, and we're out of here. I hear Las Vegas is warm this time of year. We'll get some new identities, and you, my lovely, will sip margaritas by the pool come Sunday."

"But I need to be with you," Emily whined.

"No, the two of us together will stand out too much. I'll leave early in the morning and take the back streets on foot to the hospital. I'll go in the back entrance. There's security at the front, but not the loading dock. By ten o'clock I'll be ready when all the visitors come to the hospital."

Emily sighed. "You've got it all planned. But it's suicide. Why can't we make a run for it now?"

"Because our people will kill us back home. You know what master said if we failed. And, besides, do you want to jeopardize the life they promised us?"

"You mean all that crazy talk of us being the heirs of the alternative world, that we have the blood of the ancients of Ireland in our veins? Look, Dylan, I might have believed that once when we were kids, but I'm getting older now. This entire mission has been a cock up. I'm tired of it."

"We're close to the finish. Be strong, my love," Dylan said. He reached across the table and kissed her hard on the lips.

21

BERNADETTE CAME out of the bathroom wearing her t-shirt. She lay down beside Chris in bed and put her head on his chest. "That was a memorable family dinner."

Chris kissed the top of her head. "No blood was spilled, so I'd say it was a success."

"What about the crap of me being the daughter of an Irish gypsy?"

Chris blew out a breath. "The only way to be sure other than to do a DNA test."

"Like you did? What if Cahal is right, that I'm one hundred percent Irish? It means my father and mother smuggled me into Canada and falsified my records? I used the record to get into the police force."

"Why not cross the bridge when we come to it? I ordered a DNA kit for you and it came in the mail today," Chris said. He reached into the nightstand beside him and pulled out a box.

Bernadette opened the box and pulled out the tube. "This is it? How do you use it?"

"You spit," Chris said. "You see the line there, you spit up to it, and you're done. We send it in and in several weeks, we find out just how you arrived on the planet."

"Do I really want to know?"

"Can you live with the uncertainty? You're like a cat with a ball of string with things like this. This will gnaw at you forever."

Bernadette looked at the tube. "You're right. It's the only way to be sure. But what if find out he's right, and I'm not my mother's daughter? Then I've been living a lie for all my life?"

"You mean like me finding out I'm Jewish?" Chris asked with a chuckle.

"Oh, yeah, sorry. How are you dealing with it?" Bernadette asked as she rubbed his chest.

"I'm fine with it. I found more relatives back in Greece who are Jewish. They were from a sect called the Romaniotes. One of my cousins informed me on Facebook they survived the holocaust mainly because they spoke Greek and blended in, so the Nazi didn't take them off to the camps in Europe."

"Wow, you have one hell of a past. Have you told your mother yet?" Bernadette asked.

"I'm going to call her in the morning and tell her about our wedding plans. She's going to make a big stink about the wedding not being in Toronto with two hundred Greeks. I'm going to inform her I have two cousins coming from Greece —one of them is a Rabbi," Chris said with a deep chuckle.

"You think that's kind of cruel?"

"No, it's time I took control and live my own life. She must deal with it."

Bernadette looked at the clock. "It's getting late. We'd best get some sleep. I'm doing some work tomorrow in tracking our suspects."

"Oh, yeah, there's one more thing I forgot to tell you."

"What's that?"

"I got a call from your detachment today. They said they're short of personnel right now and asked if I'd pull some guard duty at the hospital tomorrow."

"What? Did you accept?"

"Well, yeah. They could use the officers at the hospital for the streets."

"But they have security officers at the hospital."

"They're not allowed to carry a weapon. I've been out of the RCMP for only a year, so my qualifications are still valid."

"Well, if it's what you want. Who's taking care of Cahal tomorrow?"

"Harvey will watch him, your grandmother is fine on her own, and I could use some time away from all of them."

Bernadette laughed. "You're right. You've been doing all the heavy lifting at home. I really appreciate it."

"Really," Chris said, moving his hand down her back and massaging her buttocks.

"If you keep it up, you're going to get laid."

"I was hoping it would."

Bernadette sat up, pulled off her t-shirt and pulled the covers over them.

22

RONAN BRONAUGH STEPPED out of the back of his chauffer driven Bentley onto the curb. A light rain was falling. His chauffer held an umbrella for him as he walked to the door of the Westin Hotel.

He frowned at the attention of the chauffer; no self-respecting Irishman needed an umbrella unless it was a monsoon type rain. Good chauffers were scarce. This one was worth the mild annoyance.

The doorman opened the door with a tip of his hat and Ronan made his way to the Moreland Grill where he'd reserved a quiet table. As it was Saturday, the business crowd wouldn't be there. He'd have privacy.

The manager of the Grill took his coat and hat and led him to his table. Ronan Bronaugh was sixty-three years old, tall, good-looking, twice married with no children and one of the richest men in Ireland. He'd made his millions first in pharmaceuticals and parlayed that into billions in the genetic sciences. Several newspapers accused his company, Odin Genetics, of '*playing god with our genes;* ' he loved the sound of that. He had the newspaper column placed in a glass frame on the wall in his office.

Brandon Millhouse, a thin man with thick glasses and wispy brown hair, sat hunched at his table. He rose with a halfhearted attempt to greet Ronan but did a poor job of it and sat back down again.

"Mr. Bronaugh, always a pleasure," Millhouse said in his nasally upper-class British accent.

"Yes," Ronan replied. He disliked Millhouse intensely. He was always ill at ease and looked like a frightened rabbit, but that he was English, the very people his forefathers had fought to keep the south of Ireland free. But Millhouse was the best accountant there was. If you wanted to keep your fortune hidden from the prying eyes of the taxman, Millhouse could sink it deeper and keep it more hidden than any accountant he'd ever known.

A waiter brought them menus, and Ronan waved him away.

"I have made the deposits you requested," Millhouse said.

"What's the total?" Ronan asked

"One billion."

"Can it be traced back to me?"

"I washed it through several of your other companies," Millhouse said.

"You've done an excellent job. Please take your usual fee."

"Yes, of course. Is there anything else you'll need?"

"No, that will be all for the moment. On your way out, would you tell the gentlemen sitting in the lobby I'll meet him now," Ronan said.

Millhouse didn't flinch at being so abruptly dismissed by Ronan; that was his usual style. He used him for his knowledge of how to transfer money. He got up from the table, nodded slightly, and left.

Ronan motioned for the waiter to bring two coffees to the table.

A well-dressed man in his mid-fifties joined him at the table. He was well groomed with an aquiline nose and high cheekbones. He carried himself as if he thought he was much more than he was, or wished he were.

"Mr. Bronaugh, thank you for seeing me," Brendan Shannon said.

"How are things in parliament these days?" Ronan asked as he rose and shook his hand. "I ordered you a coffee."

"Thank you, much appreciated," Brendan said as he sat at the table.

The waiter dropped off menus, and they ordered the Sunday special and stirred their coffees.

"The wife and children are well, I hope?"

"They are splendid, thank you for asking," Brendan replied. He stirred his coffee and wondered what Ronan was getting at as he was never this cordial.

Ronan looked around him. "Now, listen carefully, I've sunk a lot of money into your campaign and your party. I do not see the votes in the house going our way. What's it going to take? Who else do we need to pay off?"

"The bill you're asking for is controversial," Brendan replied. "I have the religious right up in arms. They view the bill as playing God with genetics. I think I can get it through wrapped in the new protection bill."

"I need that bill made law. Don't you understand that allowing us to edit the human embryo will not only eliminate disease for all mankind but also eradicate violence? What we're doing here in Ireland will be the vanguard of a new world for humanity. They will hail you as a hero when we publish the results. They'll be calling for you to lead your party, and all of Ireland will want you as Prime Minister."

Brendan couldn't help but blush. "That is a happy scenario. However, it will be a hard road to get there."

The waiter brought their breakfast of eggs, bacon, toast, and tomatoes. Ronan bit into a piece of toast and sipped his coffee. His eyes regarded Brendan for a few beats.

"There are always hard roads. But I selected you to get this done and get it done you will. The vote happens in ten days. All of Ireland will be watching you. I will be watching you," Ronan said.

"With all the troubles re-igniting in the North, it's been hard to concentrate on these things."

"You must impress upon parliament that when the new DNA law is in, we will start a worldwide campaign of eradicating violence from human genetics. It's in the research. Wrap that in your protection bill, this country and all countries will be safe from violence forever."

"Yes, I'll get it done," Shannon replied. He'd suddenly lost interest in his breakfast.

"Excellent. Now, I must be off. I look forward to your results," Ronan said. He got up, threw some euros on the table, and walked out.

Brendan Shannon observed him leave and wondered what he'd got himself into. There was a saying about being in league with the devil, but to Brendan, being in league with Ronan Bronaugh could be worse.

RONAN WALKED TO HIS CAR. His chauffer had left it idling by the curb. Sitting in the back of the car was John Dunne. He was in his mid-fifties, heavyset with dark features and a broad forehead and bushy eyebrows that overshadowed two blue-green eyes that missed nothing.

He'd become Ronan's chief officer of security. He'd spent time in the Irish Army in the special operations force, then did some of his own private security work. When Ronan wanted something or someone taken care of, John Dunne made it happen in a matter that left no details. John would say, *"They won't see a ripple in the water when I'm finished."*

Ronan liked that about him. He slid into the back seat and nodded to the driver. The Bentley moved into traffic and made its way down the street.

"Good morning, Mr. Bronaugh," John said. "Here is a copy of the reports."

John handed Ronan a one-page piece of paper with the recent troubles in Northern Ireland. Most of it was a recap of the news. There was nothing incriminating to his company in it.

"Is there anyway any of this could come back to us?" Ronan asked.

John shook his head. "Every cell that is operating knows nothing of the others. They believe they are working for an ancient ancestry sect, set up by the figurehead you arranged."

"What about the priests who were writing their memoirs?"

"I have a team working on it. They'll have it taken care of."

"Very well, excellent job."

Ronan motioned for his driver to pull to the curb. Dunne was about to get out of the car. He stopped and turned to Ronan. "I'm concerned about the man you have acting as the leader of the sect."

"Why is that?"

"Well, for one, I've never seen his face. He seems to be demanding more loyalty from the followers. He might go too far in some of his reprimands with them. I hate to see him maim or kill some of them—a waste of talent," Dunne said.

"Leave that to me, Dunne. I have the situation in hand. Ramp up the cells, bring hell fire to the island in the form of the Troubles, and I'll have my company goals put in place," Ronan said.

"Aye sir, let loose the dogs of war?"

"Yes, those are my orders."

Dunne stepped out of the car and onto the street.

Ronan sat back in his seat and thought about the recent events. He was setting everything in motion. If everything went as planned, he would become one of the most powerful men, not just in Ireland but also in the world.

He felt the ancient DNA in his veins. It linked his heritage to the kings of not only Ireland but of the Nordic realms. He was destined for greatness. His ancestors would have nothing less.

23

DYLAN HADN'T SLEPT. He'd lain in bed beside Emily and kept hearing the house creaking as if someone was walking about. He'd taken his gun and walked into the living room several times. The old woman had stared at him with unblinking eyes. She didn't seem afraid of him. That bothered him. He couldn't wait to leave.

He now sat in the kitchen watching an old electric clock on the wall sweep its second hand around the face of a sun, a moon, and a rooster. He hated the clock.

Emily came into the kitchen. "Are you going then?"

"Yes, it's almost five. I want to walk there through the back alleys in the dark."

"What will you do if the police stop you?"

"I'm wearing my janitor uniform, aren't I? But I'll keep my face covered with this balaclava. It's so deathly cold outside no one will notice."

Emily looked at the window at the outside thermometer; it was so old it still registered in Fahrenheit. "Bloody hell, it's minus fifteen degrees, you'll freeze your bleeding arse off well before you get there."

"No worries, love, I found some long underwear that woman's husband must have used. The stuff is wool. And I found this old parka in the basement," Dylan said holding up a ski parka with a Swedish flag on it.

Emily tousled his hair. "Be careful, okay? And promise something?"

"What's that?"

"That you'll get right close to him before you shoot. Last time you were shite!" Emily said, making her hand like a gun and pointing it to Dylan's head.

Dylan shook his head in disgust, finished his tea, put his other clothes in a packsack he'd found in the basement and stuffed the gun in his jacket pocket.

Emily hugged him and kissed him hard. "Be careful. Shoot the bastard quick and run like fock, you hear me?"

"Aye, here's to that. Keep your phone close by. Mine's good and charged, I'll call you or text you when I'm done. I may have to hide out for a bit. I saw some places by the river I might use. I'll let you know how it goes," Dylan said.

He slung his pack over his back, pulled his balaclava over his face then covered his head with his parka hood.

"You look like you're about to trek to the North Pole," Emily said as he went out the door.

After he left, she went in to check on Anna. She was lying there with her eyes closed. As Emily approached, she opened her eyes.

"Do you need to pee, then?"

Anna nodded and Emily took off her bonds and led her to the bathroom, then into the kitchen for tea.

"Your man's gone then?" Anna asked.

"Yeah, he's gone to do some business." Emily replied.

· · ·

DYLAN WALKED QUICKLY down the dark alley and made his way to the main street. The street-lamps cast pools of light from one side to the other as he made his way over the hard snow. His feet made a crunching sound on the snow. He'd never heard anything like that before in his life. And he'd never been so cold.

His phone's GPS showed a thirty-eight minute walk of three point two kilometers over the Taylor Bridge. He took a longer route over Fifty Avenue Bridge. It was longer but less open.

As he walked over the bridge, he looked below him. The river had frozen completely over. "*Focking miserable country, this Canada.*" He muttered as he quickened his step to his destination.

24

BERNADETTE WOKE UP AT SIX. She was tired, but her day was tugging at her. She felt like they'd left a lot of things undone last night. The evening shift of detectives and police would continue the investigation, but she was eager to get to work and continue the search.

She rolled out of bed, threw on her bathrobe and walked into the kitchen to make coffee. Sprocket was up already, eyeing her to see if she was going to take him for a run.

She knelt down and wrapped her arms around the dog while she rubbed his fur. "Sorry, big fella, I'm heading to work early. Chris will take you for a run before his shift."

She made coffee and waited for the door to the guest room to open and her grandmother to come out.

She opened front door to pick up the newspaper and looked at the driveway; it was empty. She ran inside to the guest room. Her grandmother had left.

Chris walked out of the bedroom, rubbing his tummy. "What's up, Bernie, you look like you've seen a ghost."

"Grandma Moses has left already."

Chris shrugged and continued to the kitchen to get a

coffee. "Doesn't she do that often, coming and going as she pleases?"

"Yeah, you're right," Bernadette said. "I'll call her tonight to make sure she got home okay."

Bernadette poured some coffee and went to get ready.

SHE MADE it to the detachment before eight am. The night shift was being debriefed and the morning shift was coming in. To her surprise, Evanston was already at her desk.

"Did we have any positive hits from the store cameras last night?" Bernadette asked Evanston.

"Not a thing. I've called three taxi companies, and they've said they'll do a quick scan of their trips from all stores yesterday to elderly residences."

"Great, I'll get on the phone to the others." Bernadette said as she got to work.

IT DIDN'T TAKE LONG before the information came in. The taxi companies had been busy the day before with pickups at the malls and food stores and pharmacies. Dispatch at each company contacted their drivers to verify how many had picked up single fare elderly.

By nine o'clock they had twenty leads where the people at the addresses did not answer their phones when called.

Bernadette got Durham to approve three police cars to check five addresses each. She and Evanston would take the other five.

All units had strict instructions: If there was no one home, they stayed until someone in the neighborhood told them of the occupant's welfare. The SWAT team was on standby if they found suspects.

The first three they checked were okay. People had failed to answer their phones. They were all glad the police had come by to check on their welfare.

The next two checked out. Bernadette felt like they'd chased another dead end. Then her radio came on with a call from a unit on the west side.

"What have you got?" Bernadette asked the Constable.

"We're at fifty-eight, twenty and fifty-nine street. No signs of inhabitants, but a neighbor kid said he'd just shoveled her walk the other day. He said it's a lady named Anna Lindkivst who lives alone with her two cats. He saw a taxi bring her home with groceries yesterday, and he saw two strange young people wandering in the street."

Bernadette turned to Evanston. "I think we've found our suspects."

"You sure?"

"Can you check the garage, see if there's a white Honda van in there?" Bernadette asked.

"Ten-four. Give me a minute to check it," the Constable replied. A few minutes later he came back on, "There's a Honda van in the garage. The kid says the resident doesn't have a car."

"We got them. I'm going to roll the tactical team," Bernadette said.

Evanston and Bernadette turned their siren on and headed for the address. They were fifteen minutes away.

EMILY HID behind the picture window in the living room. Two large policemen knocked on the door, walked away, then came back. A second police car arrived, then a third. She ran to the back of the house. Two police appeared by the garage.

Anna Lindkvist sipped her tea in the kitchen. Emily left her there with her legs tied together with her hands free. I crossed her mind to pull the duct tape off her legs and bolt out the back door. She was still agile for her age, but she knew jumping out the back door might get her shot by a policeman. A silly way to die, she thought. She sipped her tea and watched the events unfold. The drama was better than anything she'd ever seen on television.

A large military vehicle arrived with the words RCMP Tactical unit on it. The backdoor opened. Men and women dressed in black with helmets and bullet-proof vests poured out of the back of the vehicle, brandishing automatic weapons.

"*Ah shite, Emily, you're done for now,*" she muttered to herself as she ran to the back window. Two of the tactical team guarded the back. They had their weapons trained on the house.

"Perhaps you should surrender," Anna suggested.

"Shut it, granny," Emily shouted to her. "I've got you as my hostage, don't I. I could slit your throat while I stand at the front door. They'll never get to you in time. They'll give me what I want as long as I have you."

"That only happens on television, my dear. There are snipers out there that will shoot you when you appear at the door with me. That's what they do."

"How would you know? You're an old woman who knows nothing," Emily snarled at her.

"One of my nephews was a policeman. They always negotiated with hostage takers but never let them leave. And where could you go? You're a two hours' drive to an international airport. If you negotiate a plane, the place you land would take you into custody."

Emily grabbed her phone and sent a text to Dylan. There was no answer.

DYLAN HAD MADE it to the hospital just past 6 a.m., He'd had to hide in back alleys as police cars went by, but he made it to the loading dock. He watched as trucks backed in and delivered food and pharmaceuticals. It took him over an hour hiding behind a garbage bin to see an opening. When the trucks finished unloading and the drivers went inside to present their bills of lading, Dylan ran inside.

He hurried down a corridor, nodded to other hospital staff. He kept his head down, making like he was late for his shift. His green janitor's uniform made it look like he belonged on staff.

At the end of the hallway, he found a maintenance room —locked. He swore to himself and moved on. As he rounded another corner, he saw two maintenance men walking towards him. They wore utility belts for electrical work. He kept his head down and muttered a "good morning," to them as he hurried by. They barely noticed him.

After checking another door, he found one that was open. He went inside and locked the door behind him. He waited there for three hours. Sometimes dozing off. As his phone showed 10 a.m., he left his backpack in the room, grabbed a rolling janitor's bucket and a mop, and pushed his way out of the room.

He placed the handgun in the squeegee part of the bucket and placed the mop head on top of it. Having it in his pants pocket made it too obvious. He pushed his way towards the elevator and pressed the number for Father Dominic's floor.

. . .

CHRIS WENT for a run with Sprocket at 7 a.m., showered, and dressed for his shift. It felt odd to be back in uniform after a year out of the force. The uniform they'd given him fit just fine. He strapped on his bulletproof vest and his handgun.

He made a call to his mother in Toronto, which didn't go well, and realized he needed to get to work.

By 9 a.m., he was at the hospital to relieve the other policeman. They exchanged greetings, talked about the weather and how cold it was outside, and Chris took up his position. The nurses on the ward couldn't help but notice the tall and muscular constable with the bulging chest and biceps. For the first half hour of his shift, they all found some reason to walk by. Chris smiled and nodded. He'd tell Bernadette about this later this tonight to get her worked up.

He looked briefly inside to see Father Dominic resting and propped up in his bed eating breakfast. The meal carts were coming around to pick up the trays. One now filled the side of the hallway as food staff picked up trays.

The elevator doors opened. A janitor pushed a bucket ahead of him with his head down and his arms folded in. A nurse at the front desk looked up briefly, then back down to her work.

Chris noticed the janitor as he came around the meal cart. He watched him reach into his bucket—a gun appeared in his hand. Chris's hand dropped to his gun. The janitor fired first.

A red-hot pain hit his chest. His knees buckled. His brain registered what was happening. He'd been shot.

Chris pulled out his gun. The janitor came towards him with his gun raised at Chris's head. Chris fired.

Dylan spun backwards. He clutched his stomach with

his left hand, holding his gun with his right. He fired wildly, running from the room.

A second bullet hit Chris in the chest.

Dylan ran down the hall shouting, "Get back or I'll shoot."

He made it to the stairs, pushed the heavy fire door open, and started down. Sirens sounded—growing louder towards the hospital. There were shouts coming behind him.

He needed to make it to the loading dock. There might be a car or truck to steal.

He pushed the door open at the bottom. He needed to get to the janitor's closet with the change of clothes in his backpack. Resting, he put his hand on his stomach. Blood covered his hand when he pulled it away.

The room spun before his eyes. *"I'm losing blood,"* he said to himself in a matter-of-fact voice.

The backpack didn't matter anymore. He needed to get back to Emily. Making it to the loading dock, he saw a jacket hanging on the back of the door. He put it on and limped out the back of the hospital.

The hospital wasn't far from the river. If he could get there, he could walk over the ice.

"It's not far, Dylan. Come on lad, you can make it," Dylan told himself. He pushed himself to run, breaking into a stumbling gait. The sirens were all around him. One was getting close. He didn't want to turn around.

A car came to a halt behind him. Car doors opened. A voice yelled, "Stop, police."

Dylan whirled and fired his gun. Two policemen ducked behind their car to return fire.

Dylan felt a sharp pain in his right arm. He dropped his gun and ran again.

"Get to the river, you can escape across it," Dylan told himself. A cloud seemed to come over his eyes. He blinked hard and ran forward.

He made it to the bank and slid down it, finding himself under the bridge he'd come over in the morning. He made it onto the ice.

A shot rang out behind him. A piece of ice exploded into shards beside him. He threw himself forward, making it to a bridge pylon where he caught his breath.

He heard the police voices; they were telling him to surrender.

"Not going to happen," Dylan yelled. But he wasn't sure if anyone heard.

He took out his phone and called Emily.

"Dylan, where are you?" Emily asked.

"I'm trying to make it home. It's looking bad, but I think I can make it. Can you call our minder? Tell him to pick us up, tell him I shot the priest in the head. Maybe he can make a diversion so we can get away?"

"Dylan, the coppers have me surrounded. There's no way out," Emily said. She was standing in the living room watching the buildup of police outside.

"Yes, there is a way out my love. We'll be in Valhalla together," Dylan said.

Emily closed her eyes as the tears fell from her eyes, "Yes, my love, we will."

Dylan closed his phone. He couldn't hold on to it anymore with the cold, he dropped it. He turned back towards the ice and ran towards the next pylon. He saw a patch of open water and he tried to jump it. His foot slipped.

The police officers heard a scream as they approached the bridge pylon with their guns drawn.

Constable Stewart walked along the ice, following a trail

of blood until it stopped at a patch of fast-moving water. The trail stopped there.

Stewart got on his radio and informed dispatch that the suspect had gone under the ice and presumed dead.

Constable Simmons came beside Stewart. "What are the chances of finding his body?"

Stewart looked at the water. "Spring breakup of the river isn't for another two months. His body could make it all the way to Drumheller or even the South Saskatchewan River. I'm sure in the meantime he'll be muskrat and fish food."

Simmons blew out a breath that turned to steam in the cold air. "You know they'll bring in divers to look down-stream, anyway."

"Yeah, they probably will. Makes a good show for the people on television. But then maybe his body got caught on a snag," Stewart said. "Let's get some tape to mark this off."

They walked back to the car as other police arrived.

"What's happening at the hospital?" Stewart asked an officer.

"I heard some radio chatter about an officer down. It's Chris, Bernadette's fiancé. I think it's bad." The officer replied.

Stewart stopped and turned to Simmons. "Oh god, I wonder if Bernadette knows that?"

25

BERNADETTE STOOD behind the patrol car with Evanston beside her. With guns drawn, they watched the tactical team swarm around the house. The standoff could take hours. The waiting had begun.

Sergeant Desjardins was in charge of the team. He was in his late forties, a large man with a dark face and habitual frown that seemed to go with his job. His team of five men and two women officers established a perimeter of two blocks around the house.

They checked the houses on both sides. If occupied, they escorted the residents to a bus for safety.

Now, this was the game of waiting for the right moment. They telephoned the home's landline several times, no one answered.

Remote pole cameras with extensions were used to survey the kitchen and the living room by sliding them under the door. They knew where the hostage was, and they knew where their suspect was. The team was in position at both the front and back doors, waiting for a signal.

Desjardins waited for the right moment. He watched the cameras.

He saw the young woman walking out of the kitchen towards the living room. She had a knife in her hand.

Desjardins gave the order, "Go—go—go!"

A team of three officers hit the old door with the battering ram throwing in flash bang grenades. They pounded into the room yelling, "Police, get on the floor."

Emily ran to the back of the house. She wanted to put the knife at Anna's throat.

Three more police were coming in the back door. They shouted for her to get down.

Emily raised her knife and ran at the first officer.

The female officer pulled her trigger twice. Emily's body convulsed with the bullets hitting her body. She fell backwards onto the kitchen floor.

The officer bent down and checked for signs of life. Emily was dead. She radioed in the all clear and checked on Anna.

"Are you alright, ma'am?" the female officer named Sanderson asked.

"Oh, much better now," Anna said. "But I think I'll need a visit to the toilet with all the excitement."

"Let me help you," Sanderson said.

Anna stepped over the body of Emily and looked down at her. A pool of blood seeped from her body. It made its way down the long narrow hallway, staining the oak hardwood flooring a deep burgundy.

"Karl won't be happy with that stain," Anna said.

"Is there someone named Karl in the house with you?" Sanderson asked.

"Oh, no," Anna replied, putting her hand on Sanderson's arm. "My husband, Karl has been dead for many years. He came to me last night and said you'd rescue me. He told me I'd be fine, but he said you'd make a mess when you came in." She looked around her at the broken doors and the blood. She shrugged her shoulders, entered the toilet and closed the door.

SERGEANT DESJARDINS GAVE the all-clear sign and called in his information to dispatch. An ambulance arrived with a coroner's van. Bernadette and Evanston holstered their guns and breathed again.

"Well, that's over. Do we know what happened to the other one?" Evanston asked.

"I've been hearing multiple sirens across the river, but I didn't dare pick up my radio or phone or I'd lose my focus on this situation," Bernadette said. She scrolled through her missed calls, she saw two from Durham, and she dialed him.

"Hey, Chief, we got the girl, Emily, what's the situation with the Dylan kid. I heard a lot of racket across with river, what's up?"

"Bernadette, sorry, it's Chris. The kid shot him, he's in emergency, you'd best get there—now."

26

BERNADETTE TURNED TOWARDS EVANSTON. "Chris got shot.
I'm going to the hospital."

"I'll drive," Evanston said.

Bernadette didn't argue. She yelled to Desjardin, "We
got to go."

"I just heard it on the radio, I'll tell the guys to make a
hole," Desjardin replied.

Evanston fired up the patrol car with all the lights and
horns. She had to move through the crowd that had formed
to watch the action at the house. Bernadette sat beside her,
fidgeting and cursing at the slow progress.

"Always a good crowd for a hostage taking," Evanston
said. "Did Durham say how bad Chris is?"

"He didn't say, just said I need to get there fast."

"I'm on it," Evanston said. As soon as they cleared the
onlookers, Evanston hit the gas. The car's engine roared, the
snow tires spun, then caught on the road. They hit the main
street, then the bridge. The hospital was already in view.

Below the bridge, Bernadette could see the police team
searching for the suspect. She did not understand what

happened or who shot Chris. She tried to keep her mind from jumping to conclusions. It was hard not to. She focused on her breathing; she would just breathe and wait until she saw him.

As they approached the hospital, two patrol cars moved back to let them through. News about Chris rolled through the force like wildfire. The greatest concern of the force was one of their own comrades in arms getting shot. It happened too frequently, and when it did, they all felt it.

Evanston slid the cruiser to a stop. Bernadette bolted out the door of the car and ran into the hospital. Constable Stewart met her in the lobby "He's in emergency."

Bernadette set off on a run. There was nothing she could do but put every ounce of her energy into getting to Chris. Durham said get there fast. That's what she did.

A nurse directed her to a curtained area in the Emergency room.

Bernadette pulled back the curtains. Chris was lying there with his chest bare. He had an oxygen mask on his face, an IV in his arm, with two doctors standing over him.

One doctor, named Patel, turned to Bernadette. "Your guy was lucky. Both shots were in his body armor with a twenty-caliber at close range. One of his lungs collapsed from the bullet impact, but he'll be okay in a day or two."

Bernadette stood beside Chris and squeezed his arm. He opened his eyes and tried to smile. A shooting pain went through his chest from the collapsed lung. He grimaced and took a deep breath of the oxygen.

"Hey, my big guy, you're going to be fine. I'm right here." She leaned forward and put her lips to his ear. "Remember, I'm your Calamity Jane, you're my Sundance Kid, we see everything through together."

The side of Chris' lips turned up into the tiniest of

smiles. He drifted off into a deep sleep as the drugs took effect.

"He needs to rest, then we're going to run some more tests," Doctor Patel said. "You can come back in a few hours if you like."

A nurse took Chris's pulse and adjusted his blanket. Another checked on his saline drip. Bernadette backed away from the bed after squeezing his arm. She'd seen so many people in this situation, now she knew how helpless they felt.

BERNADETTE WALKED out of the curtained room to find Evanston standing there holding a notepad.

"He's going to be okay. A collapsed lung from the bullets' impact to his vest, but the little bastard didn't get him. What have you got?" Bernadette asked, looking down at Evanston's notepad.

"I spoke with Constable Stewart. One of the hospital staff who was picking up food trays saw the suspect dressed as a janitor come around her cart. She said Chris didn't have a chance. He shot him at point blank range. She heard a bunch more shots, and she ducked for cover," Evanston said.

"Did the shooter kill Father Dominic?"

"No, that's the crazy thing. The father must have turned his head—the bullet grazed his head. That priest is one lucky son of a bitch... or whatever they call him in the Catholic Church," Evanston said.

"I'm sure the Church will come up with a miracle to name after him."

"It might be Saint Lazarus, because someone said they

had killed him. That's what dispatch got from our Constable on site."

"I think we leave him as dead—for now."

"What are you thinking?"

"I'm still thinking these two had help and there's someone else in town. We'll what shakes out with the news of Father Dominic's death."

"You still think your Uncle Cahal is in on this, don't you?"

"Sorry, you got me. You remember that thing about relatives? You can choose your friends and not your relatives," Bernadette said.

"Don't I know it," Evanston said. "And as we all know, it's the people close to you we always suspect in a victim's death." She looked down at her notes. "There's something else. The officer's found a cell phone by the river. They think it's Dylan's."

"How soon until we can get some info off it?"

"An officer is rushing it back to the techs, and they have the phone from Emily. We should have a report on everyone they called inside of an hour," Evanston said.

"Good, maybe we'll get a break in this case, find out who sent them and who their handlers were while they were here," Bernadette said.

27

BERNADETTE LEFT THE HOSPITAL—EVERYTHING in her wanted to stay. Her heart did flips in her chest as she drove away with Evanston. Chris needed to recover in the expert care of the medical staff. She'd only get in the way. They drove back to the detachment headquarters and found the techs working the cell phones they'd recovered from the suspects.

Miranda Nowicki, a recruit, had the cell phone on the desks. She possessed an excellent understanding of everything about computers and technology, something foreign to both Bernadette and Evanston.

"I've downloaded all the numbers both of them used on their phones since they've been in Canada. Most of their calls went to a number back in Ireland, but there is one they kept calling that is a local number," Miranda said.

"Local, as in right here in our city?" Evanston asked.

"You got it. It's our area code," Miranda replied.

"Can you locate it?"

"I've sent a request for a ping to the phone company. They'll check the number. From there, we find the tower it's near and do a GPS check," Miranda said.

"How soon will we get an answer?" Bernadette asked.

"Hold on, I'm getting something now," Miranda said. She looked at her screen. "Do either of you recognize this address?"

"Hell yeah," Bernadette replied. "That's my address. Let's roll. Evanston, call for backup."

Evanston and Bernadette put on their vests and checked their weapons as Dawson walked into the room.

"You got something?" he asked.

"Yeah, the number called from our two dead suspects' phones is my dear Uncle Cahal. Miranda pinged their phones to my address. Time for me to go clean house," Bernadette said.

"Got it," Durham said. He ran back to his office, grabbed his gun and vest. He called in a SWAT team to meet them at Bernadette's house on his way out the door.

Evanston drove the cruiser while Bernadette sat there fuming. "He's a felon. I should have trusted my gut. My god, even Sprocket didn't like him."

Evanston looked over at her. "This might be a false alarm. Maybe they planted something on Cahal. We don't want to walk in there and shoot the guy."

"Oh, hell no, but I'd like to give him a flesh wound—just kidding," Bernadette said.

When they arrived at Bernadette's home, they found the place in darkness. The sidewalks lay covered in snow. No one had shoveled them. One set of tire tracks led up to the house.

Bernadette jumped out of the car with Evanston. They

crouched beside the vehicle with guns drawn. Two more police cruisers came up beside them. The officers crouched down beside their cars, guns ready.

"What do you think?" Evanston asked.

"Let me try my neighbor's number next door," Bernadette said. She dialed his cell. "I got no answer."

"Maybe he's out on errands," Evanston said.

"Harvey Mawer goes nowhere in the winter without shoveling his driveway and sidewalk first. I've lived beside him for three years and that's what he does. He'll answer his phone no matter what he's doing. I heard him flush his toilet once while talking to him."

"So, what's the move?" Evanston said.

Bernadette held off her response when the tactical team arrived. The big armored vehicle lumbered to a stop, its air brakes sounded. The officers clad in helmets and body armor piled out of the back.

Desjardins came over to Bernadette. "What have you got?"

"We traced the cell phone call of our dead perps to my address. Cahal Callahan is the one working with them."

"Isn't he your uncle?" Desjardin asked.

Bernadette shook her head. "I wish you wouldn't call him that. He's my alleged uncle."

"Whatever," Desjardin replied. "I'm going to send my team into your neighbor's house, then yours. Does he lock his doors?"

"Hardly ever, and never during the day. Please don't use a battering ram on them. He'll be mad as hell." Bernadette said.

"He will be if we find him alive," Desjardin said. He turned and signaled to his team. They lined up in single file, assault rifles locked and loaded. With hand signals, they moved forward in perfect formation and silence.

They split in two—one team covered the back, the other took the front. They checked the inside with their cameras first; they entered with a quick push through of the door. It took them three minutes to give the all-clear sign.

"Well, we know where he isn't. Now let's go see if he's at my place," Bernadette said.

The team reformed in front of Bernadette's door. She walked to the head of the formation, nodded at Desjardin to let him see she would lead the team in.

The team did the remote camera check, signaling no movement inside.

At the door, she turned the handle—locked. She cursed under her breath. She took her key out of her jacket, inserted it, and unlocked it. The door turned. She pushed her way inside to the dark interior.

The tactical team's laser sights on their guns threw lights all over the house.

The open door cast a bright light down the hallway to the kitchen. A form lay on the floor. She couldn't make out what it was. She swept her gun left and right as she advanced. The outline of a man in a chair came into view.

She trained her gun on it and moved toward it. A small beam of light revealed Harvey Mawer. His head lay to one side. An overturned teacup was in his hand. He looked asleep. She checked for breathing. His breath was shallow but there.

She walked into the kitchen. The form she'd seen earlier was Sprocket. The big dog lay with his tongue hanging out. There was a faint sign of breath coming from him.

. . .

"CALL THE EMT's, Harvey and my dog were drugged. Put out an APB for Cahal Callahan," Bernadette said.

Evanston stood there looking over the room. "So your uncle was in on this all along."

Bernadette turned on Evanston. "I thought that bastard was bad news from the moment I met him. I thought keeping him here would mean I could watch him. Well, he was using this place to watch us. Harvey had a police scanner. I'll bet you he used it this morning, then drugged Harvey and Sprocket to make his getaway."

THE AMBULANCE TOOK Harvey to the hospital. The EMT thought Harvey would be okay, just heavily drugged. Sprocket was another problem. The big dog was barely breathing.

Bernadette called Dr. Annette Chow; she'd been Sprocket's vet from the day she'd brought him home. Chow loved the big dog and promised she'd do everything she could to revive him. She was going to take a blood sample and text Bernadette with her prognosis as soon as she had one.

Watching the van leave one way with Sprocket and the ambulance leave on its way to the hospital with Harvey, Bernadette had a feeling of despair and then rage. This man claiming to be her uncle had caused this.

She was going to find him. He was going to pay for this, for all of this. She turned to Evanston. "We need to get back to our office and start a serious search for this son of a bitch."

28

THE RCMP DETACHMENT was a buzz of activity. Officers were dropping off pages of reports. A group of officer scanned remote highway cameras. Three officers manned phoned to airports looking for leads.

"How far do you think Cahal got after he received the information on our radios?" Evanston asked.

"The shooting happened at ten this morning. The radio report came in at ten fifteen. I'm sure he lit out soon after."

"But wasn't he supposed to pick up our two Irish assassins?"

"If he heard the radio chatter of officers in pursuit and we had Emily surrounded, then he'd give them up for lost. He'd be saving his own worthless hide."

Evanston heard that last remark and tone from Bernadette and decided it best not to expand on that. She picked up her coffee and sipped in the silence.

Constable Chen, a second-year new hire, came by with her laptop. She was a petite Chinese girl with the heart of a tiger in the combat practice ring. No one wanted to face her in combat.

"You need to see this," Chen said. "I got this from one of the parking lot videos the security companies sent us."

Chen put the laptop in front of them, hitting play on the screen. The van that Dylan and Emily had driven came into view. A man walked up and talked to them, then walked away.

"Can you freeze it and enlarge it?" Bernadette asked.

Chen enlarged the photo. It was Cahal Callahan. He spoke to Dylan for a moment. They exchanged something, and he walked away out of view.

"We got him. Now we have to find him," Bernadette said. Her cellphone binged with a text. She looked down. "My vet confirmed it's the same drug Emily and Dylan used on Father Frederick."

"Is Sprocket going to be okay?" Chen asked. She had a Burmese Mountain dog at home and loved to play with Sprocket.

Bernadette smiled. "Yeah, Sprocket is coming around. The drug is passing out of his system. He wagged his tail and licked Annette's hand."

Chen took her laptop, folded it, and tucked it under her arm. "We need to find the MF that did that to your dog. No human does that to animals. I wouldn't mind finding him myself."

She walked out of the room with Evanston staring after her. "Did she just call Cahal an MF?"

"Wow, remind me to never get on the wrong side of that Asian fireball," Bernadette said.

They spent the rest of the afternoon gazing over reports and videos until their eyes were seeing double. Every airport had a BOLO, they'd put Cahal's face on the national and international search network. It was now a matter of time until the system pulled up something.

How far and how fast Cahal could travel was the main thing. Two major airports were only two hours from Red Deer. The Calgary Airport had the most direct international flights. With the help of a team of officers, they'd checked every flight that left either airport in the past four hours.

There was nothing.

At five, Evanston and Bernadette had a meeting with Durham; they filled him in on what they had.

Evanston pulled out her notebook. "We got some cell traffic between our dead perps and Mr. Callahan."

"Any texts in there?" Durham asked.

Evanston squinted at the list. "Yes, there's one to what we assume is Callahan's number. As this is the one that pinged at Bernadette's house, and it's asking for a pickup time from the perp's number," Evanston said.

"Can we link that phone to Callahan?" Durham asked.

"We saw him get something from Dylan in a supermarket parking lot, but that's all we have." Bernadette said.

"Wait.," Evanston said. "Where did the phones of our perps come from?"

"The tech said they used prepaid cheap phones probably purchased here in Canada, so they had North American SIM Cards," Bernadette said.

"But we never found a cell phone on Callahan when we originally arrested him," Evanston said.

"We need to find where the perps got theirs." Bernadette said. She jumped out of her chair and ran down the hall to meet with the tech.

When she got to the room, her chair was empty. "Damn it, just my luck, she's gone home."

"Who's gone home?" Miranda asked, walking into the room.

"Oh my god, you're still here. The cell phones of the

perps and our suspect, Cahal Callahan—how soon can you do a search to find out who bought them?"

"I can do it right now. They register all phone numbers with purchase," Miranda said. "This won't take long."

She sat down at her computer, pulled up a database on phone numbers, and entered the names that Murray and Quinn had used as their aliases when they entered the country.

She whirled around. "They purchased both phones just outside of Calgary at the Cross-Iron Mills shopping mall."

"Did they register a third number?" Bernadette asked, then held her breath.

Miranda squinted at her screen as the names scrolled. "Yes, they did. Holy shit, I don't believe this. The number we pinged at your place. They bought that phone."

"Miranda, you are one amazing lady. Please print that file. And run a GPS tracker to that third phone," Bernadette said.

Bernadette walked the piece of paper back to Durham's office as if she'd just caught the biggest trophy fish in her life.

"You want proof? I got it right here," Bernadette said. "The phone that pinged at my home was given to Cahal by the perps."

"How could you prove it? A defense lawyer could say that Cahal Callahan wasn't near your place when the call took place."

"Miranda also did a GPS tracker on the phone. The phone took off for the Calgary Airport only thirty minutes after it received a text from our dead perps."

Durham almost leapt out of his chair. "We got aiding attempted murder and I'm sure we can bring that around to murder. I'll get the Crown Prosecutor on this right away.

With this we can issue a Canada-wide and international warrant."

"What are the chances we'll get him back if he makes it overseas?" Bernadette asked.

Durham leaned back in his chair. "If we make a strong enough case to where he's detained, if he is. You're looking at two to six months. If he gets a talented lawyer, it could be a year, or even more."

Bernadette and Evanston returned to their desks.

"Well, that threw a damper on the party," Evanston said. "If we catch him in Canada, we get to prosecute immediately. If he makes it out of the country, he sits on ice until we can bring him back. I hate justice sometimes."

"It's what we signed up for. I just want to get him back here to grill him on what exactly he was up to," Bernadette said.

"You suspected him from the beginning, didn't you?"

"Yeah, there was something about him. But I let my guard down. I won't let that happen again. Now let's get to the CCTV footage and see what we can find in airports."

For the next two hours they checked countless tapes of service stations videos, then moved onto passenger videos from airports. There wasn't enough coffee to keep their eyes from going limp.

Bernadette looked at the clock on the wall. It read 7 p.m. "My god, is that the time? I have to see how Chris is doing. Can you handle the search for a while?"

Evanston smiled. "Are you kidding? Sit here and look at pictures of people getting on airplanes without you muttering under your breath for background sound? Go on, get out of here, I'll text you if we find anything."

· · ·

BERNADETTE MADE it to the hospital twenty minutes later. She hoped Chris might be out of his drugged state, but also wanted to just lie beside him and sleep for a while.

When she found him in his room he was sitting up in bed.

"Hey, sweetie. You look good," she said as she bent down to kiss him.

Chris made an attempt at a weak smile. "Yeah, for a guy who let a killer pop two shots in him."

She squeezed his hand. It felt cold. Taking his big hand between both of hers, she kissed his hand and rested it on the side of her face.

"How could you see him? A hospital staffer said he came at you from behind a food cart. Not exactly a fair fight. And anyway, Father Dominic isn't dead. He only got grazed again, which I'm sure isn't doing his poor old skull any good, but he's fine."

"Father Dominic is okay?"

"Yeah, we wanted to keep it a secret. Well, I wanted to. I needed to see if Cahal would do anything."

Chris blew out a breath. "You still don't trust him, do you?"

"Not after what he just did," Bernadette said. She filled him in on recent events and watched his eyes widen as he learned what the Irish uncle had done to Harvey and Sprocket.

"That son of a bitch. I'll rip him apart. I was going to give him my recipe for my Irish stew," Chris said. He grabbed at his chest for a second as the pain shot through him from his collapsed lung.

"Hey, take it easy, my darling. Don't get riled up, we'll find him. You rest up, get better, and we'll get you home."

Chris lay back on the bed and let his breathing return to normal.

"You must call my mother," Chris said.

"Me?"

"Yeah, you," Chris said, taking her hand. "If detachment human resources pick up the phone and call her, we're screwed. She'd be on a plane out here in a day."

"Why would human resources call her—wait, you didn't put me down as emergency contact on your sign in form?"

Chris lowered his eyes. "I'm terrible with paperwork. I forgot."

"Oh crap. You're right. I do have to call her. But she hates me."

"She dislikes all *xenos*, her word for foreigners."

"And what's the word for a Cree slash Irish mix detective who has mesmerized her only son with her charms?"

Chris winced slightly. "You don't want to learn that word. But she may have softened up a bit. I called her before I left for work this morning. We had a brief conversation about our heritage."

"You told her you found out you're Jewish and now you want me to walk into the mix of this. She must be madder than a bear with a sore head."

Chris moved slightly with the pain in his ribs. "She was a bit vocal."

"Explain vocal."

"She told me I should let the past stay in the past. She claims we're Greek, not Jewish."

"Hum, that's an interesting take on your heritage—denial. I'll call her, tell her you're injured and doing just fine. I'll also take the time to invite her to our wedding."

Chris shook his head. "You'll be entering dark territory there, my love. She'll get even more riled up."

"What me, get your mother upset? I'm just going to ask her how she feels about us having a native shaman and a rabbi officiate our wedding. Nothing too radical," Bernadette said with a smile.

"So, you're not concerned about Cahal's story of you being the daughter of some Gypsy Irish woman?"

"You're just pushing my buttons, aren't you?" Bernadette asked. She wanted to punch him in the arm at this moment, but not in his weakened state.

Chris had a tiny smile. "Maybe a little. Did you spit in your DNA test tube yet?"

"Not yet. But I will tonight if it makes you happy. Now get some rest. I'm picking up Sprocket from the Vet. I'm sure he wants my company, and I need his—a quiet male dog that doesn't give me any lip," Bernadette said. She bent down, kissed him, and headed out the door.

Before she left the hospital, she checked on her neighbor, Harvey. She went to his ward, found him fast asleep, and left a note by his bed that she'd be by in the morning to pick him up if he needed a ride home. That was just a gesture on her part. Harvey had so many friends in the city that one phone call from him would spark a fleet of cars to his aid; most of them would be elderly widows looking for his affections.

She left the hospital and got into her Jeep. A gentle snow was falling as she drove out of the car park. She felt alone in that moment. Chris and she had been together for over a year. They'd been through a lot together, but leaving him in the hospital pulled hard on her heart muscle. It resembled an ache after a big workout in the gym, only it seemed to last longer.

She drove to the Animal Hospital and spoke with Annette Chow. Her vet was a big softy for Sprocket. She'd seen him through many injuries that were mostly self-inflicted as Sprocket needed to investigate bull snakes, porcupines, and chase down coyotes. All with negative effects.

When Bernadette came into the exam room, Sprocket jumped off the table and stood up with his two paws on her chest. She grabbed his head and ruffled his ears.

"He's happy to see you." Dr. Chow said.

"The feeling is mutual. Is he okay for me to take him home?"

"Give him lots of rest, lots of water, and don't run him for a day or two. The drug is coming out of his system. It's been about eight hours now. He'll be fine."

Bernadette took Sprocket to her Jeep. He still wasn't his usual self. His head drooped down. He moved with effort, his head hung low. She had to help him up into the back seat.

She drove home, put Sprocket in his dog bed, ate some leftovers in the fridge and poured herself a glass of wine.

The house was eerily silent as she tried to go over the day's events, and it was hard to fathom how everything had been turned upside down in her world. They had killed the two Irish assassins, Chris had been shot, and Harvey and Sprocket had been drugged so Cahal could get away.

She sighed, took a long sip of her wine, checked on Sprocket, then looked at her phone. There was nothing else to do but call her future mother-in-law.

Her phone read eight o'clock. That meant ten in Toronto. Marula Chistakos never went to bed early. She was a night owl, drinking tea at night while watching Greek and American soap operas until she fell asleep in her armchair. Marula had raised Chris and his sister

Lenia after their father had died when they were young. She fiercely protected Chris, which is one reason he'd left to join the RCMP and get some space. Marula thought any woman who got between her and her son was a threat. Especially one who wasn't Greek, like Bernadette.

Bernadette dialed her number. Her stomach did somersaults of dread.

"Yassou, hello, Marula Christakos here."

"Hi, Marula, it's me, Bernadette calling."

"What's happening, why are you calling? Where's my Christos?" Marula asked. Her English became worse when she was excited.

Bernadette took a deep breath. They'd never had a normal conversation. It always concerned an emergency which involved Chris.

"Chris is in hospital."

"What! How they injure him? He is dead?"

"No, no, he is not dead. A suspect shot him. His vest saved him. He will be out of the hospital in three days. He would have called you, but it's hard for him to speak right now."

Marula paused for a moment. Bernadette could feel she was building momentum. That was never a good sign.

"You are always a danger to him. Why he is still with you?"

Bernadette put her hand to her forehead. "Because we love each other, and we are getting married in May. May tenth, to be exact. I just got confirmation of our wedding dates."

"You are not Greek."

"Well, from what Chris told me, neither are you," Bernadette said. The moment the words came out of her mouth, she regretted them. "Look, I'm sorry, I shouldn't have said that…"

"… Christos told you?"

"Yes, he did. He said he's been talking to some cousins of his back in Greece who are Jewish."

"I… my father and even his father. We tried to protect the family. The Nazi's were killing us. You do not understand how bad…"

"I can understand," Bernadette said. The white settlers decimated her own people, the Cree Nation, but she didn't want to make a comparison.

"No, you do not understand. They hunted the Greek Jews like animals. My father swore it would never happen again. He saw his neighbors shot in front of him."

"Mrs. Christakos, I'm so sorry all that happened, but it's in the past. You live in Canada now," Bernadette said.

"Three days ago, boys put bad words on a Jewish cemetery here in Toronto. Is better we stay quiet, stay Greek."

"I cannot judge you or speak for you, but I do know that Chris will stand up for what he believes is his heritage. I don't think you can deny him that." She couldn't believe she was getting into this conversation. She should have hung up.

"No, you cannot judge, you do not know. I know. And I know you are no good for my son. He is my boy, he is Greek. I tell him he should not marry you. He should marry Greek girl, stay Greek, and keep away from people who hate Jews."

The phone call ended with a slam of the receiver on Marula's end. It made Bernadette jump. Sprocket woke up and looked at her with concern.

"That went well, don't you think, Sprocket?" Bernadette asked her dog.

She finished the dregs of her wine, washed her glass and got ready to go to the bedroom.

Sprocket wagged his tail and perked up his ears. He knew with Chris out of the house he might be able to jump on the bed with her.

Bernadette looked at Sprocket. "Okay, you can jump on the bed, but try not to shed too much so Chris doesn't find out. And don't snore."

The dog got it. In a flash, he shot into the bedroom and bounced onto the bed. He laid his big body down on Chris' side and looked up at her.

By the time Bernadette had come out of the bathroom, the dog was fast asleep snoring peacefully.

Bernadette climbed under the covers and turned off the lights. She nudged the dog once to see if he'd stop his snoring, but it didn't work.

She fell into a fitful sleep of Greek mother-in-laws and Irish assassins.

29

Bernadette woke up at 6 a.m. to see Sprocket had already vacated the bed. She would do a complete vacuum of the bed to hide any evidence of him. Although Chris always found stray dog hairs when he came home.

Only once did Bernadette say, "At least she wasn't hiding sleeping with a man." It had sounded lame. She'd just vacuumed and looked at his eye roll of disapproval when he checked the bed.

She made coffee, checked her phone and scrolled through messages. The one that made her stop was from Detective Patrick Sullivan in Dublin. He'd seen the international search for Cahal. He said he might have something.

She called his office; his line went to voice mail. There wasn't much she could do but leave a message. She informed him of the deaths of Emily Murray and Dylan Quinn, in case he hadn't read the report online.

Then she took Sprocket for a slow walk. He looked okay, but the drug GHB could act differently on a dog. Sprocket's gait was okay, and he kept looking back at Bernadette, hoping she'd break into a run.

"Sorry, fella, the vet said no running for you for a day or two. Just chill and we'll be running again soon."

His ears perked up, and at the sound of 'running,' he gave her a resounding 'woof,' and they finished their walk.

As she got in the door, her cell phone rang. It was an overseas number.

"Detective Callahan."

"Ah, I'm glad I caught you," Sullivan said. "I see from the reports you've had a bit of action down your way."

"I guess you could say that. The key thing is the bad guys died."

"Oh, and Father Dominic, he's still among the living?"

Bernadette felt a moment of panic. Should she confide in this detective or tell him the same lie they were telling everyone else?

"That's a bit of classified information at the moment," Bernadette said.

"Your secret is safe with me, Detective. I understand if you wanted to flush out your uncle. Seems he's done a runner, as we say here."

"Yes, into the wind, as we say here. He had about a four-hour head start and could be anywhere on any airplane or airport."

"We've had a stroke of luck. Once we had the actual passport photo of him you sent us, we ran all of his features through our facial recognition software here in the EU. We found a match."

"Where did it show up?"

"In Amsterdam's Schiphol Airport early this morning. He must have taken a red eye from somewhere in North America. We've checked the video feeds of all the connecting flights to the UK and Ireland, but we've come up empty on that."

"Would he head back to Ireland?" Bernadette asked.

"Hard to say, but we found both your suspects, Murray and Quinn, belonged to a strange organization of ancient believers. Cahal, it seems, was one of them."

"What beliefs?"

"That they were the direct descendants of the ancient kings and queens. Seemed they had some ritualistic mumbo jumbo they got into. Sorry, there's little more to go on," he said.

"Anything to shed light on the case would be welcome. We're still in the dark as to the motive. We'll get a warrant for Cahal's arrest on charges of aiding and abetting an attempted murder in the morning. There's a charge of giving someone GHB, but we're waiting for the victim to give a full statement."

"Once we possess your international warrant, we'll arrest him if we find him," Sullivan said. "But he's a slippery sort."

"Wait, I thought you didn't know about him when I first mentioned his name to you."

"Ah, sorry about that. We've known of him for years. He's always been in shadows, never one to show his face. He never allowed his picture to be taken or got a driver's license. There were rumors he was involved in the IRA, but no one knew what he looked like, until now."

Bernadette shook her head. "I guess if he is in fact my uncle, I'm related to one that's become somewhat of a legend. Not sure that's a comfort."

"No, I imagine it's not. But tell your force we'll be on the lookout for him," Sullivan said.

"Thanks, I'll inform my chief of detectives."

"Always happy to help our fellow officers," Sullivan said as he rang off.

Bernadette texted the message to Dawson, changed her clothes, and headed for the hospital.

She wanted to see Chris and needed to speak with Father Dominic, if he was in any way lucid. The information she'd just received on Cahal didn't surprise her. Nothing seemed to anymore. This was like having her entire ancestry run over her.

DETECTIVE SULLIVAN MET with Bishop at the long bar in the pub. He was nursing his usual pint of Kilkenny Cream Ale that Sullivan found particularly appalling. To Sullivan, only a Guinness was a proper pint. All others paled by comparison.

"What's new?" Bishop asked as he regarded his pint with great anticipation.

"I was just sharing a bit of information with that Detective Callahan in Canada. Seems the RCMP killed both Quinn and Murray. I'm not sure if you saw the bulletin on Cahal Callahan, but he's a suspect. He did a runner. I was looking at the sheets the morning, he turned up on visual ID in Amsterdam."

"My, you've been busy. Any news on that crazy ass cult of Callahan's?" Bishop asked.

"We're uncertain if he's directly involved, we only suspect he is. And we're not certain if he's a leader or a follower," Sullivan said, taking a sip of the fresh pint in front of him.

"Look, we've been chasing Cahal for years. Never had a bloody thing on him. He's been a crafty bastard, and now for him to get mixed up in this shite... what's the name of the organization?" Bishop asked.

"It's called Tuatha De' Danann, that's proper Gaelic for People of the Goddess. The man at the head of it is called Dagda or the Master. You're right to call it shite. There's about three to four hundred of them in all of Ireland and you can be sure their up to no good," Sullivan said.

"I've heard some ugly rumors. Some people got involved on the fringe of the thing, attended a few meetings and said they're scared to go back."

"Why? What scared them?"

"Some guy in a golden mask was asking them to renounce their free will," Sullivan said.

"That's scary. Sounds like some of my marriages," Bishop said, draining the last of his pint. He pushed it forward to order another.

"That aside, it seems a bit off in these times. Don't you think?" Sullivan asked.

"There's not much we can charge them with. If they're just being all crazy like and running around like daft idjits, that's their business. As long as they're not doing harm to anyone..."

"Yes, but if it involves Cahal Callahan, they must be up to something."

Bishop nodded as his fresh pint appeared. "Aye, you've got a point. What do we do, watch the streets?"

"I'd watch the morgue," Sullivan said as he took hold of his new pint. "Cheers, here's to the business of murder and mayhem as we call it in Ireland."

* * *

The Master looked out over the long table. Twenty men and women were seated in front of him, dressed in brown robes with hoods. They cast their eyes downwards at the flickering light before them and listened as their master spoke.

"We have destroyed the one link to our order. No one will learn our origin, our nature. Our secret is safe. Now, I want all of you to go out and do the duties I have given you. Do you hear me?"

"We hear you, master," they replied in unison.

"What is my name?"

"You are Dagda, you are the master."

"And who are you?"

"We are Tuatha De' Danann. We are the people of the goddess. We are the ancient ones. Our ancestor's blood flows through us."

"Excellent. Now go." Dagda commanded.

They rose as one, walking out of the room. They stripped off their robes to reveal their street clothes. Each of them had a Celtic Cross tattooed on their necks and wore an amulet of fine gold.

A young ginger-haired man threw off his robes, readjusted a Smith and Wesson gun in his belt, and looked around with a smile." Right then, let's go out and cause some right shite."

30

BERNADETTE ARRIVED at the hospital at 8 a.m.; the hallways were bustling with the large food trolleys. Plastic trays with the plastic wrapped food offerings and cups covered in paper were being delivered to individual rooms.

She walked into Chris' room. A bowl of tepid oatmeal with skim milk and juice sat on a tray in front of him.

He looked up at her in anguish.

"Are you still in pain?" she asked.

"I am at the sight of this food. How soon can I get out of here?"

"I saw Dr. Patel down the hall. He said tomorrow, if you're good."

"I'll be a freaking angel if that gets me away from this food. Who eats this crap?"

Bernadette came to his tray, uncovered the oatmeal, sprinkled some brown sugar on it and mixed in some milk. She took the spoon off the tray and shoved a big spoon full into his mouth.

"There you go. Now chew, big guy. I'll come by later to try to break you out of here. Now, eat your healthy breakfast.

I'm going to check on Harvey and then find out the status of Father Dominic."

"Sounds like you've become Florence Nightingale on your rounds," Chris said.

"Just doing my rounds and extending my mercy like the Saint Bernadette I'm named after," she said, walking out of the room.

Father Dominic was two floors up. They'd put him in a private room. Bernadette had asked for a further ban on his true status. Something just didn't feel right letting the world find out he was alive when so many wanted to kill him.

A security guard stood outside his room. She showed her badge and entered. Father Jo sat beside the sleeping Father Dominic.

"How is he?" Bernadette asked.

"He's sedated and sleeping. The bullet only grazed him, again. There was some bleeding and some mild brain trauma. But he'll be okay. The saints are with him and blessed him to fulfill his mission," Father Joe said.

"And what exactly is his mission?"

"Ah... you mean his sacred mission on earth. It's the same for us all—to serve our Lord," Father Joe said. He took his glasses off and finding a spot on a lens, he cleaned furiously.

Bernadette regarded Father Joe for the first time. He took great pains to hide his height by hunching his shoulders. His knuckles had calluses from physical activity. But there was no wood shop at the seminary. There was a gym. Those kinds of calluses could come from Karate training. Students who pounded on a Makiwara Board displayed similar hands.

Bernadette still had one at home. It toughened the elbows, feet, knuckles or any area of the body you used to strike with in Karate. The board was a heavy duck canvas fabric that would harden your skin as you whacked it over and over.

"What form of martial arts do you practice?" Bernadette asked.

"Martial arts? I don't understand what you mean," Father Joe said. His eyes darted from Bernadette to the floor, back to an unseen object of interest behind her.

Bernadette took one of Father Joe's hands and looked at the calluses. "You get these from what? Crawling on your knuckles to prostrate before the altar every morning? And remember, it is a sin in the Catholic Church to lie."

Father Joe stood upright; he looked different. "You're so correct. In the words of St. Augustine, *a lie consists in speaking a falsehood with intention of deceiving.*"

"Who were you intending to deceive?" Bernadette asked.

"The church asked me to look after Father Dominic and Father Frederick. It looks like I failed miserably with the latter. I'd no idea the killers were hiding in the seminary. Had I known..."

"—You would've dealt with them. What's your training background?"

Father Joe stood erect and saluted. "U.S. Marines, Special Forces."

"You're an American?"

"Dual citizenship. I was born in Canada with an American father. We moved back to Duncan, Oklahoma, where my dad worked for an oil service company. I got the military bug and joined the US Marine Corps."

"Then you just got the urge and joined the Monk Corps?"

Father Joe smiled. "Yeah, it was an atonement for all the people I sent to their heavenly rest in my first career. But I sensed there was more to life than marching in line and releasing a pile of hurt onto some foreign country that my government found was out of favor. No judgments on that, however..."

"But it seems the Church has used your previous talents."

"When the Church found out about my previous career, they asked me if I would join the Guardians."

"And they are?"

"We are an organization in the Church that protects members from attacks. Here, the killers were after the Father's Dominic and Frederick."

"You knew what they were writing in their memoirs, didn't you?"

"Yes, and no. I understood they were compiling a list of names of people involved in a secret society in Ireland. They came from an offshoot of Tara in County Meath, the seat of the ancient high king of Ireland. There was a man named William McGrath who was convinced the ancient high kings were descendants of Israel."

"Interesting stretch on history," Bernadette said.

"It got worse. Someone came along with a lot of cash and investigated all the DNA of the Irish and decided they were gifted and ancient. They were the people of the goddess, and Dagda was there divine god," Father Joe said.

"Okay, getting weird. But then I've seen some Netflix documentaries that are stranger sounding. So, how did our Fathers Dominic and Frederick figure in this?"

"They were both in the IRA back at the beginning. They were in some early battalions and met all the founders. We assume they met McGrath and found the identity of the new head of the society."

"And that someone, the new head, wants them killed?"

Father Joe nodded; he walked over to Father Dominic, looked at him and adjusted his covers.

"You want to tell me what happened the night of the attack on Father Dominic?" Bernadette asked.

"Did you read the report?"

"No, I want to hear what really happened. You didn't mention yourself being able to fend off the attackers."

"How do you know that?"

"Because Father Dominic is still alive. If the killer was in the chapel alone with him, Father Dominic would be dead. What happened?"

Father Joe looked up at Bernadette and held her gaze. "I was following Father Dominic that night, like always. I'd taken a seat in the back pew and watched as he made his way to the altar. I heard a gun being chambered. All I could see was a hand sticking out from behind a door. I grabbed a hymn book and threw it. It hit the assassin's hand, made the shot miss."

"Did you see the attacker?"

"No, I ran for the door, but someone slammed it shut and had thrown a long brass candlestick in the handle. I ran around to another door. By the time I got there, he was being driven away in a car."

"Did you get a plate number?"

"No, I didn't."

"Did you notice anyone else around? Like Cahal, perhaps?"

"No. There was another set of footprints leading from the chapel. He could've been a lookout for the shooter. When I chased after the shooter, Cahal got separated from them. The car took off. He had to make a run for it."

"That explains a lot. Why didn't you give that statement

to us? We could've taken Cahal into custody and charged him as an accessory," Bernadette said.

"You'd only have circumstantial evidence. We needed to find not just the shooters but who sent them. We've been searching for them back in Ireland, but so far nothing."

Bernadette stood beside Father Dominic. "So all of this is from what's inside this poor old man's memory. Did you find any copies of what he wrote?"

"Sure, he left it on the seminary computer in a file encrypted in the wonderful Cloud. No one can get to it without the password."

"Did Frederick have the password?"

"I doubt it. The assassins probably gave him the drug to dig it out of him. If they'd gotten it, they would've destroyed the file on the computer. It's still there."

"What's the file called?"

"Redemption song."

"Isn't that a song by…?"

"Bob Marley and the Wailers," Father Joe replied. "I got seriously stoned to that before I joined the Marines."

"And there's no way you can get that file open?"

"No, I was in the library trying to hack the code the night the killers attacked Father Fredericks. If I'd stayed more vigilant, he'd still be alive. But I had it in my grasp… then I lost it. The file has a failsafe on it, too many attempts at the password, and it will self-destruct. I had to stop."

Bernadette stood back, looking at Father Joe. "How do you intend to keep Father Dominic safe until he recovers and gives you the password?"

"We're hoping you'll keep him dead, at least for a time until he recovers and can give me the access to the files."

"That could be a tall order," Bernadette said, looking down at Father Dominic. He looked so peaceful lying there.

The oxygen mask was giving off a faint mist around him and the heart rate monitor was producing a gentle beeping sound.

"Any days you can give us will be of great help. I've tried to reach out to my fellow Guardians for extra help, but they're maxed out. They told me to do what I can."

Bernadette put her hand on Father Joe's arm. "I'll do what I can. I'll speak to my chief of detectives."

"Can you not tell him about my organization?" Father Joe asked. "The fewer people that know, the better."

"Sure, I love keeping secrets," Bernadette said with the arch of her brow.

"Thanks," Father Joe said.

Bernadette walked out of the room and headed back down to Chris' room. She'd need to talk to Durham, have a conference with the head of the hospital, and somehow convince everyone that they needed to keep someone dead. Not the conversations you have every day.

She went to Harvey's room but could hardly get in. His room was mobbed with elderly ladies who had brought him baskets of muffins and jars of preserves. They chattered endlessly as they fussed over him.

"I hope you don't mind, but I have to interview Mr. Mawer as a matter of police business," Bernadette said.

They looked up at her with scowls and then softened. Most of them knew Bernadette as Harvey's neighbor. They lined up to give him kisses on his cheek then marshaled themselves out the door.

"Thank goodness you arrived, Bernadette," Harvey said. "I don't think I could take another minute of that gang of ladies."

"I thought you loved female attention."

"Absolutely, but not in a group like that. I'm worried that

some of them might compare the stories I've told them. It could take me months to repair the damage," Harvey said with a wink.

"Oh, Harvey, you're quite the ladies' man," Bernadette said, resting her hand on his shoulder as she sat in a chair beside him. "But you're doing okay now?"

"I'm doing fine. That darn drug is almost out of my system. How is my boy Sprocket doing?"

"He's fine. I brought him home last night. He'll be happy to see you when you get out of here, which I'm sure is soon," Bernadette said.

"Great. And how about that guy... I think his name was Jacob Burk... something or the other?"

"You mean Jacob Burkov, the blog reporter? What about him?" Bernadette asked.

"Well, he was there. He knocked on the door as Cahal was making tea. He wanted to interview Cahal and he let him into the house. I was against it, mind you. But Cahal wanted to be interviewed. He said he had nothing to hide."

"Did he leave?"

"Not that I know of. I remember feeling all groggy like and that Jacob guy was in the chair across from me. I saw him pass out just before I did."

"Harvey, I got to go. Cahal must have taken his car and him hostage. That's how he got to the airport so fast," Bernadette said. She kissed him on the cheek. "I'll check in on you later."

Bernadette left the room while dialing her phone. "Evans, you still got the plate number of the red Honda that Jacob Burkov was driving?"

"Yeah, why? Is being a nuisance again? You want to pick him up?"

"No, Harvey Mawer just ID'd him as a victim of the

drugging at my place by Cahal. He must have taken his car and him."

"I'll contact the rental agency. They have GPS locaters on their vehicles. I'll tell them to do a locater on it. You think Burkov is still alive?"

"No idea. It's been almost forty-eight hours. We'll put out a BOLO once we have the vehicle's plates and hopefully the rental company can track the car."

31

CAHAL CALLAHAN TRAVELED AS FAST as possible. He'd arrived in Amsterdam at eight in the morning. His passport claimed him as a Canadian named Charles Manly. He listed his profession as an information technology consultant, as vague as you can get for these times. His hair dyed dark brown, his eye color changed with contacts, and he wore a hat everywhere he went. He ensured he looked down to avoid cameras as he walked.

From Amsterdam, he took the Euro Rail to Paris. He booked a first-class seat on British Rail to London through the Chunnel. Customs in Paris du Nord train station glanced at his Canadian passport, stamped it and pushed it back at him. He dined on small sandwiches and a glass of Sauvignon Blanc as the train entered the tunnel and did its fast descent under the English Channel and shot out the other side in twenty-two minutes. He timed the journey on his watch and smiled.

He got to London, checked into a hotel walking distance from where the train arrived at Saint Pancras Station. The St. Pancras Renaissance Hotel had one deluxe room left in the Barlow wing. At only $322 USD a night, he thought it a bargain.

The next morning, he rose early. He took the train from London to Holyhead, a mere three hours and forty minutes with time for a quick pint in the Irish Ferry Terminal, and he boarded the ferry and sailed the Irish Sea. The air felt crisp, the sea spray cool. But he couldn't be happier. He watched the shoreline and then Dublin came in sight after a sail of just over three hours.

He congratulated himself on his journey. He'd evaded the airport customs checks that were more thorough, he'd slipped through all of their nets and now, he'd get off this ferry and take a brief ride into Dublin town. He could taste his first Guinness. He knew the exact pub and the best barman to pour it for him.

The announcement came over the loudspeaker for foot passengers to disembark. His feet felt light as he almost bounced down the gangway with the terminal in sight.

A row of taxis lined the curb. He had his hand in the air to motion to one when a figure appeared at his side.

"Welcome back, Cahal," a Garda Policeman named O'Connell said.

Cahal started, he looked at the policeman and smiled. "I think you have me confused with someone else. I'm a Canadian citizen. I will show you my passport if you like."

"I'm sure it's a fine forgery, Cahal. And we'll add a charge of entering the country on a false document. But you're being detained on an international arrest warrant of aiding and abetting attempted murder in Canada. The Canadians have asked us to detain you." O'Connell gripped Cahal's arm. The grip was like a vice.

"How on earth did you find me?" Cahal asked.

"You triggered the facial recognition in Amsterdam,"

O'Connell said. "We lost you for a time, but then found you again at the Paris station on British Rail. A Scotland Yard detective followed you from your hotel this morning. He sat behind you on the train. He called us when you boarded the ferry."

"I must have a lawyer," Cahal said.

"I'm sure you will. Now, let's have no trouble. Come along then."

Cahal's shoulders slumped as he walked to the waiting police car. A policeman opened the back door; he had a broad face and cheery smile. The name on his badge was Flaherty.

"There you go Mr. Callahan, we saved you cab fare into town," Flaherty said as he closed the back door.

Cahal Callahan sat in the back of the police car wondering if he'd heard the policeman say attempted murder or murder. He was afraid to ask the question.

32

"They found Burkov; he's alive," Evanston said as she pushed herself away from her desk.

"Where?" Bernadette asked. She put down her fourth cup of coffee and looked over her laptop at Evanston.

"Cahal left the rental at the Calgary Airport in the main parking garage. Looks like he wanted to get to his plane quickly. That's lucky for Burkov, much warmer in there. He didn't freeze to death. He was dehydrated and cold, but he'll be fine after a brief stay in hospital," Evanston said.

"I'm sure he'll be back to his nasty blogging soon," Bernadette said.

"I saw his latest blog. Apparently, he's changed his attitude about you. The Calgary Airport Police informed him it was your quick thinking got him found so quickly."

"Really? I'm so glad. But I hope he doesn't lose his lucrative cat food sponsors by going soft on people," Bernadette said.

"The good thing is, we can add this to the list of charges against Cahal. The prosecutor is drafting it up and sending it off to Ireland today."

"That's great. Maybe that will help us spring him from Ireland and get him back to Canada. Now, I've got to go see about getting Chris sprung from hospital. That guy feels so hemmed in there, you'd think he was doing time in prison."

BERNADETTE WASN'T able to get Chris released from the hospital until late afternoon. The doctors wanted him to see the people in physiotherapy and do some exercises. They felt he'd improved enough to be discharged.

An orderly wheeled Chris downstairs to the lobby and into her Jeep. Sprocket woofed and whined in the back of the Jeep to welcome Chris back.

"I'm so glad you're okay, sweetie," Bernadette said.

"You'd think with all the cries of bed shortages in Canadian hospitals, they would have let me out sooner," Chris said.

Bernadette put her hand on his arm. "They wanted to make sure you're okay. I do too. So, now we're heading home and you can get some rest."

"Rest. If I were more rested, I'd be a slug. I've been lying in a bed for three days. I'd like to get moving. Maybe get into the kitchen and make some food. I'm sure you've been living on takeout."

Bernadette glanced at him as she drove the vehicle out of the parking lot. "Normally that would be the case. But Harvey got home Sunday and every little lady that he's ever dated or talked to has brought over casseroles and enough cinnamon buns that I've had to freeze some of it. Poor Harvey was beside himself. The food just kept coming, and so did they. He had to make room for it so we have a fully stocked fridge."

Chris chuckled. "Great, from hospital food to tuna casserole supreme. I can't wait."

They drove in silence for a while. Chris looked at the blue skies and the snow. He imagined they would cover the Rockies in snow and look amazing. To Chris they were the most beautiful things in the world, tall, majestic peaks that seemed to hold the white clouds in their grasp. He wondered how soon it would be until he could walk amongst them.

"I got a text from Emerald Lake Lodge this morning. It's decision time. We either take it or we don't," Bernadette said.

Chris turned to her. "Let's take it. Being shot gave me a fresh look on things."

"Like what things?"

"Well, I'm leaving the police force for good. I won't be doing any short time shifts and never going to consider it."

"Ah, you're thinking of being a chef?"

"I thought about that, but that means I'd have to organize people all day. As we know, people can be difficult."

"Totally, so what's on your mind?"

"I'm thinking of becoming a wildlife officer. I checked the prerequisites and one of them was a degree in criminology and law enforcement. I have that."

"Really, that's great," Bernadette said. "I think one of us ducking bullets and bringing down crooks is enough in the family."

They pulled into their driveway. Harvey's driveway was filled with Toyota Camrys and Buicks. The little blue hair army was back to take care of him. Bernadette got Chris to sit in the big easy chair in the living room. She turned the television to a nature channel he liked and left him to rest.

She picked up her cell phone, texted to the Emerald Lake Lodge that they accepted, and hit send. Only a slight feeling of panic went through her as she realized they'd set an actual date that was three months away and there was this thing called wedding planning to do.

She put her phone down. *"Come on girl, planning a wedding can't be as hard as chasing criminals,"* she muttered to herself.

Her phone pinged with a text. The message was from Sullivan in Dublin. *It read that they'd arrested Cahal on the charges of aiding an attempted murder. He was now in the Dublin jail.*

Bernadette called Durham. "Chief. They have arrested Cahal Callahan, on attempted murder in Ireland. What happened? Why couldn't they make it a charge of first degree murder?"

"The Crown couldn't link Cahal in the texts to the murder of Fredericks, only to the attempted murder of Dominic. We can't keep it a secret that Dominic is alive. The world of legality has few gray areas in dead or alive with warrants for arrest," Durham said.

"Okay, thanks, Chief, I'll call Father Joe and let him know." Bernadette put her phone away and let the whole situation sink in.

Father Dominic was once again a target. How could they protect him? Cahal was in prison. How long would it take to get him extradited? And there was one other minor problem niggling at her brain. She'd put a bond up for Cahal. His trial was in four weeks. If he didn't appear, they could get a continuance, but for how long? Ten thousand dollars was the same amount she'd budgeted for her wedding.

She went back to the living room to see how Chris was

doing. He was fast asleep; she'd work from home today and watch him. Sprocket did the same. The big dog lay to one side of Chris and lifted his head from time to time to check on him.

33

DUBLIN, MOUNTJOY PRISON

CAHAL CALLAHAN SAT across the table from his lawyer in Mountjoy Prison in the center of Dublin. They nicknamed the prison the Joy by those who'd served time and left.

Cahal's lawyer was a large man named Bryan Badderby. He wore an expensive suit with highly polished shoes. He tapped a gold pen on a sheet of paper with his manicured hands. A drop of sweat beaded on his brow. Cahal's case was not going well.

He'd been before the judge already. He'd seen the charges and the extradition request made known by the prosecutor acting on behalf of the Canadian Embassy. Cahal thought he'd either be free in no time or his council would drag the case on for years and tie them up with countless appeals.

"I'm afraid you're done for, my man." Badderby said after shuffling the papers a few more times.

"What do you mean, done? You saw what they've got against me in Canada. This would barely hold up in court here in Dublin, you know that. What the hell kind of lawyer are you?"

"The one that sees the forces greater than the ones in this room, Dublin or the entire republic of our fair isle. I see the hand of the Vatican here. You were, as the charge read, involved with the murder of an Irish priest and the attempted murder of a second. Actually, the second is a bit obtuse, there's a note here that claims this priest is dead, and I received a message he's alive. But that's aggravated assault."

"Father Dominic is still alive?" Cahal asked.

"I have the reports, yes," Badderby said.

"I need to get a note to someone."

"You know I can't do that."

"How much is he paying you?"

Badderby closed his eyes, then opened them and looked down at his papers. "Pass it to me before I leave."

"Okay, then why is my case hopeless?" Cahal asked. He placed his hands on the table and hunched over. He wrote a note on a small piece of paper with his back turned to the guards.

"Your case was fast tracked to the Minister of Justice. There's a rumor the church got involved in this. They have a problem with old priests being targets. He's allowed your extradition. Wants you kicked back to the Canadians immediately."

"What about appeals?"

"I met with my inside man in the Minister's office. He said not to waste my time. They will fast track every appeal and shoot them down. You'll be able to delay a month, two tops. But you'll be off to Canada soon. I hope you kept some woolies for the journey."

"Thanks for the travel advice, counselor, just see that note gets to my friends," Cahal said.

Badderby hoisted himself up from the table, nodded for

the guard to open the door, and left the room. He made his way to his Jaguar SUV, driving at an easy pace to a pub on the outskirt of town.

He walked into the pub, ordered a pint of cider, and passed the note with his money to the barman. He'd done his job. He hated the people who sent him to represent Cahal Callahan, but their money was good. It was almost too good.

RONAN BRONAUGH MET with John Dunne later that evening. Dunne had left a message with his receptionist that there was a vintage port in at his local wine shop. Bronaugh hated port, but it was a call sign to tell him where to meet Dunne.

They met in the back of the wine shop in a room for the very best customers to sample wines. Bronaugh sipped a twenty-year-old Burgundy by swishing it around his mouth and judging it to have gone past its peak. He poured it out and looked at Dunne.

Dunne sat there with no wine and only a piece of paper. "Cahal sent a note that Dominic is still alive."

"Is it rumor or fact?"

"Doesn't matter. If it's a rumor, we've no problem. If it's a fact, I'll have it dealt with," Dunne said.

"And what of Cahal. What do we do with him?"

"We need to get him out of prison. There is no way they can send him to Canada. They might turn him. He's still useful to us," Dunne said.

"How soon can you make it happen?" Ronan asked.

"Soon."

They got up and left the room. Rain was falling in a torrent on the street. Ronan's chauffeur stood outside the wine shop with an umbrella, escorting him to his car.

Dunne walked out of the shop afterwards, pulled up his collar, and marched down the street like he was going off to battle. In his mind, he was.

CAHAL CALLAHAN HATED everything about prison. He'd never been in one, nor visited someone in one. From the small beds to the polished cement floors, the neon lights and the smell, especially the smell, he hated every moment.

The smell was of men, sweat, and body odor; it floated in the air like a mist and mingled with the harsh woolen blankets and the acrid paint on the walls. From the moment he woke up in the morning to the time he went to bed, he tried to get the smell out of his nostrils, but he couldn't.

He lined up for breakfast amongst the other inmates that morning. He kept to himself. The best thing about him was his age. Old men in prison were no threat to the young ones. He kept his distance, and they didn't bother him.

Three days had passed, and he hadn't heard a word from anyone. How much longer would he have to wait? A large man with a shaved head and tattoos butted into the line ahead of Cahal. He merely backed off and let him in.

He would be docile here. Let them move him from one cell to another. Never make a fuss, stay in the background and bide your time—that was always his method. Things would work themselves out.

The big man in front took a step back. He passed Cahal a small packet. Cahal didn't know what it was. He wanted no trouble. He put the packet onto his tray and hid it under his plate.

He received his breakfast and sat at a table away from

everyone else. The big bald man came to his table and sat across from him.

"I don't want trouble," Cahal said. "I don't do drugs. Sorry lad, if you're selling, I'm not a customer."

The big man leaned forward. He had tattoos on his face, with two front teeth filed to look like fangs. "Listen, these aren't drugs. I got a message from outside. You're to take the packet with water and go back to your cell."

A feeling of dread came over Cahal. If he didn't take the packet, the big man would know, and he'd probably kill him. What was it? Had they decided to kill him in prison to silence him, or was it a way to get him out?

"What is it?" Cahal asked.

The big man smiled. "It's a lovely mix of an antidepressant to make your body sweat, some Viagra to make your face flush, and Digitalis to make your heart beat irregularly. Enjoy!"

Cahal's hand shook as he took the packet from under his plate. His plastic water glass was full. There was no way he could refill his glass and dump the packet.

He emptied the contents of the packet into his glass and stirred it with the teaspoon. He lifted it to his lips and hesitated.

"Be a nice boy and drink it all down now. You don't want me to send you to the infirmary the hard way," the big man said, flexing his fists. His large biceps contracted in anticipation of the work they'd get on the old man if he didn't comply.

Cahal drank the entire glass and sat it down on his tray. He got to his feet, nodded slightly to the man, and headed back to his room. He lay there wondering, trying to feel every part of his body to see what the drug would do.

Suddenly his heart raced. He broke into a sweat. A pain shot down his arm.

"Help, guard, I'm having a heart attack," Cahal yelled out. He hoped someone heard him. His chest was exploding in pain. His last thought before he passed out was, *so this is how they kill me.*

Three guards entered the room, one called the medical staff. A male nurse arrived, took Cahal's pulse, and announced a cardiac arrest. He started chest compressions and gave him a shot of adrenalin.

An outside ambulance team arrived. They were there sooner than expected.

"Lucky for this man we were in the area," the emergency medical person said.

They hauled Cahal out of the prison on the stretcher; two of the guards went with them. The guards jumped in the back of the ambulance. Neither of them noticed the extra medical staff inside.

Guns appeared at their heads, syringes plunged into their necks. They struggled for only a few seconds before their bodies went limp. The police found the ambulance on a side street ten blocks away. The guards were okay, but dazed. Cahal had vanished.

34

BERNADETTE WAS FEELING GOOD. The past three days had gone well. Chris had recovered from his collapsed lung. There was still some bruising on his ribs she had to be careful with. But other than that, things were getting back to normal. Sprocket returned to his former self and now ran beside her, his tongue hanging out, his breath rising into the cold air.

She was back in the office, finishing the reports from the incident with Cahal and the drugging of Mawer and Burkov. The completed reports would become warrants and sent off to Ireland to make their case of Cahal Callahan's extradition.

"Are you writing a novel there or a report?" Evanston asked as she walked by on her way to the coffee machine.

"Smart ass," Bernadette replied. "I'm just putting in all the details of the deeds of Cahal Callahan."

"Ah, yes, your nefarious uncle. Who knew you had such a black sheep in your family? Maybe you joined the police to make up for his bad karma."

Bernadette winced at the name uncle. "I still wish you wouldn't call him that. And you can stop the karma crap."

"Why not? How will you know unless you take a DNA test? Chris told me you were going to do one. Did you?"

Bernadette rolled her eyes. "Yes, I finally did it. I can't believe how much spit you have to put in that tube. We can do DNA tests with our lab with a simple mouth swab."

"And did you send it in?"

Bernadette nodded. "I sure did. It went two days ago." She looked up as Chief Durham walked in the room. He looked very unhappy. "What's up, Chief? Looks like you got some terrible news or your hockey team didn't make the playoffs."

"You'd both better come into my office," Durham said.

They both came in and sat down. Bernadette couldn't contain herself. "What is it?"

Durham looked at them. "Cahal Callahan escaped from prison yesterday. Sorry, I just got this email this morning. It came from the Canadian Embassy in Dublin."

"Holy shit—" Bernadette began and stopped herself. "Did the report say how it happened?"

"He suffered a heart attack. An EMS crew arrived to take him to hospital. The two guards who accompanied him were unconscious and Cahal gone."

"One hell of a slick job," Evanston said.

"Yes, it was. There is something you need to know. With all the turmoil going on in Ireland, the Dublin Garda cannot commit manpower to search for him."

"What I go after him?" Bernadette asked.

"You'd have no powers over there, and I doubt they'd help you much. I cannot think of any reason I'd send you," Durham said.

"I can think of ten thousand reasons," Bernadette said. "I've had Joe Christie push Callahan's appearance to coincide with when he returns for the other charges. He doesn't appear, I'm out ten grand."

Durham shrugged. "Sorry, that's the chance you take when you give a surety. He doesn't return, the court gets the money. Even if you went there, with the additional charges he has for escaping an Irish prison, they'll tie him up in the courts. You'll never get him back here, unless he got on a plane with you to return here."

"That's it," Bernadette said. "I go there and get that piece of crap uncle of mine on a plane back here."

Durham chuckled. "Callahan, you'd have to work a miracle to get something like that. And I can't spend a dime of the detachment's money if you want to go, and you'd have to take a leave of absence. Can I give you any more reasons not to go?"

"Give me four days. I've enough travel miles on my credit card to cover my flights and hotels. If I can't find him, I'll be back and write a check for ten big ones to the clerk of the court," Bernadette said.

Durham dropped his head in his hands. "I can't believe I'm thinking of letting you go, but I want him back to face charges. Okay, if you go, you have no weapon and no badge. You don't have a shred of authority over there. You might as well be a tourist."

"Not a problem, Chief," Bernadette said and left the room.

She pulled up her credit card's website where she had more travel points than money. Finding a flight from Calgary to Toronto to Dublin that was only thirteen plus hours, she booked it. Then she booked a car, a Mini Ford Ka with a manual transmission. She realized she hadn't driven a stick shift for ten years; how hard could it be?

The hotels were a problem; all the ones in her travel

miles program were at the airport or too many points. She settled for a hotel in the brewery and Dublin Castle area. She picked a three-star hotel for sixty-two Canadian dollars a night.

She clicked on the site to book it. *"Think of it like urban camping,"* Bernadette said to herself as she completed the booking. It was late in Dublin, but she texted Detective Sullivan so he'd know she was coming there.

Evanston came into the room and stood by her desk.

Bernadette looked up. "What's up Evans?"

"You don't think this is hasty, rash maybe?"

"I know it is. But ever since Cahal got away, I wanted to be on his trail. Now, that's where I'm going to be," Bernadette said, looking up at Evanston. "If he is a true Callahan like my father, all I need to do is check the pubs in the area he once frequented. My father shined the bar of many a pub with his elbows in his drinking days. I think Cahal will be the same."

"And how do you expect to get him back here?"

"No idea. I'll make it up as I go," Bernadette said as she sent the booking files to her phone and closed her laptop. "It's five o'clock. I got to see my lovely man and tell him what I'm up to."

Evanston rolled her eyes. "Good luck with that."

Bernadette's cell phone rang; it was Sullivan in Dublin, "Hi, Detective Sullivan, I didn't expect you to call me back, I know it's late there—"

"Are you somewhat mad?" Sullivan asked, interrupting her.

"No, I'm not mad, what do you mean?"

"Ah, the word I'm going for is crazy as in mad in the head. How do you expect to find this man, Cahal? I doubt if I can help you when you come here. I've got three bank robberies and a murder to work on. Cahal is an old codger. I doubt if the department will put much more than a BOLO on him."

"That's fine, Detective. I've rented a car and I'll find my way," Bernadette said.

There was a long pause on the phone.

"Where are you staying?"

"A hotel in the brewery district."

"Most of those hotels are shite."

"Thanks for the heads up."

"You're welcome. When do you arrive in Dublin?"

Bernadette looked at her itinerary. "I arrive at just before seven on Friday morning."

Another long pause on the phone, Bernadette waited.

"I'll meet you for breakfast at zero eight hundred. There's a nice little café called Annie's in Blanchardstown. Take a right out of the airport and a right on the Northern Cross Route. Then the exit into the town; it's just past the Connolly Hospital. I'll fill you in with what I can," Sullivan said.

"I appreciate that, Detective. I'll see you in a few days," Bernadette said. She realized a meeting with the detective was more than she'd hoped for. She'd called him, as it was the correct protocol to tell him she'd be looking for Cahal, but at least she might get the lay of the land.

"Are they going to help you out?" Evanston asked.

"I got a breakfast meeting when I arrive. That's it. I doubt if they can do anything for me but give me directions and tell me not to get in their way."

"Better than nothing."

"Okay, I gotta make tracks. My plane is tomorrow, and I have a bunch of things to do," Bernadette said. "I'll see you next week."

"Hey, take care, and I mean it," Evanston said. "I just lost Sawchuck as my partner, now I got you. Don't go doing anything silly over there."

"Like getting killed?"

"No, I meant like a traffic accident. They drive funny over there, don't they?"

"Yeah, it's called the left side of the road."

"And that's driving funny," Evanston replied while crossing her arms.

BERNADETTE LEFT the detachment and drove to the hospital. She wanted to speak with Father Joe before she left. She found him in Father Dominic's room. He'd put a cot in there so he could be with him twenty-four seven. A guard was outside the room, and another at the front elevator.

"Hey, Father Joe," Bernadette said as she entered the room. "How is he doing?"

"Looks like we need to keep him longer. He has a bit of a fever and they don't want to move him until it goes down," Father Joe said. He looked tired and disheveled. He'd gone without a shave for many days and his eyes were bleary.

"I wanted to tell you that Cahal escaped from prison in Dublin, and I'm off to search for him. I'm here to ask if there're any leads you can give me on what Fathers Dominic and Fredericks were looking into in Ireland."

Father Joe ran his hands over his face and sat down in a chair. "Somehow it starts with some ancient stones of Tara. I heard the two of them speaking about it at the computer one night."

"Any idea what the significance is?"

"I don't have the foggiest, sorry. I only know it has something to do with ancient kings of Ireland. At first, I thought they were just writing a book of history. When people came after them, I knew it was something more."

"You knew they were in danger?"

"That's the intel we had. The church sent me here one week before they arrived. This was to be the perfect hiding place for them," Father Joe said as he turned to look at Father Dominic. "Unfortunately, someone found out about it."

"Thanks for that, Father Joe, I'll check it out. Take care of yourself and Father Dominic."

"You too. There's one more thing. When you get there, if you need my help, call me. Do you still have my number?"

"Right here in my phone."

"Great, and I'll send you another number. It's a local number in Ireland. There's a Guardian I know there called Sister Mary-Margaret. She might help you."

"You have nuns in your group? Good to hear," Bernadette said.

"We come in all shapes and sizes. Now travel safe and God Bless you," Father Joe said.

BERNADETTE HEADED OUT THE DOOR. There was one stop she needed to make on her way home. It was a total gamble, but that's what she had now.

She parked herself outside of the Corral Bar, one of the seediest, most disgusting booze joints in town. The place was busy; even with the prices of oil down and jobs scarce, the guys still found money to buy cheap beer.

A Bud Lite sign blinked in the window, and as she opened the door, the sound of the low growl of male voices with the loud shrieks of a few women filled the air.

Happy hour had been on since four. The crowd talked

loudly with cheap beers and highballs. Bernadette saw Cindy at the bar and made a straight line for her.

Cindy was twenty-two, blonde with blue eyes, and covered in tattoos with two studs in her nose and a lip ring. She'd been there for two years. Her story was a simple—bad choice of men. She'd had one child and two men she needed to keep away from.

Bernadette had helped her with one man. He'd been a total loser and drug dealer, she'd been able to focus enough heat on him, so he did some serious time.

Cindy saw Bernadette as she came up to the bar. "Hey, Detective, what can I pour you. It's on the house," she said with a smile.

"Just a Diet Coke, Cindy." It amazed her at how pretty Cindy was, which was her problem. She attracted men in droves, and she had the worst taste in the ones she chose.

"Sure thing, Detective. What brings you in here?" Cindy asked as she put a coke in front of Bernadette.

Bernadette leaned forward on the bar. "You once told me you had a unique way of controlling your rowdy customers. You said they became like putty in your hands. I got a feeling you sprinkle a little something in their drinks. Am I close?"

Cindy looked left and right, watching as her manager walked by and went into the back. "How much trouble am I in?"

"You're not in any trouble, Cindy. I know you've got to control this crowd and I don't see a bouncer at the door. I need some of that sprinkle you use for a trip I'm taking. No questions asked," Bernadette said in a low voice.

Cindy looked behind her. The manager was pulling out a fresh keg of beer and rolling it towards the other side of the bar. She pulled out a packet of green pills and pushed it across the bar.

Bernadette placed her hand over it. "Is it GHB?"

"Sure it is. A guy came in here once and tried to put it in some girl's drink six months ago. I saw him, and the manager threw the guy out, but he dropped it. I kind of figured I could use it to settle down some rowdy's—only the nasty one's mind you," Cindy said.

"You know it's illegal, right?"

"Sure I do, but what are you going to do in here? Those jerks will take the place apart. I sprinkle a little of this in their drink, then we call a cab to take them home."

Bernadette smiled. "Thanks for this. I won't tell a soul."

"Anything for you, Detective, you've really saved my ass a few times."

"I could save it more if you got out of this place."

Cindy gave a sly grin. "Are you kidding? With the tips I make here? All I got to do is show these guys a bit of cleavage and I pay for my daughter's day care every month."

Bernadette shook her head and walked out the door. The smell of the beer and male testosterone lingered in the air until she got into her Jeep. She put the packet into her inside pocket and thought *one down, one to go.* The next adventure was Chris.

35

SHE ARRIVED home to see lights on in the house. She parked and walked in to find Chris back in the kitchen, his second love in life after her. He was such an excellent cook it made her pale by comparison—when the comparison was; she knew how to order food for delivery and microwave something.

Chris smiled as she entered. "How was your day?"

"Good, catching up on paperwork. How was your day?"

"Great," Chris said. "The Rocky Mountain Forestry Management Division wants to interview me in two days. I had a great talk with their human resources department. They've had a bunch of guys retiring this year." He poured her a glass of wine and kissed her on the lips.

"That is great, sweetie," Bernadette said, taking a big sip of her wine.

"Whoa. What's up?"

"What do you mean?"

"You've got that look on your face. It's that look that says you're about to drop something on me. Something that you know I will not be happy with."

Bernadette put her hand to her head. "Am I that easy to read? You think all those years of playing poker—"

"You're not playing poker, you're about to convince me you're going to do something you think is right and I'm going to say is crazy. Why not cut to the chase," Chris said. He pulled off his apron and led her out of the kitchen to the living room, where they sat together with their wine on the sofa.

Bernadette blew out a breath. "Okay, Cahal escaped prison in Ireland. I'm going after him."

"Not authorized by the detachment, I assume?"

"You assume correctly. I used my points on my credit card," Bernadette said, taking Chris' hand. "Look, I've got most of it covered except for some hotels. It's only four days."

"Is it the ten grand you think you'll lose or something more?"

"It's far more than the ten thousand dollars. This man lied to me. He was in our house. I made the worst call of my life in accepting him. He turned out to be a killer."

"Helping a killer and being a killer are different under the law."

"They're the same to me. I want him back to stand trial. I want to know why this man, who says he saved my father from being killed in the Troubles in Ireland, would come here and try to kill two priests."

They both took a moment. The tension in the room was electric. Sprocket looked at them, his eyes searching to see what was going on.

"I can't stop you," Chris said finally. "I can only ask you to be careful."

Bernadette leaned forward, and they collapsed into each other. Bernadette felt some tears falling. "Look, my big man, you know I'll come back. But whether I bring that bad ass uncle of mine back dead or alive is another matter."

They both laughed. Sprocket jumped up putting his paws on the sofa and began licking their faces with the release of tension in the room.

Bernadette stroked Sprocket's head. "Okay, we were getting a little tense, now it's over."

Chris returned to the kitchen to continue making dinner. "When do you leave?"

"My flight's at noon tomorrow to Toronto, then the redeye to Dublin."

"That doesn't leave us too much time," he said with a wink.

"How sore are your ribs?"

"I'm sure my ribs can handle it," he said with a smile.

Bernadette came off the couch and kissed him, "I'll be gentle."

36

CAHAL CALLAHAN WOKE up in a darkened room. A light came on, John Dunne stood over him.

"Ah, you're among the living, I see, Cahal," Dunne said.

"Where am I?"

"Does it matter? You're alive, you're out of prison, and you've a lot to answer for."

"Look, I heard Dominic was dead on the police scanner. They claimed he was a victim of a shooting. How was I to know? I legged it out of there before they discovered me."

Dunne shook his head. "Good answer, but I doubt if the Master will accept it. You know how he gets."

Cahal's face went white. "Does he want to see me?"

"Yes, he does."

"Do I have to go back to Canada to finish the job?"

Dunne put up his hand. "No, we'll send another team in a few days. We have so many other projects, you know, the general mayhem."

"It's starting then, the uprising?"

"We'll make it seem like it has. All of Ireland, England,

and Europe will think the Troubles are back. It'll scare the bejesus out of them."

"Am I to take part? I can, you know. I'm good with a bomb," Cahal said.

Dunne shook his head. "No, you've more important things to do."

"What's that?"

"That detective in Canada, the one you call your niece..."

"Bernadette Callahan. Yes, what of her?"

"We hear she's coming here."

"To Dublin?"

"Don't be daft, man, where else do you think?"

"I don't understand. Why?"

"For you. She wants to bring you back to Canada to stand trial."

"She can't be serious. She's not a lick of authority here," Cahal protested.

"But she can cause right shite now, can she not? Your job is to find her when she arrives and kill her. This time don't muck about. Do it right. If you cock it up, you know the consequences. You won't wake up next time."

"I understand, I'll make sure she's dead," Cahal said.

"Yes, you will. Now, here's a phone. Make whatever calls you need, but make sure it's done."

John Dunne left the room. Cahal sighed and got out of bed. He found a teakettle on the table. He plugged it in, waited until the water boiled, and made a strong cup of tea.

He almost burnt his tongue on the hot tea as he dialed a number.

"Who's this?" a voice asked on the end of the line.

"Cahal here, don't ask questions, we got a job to do."

37

THE NEXT DAY was a blur of activity. Bernadette woke up at five, ran with Sprocket, showered, and packed a bag. Chris took her to the Calgary airport with Sprocket in the back of the Jeep.

They left at eight for the hour and a half drive. The sun rose in the brilliant blue sky. The outside temperature gauge read a frigid minus twenty centigrade. It encased the Rocky Mountains in a blanket of snow as they got closer to Calgary. They looked like sentinels guarding the way to the western ocean.

There was so much Bernadette loved about moments like these—the silence of the morning, the hum of the tires on the road, the feeling of just being with Chris.

There were things tugging at her brain. It was the last phone call with Grandma Moses. She called to tell her she was going to Ireland and Grandma Moses had said, "You remember that dream I told you about? I had it again last night."

Bernadette had to reflect on it for a second, it had been last week. So much had happened since then. It was something about a castle and the ocean. She promised her grandma she would avoid both places, told her she loved her, and got off the phone.

The airport was busy when they arrived; she hugged Chris gently because of his ribs, wrapped her arms around Sprocket, and headed for her plane.

She had only a carry-on bag that contained two pairs of jeans, t-shirts, two sweaters and a rain jacket along with underwear and some makeup.

The flight to Toronto was three hours and forty-five minutes. Businesspeople occupied most seats and those trying to get to Toronto for a long weekend of theater and music.

The two women sitting beside her were doing just that. They talked incessantly about the shows they were going to see and all the shopping they were going to do. Bernadette put in her ear buds and watched reruns of *Cagney and Lacey* on her iPad.

The Toronto airport was busy. She wondered just where the hell everyone was going in February in Canada, but the answer was easy. South. Canadians flocked south to the beaches of the Caribbean, Mexico, and the U.S. that earned them the name snowbirds.

Bernadette found a bookstore, wandered in, and browsed the aisle in history. There was a book on Ireland, called *Voices from the Grave*. She leafed through it and found it to be a biography of two dead men. One had been in the IRA, the other on the Loyalist side in Northern Ireland.

She bought the book and headed into the international boarding area to board the Air Canada Airbus. The plane was half full as this was not tourist season in Ireland.

Most of the passengers looked to Bernadette like business types, some in suits, some in expensive jeans and designer sweatshirts and wearing shoes that had been in the last issue of Vogue magazine. They were some kind of new techie entrepreneur or had figured out a way to run another scam on bitcoin.

She took a window seat in an unoccupied row and opened her book. The plane took off at 8:45 p.m. The flight was six hours and forty-five minutes, and she doubted she would sleep.

The cabin personnel helped in that. They brought by coffee, and then drinks, then food followed by duty-free items for people to make purchases of things they never knew they wanted. By the time they'd finished and shut off the lights so people could sleep, it was well past midnight Toronto time.

Bernadette hit the call button for a coffee and kept reading her book. She got to the part when the Troubles started. They'd decided that marches no longer worked. They, being the IRA, decided violence was the answer.

She sipped her coffee and kept reading. There was a place in Belfast called Shankill Road where some violence started, then it spread throughout the city until people were hiding behind barricades or in their houses from snipers and firebombs.

After several hours of reading, Bernadette got a sense of her ancestry. Ireland, this lovely ancient land of myths and legends, had become a pawn of kings and queens. The planting of English Protestants in the North to act as a buttress against an invasion of England in the sixteenth century had set a smoldering ember of resentment that would erupt in violence on a regular basis.

As the big plane droned its way to the little island, Bernadette hoped that this place would never erupt in violence again. She felt her eyes droop. Putting her book on the seat next to her, she stuffed her jacket against the window and fell asleep.

The lights came on in the cabin, the flight attendants announcing the plane was landing in twenty minutes. Bernadette rubbed her eyes. She'd been asleep for fifteen minutes.

She made her way to the toilets, washed her face, and looked at her herself in the mirror. "Wow, you look awful," she told herself with a laugh. She brushed her hair and put on a bit of makeup, so she didn't resemble a character in the *Day of the Dead*.

The plane landed in Dublin in a rainstorm. As the big plane taxied to the terminal, the rain pounded the runway making it seem like a sea had taken it over.

Bernadette sailed through customs. She claimed on her entry form that she was visiting family. She even put her aunt's name as her contact in Ireland. She planned on meeting her in the next twenty-four hours to hunt for Cahal.

When she found her rental car, she had a realization. This was the smallest car she'd ever seen. She drove a Jeep back home. She'd grown up driving trucks on the reservation in the north; the cars the Canadian police used were big Fords. This was smaller than small.

She opened the back hatch and dumped her bag in. Then she went to get into the driver's door and realized it was the wrong door. *"Okay, Bernadette, wrap your head around it—left. They drive on the left,"* she said aloud with a laugh.

An Irish couple was getting into a car beside her; they looked at her only briefly wondering who the crazy lady was talking to.

She got into the driver's side and the reality sunk in; she'd have to manage a four-speed stick with her left hand.

How weird was that? She'd driven her grandma's old Ford that had a three on the column shift and some water trucks for an oil rig to make money before college, but this would be different.

She put the car in reverse and backed out—the wrong way. Pulling out of the parking garage, she almost ran into a bus as she'd slipped into the right lane on her exit.

The bus sounded a large horn that woke her up. *Left, remember, it's left.*

She used her cell phone GPS map to locate Annie's Place.

"Okay, turn right," Bernadette said as the GPS voice told her to enter the motorway.

Her hand grabbed the gearshift. Her foot hit the clutch, and the gears made a grinding sound.

"Wrong!" She yelled to herself.

Her foot pressed the clutch in again. She looked at the gearshift; she'd gone the wrong way by dropping the gear into second instead of third. This time she went from second, pushed it up to third and let out the clutch while hitting the gas.

The little car lurched forward.

A loud horn sounded behind her. A massive truck was coming behind her fast, hitting its horn and brakes at the same time.

She pushed in the clutch, popped the gear into fourth and hit the gas. The little car's tires squealed as it lurched forward. In seconds, the car put distance between the big truck and impending doom.

"Holy crap, girl. You need to wake up,"

She found the turnoff to Blanchardstown and made the exit by threading the car between two large trucks and not hitting anyone. Moments later, she parked the car in front of Annie's Café and turned off the engine.

The café was full. A sea of fully awake people huddled over piles of toast, eggs, bacon, and beans.

Bernadette was instantly hungry. She'd pecked at the airline food that comprised a sandwich wrap and salad with an unidentifiable dressing.

A man waved at her from a table by the window, and as she approached, he stood up. "Good morning, I'm Detective Patrick Sullivan. I recognized you from your detective photo. I hope you had a pleasant trip over."

Bernadette shook his hand and then sat at the table. "It was fine." She didn't want to give him the long details of lack of sleep and terrible food. That was a given in air travel.

A waitress with purple hair and a tattoo of three roses on her arm dropped menus and water on the table.

"The full breakfast is what you want if you've just had a sleepless night on a plane," Sullivan said.

Bernadette sipped her water. "It's that obvious?"

"The transatlantic crossing can be a bit much with the time change. How much is it for you?"

Bernadette looked at her watch. "It's midnight in Calgary where I left from. So, an eight-hour time difference. I might need the full breakfast."

Sullivan ordered tea and Bernadette coffee with breakfast. There may be something to the Irish breakfast tea, but she was having nothing to do with it.

"I'm sorry we couldn't meet at the station," Sullivan said.

"I totally get it. I'm a Canadian tourist as far as your force is concerned, no badge and no authority."

"Well, yes, and my boss doesn't take well to other detectives dropping in to find an escapee from our jail."

"Ah, a stickler for regulations, is he?"

Sullivan leaned forward. "Well, yes, a bit, but we are under a lot of pressure. Two murders in the past week and several bomb threats with a bank robbery. We're about over our quota for the year."

"Any leads on the murders? Sorry to ask, but it's my detective on vacation speaking. I hope you don't mind," Bernadette said.

"I don't mind at all. The two victims were both retired IRA men. We have no leads to go one other than two children saw their grandfather being led away by two young men in a small blue car. The only thing the children gave us was the hair color of the men, red and black. No number plates and no other description."

"What was the murder weapon?" Bernadette asked.

"The ballistics figures it's a Smith and Wesson center model. Both nine millimeter bullets, standard load, not hollow point. As I say we're stumped by this."

"Does it connect your murders and the ones in Canada?"

"That's a possibility, but why? Who would want to kill off old IRA members? The Troubles have been over for some five years, but there's been rumors of a resurgence throughout the country."

"What rumors?"

"A group calling themselves the New IRA have been planting bombs and doing robberies. But the word we get from our informants is these aren't the IRA at all. They are using it to scare people."

"Are they the same group that did the recent murders?"

"We assume so, but we can't put our finger on it. We've had no informers, which is strange. By now I'd have a dozen suspects. I have nothing."

"I hate to mention it," Bernadette said, sipping her

coffee, "but could this be the work of that ancient clan, of whatever you call it...?"

"Ah, the Tuata De' Danann. I hope it isn't something as crazy as that. Cults are hard to deal with. I can deal with criminals. They are selfish and lazy without morals. The cults I've dealt with have ideals that can make them unpredictable."

The waitress arrived with their breakfast and set it before them. Bernadette looked down at a pile of food. Two sausages, a sizeable chunk of bacon with French fries piled onto baked beans, swimming in sauce with a fried egg on top. It made her lose her train of thought.

"The Irish know how make a substantial breakfast," Sullivan said. "Now, tuck into that and I'll give you a rundown on where you might find Cahal."

Bernadette needed little encouragement; she cut off some sausage, slid it through the bean sauce, and chewed. It tasted fantastic.

Sullivan brought out a piece of paper. "Here are the pubs that your uncle would go to if he wanted to find people to hide him in Dublin."

"What about out of Dublin? Would he go to Kildare?" Bernadette asked between bites.

"Why Kildare?"

"I saw a picture outside the John Nolan Pub, the picture was supposedly from there."

"I believe I've seen such a place. There are a lot of pubs in Ireland."

"I have a lead of my aunt Aideen. I spoke to her from Canada. She says she lives in a town called Kilmeague. I'm going to visit her after I leave here. I don't think it's too far."

"Nothing's far in Ireland," Sullivan said. "The whole

place is two hundred miles long and you can drive the width of it in day."

"That's where I'll start then," Bernadette said

Sullivan took a sip of his tea. "Look, I know my people can't give you much support, but the moment you need some backup or you run into anything that you think is suspicious, I want you to call me."

"I will, you can bet on it," Bernadette said.

"And be very careful. These are troubling times here right now. We're not sure who's behind the killings and the bombings, but they are serious."

"So am I," Bernadette said as she paid the bill for both of them and got up to leave.

38

BERNADETTE GOT in her car and headed south on the M50. She'd put the town of Kildare and Kilmeague into her GPS and let the lady's voice on her phone give her directions.

This time she took extra care to ensure she was in the right gear as she shifted. The clutch felt funny. It was small for the boots she wore. The clutch was also quick. It wasn't like that big one on a truck, where you punched it down with your foot and did a slow release. This thing was fast.

She got the feel of the little car. The model had pep. Before long she was zipping in and out of traffic and passing all the large transports. She found the N4 turnoff that took her out of Dublin and then onto the minor roads of the R403. She breathed a sigh of relief. She was now in the Irish countryside.

Even in February, with rain pelting down, it was green. Most of the trees were bare, but the grass, it was that emerald green that gave the island its name. She felt instantly comfortable here. It was as if she'd found the other half of herself, the Irish half that her father had given her.

She opened the window a crack and let the cool air flow

in. The air smelled clean. All of her senses woke up, and she felt refreshed.

As she gazed around the countryside, she almost giggled. Here she was playing tourist on the island, looking for her uncle wanted for aiding a murder. How freaking odd was this?

A half hour later, she took the R415 and came upon the town of Kildare. She drove slowly by the John Nolan Pub. The sign on the door stated it opened at ten-thirty in the morning. Her watch read nine-thirty. She stepped on the gas and headed for her aunt Aideen's place.

In another forty-five minutes she drove into the village of Kilmeague, population 947. There wasn't much there: a large church, a pub, and a few small stores.

She found the address of a small, isolated house on a street on the edge of town. It was stone with a steep tile roof and wooden shutters. The home looked neglected.

Knocking on the door, she heard a shuffling of feet inside. The door opened slowly, revealing an elderly woman with a wrinkled face underneath a cascade of gray curls. "Yes, how may I help you?"

"It's Bernadette Callahan. Is this the home of Aideen Callahan?"

The door opened wide to reveal a little wiry body attached to the wrinkled face. "Why, Bernadette, what a joy to see you. Yes, it's me, your aunt Aideen. Come in, come in."

Bernadette walked into the little house. The rugs on the floor were threadbare. There were few pieces of furniture in the home. A small sofa with a wavy surface that showed its lack of springs sat in the living room with two bentwood chairs. A small coffee table occupied the center of the room. One leg looked ready to give way, the other's looked like they might follow..

Aideen disappeared into the tiny kitchen and made tea. A moment later she shuffled out with a tray with teacups and biscuits.

"I did not know you were coming, Bernadette, I would have gone 'round to the shops and bought some proper scones."

Bernadette sat in one of the bentwood chairs, not wanting to chance a stray spring in the sofa. "This is fine. I should have called first, but I just got into Dublin this morning. I thought I'd surprise you."

"Well, my dear, you have done that."

Bernadette watched Aideen's eyes as she placed the tray on the table. Was there something more to that statement?

"Do you take sugar?"

"Yes, two please."

"A bit of a sweet tooth, like your father," Aideen said as she dropped two cubes of sugar into her cup. "Do you take milk?"

"Yes, a large splash if you please."

"Again, just like your father. I used to say he wasn't having tea; it was a milk shake I was making for him."

Bernadette stirred her tea and regarded her aunt. She looked barely five feet tall. She wore a wool dress, heavy stockings, and a cable-knit sweater. The heat was barely on in the house, if at all. No wonder she had to wear so many clothes. A small fire burned in the hearth, throwing a bit of warmth in the air.

"I hope you don't mind me asking a few questions," Bernadette began.

"Not at all, my dear. I'm sure you have so many about the Callahans."

Bernadette decided not to lead with her questions

regarding the whereabouts of Cahal. She didn't want to put the old girl on the defensive.

"Cahal showed me a picture when he was in Canada. It was of me with my dad and Cahal. We were standing outside a pub in Kildare."

Aideen sipped her tea and pushed a biscuit to one side of her plate. "Oh, yes, I remember that day. It was the day your father came to take you home."

"Was I living with you or Cahal?"

"Oh no, it was when your birth mother gave you up."

"Ah, excuse me. What are you saying?"

"Oh, my dear, I'm so sad you didn't know. Your father had a bit of a fling with a traveler. We sometimes call them Tinkers I think you call them Gypsies in your country. You resulted from that brief love affair. We had to bargain with that woman something awful to get her to give you up. But she finally saw the reasoning." Aideen leaned forward. "Which was in the form of money, I dare say, but she came to her senses and your father came here to claim you."

"Is this lady still around?"

"Yes, she is, her name is Francine Dooley. She lives in a camp on the west side of town. The place is a bit run down, but that's their way of life."

Bernadette finished her tea. "Well, that's interesting. I must check it out. Now, Aunt Aideen, have you seen Uncle Cahal?"

Aideen dropped her teacup into her saucer. "Why don't you tell me the real reason you're here? I know you're a Canadian detective. You're here to capture my poor brother. You know he'd do nothing of what they've charged him with. And you, his kin, after him to put him in shackles and take him like a criminal back to Canada. Are you not ashamed of yourself?"

Bernadette stood up. "Not at all, Aunt Aideen. I'm an officer of the law and your brother—my uncle has broken that law. I will do everything in my power to take him back to Canada. I'm sorry we had to meet this way. Thanks for the tea."

Bernadette walked out of the little house and got into her car. "Well, that was a pleasant family reunion," she said as she started the car.

She reversed round and drove down the road. A blue car parked by the side of the road. Two men sat in it, watching her. One was red-haired, the other dark. They looked away as she passed—a dead giveaway. She drove on.

39

BERNADETTE DROVE down the road towards the Gypsy camp, occasionally glancing into the rearview mirror. The car was a small blue Volkswagen. It came into view about a mile into her journey. The guys in the car were rank amateurs in tailing someone, but that suited Bernadette. Their poor technique kept them visible.

The thought crossed her mind of the thumbnail sketch of the men being sought for murder. Compact car and red hair came to mind. But red hair and compact cars were everywhere in Ireland. She'd wait to determine what the car did next before she made any judgments or got worried. She would call Sullivan for backup if she thought killers were stalking her.

The camp of caravans or trailers, as they would call it in North America, appeared on the left. There was no sign of what it was. Two white posts stood on either side with reflectors to find the entrance at night.

A small hill rose behind the caravans, crammed into the barren trees. They looked forlorn, well used, and they had kept some up and some not at all. Columns of smoke rose from a few outdoor campfires where children were playing with sticks and throwing things into the flames.

Bernadette drove in and parked. The blue Volkswagen stopped down the road. She tried not to laugh as she stepped out of her car. The worst tail ever. These two seemed more like chaperones than killers. If they were meaning to kill her, they would surely have made a move by now.

Three small children approached. "Watcha wan?" a little boy asked.

Bernadette shook her head. The language was incomprehensible. "I'm sorry, I don't understand you."

A little girl with dark hair and blue-green eyes came forward, "We want to know what you want?"

"I'm here to see Francine Dooley. Is she here?"

"Where are you from? You speak funny," the little girl said.

Bernadette knelt down beside the little girl. "I'm from Canada, and my name is Bernadette Callahan. What's yours?"

The girl smiled. "My name's Naomi. You have an Irish name, but you don't sound Irish."

"No, but my father came from this area. I was born in Canada," Bernadette said.

Naomi took Bernadette by the hand and led her to the back of caravans through a crowd of people who'd come out of their trailers to stare at the stranger. A single caravan stood on its own. It was twenty feet long with two metal chairs on a rotting wooden porch. A kitchen table with chrome legs and faded formica top sat to one side, covered in pots and pans.

Naomi knocked on the door and called to Francine. The

language she used sounded foreign to Bernadette; the only thing she recognized was the word Francine.

The door creaked open only enough for the woman to peer out. Then the door swung wide. A woman of Bernadette's height with red hair fast going gray, green eyes and full round face stared down at her.

"Are you Francine Dooley?"

"Ai, that be me, and you are?"

"Bernadette Callahan."

Francine's' shoulders dropped. "Ah, shite, they said you might come round. Come in, come in. I'll make tea."

"Who said that?" Bernadette asked.

Francine dropped her eyes to the floor and went to the kettle. She poured some water into it from a plastic jug and plugged it in. A gas generator hummed outside, and the kettle boiled.

Francine placed two mugs on the table and sat down across from Bernadette. A soft light from the window highlighted her face. Her eyes darted back and forth; she wouldn't look Bernadette directly in the eyes.

"You said someone told you I might come here—who was it?" Bernadette asked.

"I don't recall."

"Was it a recent conversation?"

Francine reached for a packet of cigarettes on the table. She pulled a cigarette out and put it to her lips. She struck a match, inhaled deeply, and blew smoke upwards into the air.

"I think I got a bit confused. It was years ago. That's it. Someone said the mistake I made in having you would come back to me. Here you are," Francine said, pulling the smoke into her lungs and letting it exhale slowly.

Bernadette sensed she was using the smoke as a cover. She filled the air as if she was trying to hide behind it.

"Cahal and Aideen Callahan both told me a story of my being born to an Irish woman near their town."

"They say I'm an Irish Gypsy?"

"I believe so. You want to tell me how I was supposedly born here?"

"There's no suppose about this, dearie. Your father, Dominic Callahan, gave me a right good shagging outside the pub one night. There was no proper romance, just a knee trembler up against a wall in the alley and nine months later out you come to add shame to my stupidity."

"I see. And you gave me up for adoption? Is that it?"

"If that's what you want to call it. I went to Aideen and Cahal straight away, told them what that little bugger Dominic had done. They agreed to give me cash, and I handed you over. There, that's the story."

"Interesting story. How did you meet my father?"

"He was a singer in a band. A lovely voice, he had. I was young, I got as near to the band and flashed me eyes at him. The rest is... well, the rest is you..."

"I guess that's a believable story," Bernadette said.

"Why wouldn't you believe it? Maybe you don't want to because you'd be the child of a Gypsy woman. We have a long and good tradition in this land. You could do worse than have the blood of my ancestors in your veins."

Bernadette raised her hand. "I'm sorry if I've offended you. This is all new to me. Until today, I assumed I was the child of my native mother in Canada."

"Well, the Callahan's have a way with lies now, don't they? Your father would have sung a sweet song to weave his story, he would."

Bernadette sipped her tea. "Tell me about Cahal Callahan."

Francine's eyes flashed before she closed them and looked away. "What's to tell? He's a Callahan, like your father."

"When did you see him last?"

"Years ago, at a market. I remembered him hanging about with your da so he could get some girls. He wasn't the looker your da was. But he could talk the girls' nickers off just as well."

Bernadette paused. She let the silence fall over the little trailer. She stirred her tea and looked at the table. The match book that Francine used lay beside her cigarettes. There was a Canadian maple leaf on the front of the packet. She'd seen those same matches in Duty Free at the Toronto airport.

Francine noticed her staring at the packet. She swept her hand over them and pulled them towards her.

"I must go," Bernadette said. "Thanks for your time."

"That's it then?"

"Yes, that's it," Bernadette said.

"Will you not leave your mother a few euros?"

Bernadette got up to leave. "You said the Callahan's paid you for dropping me off over thirty years ago. What do you want to get paid for now? Your story?"

"But I've told you, I'm your birth mother."

"No, my mother is a full Cree Native. She was born on the Lone Pine Reservation in Northern Canada. I was raised by her and my grandmother. Those are my true parents."

"You're ungrateful, you are."

"No, I'm very grateful. I know who I am, and if I am related to you, I'm glad I didn't grow up bitter like you. I'm sorry for you. That's all I have. Goodbye."

Bernadette walked out of the trailer. The children clustered around her and tried to keep up with her as she walked to her car. They had to run to do so.

She got in her car, revved the engine, and popped the clutch making the car fishtail out of the dirt parking lot throwing grass leaves and dirt from the tires.

The car hit the road. She accelerated. Looking in her rearview mirror she could see she'd lost the little blue Volkswagen. She smiled.

40

BERNADETTE DROVE over the speed limit. The car took the corners well. Nothing about the conversation with Francine made sense. Her story didn't jibe with Cahal's story, but lies never do.

Cahal said he'd put her father on a freighter when he was young and never seen him again, and then he said he'd come back to Ireland. Francine's story of her father playing in a band made sense, but it would have to have been over thirty years ago.

"Okay, Bernadette, give your head a shake. You're here to find Cahal. Not to examine your birth," she said to herself. She needed to focus. The past few hours in Ireland were more than she expected.

The James Nolan Pub had few cars outside as she parked across the street. She pulled the picture of Cahal from her pocket and entered the pub.

The place was old, with wooden beams in the ceiling painted black. The floor was old plank, laid before the turn of the century. Everything about the place spoke of age. The place smelled like a lake full of beer had seeped into the floors over time.

Bernadette walked up to the bar and sat on a well-worn wooden bar stool a century of bottoms had smoothed.

The barman was in his mid-fifties, round and stocky with a full beard and bald head. He looked like he'd always been there, as if he'd come with the place. Born with the beard and a taste for beer.

He wiped his hands on his apron and came over to Bernadette. "What can I get you?"

Bernadette looked over at the long row of beer handles that pumped beer.

"I'm new to Irish beer, what do you suggest?"

The barman's face brightened. "Ah, a tourist to our fair Isle. I always suggest a Kilkenny, as a Guinness may be a wee bit harsh at the first."

"Sounds good, but a small one. I've just got off the plane."

"A half it is."

The barmen pulled the pint at the handle and smiled at her again. "Where are you visiting from?"

"Canada."

"I have relatives in Toronto. Are you near there?" he asked as he placed a coaster and the beer in front of Bernadette.

"No, I live thirty-five hundred kilometers west of Toronto."

"Oh, that is a big country."

"Very big," Bernadette agreed, taking a sip of the beer. It was creamy and smooth with a bit of hoppy taste. With her jet-lag, it was just the thing to take the edge off.

"We don't get many visitors this time of year. What brings you here?"

"Looking for a lost relative," Bernadette said, pulling a picture of Cahal out of her jacket pocket and placing it on the bar.

The barman walked over. He looked at it for a second. "Looks familiar."

"Have you seen him in the past few days?"

"No, not recently, but a month ago, I think I saw him come in here."

"Is this his regular pub?"

The barman paused for a moment. "You a cop?"

"Yes, I am a cop. I'm a detective in Canada. I have no authority here. But this is my uncle Cahal Callahan, and I need to get in touch with him."

The barman chuckled. "Did he win the lottery back in Canada?"

"Yes, you could say that," Bernadette said. She pulled a piece of paper from her pocket and wrote her cell phone number on it. "Here's my cell phone number. If you see him in here, call me."

"Should I tell him you're looking for him then?"

"No, I want to make it a surprise," Bernadette said. She dropped a five Euro note on the bar. "Keep the change."

The barman smiled. "Come back again."

She walked outside. It had stopped raining. The beer was wending its way nicely into her brain and smoothing her jet-lag. It was now just past noon. She thought she might find lunch somewhere on the way back into Dublin, then her hotel and a bed. The bed sounded like a good idea.

Out of the corner of her eye, she saw two men approach. One had red hair. She turned to face them.

41

BERNADETTE QUICKLY ASSESSED HER SITUATION. She had no weapons, only her hands and feet. There was nothing around her but the brick wall of the pub. She took one step closer to it.

The men came to three feet away and stopped. "We want you to come with us," the red-haired man said.

Bernadette stood there. Raised both her hands with palms towards them. "I don't see that happening."

The red-haired man opened his jacket to reveal his gun. "But Mr. Smith and Wesson says it is. Get in the car."

Bernadette stared at the man, locking eyes. He didn't have his hand on the gun. His mistake.

She lunged forward stomping her size eight boot on the top of his foot. His face registered the pain. With open palms she slapped his ears as hard as she could, hoping to break his eardrums. He staggered forward. She grabbed his ears with both hands, pulled his head down to meet her knee. His nose made a crunching sound on her knee. She followed the move with her right elbow to the back of his head. He hit the ground.

The second man stood paralyzed by her actions—then he came at her.

She turned to face him, the brick wall behind her.

He charged at her, placing his hands around her neck. Her hands came up between his arms grabbing him by the collar. She pulled his head forward towards the wall while ducking down and moving to the right. His head made a crunching sound with the wall.

The barman came out of the pub and stared down at the two men. "What's this then?"

"Sorry for that," Bernadette said. "These two wanted to offer me a ride, I refused." She reached down, taking the gun from the red-haired man's waist. It was a Smith and Wesson 986 center model, called a wheel gun by some.

She got into her car and threw the gun in the glove compartment. She put the car in gear and shot out of the town.

It took a half hour to get back into Dublin. The traffic was light on the Friday afternoon. She made a delivery before going into her hotel. Checking her Google maps, she found a donut shop in downtown Dublin. She ordered a half dozen donuts but asked for a one dozen box. The young man behind the counter was happy to comply.

Punching the address of the Special Detective Unit of the Garda into her maps, she arrived outside the building fifteen minutes later. She dropped the donuts off with the gun underneath the first layer. She placed a note to Detective Sullivan to check the gun as the possible murder weapon and included the license number of their car. Only then did she head for her hotel, which was easy to find. It was finding a parking space for her car that took a half hour.

The hotel was, as Sullivan had said, a bit 'shite' but it was clean, with almost usable towels and bar soap that lathered. She took a shower and decided on a quick nap. Her body now vibrated with fatigue. Her watch read two o'clock Dublin time. She lay on the bed, her eyes couldn't stay open —she fell into a deep sleep.

When her phone rang, it pervaded her consciousness for a long time. She kept telling someone to answer the phone, but no one seemed to hear her. Finally, she opened her eyes and grabbed her cell phone beside the bed.

"Hello, Callahan here."

"Where did you get the gun?" Sullivan asked.

"Oh... hi," Bernadette said, rubbing the sleep from her eyes. A bedside clock showed 4 p.m.

"Why didn't you call the police or me?" Sullivan asked.

"I'd be spending the entire day in questioning at your station, which means day lost in finding Cahal. He knows I'm here. He sent those men to take care of me."

"Did you get a good look at the two men?"

"Yes, I did. What about the gun? Did you run it through ballistics?"

"It's a match for both murders. When can you come to the station to make an ID of the men?"

"So, here's the problem with that. Cahal's people know I'm here. They were after me. The red-haired man knew my name. Isn't it obvious to you our murders are connected?"

"Yes, that's obvious. When we catch the two men, we solve all the murders," Sullivan said.

"I don't think so. Cahal is at the center of this. Those two were low level and dumb. That they could take out two old men is even a wonder. I want Cahal, and if you help me get him, I'll help you get your two boys who think they're men."

"You know I could bring you in?"

"For what, finding a gun on the streets? Happens all the

time. I was being a concerned citizen as I toured your lovely land."

Sullivan paused for a moment. Bernadette waited him out.

"What do you want?" Sullivan asked.

"Help with a stakeout of a Gypsy camp outside of town. And I also want to know who in your department let it slip I was coming to Ireland."

"I'll find out. Then we must meet. Can you give me an hour?"

"Sure, I'm going to continue my nap, call me," Bernadette said. She lay down on the bed, falling into a deep sleep again.

42

RONAN THREW his full weight into the strike with the broadsword. The heavy steel made a loud thwack sound as it met the wood pole in the center of his workout studio.

His gymnasium was the medieval equivalent of a weapons room. Shields, lances, pikes, and swords lined the walls. Large banners of ancient Irish kings hung from the wooden beams in the ceiling. An enormous stone fireplace roared with logs.

John Dunne entered the room through a wooden door set with brass. He stood watching Ronan. He never disturbed him, but this was important.

Ronan stopped at the sight of Dunne. He was breathing heavily, sweat glistening on his face. He grabbed a white towel and mopped his forehead.

"What is it?"

Dunne advanced into the room slowly. He hated this place. The weapons were ghastly, with sharp edges and spikes. He preferred a gun. Much more civilized. In his opinion—you killed a person, you didn't maim them.

"Two of our people contacted Bernadette Callahan."

"And?"

"She seems to have escaped capture."

Ronan wiped his hands with the towel. "How could she have got away if they made contact? What did they do—introduce themselves? They were to take her to the sea and kill her. What manner of imbeciles do we have?"

Dunne shuffled uneasily from one foot to another. "Mr. Bronaugh, they are all conscripts from the group you started, Tuata De' Danann. The master you have at the head of it has full power over them. I'm sorry they've disappointed you."

Ronan dropped his towel. "Yes, you're right to point that out. They are in the master's command."

They paused and stood there. The logs crackled and snapped in the fire.

"We must do the best we can," Ronan said. "If our people cannot defeat her, they must stop her in another way. I'm sure you can think of something, Dunne."

"Yes sir, I will do so," Dunne said as he walked out the door. He had an idea how that would happen.

"Oh, one more thing, Dunne."

"What is it?"

"How is our grand finale doing?"

"The grand finale, sir?"

"You know, the bombs that are being delivered."

"Oh yes, sir, the bombs. They left for England this morning. They are safely on their way."

Dunne walked out of the room and sent a text to make sure the bombs were on their way. He doubted he'd live through another major disappointment.

～

THE TWO LARGE transports rumbled off the ferry at Holy Head, making their way on the A5 to the M54 where the motorway spliced through Birmingham and merged into the M6 until it became the M1 after Coventry. The men in each transport didn't acknowledge each other at a petrol stop.

They got out, picked up tea and sausage rolls, and moved on. Just outside of London, in a town called Watford, they pulled into an industrial area. They backed the transports into a large bay and got out. Three men waited inside.

They greeted each other and unloaded the cargo.

"Careful now," a man named Finn said. "You'll blow us all to fock if you jiggle it too much."

"It's not armed, you silly bastard," a man named Declan said.

"I don't like taking chances," Finn said.

Declan laughed. "You afraid you'll get to Valhalla before us?"

"Everything in its time," Finn said, guiding the large carton onto the platform.

They unpacked the first carton. Inside there were wires and a central control linking four cylinders with a transmitter.

"This is PETN, a nitro derivative," Finn said. "This is more powerful than TNT and will cause one hell of hole in any place we put it."

"Roll out the copier," Declan said.

Two men rolled out a large photocopier; it measured some eight feet long by four feet high. They pushed it onto the platform and opened the inner doors. It was empty inside.

"This will work." Finn said. "What's the other one going into?"

A man rolled a large industrial laundry basket onto the dock.

"You've got to be joking." Finn said.

Declan waved his hand. "What, you've never seen a commercial laundry delivery? They roll these off without question."

"How are we to get it into the banquet room?" Finn asked.

"Easy, we tell them we have a special delivery of table linens. Our men roll it right into the dinner and leave. Five minutes later, as they're leaving, our mate hits the detonator on his phone and boom," Declan said.

"When does it all happen?" Finn asked.

"We lie low for a few days; the Master wants it to happen at a special time."

"Why, what's up with the time?"

"You bleeding idjit, it probably coincides with the sun, the moon or the stars in some ancient realm. That's how the master works and we don't question it," Declan said.

A large man in overalls, named Max, stood beside them. He had a Celtic cross tattooed on his shaved head. "No, it doesn't. There's a meeting of a bunch of European big shots at Canary Wharf and the other is a hotel in Brighton with the entire British Cabinet. We're going to take them all out with these two bombs."

Declan and Finn raised their eyebrows in recognition of the information. "We're going to cause some right shite we are," Finn said.

* * *

Ronan left his practice hall for his shower. He'd once hired a young woman as his butler, to help him bath, however, his advisor warned him how the media might report such behaviour. Dismissing the young lady had grated on him. They bathed ancient kings. Why not him? With a nod to reason, he now took showers on his own.

He toweled himself off, pulled on a plush bathrobe, and padded his way over a deep carpet to his private chamber. He allowed the maid in to clean. No one else entered his room. Some things must be kept sacred. He picked up his phone and dialed the number of Brendon Shannon.

Shannon answered, "Mr. Bronaugh, a delight as always to speak with you."

"How close is the vote on the protecting Ireland bill?"

"Ah, well, not as close as we'd like, but there is hope on the next round of voting," Shannon said.

"In two days, there will be something in the news to convince them," Ronan said.

"I see. Would you care to give me an idea of what to expect?" Shannon asked.

"No, but I expect you to do your job. Convince the undecided members, they need to vote in favor of the bill. Once this bill is in effect, my company can screen all violent behavior from all embryos in Ireland and then the world. Don't you see how safe the world will become?" Ronan asked.

"Clear as a bell," Shannon said.

"Then you'll have no problem in getting it done," Ronan said, disconnecting the call..

He walked to the full-length mirror and stood before it. "One day, they will bow before this form as their king," he proclaimed to the room. He felt good.

43

A RINGING PHONE pierced Bernadette's consciousness. She was sure she answered it. She said hello several times. There was no one on the other end of the line. She put the phone down and fell back to sleep.

It was only after her cell phone rang again and again that she realized she was dreaming. She sent a message to her conscious brain, "Wake the hell up and answer the phone."

She threw her arm across the bed and picked up the phone. "Hello, Bernadette here."

"I hope I didn't wake you from a deep sleep. Getting up from a jet lag sleep is horrific," Sullivan said.

Bernadette rubbed her eyes and checked the time. It was 6 p.m. "It's late, I thought you were going to call me in an hour."

"I had some things to sort out. It seems the leak in our department came from my partner, Bishop. He's a bit of a lady's man. He chatted up a girl in the pub last night and told her about some Canadian detective coming to Dublin to look for her uncle."

Bernadette sat up in bed. "Don't be too hard on him, I'm sure he meant no harm."

"He mostly does harm to himself." Sullivan chuckled. "I doubt he got to first base with the girl."

"So, where are we on this? Do you want to meet?"

"Yes, meet me in a half hour at the Brewery Inn. It's only a few doors down from you."

Bernadette took the time to hang a few clothes up on the three hangers in the small closet. The place didn't have much of anything except a bed, a small chest of drawers, a tiny closet, and a small bathroom with a shower, toilet, and sink.

She squeezed into the bathroom and confirmed that she looked as exhausted and jet lagged as she felt. She pulled some things out of her makeup bag and attempted to do some reconstruction to her eyebrows and throw some color in her face. At the end, she smiled; she no longer looked like a cadaver—success.

She walked down the three floors by the stairs. The elevator was so slow it seemed to be a joke amongst the hotel staff. The evening foot traffic was building on the street, with young Dubliners out to party and get seriously happy or drunk, the latter being the likely outcome.

Bernadette found her way to the Brewery District Pub. It was a rather bland looking place with little ambience. Tables and chairs seemed scattered about the place. A dart board occupied one corner, and if Bernadette's eyes did not fail her, there was a jukebox. Two young people were trying to figure out how it worked. Someone finally showed them how to put in a Euro and punch a song on the playlist. A song emanated from the old relic.

At first, Bernadette couldn't recognize the song, then it came to her. It was the Commitments singing "Mustang

Sally" from the 1991 movie with the same name aptly called, *The Commitments*.

Bernadette wasn't even a teenager when she saw the movie. It was totally against her grandmother's wishes, but she loved it. She hardly identified with being Irish at the time until she heard the one line in the film: "The Irish are the blacks of Europe." That was the one thing that made her see her Irish roots.

Sullivan was at the bar nursing a pint of Guinness. She approached as he got off his stool and came towards her.

"What can I can get you?" Sullivan asked.

"A half of Kilkenny would be nice," Bernadette said.

Sullivan raised his eyebrows at her choice before turning to the barman and placing her order. They walked to a table far away from the others to talk.

Bernadette sipped her beer, taking the place in. "A bit of an unusual place."

"They know how to pour a proper pint of Guinness here. It shouldn't be in a frosty mug like they do now. The Europeans and their strange ways." He sighed as he looked at his pint, "they should leave some things alone."

Bernadette regarded the middle-aged detective over her beer glass. There was a lot to like in this man. If he lived in Canada, he'd be a good drinking buddy.

"So, did you learn anything else in the past few hours?" Bernadette asked.

"There was a report of two men being accosted by a Canadian woman in Kildare this afternoon," Sullivan said, putting his pint down and staring at her.

"Oh. Really? Do the two men wish to press charges?"

"No, actually. They made their complaint to the barman of the James Nolan Pub. They said a lady jumped them and began beating on them. The barman reported to the local constable but failed to get the names of the victims," Sullivan said as his body convulsed with laughter. "You gave them a right pounding, it seems."

"They came at me with a gun. That's improper etiquette as far as I'm concerned."

Sullivan smiled. "We matched the car's number plate to Sean Murray. He has a mate he hangs with, Jamie Kelly. Both are low-level criminals. Here's a picture of both of them. Do they look familiar?"

Bernadette looked at the two pictures Sullivan placed on the table. "That's them," she said.

Sullivan placed the pictures back in his pocket. "You'll be happy to know that Sean Murray is Emily Murray's cousin and hangs about with Dylan Quinn and Cahal Callahan."

"I knew there'd be a connection to the murders in Canada and here in Ireland. Someone is trying to silence something."

"That's exactly what we're thinking."

"Who in your department thinks this?" Bernadette asked.

"The special detective unit. After running the gun and the license plate, we can see the dots connect. I spoke to my detective sergeant, and he agrees we need to help you find Cahal."

Bernadette sipped her beer and stared at Sullivan. "Now wait a minute. That's a fast turnaround; even my people wouldn't see things that quickly. This isn't because I'm a target and all you have to do is dangle me about like bait, is it?"

Sullivan coughed into his hand. "Well, not exactly bait, but you have received the attention of the people we're looking for. My chief reasoned if we put you on the hunt, they'd come to you."

"I might need a full pint to digest this," Bernadette said, pushing her empty half pint forward.

"Let it be my honor," Sullivan said.

He returned with a full pint of Kilkenny and a pint of Guinness for himself. The noise in the pub was growing. Young people had crowded around the jukebox, finding the relic a fascinating toy. They punched in tunes from the oldest Van Morrison albums and some Cat Stevens.

Bernadette took a sip of her new pint. "Okay, I'm ready to be your bait, if that's what you wish, but for tonight, I want you to join me at a stakeout for Cahal."

"Where?" Sullivan said, leaning forward to hear her through Van Morrison's "The Healing Game."

"There's a Gypsy camp south of Kildare. I'm sure Cahal has been there with his old girlfriend."

"Who is this lady?"

"She claims to be my Irish birth mother."

Sullivan pulled a face. "Your what?"

"Long story. Let's just say we had a talk and that one, she's probably lying about being my mother, and two, she's seen Cahal recently."

"Why are you so sure she's seen Cahal?"

"Easy. She said that in the past, he wasn't that handsome, but he had a way in talking girls' knickers off. She put an emphasis on the word, knickers."

"That's it? That's all you have? A woman puts an inflection on naming her underpants and it's a code word for she's been having it off with an escaped convict?"

Bernadette leaned forward and held Sullivan's gaze. "Don't tell me you haven't worked with less?"

Sullivan blew out a breath. "You have me there—intuition is a detective's greatest asset. Those without it never make it in this profession. Okay, I'll arrange a stake out —when?"

"Tonight."

"Tonight. Why would you go tonight? You've just bested his goons. He'll go into hiding. You'll never find him there."

"He guessing I'm tired. He knows when I arrived in Dublin. He'll feel safe at the caravan tonight. He'll move tomorrow."

"You must be joking," Sullivan said. "You've hardly had any sleep; you look like you can hardly see. How will you able to sit in a car and do a stakeout?"

Bernadette leaned forward. "That's easy. I won't be using a car. It's too obvious. There's a small hill above the place with perfect sightlines. I'll park myself in the trees for the night and watch. I'm positive Cahal will make an appearance."

"Are you convinced this is your plan for tonight, then?"

"Yes, I am."

Sullivan drained his pint. "Then we'd best make plans. I'll let the Garda know. I doubt we'll get much backup other than a few officers on the road. I'll put together some sandwiches and tea. I'll also get some infra-red field glasses and a pair of wellies for you."

"What are wellies?"

"You call them rubber boots. All of Ireland is awash in rain this time of year. I hope you've a good rain jacket."

"I do," Bernadette said.

"Good," Sullivan said, "let's get your things. My car is just up the road."

Bernadette got up from the table. She felt wobbly. She'd

had only one and half pints of beer, but it had gone to her head. She steadied herself and realized it was the jetlag.

They left the pub with Van Morrison's song "*Into the Mystic*" playing in the background.

44

THE MOON WAS PEEKING out from behind the clouds as they drove towards Kilmeague and the Gypsy camp. The rain unleashed a torrent and then softened to a light patter. An Irish folk song played on the radio as Bernadette sat in the passenger's seat watching the countryside and houses go by.

The stone houses with wooden shutters looked picturesque in the rain. Some streets in the towns had cobblestones. There was a calm and idyllic quality to the place. Bernadette couldn't imagine Ireland to be anything but a peaceful island, almost suppressing some of its dark past.

They arrived a few kilometers up the road from the Gypsy camp to meet with a Garda Police car. Sullivan got out to have a word with them. He spoke with them for a minute and got back in the car.

"They'll sit here on the side of the road and be our backup. I told them not to come until I call," Sullivan said.

Bernadette looked at the two young officers in the car. They appeared to be in their early twenties. She looked over at Sullivan. "What weapons are they carrying?"

"Oh, the Garda doesn't carry guns. I didn't have enough time to make the request for weapons for them," Sullivan replied.

"Then what's the use of these guys for backup?" Bernadette asked.

"I have a gun," Sullivan said. "That will suffice for now."

Bernadette looked at him in wonder, then back at the road. "Okay, I'll find a big stick if I need it."

They drove down the road. Bernadette gave directions to pull off the road five hundred meters from the camp. They parked the car, took the binoculars, sandwiches, and a thermos of tea from the back and headed into the forest.

The wellies Bernadette received were a few sizes too big. She'd put on two pairs of extra wool socks. It almost solved the problem, but her feet still rubbed back and forth. But the journey up the hill wasn't far.

The forest was thick with underbrush. They slogged through, pushing wet branches out of the way. After twenty minutes, Bernadette found the perfect spot in a clearing with a large willow to use as cover.

Sullivan pulled a waterproof tarp from a backpack and laid it on the ground. He placed the sandwiches and tea on the tarp and took up position.

"I see you've got this situation figured out," Bernadette said.

"Almost every stakeout is in the rain. It's raining or will rain. There's an old saying that there's no poor weather, only the wrong clothing."

"I think we have the same saying in Canada, only it's with frigid cold," Bernadette said. She picked up a pair of binoculars and focused on Francine's place.

"You see anything?" Sullivan asked.

"There's movement inside the trailer. Hold on, someone's coming to the window. Damn it, that's Cahal. He's looking right up the hill at us."

"I'll call the backup."

"No, you won't," a voice behind them said.

Bernadette whirled around. Sean Murray and Jamie Kelly stood behind them. Jamie had a double-barrel shotgun pointed at them.

"Ease off that gun and throw it here, copper. I'll put a full blast of twelve gauge shot in you. Make a hell of a hole at this range."

Sullivan removed his gun and tossed it to Sean.

Jamie smiled. "Cahal told us you'd be back. Now, put your hands behind your backs. Sean, tie their hands, and watch that wicked bitch. Don't let her try any of her funny stuff."

Bernadette and Sullivan stood up on the tarp. There weren't many options. Jamie had the shotgun pointed at them. Sean took Sullivan's radio and cell phone and tied his hands.

When Sean came to Bernadette, he told her to turn around. He wanted nothing to do with the business end of her hands or feet.

"Now, march down the hill," Jamie commanded while waving the shotgun.

Sean had the handgun pointed at Bernadette's torso. He had an evil look in his eyes, like he was looking for any excuse to pull the trigger. His head had a large bandage where his forehead had met the wall. Nothing in him looked grateful for the experience.

"You know I'm a Garda detective, don't you?" Sullivan asked as they walked down the path.

"Yeah, what of it?" Sean asked.

"Serious time is what you'll get for harming an officer of the law."

"Hear that, Jamie? He thinks we're scared. This man doesn't know we have people in high places and well fixed. In two days' time we'll be right up there with you lot, we will. You'd be wondering why you never bowed low to us before, but then you'll be dead tonight," Sean said.

They walked on in silence down the narrow path toward the Gypsy camp. Bernadette noticed a clearing on the right. A little cross surrounded by flowers was in the center. They came to the camp, and a door opened from Francine's trailer.

Cahal stepped out. "Well, if it isn't my niece, come to pay me a visit."

Bernadette stared at him, her face flushed with anger. "Cahal, you're only charged with aiding a murder in Canada. If you kill us, you'll never get out of prison."

Cahal smiled. "That is true, if I'm caught, but I don't see that happening."

"We have policeman down the road. They'll be here soon," Sullivan said.

"Really, now that gives me a bit of a fright, it does. Two young men dressed in uniform with no weapons. What are they going to do, call Dublin, then run and hide? All Jamie has to do is fire his shotgun in the air and they'll be off like rabbits."

"Where do we take them?" Jamie asked.

"To the cliffs, and make sure you leave them at the bottom this time, none of the foolishness you did with O'Dea," Cahal said.

"Aye, we hear you," Sean said. "We'll take them all the way to the Cliffs of Moher and drop them off."

Cahal smiled. "That's a grand idea." He turned to look at Bernadette. "Those cliffs are on the western side. Maybe you can throw a kiss to your lover back in Canada as you plummet to the ocean."

Bernadette fists clenched in her bonds. If she could free herself, she'd take his eyes out with her favorite karate move. Seeing her fierce gaze, Cahal stepped back.

They took Bernadette and Sullivan to the back of the van. They tied their feet and hoisted them in. Sean and Jamie said goodbye to Cahal, and they started off.

They felt the van pull out of the caravan park and take to the roadway. They sat in silence for a while as they listened to the two men arguing in the van's front.

"The Cliffs of Moher are too bleeding far away. That's a two-and-a-half-hour drive," Jamie said. "I say we shoot them and dump their bodies over the cliffs of Brayhead."

"But it's not steep enough," Sean argued.

"The gun will kill them, not the fall. Don't be daft."

"But what will the Master say?" Sean asked.

"That's easy. Remember, there are toll roads all the way to the Cliffs of Moher. We say we saw coppers everywhere and disposed of them closer to Dublin."

"I like how you think," Sean said with a smile. He made a right turn, and they continued their journey.

Bernadette moved herself to a sitting position beside Sullivan. "Where are they taking us?"

Sullivan leaned over to whisper in her ear. "It's a long series of cliffs south of Dublin."

"How long until we get there?"

"Probably take an hour on the back roads."

"That should be enough to get out of these ropes," Bernadette said. "How about you?"

"Might take me a bit longer. I've a buggered wrist, but I think I can manage. What are you planning?"

"Not dying."

"Good answer."

45

THE VAN CONTINUED through the night. The men in front became quiet. Bernadette and Sullivan listened for additional information. There was none.

They felt the van slow down, turn and go over a rocky road. Bernadette smelled the sea. The air was colder; it made its way into the van and chilled her.

She focused, slowing her breathing, feeling her hands and feet. They were her weapons. She had loosened hands minutes ago. Sullivan had done the same. When the door opened, she would look for opportunities.

The van came to a stop. Feet crunched on stones; the back door opened. Two guns pointed at them through the open door.

"Get out," Jamie yelled.

"You have our feet tied," Bernadette said.

"We'll untie your feet, but one kick from you and I blow your head off. You hear me now?" Jamie said.

"I hear you," Bernadette said. She moved her feet towards Sean. He cut them loose with a knife. He did the same with Sullivan.

"Out you get now," Jamie yelled. "The first one that gets funny is the first to die. Now move."

Bernadette shuffled her way out of the van with her hands behind her back. Sullivan followed her out.

"Now, move slowly in front of us. The cliffs are two hundred meters distance. I'd rather you walk there than I carry your dead bodies," Jamie said.

Bernadette bumped into Sullivan. "Are you a leftie or a righty?"

"I prefer left," Sullivan said.

Bernadette placed her foot in front of Sullivan's. He collapsed to the ground.

"You bleeding idjit, what the hell do you think you're doing? Get up," Jamie screamed at him.

"His hands are behind his back; you must help him," Bernadette said.

"Shoot him now," Sean yelled at Jamie. "They're just play acting. Kill them before they try something."

Jamie bent down to help Sullivan up. He put his hand on his shoulder. "Get up old man."

Sullivan rose to his knees. He reached both hands back, grabbing the back of Jamie's head—throwing him over top of him. The shotgun fired.

Sean raised his gun. Bernadette came at him from the side, throwing a phoenix punch into his temple. With one protruding knuckle on her fist, it produced an explosion of pain in his head.

Bernadette followed through with her right foot to stomp the outside of his right leg just above the knee. She only needed four kilos of pressure. He screamed, falling to the ground with a broken leg. He dropped the gun.

She picked up the gun. "If either of you move, I'll end your lives right here."

Jamie lay on the ground, moaning.

Sullivan got up from the ground. He moved towards Jamie, taking the shotgun as he did, looking down at him.

"He's taken a shotgun blast to the stomach. Rather bad I think."

"I'll guard these two while you call it in," Bernadette said.

"I'll get my radio and cell phone. They left it in the van," Sullivan said. He made his way to the van.

Jamie rolled over and called to Sean. "I'm done for, Sean."

"Don't worry, they'll get you help," Sean said.

"I don't need their help. You know what we have to do."

"You're talking shite, you are, Jamie. There's no way I'm doing that."

"You know what happens to those who get caught. They kill everyone in our family. That's the code. You want your girl dead? I don't want my ma to die."

"Aw, Jesus, Jamie. You had to mention that."

"You know it's true," Jamie said, lifting himself up off the ground. "You must man up. It's the only way to Valhalla." He moved his left hand to his neck. An amulet of silver hung there with a silver chain.

"I'm not doing that," Sean screamed at Jamie. "You can't make me."

Jamie coughed. Blood came out of his mouth. "No, I can't make you. But do you really want your entire family to die?" Jamie placed the amulet between his lips. He bit down hard on it and sucked it into his mouth. He was foaming at the mouth in seconds.

Bernadette ran over to him. His body was convulsing. His eyes rolled back into his head. There was nothing she could do.

She turned to look at Sean. Tears were in his eyes as he put his own amulet in his mouth. He bit down on it.

"No, wait, don't," Bernadette screamed at him.

It was too late. Sean was foaming at the mouth like Jamie. Sullivan came back from the van on his phone. He put it down. "What's this then?"

"They committed suicide. Jamie said the cult would murder their families if we took them prisoner," Bernadette said.

"Sounds worse than the Mafia," Sullivan said.

"Who are these people we've run into?" Bernadette asked. "This is not your normal criminal behavior."

"The Garda patrol will be here soon. Would you mind coming back to our headquarters to go over a few things?"

Bernadette looked down at the two bodies. "Sure, I hope there's a stiff shot of whiskey at the end of this night, because this is strange."

They both turned as two ambulances followed by several Garda police cars came blaring up the roadway. Bernadette sighed; this was going to be a long night.

46

BERNADETTE SPENT several hours at the Garda Headquarters. Detective Sullivan took her statement and passed on to his detective sergeant, James Gallagher, who requested a meeting after he read it.

Gallagher was tall with an athletic build. He wore no jacket and his tie looked like it had been through two days of use. He had a thick head of red hair and bushy eyebrows that both showed a touch of gray. He looked all of fifty. He chewed a small toothpick as he glanced over the report.

"This seems most unusual, Sullivan," Gallagher finally said, looking up from the report.

"Which part?" Sullivan asked.

"All of it," Gallagher said, throwing the report on his desk.

"Yes, at the face of it, this sounds farfetched, but I can assure you, what Detective Callahan overheard them saying sounds about right."

"But you didn't hear them say anything about this Valhalla business, did you?"

"No sir, I did not, I recorded the conversation from the detective," Sullivan said looking at Bernadette.

"And, you're certain, Detective Callahan, you heard this man, the deceased Jamie Kelly, talk about going to Valhalla and they'd better do it or have their families suffer?"

Bernadette sat upright. She felt like she was being grilled by her own chief of detectives back home. "Yes, sir, that is exactly what I heard."

"Hard to fathom," Gallagher said. "How am I supposed to report this to my superiors?"

"You could begin with the toxicology report of their bodies once they're completed. I'm sure the report will come back as cyanide poisoning. That should convince them," Sullivan said.

Gallagher raised his thick eyebrows. "Yes, that is a good point." He stared at Sullivan. "What's your plan? How do you expect to sort this out?"

"We will interview all the people acquainted with the deceased to find links that will lead us to who is behind their organization," Sullivan said.

Gallagher looked at his watch. "Is that the time? It's past midnight—well, I guess that's a good a plan as any. Carry on and keep me informed."

Bernadette and Sullivan walked out of Gallagher's office. The evening shift of detectives and police was moving about the building with phones ringing in the background.

"How about if I drop you back at your hotel? I'm sorry I can't take you to a pub. They shut at half midnight. We're a bit old-fashioned that way here. There're nightclubs open but none of them suitable for a quiet drink."

Bernadette rubbed the back of her neck. "That's fine. I need some time to relax. How about I see you in the morning?"

They drove through the streets of Dublin. People walked through the streets in crowds as the pubs were closing. Another drizzle of rain hit the streets. The people hardly noticed the rain. They seemed young and slightly intoxicated. Sullivan drove to the front of her hotel.

Bernadette opened the car door to get out. "What time should we meet tomorrow?"

"I'll pick you up at half seven. We can talk about our plans over breakfast. I'll draw up a list of people to interview."

Bernadette turned and looked at Sullivan. "I have a feeling all these people met somewhere long ago. I doubt they read a bulletin board looking for murderers for hire. Something in the way the two men talked at the cliffs. That kind of thinking is in ingrained in you."

"I see where you're going with that. Some excellent discussions for tomorrow," Sullivan said.

"Yes, until tomorrow," Bernadette said. She got out of the car and entered the hotel. A walk up the three flights of stairs to her room became a major workout. The combination of jet lag and lack of sleep pushed her to the limit.

She got to her room, entered, and shivered at the chill. There was no thermostat to raise the temperature. She pulled out a small bottle of duty-free Scotch she'd purchased in Toronto. She poured herself a stiff drink and put in a few drops of tap water in a glass she'd found the bathroom.

She sipped and let the scotch roll over her tongue before allowing it to slide down her throat. She let herself exclaim a heartfelt *hum*, then kicked off her boots and lay on the bed.

Everything in her wanted to sleep, but she checked messages on her phone. She knew it was the last thing she should do if she wanted to get to sleep, but in her heart, she wanted to reach out over six thousand kilometers to Chris. She'd come close to being killed. Two young men had died in front of her for no sane reason, and she was in a room that really was shite.

She had a text from Chris asking her how she was doing, and one from Evanston asking if she'd tried Guinness yet and she should get her ass back to help with the caseload.

It was one in the morning in Dublin, which meant four in the afternoon at home. Bernadette dialed Chris's cell. He picked up on the first ring.

"Hey, sweetie, so glad you called. You okay?" Chris asked.

"Ah, yeah, just kind of tired. How about you?"

"I'm great. I miss you. How's the search going?"

Bernadette filled Chris in on the meeting with Aunt Aideen and the Gypsy woman, Francine. She omitted the near-death experience on the cliffs.

"Any sign of Cahal yet?"

"We've run into some friends of his, but they weren't very helpful," Bernadette said, taking a sip of her scotch.

"Just be safe over there. You know I worry about you."

"Aw, you're so sweet. What have you been up to?"

"Remember, I'm the wedding guy, you left me in charge. I've talked to the lady at Emerald Lake Lodge, I have the menu planned, and picked the banquet room."

"Wow, you've been busy. So glad you could do all that."

Chris laughed. "It's easy when I'm making all the decisions. I just ask myself if you'd agree, I say yes, and it's done."

"My God, I love you," Bernadette said, breaking into laughter. She took another swig of scotch and smiled. "That's the first laugh I've had all day."

"Good, because you won't like the conversation I had with my mother."

Bernadette put her hand to her forehead. "Tell me."

"She called to tell me she wouldn't come to our wedding. That's it—she won't budge. She ranted and raved about what a lousy son I am, and I will not go into the words she used for you."

Bernadette took another sip of her scotch. "Don't worry, my sweet. I'll call her."

"You're kidding, right?"

"No, I know just what to say to her. Listen, I need to get some shut-eye. I'll call you later tomorrow. Okay?"

"Okay, love you madly. And don't take what my mother says seriously."

"No, problem. Goodnight," Bernadette said. She was going to put her phone away, then called her soon to be mother-in-law. She'd survived almost being shot and thrown off a cliff, Maroula couldn't be that bad.

Bernadette dialed the number of Maroula; it was 6 p.m. there. She answered after a few rings.

"Yassou, hello Maroula here."

"Maroula, it's Bernadette."

"Why you call? I say I no go to your wedding."

"That's fine. No problem. But I want to tell you something. My mother gave birth to five boys and one daughter, me. My grandmother had seven children, five boys and two girls. You know what that makes me if Chris and I have babies—a baby boy factory. That's the odds—I did not make that up. And, if I have a child, I will never let you see him and I will never name him after your husband, which is the Greek tradition if you do not attend our wedding. Do I make myself clear?"

There was a long pause on the other end of the phone. Bernadette poured herself more scotch and waited.

"You would do this? You would have a baby?"

"I'm not sure how this translates in Greek, but never say never. Yes, there's a good chance we might have a child. And, as my mother and grandmother had mostly boys, chances are it's going to be a boy."

"You would not let me see him?"

"You coming to the wedding?"

Bernadette let the words sink in as she sipped her scotch. She looked at her watch as the second hand swept around the face. She felt at that moment like she was sweating a suspect. The next person to speak would lose.

"I will come to the wedding," Maroula said in a quiet voice.

"That's wonderful news. I look forward to seeing you. How about if I call you Midera? Is that okay?" Bernadette said, using the Greek word for mother.

"Yes, thank you. I will call Christos," she said.

Bernadette pushed the end button on her phone. She finished her scotch and went to the bathroom to wash her face and change. For this trip, she'd chosen a pair of flannel pajamas. The chill in the room told her she'd made an excellent choice.

By the time she got into bed, there was a text from Chris. It said, *Good news, my mom is coming to our wedding. Did you really promise her a grandson?*

She stared at the text. Damn, what the hell? How did her future mother-in-law get that conversation as a promise? She smiled. That old woman was still pretty sharp, even when cornered she could come up with a win.

As Bernadette turned off her light she muttered, "Well played, Midera, well played."

47

Bernadette awoke to the sound of her cell phone alarm at 7 a.m. She crawled out of bed, looked at the rain-filled sky, and went into the bathroom. On the way there, she noticed the empty bottle of scotch on the bureau.

Now she knew why her head felt not only jet lagged but slightly buzzed by a hangover. What the hell had she been doing? Twelve ounces of scotch in a long evening might be okay, doable, but still a lot. In the one hour she'd been back in her room and on the phone, she'd binged. And damn it hurt.

She hit the shower. It felt almost warm, as in not entirely cold. She did the thing called washing the most important parts and got out as fast as she could. Wrapped in a towel, she scrolled the texts again on her phone.

See found the text from Chris asking if she'd told his mother they'd agreed to have a child. They had discussed that issue at length, deciding that two people in law enforcement should not have a child, too much stress, and the chance of leaving the kid with only one parent.

But the dynamic had changed. Chris wanted to enter

forestry management, where the worst he could face would be an angry moose or bear. In most cases, they'd be preferable over a criminal with a weapon.

She changed into fresh clothes, took some mud off her boots, and threw on her wool sweater and jacket. Today, she'd prepare for the elements.

Taking the stairs down to the lobby of the little hotel, she found Sullivan waiting for her.

"You look like you've been asleep at a train station," Sullivan said. "Did you get any rest?"

Bernadette shook her head. "Did anyone tell you the Irish could be too honest?"

"I have just the thing, cures jetlag, hangovers and botched detective stakeouts," Sullivan said. "A little café that serves the best black pudding in the city is down the street. I parked my car beside it."

Bernadette winced only slightly. She marched in step with Sullivan in the brisk morning air. "I take it this pudding has some ingredients that make it black?"

"Blood," Sullivan answered in a matter-of-fact tone.

Bernadette raised one eyebrow. "I've eaten venison and seal meat raw. I'm sure some cooked blood won't hurt me."

They entered the busy café, made their orders at the counter and found seats near the window.

"I ran some queries last night after we parted ways," Sullivan said.

"What kind?" Bernadette asked, sipping her coffee.

"You'd said our recent dead suspects had to have met somewhere. I ran a search on all their files. None of them had served time in jail, but several of them lived at the same orphanage."

The breakfast arrived and Bernadette had to focus on

Sullivan's words as the pile of eggs, blood pudding sausage, and chips appeared.

"Where was it?"

"An orphanage. The Poor Sisters of Nazareth. It no longer looks after children; nowadays they take care of the elderly. Back then they took care of the neglected waifs until they turned eleven, then they shuffled the boys off to the Christian Brothers of Kircubbin, in County Down."

Bernadette took a test bite of black pudding, decided it tasted delicious, and cut off another bite. She chewed for a second and swallowed. "Wasn't there a story of child abuse in one of those places?"

Sullivan put his hands on the table. "All of them, I'm afraid. They accused both the sisters and the brothers of sexual abuse and cruelty."

"Would the attacks on the priests in Canada had anything to do with that?" Bernadette asked.

"Your priests in Canada came from a different order. They had nothing to do with children. How do we explain the murders of the two old IRA men?"

Bernadette looked at the window at the Saturday morning traffic. People walked down the road, heads down, heedless of the light rain. It didn't seem to bother them; just a regular occurrence of everyday rain.

"What about Cahal? Did he come through the orphanage?" Bernadette asked.

"No, but the other four did. That's the only pattern I can see."

"We need to get their records. See where they ended up working, where they lived," Bernadette said.

"That's the interesting part; they all worked for Odin DNA that has an address near the wharf. We can drop in there after breakfast."

"Sounds good. What have you done with Francine Dooley?"

"She's in custody awaiting a hearing on harboring a fugitive. Her bail hearing is on Monday."

"Did anyone question her on the whereabouts of Cahal?"

Sullivan chuckled. "Yes, a female Garda officer did. She got an earful and some distinct instructions on where to go and how to get there."

"That sounds like her," Bernadette said as she pushed a fork full of fries through the egg yolk. She found Irish breakfast the best cure for hangovers and jet lag.

They finished their breakfast and drove to the address of Odin DNA at the wharf. The building had an impressive sign with graphics of test tubes and people looking onto a landscape of an idyllic Irish countryside. The building showed no signs of activity.

Sullivan and Bernadette walked up to the building. The parking lot was empty.

"it's a Saturday, perhaps they don't work weekends," Bernadette said.

Sullivan rattled the doors and looked inside. "They haven't used this place for some time."

"Maybe it's just a front?"

"Perhaps," Sullivan said, finding a small brick to smash in a window.

"Really, detective, breaking and entering," Bernadette said with false admonishment.

"I'll call it in later, after we're gone. I'll inform the Garda we've seen a suspicious break and enter."

They walked into the deserted building. A few birds flew in the rafters. A row of long tables stood empty in the center of the room with overhead fluorescent lights. An office at one end had desks and chairs with papers scattered on the floor.

Bernadette took a paper off a desk. "There are DNA records here. Someone named Constance Finery, and how about that she's eighty percent Irish and twenty percent Norwegian."

Sullivan picked up a few more. "Here are the same results from these three, all have the same percentage. That is strange." He turned to Bernadette. "The odds of that happening with four people are infinitesimally high. Have you had your DNA done?"

"Mine's in the mail."

"Unless these four people are siblings, Odin DNA is making things up," Sullivan said. He pulled out his phone and opened his Google app. "Yes, Odin DNA is owned by Odin Genetics."

Bernadette wandered around to the back area. "someone used this place recently. There's no accumulation of dust, the place is clean, I'd say it's been vacant for maybe a week or two tops."

"But why clear out now?" Sullivan asked. "The DNA business is booming. I had my own done after my wife's constant nagging. She wanted to know if Genghis Khan or Attila the Hun were in my family tree."

"What did you find?"

"Oh, Irish, mostly. But every country that could put a boat in the water invaded Ireland at one time. I have some Danish, a bit of German, and a little Welsh just to make it interesting."

They found little more to look at. They left the papers behind as they had no search warrant and got back into the car.

"Where to now?" Sullivan asked.

"You're asking me?"

"At the moment I don't have a clue, except to go back to the office and pore over countless files to search for the owners of Odin Genetics."

"How about a visit to my aunt Aideen in Kilmeague? There's a lot she has to answer for. I believe she knows where to find Cahal. That might lead us to the den of this crazy cult."

"Wonderful idea. There's a good pub in Kildare that serves a decent pint and a pleasant lunch."

Bernadette sat back in her seat and smiled. "I'm glad my idea meets with your approval."

The trip took forty-five minutes in Saturday traffic. They pulled up to Aideen Callahan's house. Bernadette went to the door, rapping on the door knocker. There was no answer.

She rapped again and waited, still nothing. Pushing the handle, the door opened. She called to Aideen. No answer.

"I'm going in," Bernadette said.

Sullivan walked in behind. "This place is cold. There's no fire in the hearth. Perhaps she'd gone on a trip?"

Bernadette walked into the bedroom. "There's not a stitch of clothing in the closet. There's not even a bed in here." She walked out of the room and back into the small reception.

"Did you see a there a bed in there before?"

"She had the door closed. Come to think of it, I only sat in this room. She brought out tea and biscuits," Bernadette said. She walked into the small kitchen off of the main reception. She opened drawers and then the little refrigerator.

"There's nothing in here. No one lives here. They never did. This was a setup," Bernadette said.

"There's one way to know for sure." Sullivan said.

"Check the local police station?"

"No, the local vicar. In a village this small, they know everyone."

"Let's go."

The church was a few blocks down the road. They found the local priest in his rectory. His name was Father Shannon, he was an older gentleman, with silver gray hair and slight goatee and wire rim spectacles that gave him a scholarly appearance.

"Sorry to bother you, Father, we're looking for Aideen Callahan," Bernadette said.

"You've come from America, have you?"

"Ah, no Canada," Bernadette replied.

"Isn't the same thing?" Shannon said with a wink.

"Well, Father, that would be like us saying the Irish and the English are the same, because you live close by and both speak English."

"Ha, good point. I like your spunk. You've come to visit your aunt's grave, have you?" Shannon asked.

"Her grave? But I just saw her a few days ago."

"You must be mistaken, my dear child. She passed away over thirty years, and somewhat tragic it was," Shannon said.

"How tragic?"

"No one really knows the complete story, a lot of conjecture over the years, but it's said she was in love with a man name of John Dooley, a Tinker from the camp down the way."

"Was he related to Francine Dooley?"

"Her brother, I think. Now the story goes that John Dooley and Aideen were deeply in love, but both families were totally against the union. They found the poor souls dead in a pond some days later. The police investigated, said they'd gone swimming and couldn't get back to shore. So very sad. Some people said it was suicide, but I wouldn't let that besmirch their names. But so sad it was."

"May I ask who identified the bodies?" Bernadette asked.

"Now, let me think, that was long ago, but I'm certain the brother, Cahal Callahan, identified Aideen, and Francine Dooley identified the body of her brother," Father Shannon said.

"May I see her grave?"

"Yes, follow me, it's right this way."

They walked out back into the graveyard. They passed by graves from over one hundred years, some so old the lettering had worn away from the elements. All that remained were stones with indents of letters and a body beneath it.

"There we are, your aunt Aideen Callahan. A lovely lass, always full of fun. And a splendid cook. A sad loss at an early age," The priest said.

Bernadette looked down at the stone—the stone next to it caught her eye, "That says John Dooley."

"Aye, it does. Cahal wanted them buried together, and the sister Francine agreed. At least here they are together in the everlasting peace," Father Shannon said with his hands clasped together.

"I need to see the medical examiner's report on these two deaths," Bernadette said, turning to Sullivan. "How soon can we see them?"

"I can bring up the files back at Garda headquarters."

"Good, let's get back there. I want to see what John Dooley looked like."

"Why?"

"I have a hunch that we might have the wrong man on the tombstone," Bernadette said.

"You suspect that's Cahal Callahan buried there?"

"I'm not sure, but it wouldn't surprise me," Bernadette said

48

"THEY'VE PLAYED ME," Bernadette said as they drove back to Dublin. "Cahal told me the story of me being born to a Gypsy woman, then he gave me the name of Aideen in Kilmeague. He knew if I chased him to Ireland, I'd search for her. The woman posing as Aideen gave me the name of Francine, so I'd go to meet her. He'd set a perfect trap. The Canadian matches on Francine's table were a clue he left to get me to return. I took the bait—he was waiting for me."

"We have a clever adversary on our hands," Sullivan said. "He's one step ahead of us."

"Well, we're about to catch up," Bernadette said. She sat in silence for most of the ride into Dublin, wondering where the hell her instincts on Cahal had gone. She'd had misgivings about him from the moment she met him. The whole relative thing had reared its head, and she'd let her guard down. Damn, she felt stupid.

Now, if the priest's version of events were true, then she wasn't even a Callahan, she was a Dooley. She let that information drop into the back of her mind to help her focus.

They entered the Garda headquarters, Sullivan signed

her in, and they went to his desk and pulled up the medical examiner's website. Sullivan entered the name of John Dooley and the date of death.

"There's no picture in the file," Sullivan said.

"Is there one of Aideen Callahan?" Bernadette asked.

"Yes, here it is," Sullivan said as he pulled it up.

Bernadette stared over Sullivan's shoulder at the corpse of her long dead Aunt Aideen. Even in death, with eyes closed, she saw the resemblance of her father.

"How could one picture be there and not the other?" Bernadette asked.

Sullivan sat back in his chair. "No idea. Let me search John Dooley with his date of birth. I might find a picture of him." He ran the search. It came up empty.

"How about that? What are the chances of two men being ghosts like that? No previous pictures on file," Sullivan said. "And the most troubling is, the coroner's photos do not exist."

"A wonderful coincidence if you wanted to murder someone and take their identity," Bernadette said.

"Do you think Francine Dooley will tell us about the death of her brother?" Sullivan asked.

"We'll ask. I doubt if we'll get anything." Bernadette said.

They made their way to the prisoner's cells for those recently brought in and awaiting trial. It took over a half hour to get Francine out of her cell. She looked a mess when they brought her in. A female guard placed her in an interview room. Sullivan and Bernadette came in and sat in front of her.

"We found about Aideen Callahan and John Dooley," Sullivan said.

Francine laughed. "What did you find then?" She pulled a cigarette from a pack, lit it and sucked the smoke deep into her lungs. When she exhaled, she blew smoke towards their faces.

"It's Cahal Callahan in that grave, not John Dooley," Bernadette said. She was fishing, hoping she'd get a reaction from Francine.

"Did you pull him up? Did you do one of those fancy DNA things on the bones? Is that what you did?" She looked at both of them. "Of course you haven't, you're here to fish. Put me old bones in the lock up forever with your copper lies. Well, you'll get nothing from me, I'm no tout." Francine faced them both down. Her expression gave nothing away but the hatred she felt for them.

Sullivan turned to Bernadette. "For your information, a tout is someone in Ireland who tells on the others."

"Thanks, I guessed as much. So, Francine, you're saying you know the truth but you're not telling the truth, is that it?"

"You're twisting my words, you are. Coppers all do that. Twist an honest person's words."

"But you're not honest, are you Francine. You're holding onto something? You aided Cahal as a fugitive. You'll go down for that, you'll do time for that," Sullivan said.

"I told my story. I said he came by to visit; I'd no idea he was an escaped fugitive. My solicitor says I'll get out in a jiff. You won't have these old bones in your lock up."

Sullivan turned to Bernadette. "We might as well go. She will not tell us much."

Bernadette looked at Francine, her eyes stared back with hatred, her jaw set in a hard line. They had no leverage on her. They'd need the DNA evidence from the grave of John Dooley, and still, would it be enough?

They walked out of the interview room with Francine

yelling curses at them. They could hear her as they got into the elevator to go back upstairs.

They got coffees and sat at Sullivan's desk to look over some more files in search of Cahal until they were both exhausted.

Sullivan finally shook his head. "I'll have them dig up the graves once we get a court order."

Bernadette nodded and then stopped in her tracks. "There's also a grave marker I noticed at the camp when we were being marched to meet Cahal. Could we get a warrant to open it up?"

Sullivan looked at her. "You saw a grave there?"

"Yes, it was in a clearing. I just remembered it now. It looked well-tended. If they don't have the authority to bury the dead on their land. That could justify a warrant to check it out."

"It might have been an animal's grave. People do that now, you see. My brother's kids have a little pet cemetery in his back garden," Sullivan said.

"How about if we err on the side of a crazed female detective from Canada and find out what happens.".

"Okay, fine, I'll make an enquiry for a warrant. It's going to depend on the manpower we have. Cahal and his people have the entire island tied up with the troubles they've been causing."

Bernadette rubbed her forehead. "You're right. This proves the man called Cahal is more complex than we realized." She took out her phone and scrolled down her numbers.

"Before I left Canada, I received a phone number of a nun here in Ireland who might help us," Bernadette said as she dialed the number.

The number rang several times before an old voice that

was barely audible answered the phone. "Hello. Who's calling?"

"Bernadette Callahan. I'm calling for Sister Mary-Margaret. Do I have the right number?"

"Hold the line please," the voice said. There was the sound of a door closing. "Yes, you have the right number." The voice changed, it sounded younger. "You must meet me tomorrow morning after mass. I'm in the Sisters of Charity Nursing Home under the name of Grace Gordon. Make sure you're not followed when you come here."

The call ended.

Bernadette stared at the phone. "I do not understand what that was about, but I have an appointment with a nun in a nursing home tomorrow morning. What times is mass in this city on Sunday?"

Sullivan arched an eyebrow. "My parish is from nine to ten, and others may be different. I'd say you're safe after half ten. Will she have some useful information?"

"I'm not sure. She's in a nursing home using an alias and her first phone voice was a fake. She's undercover, but I have no idea why."

"Perhaps someone in the home is stealing all the pudding? I'm sorry, a poor joke. We've been at this for hours, we've both missed lunch, and it's now past five," Sullivan said.

"I'm buying," Bernadette said.

THEY HEADED out of the building to a local pub that Sullivan liked. The pub was full of regulars enjoying a drink before dinner. They found a small booth in the back and placed orders. Sullivan ordered his usual Guinness; Bernadette ordered a Perrier and lime. Her little binge last night needed some space.

"The beef pot pie is braised in Guinness, a delightful dish," Sullivan said.

Bernadette smiled. "Don't they braise everything in Guinness in Ireland..."

Then the earth shook. A blinding light followed by a cloud of dust and debris descended over them. For a few seconds, Bernadette couldn't make out anything in the room.

"A bomb hit us—are you alright?" Sullivan asked.

Bernadette's ears were ringing. The explosion had concussed her entire body. Slowly the ringing ceased, and she got her bearings.

She stood up. The solid wooden booth had saved them. There were people everywhere, wandering around the pub, with their cloths in tatters.

Sullivan took her hand; they moved to the front of the pub and directed people out of the place through the back. The fire trucks and medics arrived.

Detective Denis Bishop met them as they were standing in the alley outside with the other patrons. People in in blankets stood shivering in the cold.

"You're a lucky bastard, Sullivan," Bishop said.

"How many causalities?" Sullivan asked.

"They placed the bomb on the outside of the building. It was more of a sound wave explosion. Many people might have some hearing loss and glass fragment injuries, but no fatalities. You two seem better than most," Bishop said.

"We were in a back booth. Saved us from everything but the concussion wave," Sullivan said. "Anyone call in to claim his or her handiwork?"

"Someone called a half hour ago, said Dublin was going

to be shook up tonight. Three more of these have hit pubs in the past ten minutes. The same type, mostly flash bangs, made to scare more than injure."

"Who would do this?" Bernadette asked.

"We're not sure. If it was the real IRA, they make sure they call in before, then pull the trigger. This seems set to scare," Sullivan said.

It took several hours before they could leave the pub. They made sure the other patrons were okay before they left the scene. Sullivan returned to the station to file his report. Then they searched for another pub.

Most of downtown Dublin emptied. The police cordoned off most every street into the core. They had to go back to Bernadette's brewery district, where things were quiet if not downright subdued.

This time, Bernadette ordered a glass of Jameson's whiskey. Her ears still had a ringing in them. She hoped it would subside with the addition of alcohol.

Sullivan ordered a Guinness. Bishop joined them with a Kilkenny. They sipped their drinks for a second and let the alcohol drown the weariness they felt.

"This really is shite," Bishop said. "I thought all of this was behind us."

"Perhaps it really is in the Irish DNA to always be in the troubles," Sullivan said. "Isn't some member of parliament trying to push a bill to take out the aggressive strain in a newborns embryo?"

"It's called genetic editing. The church is having a fit with it. But a politician named Brendon Shannon is having a vote this coming Tuesday. He claims the bill will edit the aggressive gene from future Irish," Bishop said. He sipped his pint. "Imagine that, taking the aggression out of the

Irish. All us coppers would be out of a job in twenty years' time."

"We couldn't do it in Canada," Bernadette said.

"And why exactly is that now?" Bishop asked.

"It would put an end to our hockey games," Bernadette said.

Sullivan raised his glass. "Cheers to that. A bit of healthy aggression is good, does a body good to get things cleared up I say, but then again when it goes over the top...."

"—We get called in," Bishop said, finishing Sullivan's sentence.

They drained their glasses, ordered some food, and left the place as it was closing. Bernadette checked her cell phone as she climbed up the three flights of stairs. She'd received three texts from Chris; he'd heard about the bombing in Dublin and he wanted to know if she was okay. She'd been so busy making sure everyone else was okay, then trying to come down from the trauma of the blast, she'd forgot to contact him.

She texted him back to tell him she was fine. It had been a long day; she was going to get some sleep. She entered her cold room, bolted the door shut and turned on the shower. Stripping off her clothes, she got in and soaped herself up to get rid of the dust and smell of the cordite. She had to wash, rinse, and repeat until she no longer reeked of a bomb blast.

She dressed in her flannel pajamas and climbed under the cold covers. As she dozed off to sleep, the ringing was still in her ears.

49

THE RINGING BERNADETTE woke up to wasn't in her ears. Thankfully, it was the sound of church bells. She stared at her watch; it was half-past eight in the morning. She'd overslept but seemed refreshed. The jet lag was ebbing out of her body, and now she was in the right time zone.

A few clouds scudded about in the sky, the sun tried to shine, and rain had stopped. Checking her phone, she scrolled the news feed from last night. They had bombed seven pubs in the night, and some mailboxes and two banks. The targets were in Belfast and Dublin. It looked like someone was trying to create panic, but why?

The cities were in lockdown. Checkpoints were everywhere, and many pubs and businesses would remain closed. Bernadette checked the address of the nursing home and then plotted it on her phone map. The home was four kilometers from the hotel. She'd walk for the exercise and the chance to see some of Dublin.

Sullivan told her last night that he'd be going into the office this morning to look at reports, so she was on her own to speak with the nun who had acted strangely on the phone.

After getting dressed, she made her way downstairs to the lobby. The young man at reception told her where to find breakfast on her journey. He directed her to a little hole-in-the wall café with only a few people in it.

Avoiding the traditional Irish breakfast, as her stomach was still processing the blood sausage from the previous day, she chose an Irish scone with jam and tea. She decided on tea, as scones and coffee seemed wrong.

The scones were fresh and fluffy with a flakey layer, crunchy outside and a soft center. Her senses went on a bit of a rampage as she swallowed the first bites. The scones were like traditional bannock bread that native's baked in Canada, but this was more refined.

She finished her breakfast quickly. She would have loved to linger over tea and a second scone, but she made her way out the door and down the street. The mysterious nun's secrecy was calling to her.

The police had checkpoints at major intersections. Passing through them wasn't too hard. She gave her reason for travel and where she was staying. At one checkpoint, the Garda didn't understand why she was heading out of the common tourist area. She told them to call Detective Sullivan at Garda Headquarters, and they let her pass.

The Sisters of Charity Nursing Home looked run down. The outside was brick with cracks. The paint was peeling off the windows, and the sidewalk leading up to it had pavers missing.

Bernadette made her way to the reception desk to find Grace Gordon. They gave her a room number. No one escorted her or asked about her visit. The room was on the second floor. There was an ancient elevator with elderly residents in walkers and wheelchairs in front of. Bernadette couldn't be sure if they were waiting to get on or merely waiting to see who came out of it.

Grace Gordon's room had a number and her name on it, and Bernadette rapped the door as hard as she could to get the attention of Grace, but not too loud in case some residents were sleeping.

"Come in," a voice said.

Bernadette opened the door and peered in. "Grace?"

"Come in, come in. Close the door behind you."

Bernadette walked inside the low-lit room. A figure in a wheelchair sat in the center of the room.

"Bernadette Callahan?"

"Yes, Sister, it's me."

"Good, I'm Sister Mary Margaret. Now I can stop this charade," she said, getting out of the wheelchair and throwing off a blanket.

The woman appeared in her sixties from her gray hair and wrinkles on her face, but as she moved and turned on a lamp, Bernadette could see she was much younger, perhaps in her forties. She had done some wonders with makeup.

"Can you tell me what's this is about, Sister?" Bernadette asked.

The nun directed Bernadette to a chair and sat beside her on the single bed. "I've been in Dublin for eight months investigating the cult of the Tuatha De' Danann. I've found everything about them except who the leader is. Ronan Bronaugh funds the organization and the lot of them have some kind of brainwashing."

"What kind of brainwashing?"

"They believe they are the direct descendants of both Irish and Norwegian royalty."

"Yes, that is odd, but what are they involved in?"

"We have several ideas, but we've not found out what they're trying to accomplish. They are up to something sinister as we've been seeing many codes on Facebook and Twitter feeds, but there's no pattern yet other than all the bombings."

"Is this group behind it?"

"Almost sure of it. But we've no smoking gun, as you say in North America. We surmise this is to do with the genetics editing bill. Parliament will vote on it this week," Sister Mary Margaret said.

"What's the connection? Why would it matter to the group?"

"One of our members gained access to Odin Genetics. He found out the genetics edit for aggression was a fake, they were putting a code to make people open to subliminal commands."

"You can do that in an embryo?"

"Our scientist in the Vatican say it's possible."

"Did your member bring back proof?"

"They murdered him. His body dumped over a cliff. We only discovered him a week ago washed up on the shores of the western coast."

"Why haven't you gone to the authorities on this? If you have even some allegations, the government could start an enquiry," Bernadette said.

"I did. I visited the office of Public Security. I gave them our concerns, but it fell on deaf ears. They even had a member of parliament there."

"Who was that?"

"Brendon Shannon."

"Isn't he the one spearheading the genetics editing bill?"

Sister Mary Margaret stared down at her hands. "I didn't know that at the time. I should have checked. But yes, he is."

"And you got no answer from them? From the people you met?" Bernadette asked.

"Oh, we got an answer all right—they ambushed us. They badly injured two of the sisters with me in the attack. I sent them to Paris to recover. The other Guardians brought me here under an assumed name so I could wait for you."

"Wait for me? What do I have to do with this?"

Sister Mary Margaret held her gaze. "There're some things we can foresee."

"You can foresee the future?"

The sister shook her head. "Oh not at all, but from the moment we heard about the incidents in Canada and Father Joe told us it involved you, he gave a high probability that you would follow Cahal Callahan here."

"And you expected me to follow?"

"We looked at your profile. You're of mixed race, from an Irish father and a Cree Native mother, the youngest of six children, which makes you a total over achiever. The last part we factored in because of your alcoholic father and being a woman in the RCMP in Canada, which is a militaristic style police force."

"No idea where you get your ideas from," Bernadette said.

"I studied psychology with MI-5 before I entered the monastery and became a Guardian. I trained in profiling, primarily of criminals. But it became useful for other fields, as in identifying recruits for our force," Sister Mary Margaret said, staring hard at Bernadette.

Bernadette put up her hand. "I'm a lifer with that militaristic force you call the Royal Canadian Mounted Police, and I like sex way too much to give it up to be a nun."

Sister Mary chuckled. "Sorry, it was worth a try, so let's

get down to business. Do you want me to tell you how to find these people?"

"You found out where they are?"

"Yes. Before they murdered our guardian, he sent us an encrypted message of the password into their computers and their location We only broke the encryption code last night," Sister Mary Margaret said. "Now, we have the location of where they are doing the secret genetics testing. If you can get in there and retrieve the files with the password, you could expose them."

"You mean going in totally illegally with no search warrant?" Bernadette said.

"That might be the case, yes."

"Everything I find inside is of no value if I do it that way."

"But you're working with the Garda. You have detectives with you."

"I love your angle, but I doubt if any Irish judge would go for it. Unless...."

"Unless what?"

"It's better I leave that unsaid. Often the best lies are the ones left with the fewest to tell the tale," Bernadette said.

"Now, where is this place and who can I expect to find there?"

Sister Mary pulled an iPad from under her bed and brought up a map. "This is Leamaneh Castle in the west of Ireland, just twenty-five kilometers from the Cliffs of Moher. It sits on private land, and the owner is a subsidiary of Odin Genetics. They've surrounded it with an electrified fence to keep people out."

"Great, anything else to be aware of?"

"Are you afraid of ghosts?"

"Only the ones on television. Who's haunting the place?"

"A vicious old ghost named Red Mary, but no one's died yet. Since no one has entered the place, I guess that's hard to say if it's a certainty."

"Ah, you're making this sound like fun. Where's the lab?"

"Underneath the main hall. There is a secret door in the back that will take you down. They've been able to work there for years by tunneling from the buildings in the back. There is a self-contained living quarters down there for fifteen to twenty people."

"And there's a friendly ghost to go with the place?"

Sister Mary leaned forward and said in a low voice, "Not so friendly. There are many haunted Irish Castles, but none this famous. Both the castle and Red Mary, the most famous of its residents, are in Irish folklore because of a bloody past. This was a stronghold of the O'Brien clan and passed to Mary MacMahnon. She was called Maire Rua or Red Mary. They named her for both her red hair and extreme temper. They hung servants who displeased her out of the castle windows, men by their necks and women by their hair. If castle maids were disobedient to her, she punished them by cutting off their breasts. Her ghost still haunts the castle according to the locals."

Bernadette felt her stomach churn and a shadow pass over her mother's grave, but she steeled herself, swallowed hard and tried not to flinch. Deep inside, she disliked ghosts. Her mother had talked about them, so had her grandmother. Now, here she was in Ireland, about to visit one.

"Alright then, thanks for the lay of the land," Bernadette said. "I should go if I'm to get there in daylight."

"You must go in the night," Sister Mary said.

Bernadette rolled her eyes. "Is that when the ghost is asleep?"

"No, they have cameras all around the place. You're better off during the night. Dress in black, approach from the west side, not the road. They don't have cameras on that side. There is a fence there, but it's usually turned off to allow their own people through. Go slow and do it at midnight. They'll never expect that."

"And what of Red Mary?"

Sister Mary shrugged. "I expect she never sleeps."

"That's just lovely," Bernadette said with a smile. "I best be on my way."

"Yes, you must. Now, go with my blessing, not that you'll need it. You're a headstrong woman who sees her own way through danger. You'll be fine."

"Another of your profiles, is it?"

"No, my intuition," Sister Mary Margaret said. She handed Bernadette a piece of paper with the password and leaned forward with a powerful hug.

Bernadette felt the strength of the woman. There was no telling how old she was; she'd guessed forty, but a tough forty.

She walked out of the nursing home into the late morning sun and texted to Sullivan that she had a lead. Twenty minutes later, his car pulled up, and she jumped into the passenger's side.

"What have you got?" Sullivan asked as she got in.

"I have our next adventure. Castles, ghosts, and the answers to our case. I expect you'll need a Guinness," Bernadette said.

Sullivan looked at his watch; it had just gone past eleven. "You're right. It's been a brutal morning. A good pint would be excellent right now. I have just the place."

50

Sullivan found them a pub on the outskirts of Dublin in a small village. The Guinness was the temperature that Sullivan preferred, and Bernadette found a lager that suited her. They sat with their pints; Sullivan took his first good pull of his Guinness and looked expectantly at Bernadette.

"You've kept me in the dark all the way here, so spill."

"I've discovered the secret lab of Odin Genetics," Bernadette said..

"And that helps us how?"

"I was told there's a secret file that claims what they are really up to. If we get the file, we could expose the group." Bernadette leaned forward. "Sister Mary-Margaret tried to take her concerns to Brendon Shannon in your parliament and someone attacked on her return home."

Sullivan drained half his pint and looked at Bernadette. "I trust no politicians, and Brendon Shannon, I trust the least of all. But how are we to get into this place? I doubt I'll get a search warrant for a hidden place in a haunted castle. I'd be thrown out of the judge's office in an instant."

"I have an idea," Bernadette said as she leaned forward.

"I go alone in my car. I head out so I'm there at midnight. I creep in, and when I find the secret door and get inside, I call you on my cellphone to say I'm lost and need your help."

"And me and a few Garda are in the area, searching for what now?"

"Ah, you've had a sighting of the escaped convict, Cahal Callahan," Bernadette said with a smile.

"Splendid. And how did I get that information?"

"I'd call it in as an anonymous caller," Bernadette said. "There must be a pay phone in a village somewhere."

"You'll find a leprechaun long before you'll find a payphone in rural Ireland, my dear girl. This part of the country has advanced with the times," Sullivan said. "I have a throwaway phone, so your caller ID won't show on the Garda incoming line. I'll make sure the notification comes to me. I'll book myself out to a search of bombing suspects in the western townships and I'll be there when the call comes in," Sullivan said, handing Bernadette a new phone.

"Do we have a plan?" Bernadette asked.

"It's better than mine, which is nothing. I've been looking at reports all morning. We've looked at every piece of CCTV footage we had from yesterday. The bombers were good. They worked like a team of football players by using others to walk in front of them to hide them and dropped the packet off. Once they were clear, they set the bomb off. I've seen nothing like it."

"And there were no causalities?" Bernadette asked.

"Nothing more than cuts from broken glass. The bombs weren't packed with fragments, only made to give the maximum amount of noise with a sound wave that broke glass. It's like they are trying to scare more than injure."

Bernadette took a sip of her pint and looked away for a

second. "This may be a crazy analogy, but this seems like an old-fashioned Buffalo Jump scenario."

"A what?"

"You must bear with me on this," Bernadette said. "On the prairies in western Canada, there's this cliff that the native tribes of Canada used to chase buffalo off of for several thousand years. They lit fires on a path to channel the herd, and made loud noises as they chased them. The buffalo had only one way to go—over a cliff to their death."

"You're comparing terrorist bombers to Indians chasing buffalo?"

Bernadette nodded her head. "Sometimes, old tactics are new again. Someone is trying to form public opinion. Have you had any calls from anyone asking for anything?"

"Someone calling themselves The Real IRA has called and said they are to blame."

"Did they make any demands?"

"Nothing, no demands, but there're rumors of two bloody great bombs."

"Well then, we best get to work," Bernadette said. "I've got to find myself some black clothes for tonight's mission."

"I know just the place; I'll drop you off there," Sullivan said.

"Great, let's make tracks." Bernadette said.

"But not towards the cliffs like buffalo," Sullivan said with a grin.

51

SULLIVAN DROPPED Bernadette off at a shop that sold hunting and camping gear. She found the black clothes that included a woolen cap and a rain jacket. She felt like she was embarking on a Navy SEAL mission. With that in mind she found an all-black tactical hunting knife with a black sheath, and added one more knife, a Smith and Wesson boot knife. A small black backpack completed her mission.

If I can't have a gun, I'll carry a double team of knives, she said to herself as she headed to the cash register to pay for everything.

She walked back to her hotel, picking up a sandwich to put in her backpack. One block away, with the hotel in sight, she had the sense she was being followed by someone on the other side of the street. She slowed her steps and looked in a store window.

A young lady stopped in their tracks. She turned around, heading back down the street with her head down.

Bernadette crossed the street and headed after her. The girl hurried down the street, looking behind her every few steps. As the girl got close to a corner, she looked ready to run. Bernadette quickened her pace.

The girl broke into a full run at the corner. Bernadette put on speed. She'd excelled in track and field as a child. If she kept her quarry in sight, she could run all day. Few subjects she chased could match her stamina. Even with the backpack, she had an easy pace and was gaining on her.

The young lady looked behind her with terror in her eyes. She picked up speed, her steps went out of sync. She fell.

Bernadette ran up beside her and extended her hand. "You need a hand up?"

"You will not kill me?" She was slight and tall with sandy blonde hair and bright blue eyes. She wore jeans, boots and a woolen jacket. She had the looks of a fashion model if she'd had a chance.

"Nope, hadn't planned on it," Bernadette said. "What's your name and why are you following me."

"My name's Claire McCann, and I wasn't following you."

"Why did you run from me?"

Claire's shoulders dropped. "Okay, I was following you. But I mean you no harm."

Bernadette looked her up and down. "Doesn't seem much chance of that. What do you want?"

"My boyfriend, his name is Burnell Quinn. He's one of them."

"One of who?"

"The silly group that calls themselves the People of the Goddess," Claire said.

"The what now?"

Claire shook her head. "That's the translation of Tuatha De' Duanann in Gaelic."

"What's your boyfriend's involvement with them?"

Claire pulled out a vaping device and ignited it. She blew out a stream of vapor into the air and looked at Bernadette. "He thinks he's being trained to be an assassin. He's a total lad, he is. Figures he's grand stuff, but he's an idiot."

"And you love him and want to look out for him?"

Claire smiled. "Yeah, I'm stuck on the little shit. I tell him that all the time."

"How did you know who I was?" Bernadette asked.

Claire's eyes dropped. "Burnell had a picture of you on his phone. The lot of them have it in for you. Cahal Callahan wants you dead. He put a price on your head. The first one to kill you gets some kind of special favor with that bloody masked man they call their leader."

"I'm so glad I'm considered a prize," Bernadette said.

"Sorry about that."

Bernadette shrugged. "How can I can help you?"

"I've gathered you're good in a fight. They're right pissed that you killed off Sean and Jamie that were after you."

"They took themselves out. How do you about all of this? You could be an accomplice to their crimes with your knowledge. Did you realize that?"

Claire shook her head. "I work in a pub they drink at. They come in there and gab about their exploits."

"Why haven't you gone to the police with all your knowledge?"

"I assumed it was all talk until I learned about the bombing on the telly. They'd said they were going to do something like that."

"So, now you recognize they're serious?"

"They are that. They call themselves the deadly ancestors. My Burnell believes he's the reincarnation of an ancient Irish warrior. The more people he kills, the greater his abilities will become. I thought this was just some shite like on a video game. I noticed he had a photo of you—I took his phone when he wasn't looking and sent your picture to my phone, hoping I might find you."

"You wanted to warn me they are out to kill me, is that it?"

Claire stared down at her foot, "Well... yeah, and to talk some sense into my Burnell." She looked up. "He's a good lad, he is. He had a promising career in computer programming, would've got a job with Google here in Dublin if he hadn't gotten mixed with these arses." Claire reached up and took Bernadette's arm. "Please, will you talk some sense into him? Here's his photo. I'll send it to your phone if you like."

"Whoa, I'm not on any rescue mission for someone who thinks he's an ancient hero. I don't know where to look for him, anyway."

"Cahal said you were coming for him. He wants all of them to gather around him for protection. Burnell will be one of his protectors. If you can talk to him, tell him I love him, that might put some sense in his thick head. If he snaps out of his stupid dream, he could help you."

Bernadette chuckled. "Your proposal makes sense. Here's my number, send it to me."

Claire sent the number to Bernadette and put her hand on her shoulder. "Please don't judge them too harshly, they've been brainwashed by that man in the mask. He's a total shit."

"Thanks for the heads up. I'll do my best if I meet Burnell," Bernadette said.

Claire turned and walked down the street.

Bernadette walked the other way. That was one of the weirdest conversations she'd ever had.

. . .

BY NINE IN THE EVENING, she was ready. Dressed in her black trousers and top with the black boots she brought with her. She fitted her hunting knife into a web belt and fixed the small knife into her boot.

She found her way to her car and threw her rain cape and a small pack into the car. The flashlight she bought had an infrared setting for nighttime. There was no way to know what she was going to face. The Google map had the castle close to the road, with several houses in a field on the west side. She hoped they didn't have trip wire sensors positioned in the field.

She started the car and began her journey out of Dublin. Sullivan and two Garda units would follow her at a distance. This now felt more than a capture of Cahal. This was to shut these people down. Their bombs had stirred anger deep inside her. Perhaps it was her repressed Irish anger. It felt good to care for this side of her ancestry.

The rain started slowly and became a torrent mixed with wind. An hour into her journey a thick wet snow fell.

52

WET SNOW FILLED THE ROADWAY. The traffic slowed to a crawl and Bernadette kept going. She pulled into the passing lane and put the car in third gear. She drove slower, but not by much. Driving in snow was nothing new to her. She lived in it six to seven months of the year. To her, it was just another kind of snow. Wet snow was easy, don't speed up, don't hit the brakes too fast, and no sudden movements.

Just before midnight she entered the tiny village of Leamaneh North. The houses were in darkness. No streetlights shone, and only a solitary beam came from somewhere in the distance.

She drove past the Leamaneh Castle. It was a shell of ancient walls with no floors inside. All that remained were the stone walls with the wet snow falling in. The structure looked foreboding.

There was a small layby a kilometer away. She parked her car, took out the pack, and strapped it to her back. She checked her knifes and glanced at her phone; she had a signal.

There was a small fence to climb over. She tested it with

a stick to make sure it wasn't electrified. It was fine; she climbed over and made her way into the field. A few sheep regarded her with mild interest from a stand of trees, then lay back down again.

The ground was wet and covered in grass. She bent low and crept up on the castle from the back. As she approached the walls, they looked ominous. A small sliver of moonlight shone down, showing the walls blackened with age. Moss stuck to the brick with rivulets of water flowing down them.

She found her way into the once grand hall. It was two story's high opening to the sky. Snow and rain had fallen down into the center. Bernadette shuddered uncontrollably as she entered.

"Calm yourself, girl," she whispered to herself. "Just some old ghosts floating about. They don't have guns."

Making her way to the back of the hall, she found the secret door. She pulled on it—a light came from below it. She pulled it open further. Warm air and the sound of machinery came from below.

"I got it," Bernadette said as she took out her phone. She dialed the Garda emergency line.

"Hello, Garda emergency. I'm at Leamaneh Castle, I've just spotted Cahal Callahan inside the castle walls—no, I won't give my name. Oh, he just went to a door in the back. I have to go," Bernadette said.

Bernadette stood over the trapdoor. A ladder was attached to the side of the entrance. She wondered how long she could stand there waiting for Sullivan.

She looked at the phone. There was nothing—she expected to see a text from Sullivan. If they were going to be late, she'd back out of the castle and wait for them. Under no circumstances was she to go in alone.

She was about to close the hatch door and return to the

car when she sensed a presence. First a wave of cold air passed through her as if she'd just walked into a deep freeze, then she saw a form. Was that red hair?

The next thing she knew, her body was tumbling down the hatch. Her backpack caught the ladder a few times, which bounced her into the walls and slowed her descent. She landed with a thud at the bottom of the shaft.

DETECTIVE SULLIVAN WAS STUCK on the motorway. He'd followed Bernadette closely until she'd pulled into the right lane and passed several cars. A large transport had pulled into his lane, then blocked his way. A few minutes later, a car spun out of control in front of the transport, taking several cars with it.

"What a ball of shite this is," Sullivan said, turning to Bishop.

"Let me see how bad it is," Bishop said. He got out of the car and walked up the road. People were getting out of their cars. No one seemed hurt, but this would take time to get the emergency vehicles to clear the road.

Bishop walked back to the car. "Not much chance of getting around this until it gets cleared."

"Damn, I just got the call of the sighting of Cahal at the castle," Sullivan said.

"Do you think Bernadette will wait for us?" Bishop asked.

"She'd better," Sullivan said as he sent her a text. His text read, STAND DOWN UNTIL WE ARRIVE. WE'RE DELAYED.

. . .

BERNADETTE'S PHONE vibrated in her pocket. She hoped it was the text telling her they were on their way. She pulled herself up and did a quick inventory of her body. No blood, nothing seemed broken.

She looked up at the ladder. The bottom rung was well over three meters high. How was she going to get back up?

Voices came from down the hallway. They sounded like they were coming her way. She ducked inside an alcove and turned off her phone.

Two men came into the tunnel.

"I heard something," one man said. He was large with a sloping forehead, dark hair in a long braid, and a ring in his ear.

"Probably the ghost of Red Mary. She wants to get down here to keep warm," the other man said. He was smaller, with short-cropped hair and a beard.

"That ghost is shite. I've never seen it," the big one said.

"I've noticed it, I have. It's like a cold rush of air that blows over your very soul. I wouldn't mess with her," the other man said.

"Total shite," the big man said, turning around—he was looking right at Bernadette.

She came at him with a palm heel strike. Her palm struck his chin pushing his lower teeth into his upper teeth. She continued her momentum, throwing a fist into his solar plexus. He doubled over. She struck the back of his head with her elbow and he dropped to the ground.

Quickly turning to the smaller man, she advanced on him. He threw a right hook at her. She blocked it with her left arm, flicking her wrist—striking his nose. His head flipped back. She drove her elbow into his throat. He dropped to the ground gasping for air. An elbow blow on the back of his head put him in the same state as his buddy.

"Sleep well, you two. I hope you don't dream of ghosts," Bernadette said as she picked up her pack and ran down the hallway. The hum of machinery increased as she neared a set of double doors.

She entered a large room. The walls were white with a soft glow of lights. A long line of pods that looked like incubators for babies were on one wall. A series of window covered with frost made it impossible to see inside. BC-1 to BC-25 were marked on the front. Most of them had a red dot on them, only three had a green dot.

Bernadette walked by them to a small lab off to the right of the room. A bank of computers sat on several desks. She turned to a laptop, found it on, and entered the password from Sister Mary-Margaret. There it was, the Genetic Edit project. Could it be this easy?

She pulled out a USB stick, inserted it into the laptop and downloaded it. She had it. All she needed to do was get back up the ladder and find Sullivan.

She turned. Cahal was standing there with three men with guns.

"Well, my dear niece. How nice of you to drop in. I'll take that," Cahal said, grabbing the USB stick from Bernadette.

"Is there anything on that?" Bernadette asked.

Cahal laughed. "Of course not. We erased everything after that Guardian broke in here last week. You must think us daft to leave it there."

"You left this lab as a trap for me, didn't you?" Bernadette asked.

"Now you're getting it. You've become far too clever and come too close to our plans. I thought I had you taken care of, but you are a slippery thing. I must take care of you myself."

Bernadette turned toward the pods. "What about those

pods? Were you growing some more followers for your master?"

Cahal laughed. "You'll never know how close you came to meet some of your own kin, my dear. Now, we need to be on our way out of here."

"The Garda will be here any minute, Cahal, you've no way out. Give yourself up," Bernadette said.

Cahal smiled. "You've no idea, do you? This lab has many tunnels. We'll take you out of here and blow this one up. When your Garda detectives arrive, they'll set off an explosion. You've not only got yourself killed, but those who come to save you. This will be a wonderful report in tomorrow's papers." He turned to the men. "Burnell and Conner bind her up and do it good. She's good with her hands, so make sure she can't use them."

"I'll tie her hands so tight it'll make her head pop off if she struggles," Burnell said. He grabbed her, removing her knives and cellphone. He put them in his pockets.

When he finished with the ropes, she couldn't move her wrists and her hands were getting numb from loss of circulation.

Conner grabbed her shoulders, spun her around, and pushed her forward. They took her through a tunnel that led upwards. They walked for ten minutes, then climbed circular stairs. A door opened, and she walked into the room of a house. Bernadette looked out the window. The castle was seven hundred meters away.

"Get her into the boot of the car," Cahal said.

Burnell took her to the back of the car, opened the trunk, and threw her in. He tied her legs together at the ankles. Now, no blood was getting to her feet.

Cahal stood over the back of the car, looking down at her. "Have you ever read of the Cliffs of Moher?"

She shook her head. "No, can't say I have."

"A sheer drop to the bottom. So many deaths each year. Sadly, you're going to join them tonight," Cahal said as he slammed the trunk shut.

Bernadette felt the car start, go into reverse, bump over the field then onto the road. Where was Sullivan, and would he enter the lab? She had no way to warn him. She'd walked into a trap and brought others with her.

SULLIVAN AND BISHOP stood on the roadway watching as emergency vehicles and tow trucks dealt with the mess.

"I don't think we'll get through this," Bishop said.

Sullivan looked at this phone. "We must. She's on the move."

"Who is?" Bishop asked.

"Bernadette is. I put a tracking device in her phone. She's headed for the Cliffs of Moher."

"But she was to wait for us," Bishop protested.

"Not if someone has her captive. She has answered none of my texts. I assume the worst," Sullivan said.

"What do we do?"

"Improvise," Sullivan said. He ran forward to the end of the wrecked cars. A large transport truck was idling by the side of the road.

"Hey, mate, is your vehicle operable?" Sullivan asked.

"Aye, it bloody is. I've just been sitting here on me arse filling out accident reports with you lot."

"We need it for police business," Sullivan said.

"Can you drive a rig like this?"

"Ah... no," Sullivan admitted.

"Then, this rig is going nowhere then, is it?" the man said with a grin as he slouched down in his seat.

Bishop walked up. "Look, mate, it's bleeding life or death —a lady been's taken captive. We need your assistance —now!"

The man sat upright in his rig. "Well, why didn't you say so. Come on then, get in."

Sullivan and Bishop ran around to the passenger side of the big rig and jumped in. The man hit the gas and started through the gears as they picked up speed.

"How fast can this thing go?" Bishop asked.

"Any Garda going to give me a ticket tonight?" the man asked.

"Not a one. You're free to hit top speed," Bishop asked.

"Just watch me dust," the driver said. "This monster can roll."

"What are you hauling?" Sullivan asked.

"Guinness."

"Try to be gentle on curves," Sullivan cautioned.

THE TINGLING SENSATION in Bernadette's hands and feet from the lack of blood was being replaced by total numbness. She wiggled them hard to bring them back to life. She tried to imagine how she could escape when they opened the trunk. If they wanted to throw her off a cliff, they'd have to untie her to resemble an accident. She planned on fighting. Her first line of defense was her fingers—a Nukite karate blow to the eyes with her fingers spread. The blow could remove an eye—she didn't care. It wouldn't be her eye. She tried to flex her fingers in anticipation of combat.

The car came to a stop, and a flashlight shone in her eyes as the lid opened. Two sets of hands grabbed her head. One forced her jaws open. They pushed a tube down her throat. A warm liquid cascaded into her mouth—Irish whiskey.

She choked and gagged. She couldn't stop it. Her throat was on fire, she fought to breathe through her nose or she'd suffocate.

"Take it all in now, my dear niece," Cahal said "Nothing like a nice tipple of good whiskey on a chilly night."

They pulled her out of the car and stood her up. The liquor was coursing through her veins. The empty bottle lay on the ground.

"You can untie her now," Cahal said.

"I thought you said she was deadly with her hands?" Conner said.

"Not when she's had an entire bottle of whiskey down her throat," Burnell said with a laugh.

Bernadette looked at Burnell. "I have a message from Claire. She loves you. Even though you're a little shit, she said she loves you, anyway. She wants you back." Her body was becoming unsteady with the alcohol, "She said you don't have to do this." She slurred the last words as her eyes rolled back in her head.

Burnell stopped and looked at Bernadette. A glimmer of recognition came over his face. "You spoke to Claire?"

"Yes," Bernadette whispered. "She said you'd come to your senses—that you might help."

Burnell shook his head. "Well, she was bleedin' wrong, wasn't she? I'm breaking up with that skinny bitch, anyway. Now, do as we say or we shoot you right here and now."

Connor took the bonds off her feet. Burnell took the ropes off her hands. They turned her around and walked her towards the cliff.

"Don't worry, my dear girl," Cahal said. "If the fall doesn't kill you, the amount of liquor should do it inside of an hour. They'll find your body in a day or two. There'll still be enough alcohol in your body to show you had a wonderful drunken night on the cliffs."

Bernadette weaved slightly. The two men held her up. She turned towards them, trying to get her brain to form words the alcohol was making fuzzy.

"How will you... make it... an accident... how did I get here?" Bernadette asked. The detective in her wanted to solve her own death.

"Ah, we brought your car up. We found it on the road. It will be here shortly. Not a problem, we have it all figured out," Cahal said.

A vehicle's engine sounded in the distance. It was coming fast.

"That will be your car now, but you won't be needing it. Okay now lads take her to the cliff and push her over. Make sure you give her a proper shove, now. I want her to make a nice drop to the bottom."

Bernadette heard the waves crashing below. A stiff wind brushed her face. Everything in her was screaming at her to fight—the alcohol had her in its grip.

The sound of the vehicle was getting louder. Connor turned in its direction.

"That doesn't sound like a car. It sounds like a bleedin' transport. What's it doing out here?" Connor asked.

The large transport came closer. A horn blared; its lights went on high beam. The men stood there transfixed with Bernadette between them.

Cahal turned to them. "Don't stand there. Throw her over the cliff, you idiots."

"But there's a witness now. That driver has seen us. How do we take care of him as well?" Burnell asked.

Cahal took out a handgun. "I'll scare the bugger off." He fired a round at the cab of the truck.

Gunfire returned from the cab of the vehicle. Cahal ducked to the ground. "The bugger's got a gun."

The big rig came around the corner of the road and slowed down, the air brakes coming on with the tires screeching as the multiple wheels locked up. It looked like it would not stop in time. It hurtled toward the cliff.

"Shoot the damn thing," Cahal yelled at Connor and Burnell.

They threw Bernadette to the ground and took out their handguns. They fired round after round at the cab. The rig kept coming.

Bernadette looked up from the ground—she could see the front radiator, the enormous wheels barreling towards her. She rolled away to the right. The vehicle continued its momentum; it stopped with its front wheels almost over the cliff.

The men had kept firing and backing up. Both lost their footing. In a moment of panic, they realized they were in space, falling backwards towards the rocks below.

Bishop jumped out of the cab of the vehicle and advanced on Cahal. "Drop your weapon, you're under arrest," he yelled at Cahal.

Cahal was out of bullets. He put up his hands.

"Are you alright?" Sullivan asked Bernadette.

Bernadette lay on her back. She turned over and waved with her hand. "I will be in a minute." She threw up.

After several minutes, she turned back to Sullivan. "Sorry about that. They pumped me full of whiskey to make my death look like an accident."

"Did you get the file?" Sullivan asked.

"No," Bernadette said. "But we have Cahal." She stared

at him on the ground with his hands being cuffed by Bishop.

"You'll get nothing out of me. Do your worst. I won't break. In two days' time all of Europe and England will be on its knees."

Sullivan stood beside Bernadette. "He'll be a tough nut to crack. Interrogation won't get us far. We must use some drastic measures if we want to stop the catastrophe he's threatening."

"Do you have anything to persuade him with that's semi-legal?" Bernadette asked.

Sullivan shook his head. "Not really. One of my detective sergeants once used a flush toilet as a makeshift water board. We still didn't get much."

Bernadette looked down at the defiant Cahal and back to Sullivan. "I have an idea. Can you get me the Smith and Wesson I brought in?"

Sullivan arched an eyebrow. "You promise not to kill him?"

Bernadette smiled. "If he has a strong heart, he'll be fine."

53

Bernadette stared at Cahal Callahan in the interview room. He looked defiant, smug. They'd been in the room for over an hour since they'd returned to Garda headquarters from the cliffs. Cahal asked for a lawyer, said he wasn't about to say anything and that he wasn't a tout.

"You can't do anything to me, Bernadette Callahan," Cahal said. "You've no jurisdiction here, not an ounce of power, and you can't ask me questions. They will throw anything you get from me out of any court. Having you in this room is improper police procedure, isn't it now, Sullivan?" His gray hair lay matted to his head. His eyes bleary and red.

Sullivan leaned up against the wall. "I think I'll leave you alone in the room with her while she beats you senseless just for the sport of it."

"But you won't now, will you? If you put a mark on me, my lawyer will stitch you up something proper. You'd be sacked from you jobs at the end. No, you can't lay a hand on me."

Bishop walked over to Cahal and leaned on the table; he

was inches from his face. "Look, we heard there's two bloody big bombs on the way to England. You tell us where they are and we tell the prosecutor to take it easy on you."

"Easy on me? Hah, what's that to mean? Twenty years instead of thirty? At my age, this means nothing. You've only got empty threats. You've come to the table with an empty hand, lads."

Bernadette walked up to Sullivan and whispered in his ear. He nodded and motioned for Bishop to follow him out of the room.

Cahal eyed Bernadette as she stood there. They'd shackled his hands to the table—he rattled his chains at her. "And you'd love to strike me now, wouldn't you? Take your vengeance out on me?"

"I've other plans for you, Cahal. If that's your real name," Bernadette said.

"What's that mean? Of course, it's me name..."

The door opened. Sullivan and Bishop walked in with Francine Dooley. They put the shackles on her and sat her across from Cahal.

"What's she doing here?" Cahal asked.

"Ah, that's a good question," Bernadette approached Sullivan and took a Smith and Wesson revolver from him.

"What do you think you're doing with that? You've not the nerve to shoot me, do you? This is just a grand show. Do your worst," Cahal said with a laugh.

"Leave us," Bernadette said to Bishop and Sullivan. "Make sure the video is off."

Bishop and Sullivan walked out of the room. They looked at Bernadette with concern in their eyes.

Bernadette took the gun and opened the revolver and spun the gun casing. "You've heard of Russian Roulette?"

"What, you think I'm afraid of dying? Don't be daft. An

old man like me, afraid of death—you'll be doing me a favor," Cahal said.

"No, not for you," Bernadette said. She spun the revolvers' magazine, then took one bullet out of her pocket and inserted it. She closed the chamber and spun it. "This is for Francine."

"What are you're doing?" Cahal yelled.

Francine looked up at Cahal and then over to Bernadette. She seemed docile, almost content.

"Francine doesn't seem to be afraid now, does she? Maybe it's because she's had a special tea we made for her. Don't you remember the GBH you gave Harvey Mawer and my dog? Makes people somewhat docile. She hasn't a clue what's going on. She won't even feel the bullet going into her brain."

Bernadette spun the gun's cylinder, put the muzzle to Francine's head and pulled the trigger. A loud click bounced over the walls of the room.

"Bloody hell, you bitch, you f'ing bitch. What do you think you're doing? You'll never get away with this. You'll be done for murder," Cahal screamed.

Bernadette spun the cylinder. "No, I doubt it. I showed you the gun I'd taken from your hired killers and it fired. Sorry, oops—they say. No video record and my word against yours—I'd no idea it was loaded."

"The name of the bomb targets, Cahal." Bernadette pointed the gun at Francine's head.

"No, you can't do this. You'll never get away with it…"

The gun's hammer sounded on an empty chamber. The metal click reverberated in the room.

Bernadette spun the cylinder. "What are the odds in Russian, Roulette? They're good when there are two or more players, but here, it's only Francine. This is one bullet and her brain—what's it going to be, Cahal?"

Bernadette pointed the gun at Francine's head again. "You're running out of time. Well, actually, Francine is."

"Stop, I'll tell you," Cahal screamed.

Bishop and Sullivan came into the room and stood hovering over Cahal.

"There's a laundry van heading for a hotel in Brighton."

"Which hotel?" Bishop asked.

"I'm not sure. I only know it's the same one the IRA blew up years ago in the troubles," Cahal said.

"And the other one?" Sullivan asked.

"A van is delivering a photocopier to Canary Wharf."

"When is it happening?"

"Tomorrow at noon, both vans arrive at the same time. They off load the bombs then detonate them by remote," Cahal said.

Sullivan turned to Bishop. "Get that information to MI-5 and Scotland Yard."

Bishop left the room.

Francine stared at Cahal. "Oh, John, you shouldn't have told them. You're a bleeding tout you are."

"I'm sorry, Francine, I couldn't see you die," Cahal said.

Bernadette opened the chamber of the gun. It was empty "There was never any fear of that, John Dooley. I palmed the bullet. It was fake."

"I'm not John Dooley. Now you're off your head," Cahal said.

"Well, now we're going for the bonus round. You are going to tell us where the Odin Genetic's files are and who is running this crazy cult."

"Ha, well, my confession will never stand up in court.

And you'll not scare me with that fake bullet. Good luck on that."

"Here's what I have. There's two bodies in a grave in Kilmeague, and I bet you the bones of John Dooley's DNA are a match for the real Cahal Callahan's. Once I give the Garda a sample of my DNA, they'll match."

"So, what of it?"

"The police report says Francine was the last to see the real Cahal alive. And she was the one who identified his body at the morgue. When they open the cold case file, everything will point to her. Probably hang their deaths on her."

"I did it. I did them both. I killed Aideen and Cahal Callahan."

"Why?"

"Francine was sweet on Cahal. She had his baby. The Callahans wanted nothing to do with her, they only wanted the baby. Called us tinkers. I filled them full of liquor and drowned them."

"What happened to the child?"

"It was poorly from the beginning. Francine carries some bad genes; the little nipper didn't stand a chance, barely lasted two years. We buried her out back of Francine's place."

"Thanks for clearing that up. Who's running the cult and where are the files?" Bernadette said.

John Dooley shrugged. "I've no idea who the masked man is, but a guy named John Dunne does. He's the mouthpiece for all our dirty work. Find him and you'll have all your answers."

"Where do we find him?" Sullivan asked.

"Swords Castle."

"That's been in reconstruction for years." Bishop said.

"Yes, it has, financed by Odin Genetics. The castle is closed to the public and they've been making it their own little hideout for years. There's a special entrance they use the public can't see."

"Can you draw us a map?" Sullivan asked.

"Aye, give me a pen and paper," John Dooley said. He took a piece of paper and drew a diagram. "That masked bugger—he's brought all this down on us, me and Francine, he has. And make sure you guard all the exits. That place has three different tunnels; I'll draw them all, and one more thing... shoot the bugger in the head for me."

"Thanks for the information, I'll see what we can do on your request," Sullivan said. He took the paper, folded it, and walked towards the door. He turned to Dooley. "I'm sending in another detective to take your complete statement. If you mention anything of how we attained your confession, I'll make sure we press the investigation of your sister so hard her head will pop. Do you understand me?"

Dooley nodded his head in reply. "You'll get no argument from me."

54

John Dunne sat at the long table as Magda, the master, looked over reports. He hated these meetings, but Ronan made him attend. He told him it was good for him to get a sense of the history that was taking place. Dunne did not believe any of it. He only believed in the euros in his bank every month.

"Is everything going to plan?" Magda asked.

"Yes, the bombs are on their way. They left Ireland two days ago. We'll detonate them tomorrow," Dunne said. He often averted his eyes from the strange mask. The voice that came from it sounded like Darth Vader with an Irish accent. It was always a strange time.

"What will you do with the recruits who are going on the mission?" Magda asked. His gold mask shifted slightly on his face. Dunned could hear him breathing heavily underneath it.

"Would you like me to dispose of them?" Dunne asked.

"Yes, nothing gets back to me. Kill them all. Tell the assassins I'm giving them all special places in Valhalla for their service."

Dunne tried not to roll his eyes. "I'll have it done."

"You haven't called me Master. Why is that?" Magda asked.

"Ah, so sorry, slipped my mind, somewhat busy in the killing department. But, yes, Master, I will see that we execute your wishes."

The master nodded his head. That was the way Dunne knew he was pleased. His cell phone buzzed. He looked down. It was an alarm. Not just any alarm—the one that told him the police were on the way.

"We must leave—now," Dunne said.

"You didn't call me master."

Dunne stood up. "The police are on their way—Master." He hit a button that showed him the security cameras. "They are at the door. Out the back way."

The master jumped from his chair, whirled, and headed for the hidden door they used as their escape route. They had planned all of this in advance. The hidden door led to an underground bunker and several corridors.

Dunne hit the red button to open the door. It swung open. A policeman with a machine gun stood in the doorway.

"On the ground now," The policeman yelled.

Dunne hit the ground. Magda grabbed a broadsword from the wall, yelling something incoherent as he charged.

A quick burst of machine gun fire sounded. Magda dropped beside Dunne. The mask fell from his face—it bounced across the floor, exposing the face of Ronan beneath it.

"You daft bugger," Dunne said. He put his hands up as the police surrounded him.

Sullivan and Bishop came into the room. "You must be John Dunne, then?" Sullivan asked.

"Yes, that's me," Dunne said.

"A source tells us you're the key man in this whole cult. I'm sure we'll have multiple charges for you once we investigate this."

"Look, if we can cut a deal, I'll tell you everything. The man you want is lying dead beside me."

"Who is he?"

"Ronan Bronaugh, the billionaire... or least he was."

55

BERNADETTE CHANGED her return home by five days as she had things that needed closure. The final interrogation of Cahal revealed they had sent him to silence the priests in Canada because they were about to expose Ronan in their book.

They rounded up members of the cult up and put them into a home for psychiatric care. They all believed their DNA was that of kings and ancient queens. There would be a long road to reconditioning their minds.

They brought in Brendon Shannon, the member of parliament, for questioning. He claimed ignorance with the help of an excellent lawyer. Some people always get a free pass.

Bernadette called Chris and convinced him he needed to join her in Kilmeague. He took the next flight out.

They stood in the church's graveyard. The rain fell softly, but they didn't mind. They held each other close and watched the gravedigger work.

"How did you figure out that Cahal wasn't legit?" Chris asked.

"There was something in Francine Dooley's eyes when she was trying to convince me of her love affair with my father. I knew she was lying."

"How did they get the photo of you in Ireland then?"

Bernadette squeezed his hand tight. "That photo of the two-year-old girl in Cahal's arms was my cousin. The one that had died over thirty years ago. We had striking similarities."

"Why was your dad in the photo?" Chris asked.

Bernadette looked up at Chris. "John Dooley photoshopped my dad into the picture. He thought he might have a get out of jail card if we caught him. It worked."

Bernadette looked up at Chris. "There were pods I saw in the laboratory. Ronan promised Francine and John Dooley he could recreate Francine's child in a test tube. But none of them worked."

"So, you're not the love child of an Irish Gypsy then?" Chris asked.

"No, but this poor thing was," Bernadette said, looking down at the grave.

"Do you know who named her before she died?"

"Aideen named her. I received a letter from the solicitor. She wanted to use a powerful name for Cahal's child and had asked my father if he didn't mind using mine because she'd heard I was strong. The letter never got sent. Funny, all these years I thought they'd disavowed my family, and here they were, buried in this cemetery. They even left me over thirty thousand euros in their wills."

"Would that have changed anything?" Chris asked.

"I'm not sure, but I would have opened their case a long time ago if I'd known the circumstances," Bernadette said.

"I'm sure you would have," Chris said.

The priest came towards them wearing his vestments and carrying his bible. "Are we ready to begin?"

"Yes, we are Father," Bernadette said.

"Dear lord, we are here today to bury this young child, gone too soon, and we know has long been in your loving arms. Know that people who love you have now laid you to rest in your proper place."

He made the sign of the cross and sprinkled some water over the grave. "May you rest in everlasting peace—Bernadette Callahan."

56

EMERALD LAKE LODGE, ALBERTA, CANADA.

THE SUN BROKE through the clouds, making the surrounding snow-covered mountains sparkle. The wedding party gathered by the shore of Emerald Lake that shimmered with deep blues and greens.

Bernadette and Chris walked out of the lodge where they had taken part in a Cree smoke ceremony given by Grandmother Moses. They joined the guests at the altar. Grandma Moses presented them with two feathers tied together in such a way that they would never be separated. They gave each other moccasins and hugged Grandma Moses.

They advanced to the canopy where Rabbi Nahman, the newfound second cousin of Chris, blessed them and placed a glass under a cloth. Chris broke the glass by stepping on it to the cheers of the crowd.

Father Dominic stepped in to give the blessings of the Catholic Church and read only one passage from the bible and ended his ceremony with prayer to the faithful.

"Do you think we covered all the bases?" Chris asked as

they walked hand in hand back to the reception. He wore a black suit with a Jewish yamalka on his head.

Bernadette smiled. She'd worn a plain white dress with a necklace of beads. "I think all of our ancestors will be pleased."

There were forty for dinner. Chris had excelled in providing a choice of lake trout or elk tenderloin and a vegetarian selection that Bernadette only agreed to at the last minute. The wines were from the Okanagan Valley of British Columbia with a selection of cheeses from Ontario matched with fortified wines from the Niagara Peninsula.

Bernadette and Chris stayed late and partied with the guests. Chris' newfound Jewish relatives provided a hora dance, Bernadette's grandmother showed everyone a traditional native dance, and Father Dominic, once plied with enough whiskey, showed everyone a jig.

At midnight they sat on the wooden balcony of their cottage and watched the moon drift across the mountains. Sprocket nestled at their feet, snoring.

"That was perfect," Bernadette said.

Chris smiled. "Yes, I'd say it was that. My mother even got along with everyone, even Rabbi Nahman."

"I couldn't ask for anything more," Bernadette said, pulling Chris' arm around her.

"I have two things, and I hope they are not overwhelming," Chris said.

Bernadette sat up and looked at him. "What is it?"

Chris pulled a small envelope. "You remember you filled out your DNA some months ago?"

"Yeah, I wondered what happened to the results."

"They came in a week ago. You were busy, so I thought I'd give it to you now," Chris said as he handed her the envelope.

Bernadette looked at the envelope. She bit her lip. "What if I'm really not half Cree and full Irish?"

"You'll only know if you open it," Chris said.

"What if I don't? What if I just go by what I've experienced and feel?"

"You might try that. But this is you we're talking about. Having the envelope closed will make you doubt forever. Like not looking at cards dealt on a table."

"Oh my God, you know me too well," she said, tearing open the envelope.

"Well, does it say?"

Bernadette laughed. "Yes, I'm full Cree on my mother's side, but on my father's side I got Irish, Welsh, Danish, and some Norwegian."

"Looks like that guy Ronan was on to something," Chris said.

Bernadette put up her hand. "Please don't get me started on that lunatic."

"I've one more thing to show you," Chris said.

"What is it?"

Chris took out a large envelope from under the chair. "This came by courier this morning to the lodge. I opened it to see if it was anything official, and I discovered it's a wedding present."

"Who is it from?"

"No Idea. Just says enjoy," Chris said as he handed the envelope to Bernadette.

She opened the envelope. Two airline tickets fell out. She emptied the package. A brochure and two cruise tickets dropped into her lap.

Bernadette put her hand to her forehead. "These airline tickets are first class. And the cruise ship cabin is a penthouse suite."

Chris opened the brochure. "This ship has only two hundred passengers. Every cabin has a butler and a valet. How can we accept this?"

Bernadette smiled and picked up her glass of champagne. "How can we not accept it?"

"But it's in three weeks from now. The itinerary says it's from Singapore to Dubai for fourteen days. Can you swing the time off?"

"I'm owed a vacation. I've tons of overtime they want me to take instead of pay. This might be nice—a once in a lifetime experience."

"But this is a cruise for millionaires. We wouldn't fit in," Chris said.

"Who cares? I buy a black dress, you rent a tux. After all, what can happen on a cruise ship with a bunch of rich people?"

ABOUT THIS SERIES

Dear Reader

If you enjoyed this fifth book in the Bernadette Callahan series please leave a review at Deadly Ancestors on Amazon. Reviews are like gold to us authors.

If you want to read the first three in the series; Polar Bear Dawn, Pipeline Killers and Climate Killers, Bernadette takes on criminals with her own brand of justice and methods. She's not always popular with her superiors but hated by criminals.

I've written the first three books in the form of a trilogy, as I've always been a star wars fan, and love to see where a story goes. The eReader box set is it a special price of $6.99 USD for your enjoyment.

Click this link to get this set, http://mybook.to/CallahnBoxSet.

If you'd like to join my mailing list for my next book and to get a free story, please click this link, www.lylenicholson.com

WHEN THE
DEVIL BIRD
CRIES

A BERNADETTE CALLAHAN MYSTERY

LYLE NICHOLSON

WHEN THE DEVIL BIRD CRIES
CHAPTER ONE, RAFFLES HOTEL, SINGAPORE

Thomas Addington sipped his gin and tonic while watching the young blonde at the end of the bar drinking her Singapore Sling. She looked late twenties, perfect skin, and those looks that only glamor magazines portrayed, but you never see in public.

Thomas hoped his gin would give him the courage to approach her. He was a moderately good-looking man in his early thirties, with a decent head of dark hair coifed in the latest style, pale green eyes, and blemish free skin. With his group of mates back in London, he was never the draw with the ladies, but he could often talk himself into a relationship for the night.

That was his plan this evening. London, England and his girlfriend, Camilla Farnham, were a world away from here. His occupation as an investment analyst for one of England's largest banks left him with a need for excitement. Casual hook-ups in bars from Singapore to Berlin and New York were his compensation for his boring life. He analyzed numbers all day and attended dreary concerts and poetry readings with Camilla back in London.

Thomas swirled his gin, taking one last gulp before he made his way toward the beautiful blonde. He'd been turned down many times, but his track record of scoring one-night stands was excellent. As an analyst, he knew his success increased with constant advances.

The bar was getting louder. A table of German tourists were laughing at the prices of the expensive drinks and throwing peanut shells on the floor, Raffles Bar being the only place in Singapore you could litter without a two thousand dollar fine.

Thomas understood German, and he looked away from the group as he focused on his target. He timed it perfectly. An elderly Chinese couple vacated their seats just as he arrived. He slid onto the barstool next to her. He could feel her heat, smell her perfume. This beauty already fascinated him.

"Do you like Singapore Slings?" Thomas asked. He waved to the barman to get his attention, trying to avoid her beauty.

She turned her head, as if noticing his presence for the first time. Her look was one of assessment, first at his face, then letting her eyes drop from his chest to his lap, then back up again. A smile edged her lips; he'd passed some kind of evaluation. He felt elated.

"They taste fruity and herbal, but the drink is growing on me," she said.

Thomas turned to face her. "Did you know, this is the very bar that invented the drink back in the early nineteen hundreds?"

She flashed a smile with perfect white teeth. "I don't think so. You seem like an intelligent man, what's the story behind it?"

"Ah," Thomas said, "the good people of Singapore

needed to hide their afternoon drinking habits, and they frowned upon ladies drinking. Thus, a Gin Sling became a Singapore Sling. May I buy you another?"

She pushed her empty glass forward. "That would be wonderful. Does this mean you'll be sleeping with me tonight?"

"Ah, that would be—"

"Beyond your wildest dreams?"

"Well... yes," Thomas said with a broad smile as he extended his hand. "Thomas Addington, a pleasure to make your acquaintance."

"I'm sure it will be, Thomas," the blonde said.

Thomas moved slightly forward as the bartender brought them fresh drinks. "And you are?"

"Who would you like me to be?"

"I'm not sure I catch your meaning."

The blonde sipped her fresh cocktail and turned fully towards him. "We only have tonight, what does it matter who I am or my actual name? I could be any name you like. Do you have a favorite?"

Thomas chuckled. No woman had ever been this bold or this beautiful. "How about Cassandra?"

The blonde winked, placing her hand on his leg, squeezing hard. "Cassandra it is."

Thomas placed his hand on hers. He loved this; he couldn't believe how much she aroused him. "You know," he said, giving her hand a soft caress, "I'm here for a few days, we could make this into more than one night..."

Cassandra sipped her drink, her eyes going wide. "Sorry, Thomas, I can only indulge you for one night. I'm boarding a ship tomorrow."

Thomas gazed into her eyes. They were perfectly

matched almond with flecks of gray. "Ah, on a world tour, are we?"

She took her hand off his leg, placing it around her drink. "Yes and no. I'm a crew member on a very luxurious cruise ship that sets sail tomorrow afternoon."

"What's the ship?" Thomas asked.

"Can't tell you. But it has only two hundred passengers, and they're mostly all millionaires."

Thomas took a sip of his gin. "Sounds boring, I work for a bank managing the portfolios of millionaires. They can be tiresome. What are you doing on the ship?

"The most important job of all," she replied. She took a long sip of her drink. "I'm not into conversation, Thomas. I have a long three-month stretch coming up where there's no fraternizing allowed with crew or passengers. I need some action tonight. You up for it?"

Thomas pushed his drink aside and motioned for the bill. "I'm your man, Cassandra."

The bill arrived, Thomas paid with his credit card, something he almost never did as he'd have to reconcile this later with his company. They walked out of the Raffles Hotel into the heat and humidity of Singapore's night.

Taxis seemed scarce. Thomas waved at a few in vain. Cassandra was getting restless. He waved harder at the cabs.

"How about a rickshaw?" Cassandra asked.

"They aren't quick," Thomas replied. He stood there looking somewhat lost.

Cassandra placed her hand on his chest. "I'm in no hurry. Look, I'm going to make love to you all night long. A brief ride in a rickshaw will be nice."

Thomas' chest swelled. "Yes, well then, let's grab a rickshaw." He took her hand, leading her to a small bicycle-powered rickshaw with a slim young Asian driver. The driver put down his cell phone. "Where to?" was all he asked in a thick Malay accent.

"The Carlton Hotel," Thomas replied.

Cassandra snuggled up beside him, her lips brushed his cheek. "Well, I didn't know you were staying at the Ritz-Carlton."

Thomas squirmed a bit, "No, actually, it's just the Carlton. My company policy, you see…"

"Never mind, we'll be just fine. I'm sure you can order some champagne when I get thirsty."

"Why yes," Thomas said. He wondered how he'd manage that. A charge like that would be disastrous to his room account back in London. He'd have to slip the room server cash. Hoping he had enough.

The driver stood up on the pedals and they moved into traffic. They were only a twenty-minute ride away. Thomas settled in, letting the warmth of Cassandra melt away his anxiety of the expense account. His girlfriend Camilla, was half a world away and forgotten.

"We need to stop here," Cassandra said.

"What for?" Thomas asked as she directed the driver to park in front of a small shop.

"I need something for tonight," she said with a wink.

Thomas ran his hand over her thigh. "I hope it's sensual and smells wonderful."

"It's a toothbrush, you silly," Cassandra said, running out of the rickshaw.

"I could order one for you at the hotel…" Thomas said as she disappeared into the crowded store.

The rickshaw driver went back to his phone, Thomas did the same. He looked at his FB site, checking on his friends. He didn't see the black Mercedes pull up behind him, nor the two men in black suits walk into the store.

He finally looked up from his phone. It had been ten minutes. How long did it take to get a toothbrush? He looked into the store. The crowd had dispersed, and only the shopkeeper stood at the till watching a television show.

Thomas ran into the store. He yelled to the little Chinese man behind the counter. "The young blonde. Where is she?"

The Chinese man looked up at Thomas. "She gone. Go with her two men."

Thomas rushed outside. There was no sign of her. He looked up and down the street—nothing.

"Did you see the girl I was with?" Thomas asked the rickshaw driver. "Did you see her leave the store?"

"I see nothing," the rickshaw driver replied. "You want to go now?"

"I don't know, the girl I was with... I don't know what happened to her." Thomas replied weakly.

The rickshaw driver shrugged his shoulders, looking back at his cell phone.

Thomas felt stuck. What should he do? Was the girl taken by someone? Was he scammed somehow? He reached into his back pocket and removed his wallet. It was still there. He was missing nothing. How could he report this strange encounter with a woman when he didn't know her name?

A light rain began to fall. The rickshaw driver raised the passenger canopy, "You go now?"

"Yes," Thomas replied. "I go now." He got into the rickshaw and slumped into the seat. He had a bad feeling in the pit of his stomach. He knew he should call the police, but his own self-preservation of his so-called good name made him powerless to act.

He finally did something. He did a quick search on his

phone of the Singapore Police Department. Using a burner email that he used for his various hookups with ladies with a Gmail address that would only lead back to a Google IP address, he dashed off a quick email. Under the heading of a suspicious observation, he stated the store's location and that he'd seen what may have been the kidnapping of a young lady.

He sighed, hit send, and put the phone away. "Thomas, old boy, you'll get yourself into deep trouble one day," he muttered to himself.

WHEN THE DEVIL BIRD CRIES
CHAPTER TWO, HAWKER ALLEY, SINGAPORE

Bernadette Callahan felt something strange as she walked down the row of food stalls with her husband Chris. They'd arrived the day before in Singapore on a flight from Calgary, Canada with stops in Vancouver and Seoul, Korea. Jet lag was wearing on her, but the sights of Singapore were more important than trying to recover lost sleep.

She had a feeling of eyes on her. That they were being followed. She looked up at the many cameras that watched the streets. Could that be it, she wondered?

"How are you feeling about our trip so far?" Chris asked. He was a big man, late thirties, with an impressive build of muscles from his dedication to the gym. He stood out amongst the Asian crowd for his height, curly black hair, and olive complexion. Chris was Greek and Israeli heritage, with a calm disposition that complemented Bernadette's fiery nature.

Bernadette squeezed his hand. "For a girl who has never been much outside of North America, this is cool." She was five foot eight with a look of a woman who gravitated between the gym and her love of food. Bernadette was a mix of Native Cree and Irish. Her hair was red and her skin was a bronze with freckles. Her green eyes missed not one food stall as they made their way down the long alley looking for dinner.

"How's some Pad Thai sound?" Chris asked, looking over the menu of one stall.

"I'm thinking spicier. Something that goes with a good jug of Singapore beer," Bernadette said.

"You didn't get enough beer on the plane?"

Bernadette laughed. "I loved the Tiger beer they served on the plane. I just need a nice spicy four alarm curry to go with it."

"Great, the food here costs next to nothing, a jug of beer costs a small fortune."

"They're trying to keep the population from drinking themselves to death with high prices," Bernadette said.

"Yeah, with that and the two thousand dollar littering fines, they're doing pretty well," Chris said.

Bernadette stopped in front of a food stall. The food listed had several dishes with three to four chili signs, denoting super-spicy food. She let her gaze turn behind them as she scanned the food.

When she saw a little man duck into a crowd, her senses went into overload. That was not a coincidence.

"You okay?" Chris asked.

"I had this feeling we were being watched. Just now I saw a guy duck into a crowd."

"Where should I be looking?" Chris asked. Bernadette was one hell of a detective with the Royal Canadian Mounted Police in Canada. Her instincts were accurate. "You think we've a pickpocket tailing us?"

Bernadette gazed at the menu to make like everything was normal. "We aren't the usual marks for pickpockets. We don't have cameras, I don't have a purse, and both of us are carrying our money in our front pockets. And you're as big as a house compared to the people here. You'd think they'd mark someone else."

Chris looked around them. A group of elderly tourists walked by happily displaying expensive cameras, jewelry, and large handbags. "I have to agree, we're poor targets for theft—especially when this place is loaded with them."

"Let's order and see what happens," Bernadette said. She ordered a spicy pork dish and Chris chose something with only a two-chili sign as he wanted to feel his tongue later. They found a picnic table and sat down with two Tiger beers as they couldn't find a vendor selling it by the jug.

"Damn, this is spicy," Bernadette said, then took a drink of beer and wiped her brow with a Kleenex.

"You wanted hot. That's what you got," Chris said. "You see anything behind us?"

Bernadette lowered her head and put the Kleenex to her eyes and looked to the side. "Yeah, he's trying hard to be invisible behind a group of tourists. He's wearing a yellow shirt and holding a bag. Oh, no wait, he just disappeared behind a beer sign."

"Hard to believe someone could be that bad. Are you sure it's not some local guy hiding from his wife?"

"When was the last time my instincts were wrong?" Bernadette asked, taking another big spoonful of curry and rice.

"Okay, I'll tell you but only if you invoke the privilege of non-incrimination. Because I'm not about to hang myself."

"You're free. No recriminations. Go for it," Bernadette said.

"Well..." Chris began carefully, "There is this trip we're on. This is an all-expenses paid, first class cruise on a two hundred passenger ship, and we have no idea who paid for it. Doesn't that classify as going off the grid, instinct wise?"

"I thought we discussed this. It's fine. This was a gift at our wedding. There are no strings attached to the gift, and none of the convicts I put behind bars would have the money to purchase this. Besides, it could have been one of your new-found relatives in Europe."

"So, your instincts told you what? As long as you don't know who paid for this trip, it's okay to do it?" Chris asked with a smile. He knew he had her in a corner on this one.

"No, smart ass, my instincts told me the only way to find out who paid for our cruise was to go on it and find out," Bernadette said with a wink.

Chris leaned in closely to Bernadette. "So far we've been on a first-class flight from Canada and staying at the Ritz-Carlton. I'd say we've done okay for two middle income Canadians on a dream trip we're not paying for—"

"Don't move your head."

"Why, what's up?"

"Our man is on the move. He's meeting up with someone," Bernadette said.

"See, I told you. Nothing to worry about. The guy is here to meet someone."

"Yeah, you're right. The someone in the yellow shirt just handed the bag off to a guy in a white shirt. Now *he's* now watching us. It's a handoff. Looks like we have a new tail."

Chris finished his beer and gathered up the empty plates to dispose of them. "Look, I doubt if he'll follow us once we leave here."

They joined the crowd in the market, winding slowly down Hawker Alley toward the main street. Bernadette stopped once to fix her shoe and looked casually back. She couldn't see him.

"I told you, you're imagining things," Chris said.

They found a bicycle rickshaw for the return to the hotel. The rickshaw moved slowly through the night with car horns honking and the streets full of people getting ready for late nights of Singapore. They rolled up to the Ritz.

"You go on inside. I'll be right behind you," Bernadette said, stepping out onto the sidewalk.

Chris shook his head in resignation. He knew she'd be looking to see if they were followed. He walked into the hotel without looking behind him.

Bernadette stopped short, then slid in behind a pillar. She watched as a motorized rickshaw came to a stop several hundred yards away. The man in the white shirt carrying the bag got out and made his way towards the hotel. She smiled.

WHEN THE DEVIL BIRD CRIES

Inspector Lee woke to the sound of his phone ringing beside him. His watch read 5 a.m. Early morning phone calls meant homicides; his staff never called this early otherwise.

"Inspector Lee," he mumbled, waiting for the inevitable.

"Inspector, Corporal Chen here. We have a fatality at the Clarke Quay."

"Details."

"A young woman, Caucasian, maybe twenty years old. The street cleaners found her in the river. She is naked. No ID, no signs of struggle."

"Has the medical examiner arrived?"

"She will be here shortly."

"Any media there?"

"None. We've cordoned off the area," Chen said.

"Good, I'll be there in twenty minutes," Lee said.

He called his driver. It was Friday. Inspector Simon Lee was forty-one years old but looked younger. He had jet black hair, soft brown eyes and a tall frame. He always walked with a purpose, never slouching in the shoulders, with his head erect. You'd think he'd been in the military, but you'd be wrong. He'd been a police officer since he left school. That was his life.

He'd married at age thirty, late in the eyes of his mother, and after his wife had given birth to a son, she'd died. That had affected Lee. He didn't know who he loved more, his wife or his son. Now, he had no choice. His son was his major concern. The boy was eleven, growing up in a world that confused him with the absence of his mother.

Lee sent a text to his housekeeper, Imran, a twenty-one-year-old single mother who lived with her grandmother and her aunt's family. Imran was used to being on call for Lee. Many times, she brought her daughter to play with his son.

Lee dressed quickly, then made his way to the elevator. He lived on the twenty-fifth floor of one of the many expensive high-rises in Singapore. His income as an inspector was good, but not good enough to afford his own car.

He felt the warm morning air. It would be unbearable later in the day. The weather in Singapore was the same for the month of June, hot with showers in the afternoon or evening. The locals lived with it and carried an umbrella.

A white Toyota arrived at the curb. Lee got into the front. He went over his cell phone messages to see what had transpired in the evening. There was a report of a woman being taken from a store on Middle Road. He'd ask the evening shift sergeant about it later.

Clarke Quay at this time of the morning lay quiet. It did not open until 11 a.m. Singapore's bars and nightclubs stayed open until 4 a.m. The area and river seemed to breathe a sigh of relief in the morning stillness.

A body under a tarp lay on the side of the river. Chen stood beside it with the medical examiner kneeling by the body.

Lee said hello to Dr. Permata. Today, she was wearing a

bright blue Hijab. She was a slight, delicate woman in her late forties. Lee found her fascinating; they'd had dinner together once. There was a mutual interest there, but her Muslim background and his Buddhist would never have made it into the actual world.

"Is it a drowning?" Lee asked.

Dr. Permata looked up from the body. "I can't tell until I do an autopsy. If she drowned, I'll find hemorrhaging in the sinuses and airways."

Lee liked that about her, so concise. Never a conjecture, only fact. "No abrasions or signs of struggle?"

"I cannot see on visual examination. I will find much more in my lab, however, there is little rigor mortis set in. I have determined only six degrees of heat loss to the body temperature. And I've taken into account the water temperature of the canal. I estimate the time of death at midnight."

"Thank you, doctor, most helpful as usual," Lee said. He turned to Chen. "Were there any witnesses we can interview?"

Chen looked at his notebook. "So far we have nothing. This area is far from the nightlife of Clarke Quay. That never stops until four thirty."

"Yes, I see that," Lee said. "This area is just far enough away from the activity; did you find any clothes the deceased might have thrown off?"

"No, Inspector, we did a complete search of the area. We found nothing."

Lee ran his hand over his forehead. This was looking like murder. He disliked the thought. Singapore had one of the lowest crime rates in the developed world. He hated to have this arrive on his shift.

"Take a picture of the deceased and send it to our

surveillance team. Have them review pictures of the entire city immediately," Lee said.

"Yes, inspector," Chen replied. He hurried to the body, took a picture of the dead girl's face, and sent it off.

"I need to speak to the sergeant who received the report of a girl being taken away last night," Lee said.

The next four hours were the basics of police procedures working backwards from the last known lead. Someone reported a girl being escorted from a shop by two men on Middle Road at 10 p.m. The police noted a rickshaw was outside the store. They scanned every surveillance camera going back in time for the evening until they saw her with a man in a camera outside the Raffles Hotel getting into a rickshaw.

Lee looked at the picture of the dead blonde victim and the blonde in the street surveillance photos. There were a lot of similarities. The same hair color and style, the height matched, but not once did she look up at a camera. Finally, he had to let his gut and instincts tell him this had to be the same girl.

"We need to find the man she was with last night," Lee said.

The police descended on the hotel to interview all the staff of the hotel, pulling some of them from bed to do so. No one complained once told the gravity of the crime.

The barman of the long bar remembered the beautiful woman speaking to a man. He pulled up his credit card receipts. The police also found the rickshaw driver. He remembered the evening, the disappearing girl, and the man who left without her. He'd dropped him at the Carlton Hotel.

Inspector Lee stood outside room 2211 on the twenty-second floor of the Carlton Hotel with Constable Chen and three police officers. The hotel manager was at his side. They knocked on the door.

Thomas Addington came to the door, and the color drained from his face when he saw the police. "Oh, dear God," was all he could say.

"Do you think this is okay to wear for our first day of cruising?" Bernadette asked as she pulled on a yellow print dress.

Chris looked up from buttoning his shirt. "You look outstanding, girl. How did you afford that? Did we win the lottery?"

Bernadette laughed. "No, I went into Calgary last week and splurged at one of those consignment shops. It's amazing what the rich people get rid of."

"Well, you look like you'll fit right in," Chris said. He finished buttoning his blue shirt he'd matched with some casual tan cotton pants. No matter what he wore, his muscles stood out. His size seventeen and half neck barely squeezed into his collar.

"Do I look okay?" Chris asked.

Bernadette walked over to him and let herself fold into his enormous arms. "Honey, you look incredible in anything."

"You don't think we look like two law enforcement officers trying to schlep their way into the rich and famous?"

"We have a two-week cruise on a fabulous ship, let's just enjoy it and not worry about it," Bernadette said.

The doorbell of their room sounded. As the bellman took their luggage, Chris frowned. He could have hauled everything down, but Bernadette insisted they enjoy the first-class treatment. Their trip to the ship included a limo. They might as well experience it all.

The journey to the cruise ship terminal took only fifteen minutes. They felt like kids going on an adventure.

Big ships docked end-to-end formed an imposing wall of steel at the terminal. The limo cruised by the huge *Carnival Spirit, Celebrity Solstice*, and the *Diamond Princess*. All these ships carried over six thousand passengers and looked like small cities. The limo made its way past them to a separate area reserved for smaller cruise ships. There, sitting on its own in a low gleaming profile, the elegant *Orion Voyager* claimed the prize for being the sleekest looking ship amongst the giants gathered around it.

The ship was a brilliant white with four rows of sparkling glass balconies. It was small compared to others in the harbor, but it looked like an overblown yacht. Only one hundred staterooms, all outside cabins, and each with its appointment of opulent comfort. That's what the brochure had said, and that is exactly what it looked like.

As the limo parked beside the pier, two porters hustled to take their bags. A ship's agent scanned their tickets, and they followed a man who introduced himself as their welcome agent. They had their temperature and health cards checked, then presented with their ship's passes.

They walked onto the ship, did a quick security check, had their passports scanned, and were met by a young man in a white uniform.

"My name is Marcus Smith," he said, bowing. "I'll be your butler for the duration of the cruise. I will unpack your luggage for you if you wish." He was small in stature, brown skinned with dark hair. His hands looked elegant in white gloves.

"No, that will be fine, Marcus," Bernadette said. "We can

unpack ourselves." She cast a sideways glance at Chris. There was no way she wanted another man handling her clothes.

"Very well, the champagne reception is this way. I will meet you afterwards and escort you to your room."

He motioned for them to continue down a corridor lined with serving staff dressed in fine uniforms holding platters of champagne and canapés.

Bernadette walked down the line, picking up a glass of champagne and a shrimp on toast with a napkin, and proceeded towards the reception area where they met the ship's crew. They wore impressive white uniforms, giving fist bumps with their white gloves. At their center stood the captain, a tall man with piercing dark eyes and just enough gray hair to make him look distinguished and elegant. He introduced himself as Captain Nicolas Prodromou. He had a slight Greek accent that Chris didn't recognize. They moved on down the line until Bernadette stopped in front of a female security officer.

"Cynthia McCabe, what the hell! I haven't seen you since basic training," Bernadette said to the female officer standing ramrod straight and holding a glass of water. Cynthia was mid-thirties, the same height as Bernadette, with blue eyes and mid-length blonde hair tied in a tight ponytail.

Cynthia looked stunned. "Wow—Bernie, of all the cadets to make it out of the RCMP, I never thought I'd run into you."

Bernadette wanted to give her a good old-fashioned Canadian embrace, but the place seemed stuffy, and Cynthia was working. She gave her a double fist bump before turning to Chris.

"Chris, this is Cynthia. We did basic training in Regina

together, I helped her pass firearms training and taught her how not be a pussy in combat."

Cynthia suppressed a laugh. "Nice to meet you, Chris. Bernie's right on both counts. But I taught her how to write a proper citation and type. Her handwriting equated to hieroglyphics. Actually, if she'd gone into medicine, she'd have been fine, but not so much in the legal system."

Chris smiled, "Yes, I'm still trying to decipher her notes to me. It's nice to meet you."

"How did you end up here? I didn't know you left the force?" Bernadette said.

"It's a long story that would take a few beers, but the short version is I tired of my life in Canada. I loved police work, but not the small towns they posted me to. I wanted to see the world..." She leaned forward and whispered, "...and not have to pay for it."

"Sound like a cool gig," Bernadette said.

A security officer walked up to Cynthia, touched her shoulder, and spoke and spoke close to her ear.

"I have to go. Seems we have the Singapore police at the pier. They have a question regarding one of our passengers," Cynthia said. "We'll catch up later."

Cynthia joined the other security officer who had just briefed the captain. They left together to the frown of a well-dressed lady who was regaling the officers with her previous voyages.

"That seems serious," Bernadette said.

"Well, I'd like to see our room, maybe stretch out on our own private deck and get some rest before dinner," Chris said. He paused for a moment. "Are you going to check the situation with the Singapore Police?"

Bernadette placed her empty champagne glass on a

table. "I think I'll take a quick walk about the ship. I'll see you in the room shortly."

"Always the detective," Chris said. "Enjoy yourself." He kissed her and went to find Marcus.

Bernadette made her way down to the deck where they'd embarked. Cynthia was there with the captain and the other officer. A tall, thin policeman with the name tag of Lee was speaking to them. She stood off to the side and behind a lifeboat to hear them.

"I must know if any of your crew is missing. We have a murder victim who claimed she was to board a ship today before she was killed. This is the only ship that matches the description she gave our witness." Lee said.

"And I'm telling you, Inspector Lee, none of our crew are missing," Cynthia said.

"What about passengers? Any missing, any not show up?" Lee asked.

"Again, no, we do a complete scan of every crew and passenger's ship pass. We have one hundred percent accounted for," Cynthia said. "I'm, sorry, but perhaps your victim was telling a story, perhaps too much alcohol."

Lee looked from the captain to Cynthia and down to the picture he held in his hands. "You have never seen this woman before?"

"No, Inspector Lee. I've already told you, we've never seen her, and our ship is getting ready to set sail," Cynthia said.

Lee shook his head; he had a muted conversation with his officers, then turned and bowed to Cynthia and the ship's officers. "Thank you. I'll be leaving now."

Bernadette watched them leave. The inspector bounded down the gangplank and into a waiting car. She saw the car speed away and was about to turn away when she spotted something.

The little man in the white shirt, who had followed her in the market and then to their hotel, was on the pier, standing behind a large box. The ship's horn sounded. Lines were being cast off. They were getting under way.

ACKNOWLEDGMENTS

I'd like to thank Dennis O'Sullivan and Patrick Bishop. One for allowing me the use of their names, although somewhat changed, but more for their insights into Irish Culture and law enforcement.

I also wish to thank Brad Chapman and Joe Nahman for their guidance in the legal system of the Province of Alberta, Canada.

ABOUT THE AUTHOR

Lyle Nicholson is the author of eight novels, two novellas and a short story, as well as a contributor of freelance articles to several newspapers and magazines in Canada.

In his former life, he was a bad actor in a Johnny Cash movie, Gospel Road, a disobedient monk in a monastery and a failure in working for others.

He would start his own successful sales agency and retire to write full time in 2011. The many characters and stories that have resided inside his head for years are glad he did.

He lives in Kelowna, British Columbia, Canada with his lovely wife of many years where he indulges in his passion for writing, cooking and fine wines.

If you'd like to contact Lyle Nicholson, please do at lylehn@shaw.ca

ALSO BY LYLE NICHOLSON
THE BERNADETTE CALLAHAN MYSTERY SERIES

Book 1 Polar Bear Dawn

Book 2 Pipeline Killers

Book 3 Climate Killers

Book 4 Caught in the Crossfire

Book 5 Deadly Ancestors

Book 6 When the Devil Bird Cries

Prequel, Black Wolf Rising

Short Story, Treading Darkness

Stand Alone Fiction

Dolphin Dreams, (Romantic Fantasy)

Misdiagnosis Murder (Cozy Mystery)

Non Fiction

Half Brother Blues (A memoir)

Manufactured by Amazon.ca
Bolton, ON

21560070R00222